# FINDING HARRIET

## Maria Teanby

Strat              s Co.

D0417880

LINCOLNSHIRE
COUNTY COUNCIL

05103350

Donation

GNR

Copyright © 2013

All rights reserved – Maria Teanby

No part of this book may be reproduced or transmitted in any form or by any means, graphic, electronic, or mechanical, including photocopying, recording, taping, or by any information storage retrieval system, without the permission, in writing, from the publisher.

Strategic Book Publishing and Rights Co.
12620 FM 1960, Suite A4-507
Houston, TX 77065
www.sbpra.com

ISBN: 978-1-62212-365-0

*Dedicated to my two children, Kristen and Nathan*

# CONTENTS

# ACKNOWLEDGMENTS

My thanks go to the North Lincolnshire Museum at Scunthorpe for their help with my research on iron working in Victorian England, to Ancestry.co.uk for their tireless telephone support during the hunt for Harriet, to the Scunthorpe Evening Telegraph for their invaluable 'Bygones' and 'Nostalgia' features and to Caroline High for her wisdom and thoroughness.

# PROLOGUE

I tried hard to concentrate on the television report yesterday but it's not easy from the pale cocoon of a hospital bed and even less easy when you are dying. Yet that was what caught my eye in the calm, post-visitor hum of the ward, above the random rattles of cups and the swish of curtains. A death.

The camera had panned over slate and tile roofs, a Google Earth view of anytown, anywhere. Except that it was my town, the town where I was born, and a place I tried so hard to leave behind. Onwards across a ragged scraping on the landscape to the northeast, where rail lines knitted and crossed to weave themselves into a single purpose — the ugly, ungainly transport of iron, steel, ore and slag around the steelworks. Switching to a full view of the works themselves, vast and carbuncular upon the town's eastern fringes, the camera closed in on the reporter in the inevitable stance by the blue and white sign at the steelworks entrance. A few trite words to snare and sweeten the interest of the watcher followed by a little pill of history, and the scene was set for the main story to unfold.

A skeletal human hand protruded from a pale mound of ashes and dust, clawing at the air from a scarred hill where gigantic machinery rasped and raked.

'And scientists have dated the remains to around the late 1800s. They believe it to be the body of a worker who was employed at the old Appleton Iron Works that stood on this site over one hundred years ago. The body, a male, was found still wrapped with the tell-tale leather apron of a pig iron carrier which protected the wearer from the splashes of molten iron as it poured into sand moulds known as pigs.'

I had strained to catch more details. It could have been him but then it could have been anybody.

'Much of the skeleton is charred, suggesting the unfortunate worker met with a gruesome accident.'

The date was right but then there were so many deaths in the local iron industry at the end of the nineteenth century. It would have been unremarkable, almost commonplace, tragic only to the little family left without means of support and iron-marked by grinding poverty. For them, it wasn't just the death of a father or a husband. Working at the Appleton Works and living under the low, grimy roofs of nearby Sereton Terrace, it meant being turned, widowed and penniless, out of the worker's house that was tied to the job.

I had thought then, grimacing beneath my oxygen mask, how iron and steel had left their rust marks across my design too. Growing up so close to a steelworks had never really left me; I'd felt stained, dirty and grimed to my very bones even when it was far behind.

No way of knowing if it was him. And I would never know now, although I'd spent a night punctuated with visions of that hand which, at times, rose up with its owner to beckon me close, as if to give up a secret or draw me into a past that had forgotten it for so long. No, no way of knowing and no time to know, although it would settle so many things.

My own death, now it is nearly upon me is, in the present scale of things, also unremarkable.

I have heard them whispering. Pneumonia, old age and the house of cards organ collapse that goes with this state of affairs will probably finish me off today or tomorrow, they said. An ordinary death really, I think, falling slowly through layers of consciousness, eased by palliative care. No life curtailed, no tragedy, no mystery and, I hope, not too much fuss.

But I have heard tears.

It's hard for them, I know. We want to keep the people and the things we love for as long as we can, no matter how old and broken they have become, but they will have to let me go in the end.

'Keep me comfortable, that's all,' I said. It's what I want.

I have heard protests. Grasping to hold up the sinking form before them, my family can't see that the natural process of death is a stripping away of this world, a gradual letting go, one by one, of the people, places and things you have cherished, until you stand naked, alone and ready.

I *am* ready but I know I am not quite alone. Well, death and I *are* old acquaintances, after all. That's why I want to be as aware as I can be when he pays his final visit. That skeletal hand has reminded me once more that we have rubbed shoulders a time or two and parted ways again.

The first time I was just a baby with an unfortunate case of tuberculosis. The poverty of the 1930s had turned both my grandmother and my father into a wonderful home for this opportunistic bacterium. Both of them had, after a spell in the Spartan regime of a TB sanatorium, recovered. Then my father's three-year detention in a POW camp during the Second World War gave it a second chance to break out from where it hid, deep in his lungs. A proud father, he kissed his baby daughter born in an optimistic 1948 on the crest of a baby boom. He kissed and dandled her and chewed her scraps from his plate, unaware he was giving her much more than his love. The silent killer had a preference for the weak and defenceless, and the first in line was me.

I lay in my hospital cot, sweating and whimpering from the throb of a large suppurating abscess on my neck, sheets and blankets drenched, blonde curls matted around my head. There was no one nearby, nothing to distract or comfort a fevered child; you didn't cosset babies too much back then. Routine and discipline were needed, they said. In unfamiliar surroundings, and in pain and fear I mewed into the dim stillness of the children's ward, my chin wobbling as I sucked on nothing, nuzzling for any kind of comfort.

I remember I cried out and a bright ball of light came in answer, hanging above me, the brightest thing I had ever seen. I so wanted to touch, to reach and to hold it as it called me; a mother's call, a sweet, heartrending song of love and belonging. It stayed there all night, a gentle guardian as I drifted in and out of fevered sleep.

Luckily for me that it *was* 1948, and that the recently invented wonder drug penicillin did its work before I could gather the brightness up. I often looked for that ball, though, at night in my bed, trying to conjure up its comfort and brilliance; until I saw it again, that is.

My baby son was just three weeks old when I gazed at the kitchen floor and saw blood oozing down my legs into a black pool at my feet. Spread-eagled on a rapidly spreading stain, I complained to the doctor as he desperately clenched my stomach in both his hands, that I could not see his face anymore.

'Talk to her,' someone snapped at my husband. 'Hearing is the last thing to go.' But my young husband didn't, or couldn't, and I did so need comfort and I wished that he would. My tongue pressed against the roof of my mouth with that telltale sucking, sucking, sucking. Then a grey fog cleared in the back of a wailing ambulance and I looked down on myself, held mummy-bound to a stretcher, red blossoms of ebbing life leaking across my lap. At a distance, through the back windows of the speeding vehicle, I saw him following in our car, his mouth twisting and working and speaking out loud words that I would never hear.

Then I remembered. Everything. My entire turbulent world from its beginning to its imminent end revolved around my suspended form in that ambulance. Moments of love, oceans of grief, a wonderful meal, the silk of a lupin flower in my hand, a train journey; it was all there. I was dying and, watching myself, I really didn't mind at all. Snuggling into a feeling of great peace, I turned my cheek to see my beautiful ball again.

I can feel the yearning still. It's hard to know whether the pain in my chest now is the pneumonia or that aching moment of loss when it vanished. It had come for me, larger and brighter this time, spinning a little beyond my reach as it gathered in the writhing strands of light that were the whole of my life. I could almost touch it, yet it was so far away. I knew I had to give *everything* to get to it, but I *so* wanted to give. I didn't have to that time, either — give, that is.

There was a better chance to observe death's finer intimacies many years later when my elderly aunt died. Pneumonia and old age had taken their inevitable hold on her too, so I *do* know a bit of what's coming although, back then, a cocktail of drugs meant to try to save her life, merely painfully prolonged her going. It was difficult watching her and I wept silently by her hospital bed, her cool, paper-skinned hand cherished in mine, through a bright, sweltering July day and on into a heavy, thick, velveted night as she motioned for dabs of water on lips parched by her oxygen mask. Among the fetid rustles, farts, mutters and coughs of the ward, I dozed and shifted uncomfortably on the green plastic chair until a moment when I awoke fully and instantly and sat bolt upright, every single body hair erect.

At the foot of her bed was my ball. Except I knew that it wasn't mine, it was hers. Her hand was still clasped in my own and I felt every last ounce of energy, living, love and life drain from her and speed towards its glowing threads. In a kind of slow motion, I watched the threads of her life and little echoes of her past as they sped past me. A first kiss, a baby's cry, her mother's face, the scent of lilacs. Then it was gone. My aunt's painful shallow breathing continued for a few minutes more inside her shell… what a wonderful piece of work the human body is to cling on, a husk without its grain. Then a gasp, a pause. Time at last to call the nurse.

'Are you sure you're all right?' she queried, leading me away while I babbled on happily about my aunt dying.

'Yes, I saw her go,' I beamed at her, my face wreathed in happy smiles. She nodded sympathetically, without understanding.

Like the process of birth, I think death can be easy or difficult. Either way, it's still traumatic if you are the one making the journey. Warm, welcoming arms and a new world are waiting at the end of it when we are born. I have a feeling it may be something like that when we die and I do so want to be gathered up into that bright warmth.

A bubbling cough forces itself painfully upwards and arms rush to lift me from my pillow. They should take this sinking ship and point it home, not try to urge it towards their own safe shores but they can't do it. They have to try to save me. It's only natural.

Death from pneumonia used to be commonplace but not easy, even though it was called 'the old man's friend'. Lungs gradually fill with fluid and frail hearts pump faster and faster to try to circulate oxygen around the body. It's a slow drowning but I'm content and detached. I've started peeling myself away from all that was my life. I've signed the DNR order and the refusal of all drugs so it will be relatively quick, no matter how hard they cling to me. At ninety-seven I'm quite ready to go.

I remember that skeletal hand once more and yet other tinier hands that caught at me; and then, with a lurch that shakes my old frame: Harriet.

Her death was unpleasant.

*Carcinoma of the bowel,* the death certificate said. That is how I found Harriet, through her death certificate. She had been deliberately expunged from memory until I read her name and spoke the words that carried with them a glimpse of her suffering. Glanrigg Workhouse in 1937 could not have been a good place to die. No pain relief, inadequate food, little nursing, no visitors. Would anyone have lifted her back on to her pillows from the bottom of the bed where she had crawled in screaming agony? Would anyone have cared that she was soiled or her lips were cracked from thirst? I heard the stories of such deaths when I was a child: stories mouthed behind hands with the word *cancer*, a mutual terror of monstrous proportions hanging between those who whispered of it. I hope death came to collect Harriet long before her body abandoned the tenacity that is life.

Hands that belong to a world I still inhabit but which seems a just a little further away now, reach to pat mine.

'Gran, won't you have a bit of pain relief? Won't you *please* take some antibiotics?' My head shakes wearily on the pillow. And there it is; what I've been waiting for. That sensation that everything I ever was is here all around me once more, filling me up tighter than the bubbles in my chest. I smile as I stare into the familiar woven strands and patterns of the life that has brought me to this point. They wind off into an unseeable distance that I know I must travel before my ball of light will be there, waiting for me. This time; this time.

'Mum, it's all right.'

Yes, it is all right, but there is so much to gather together, and so much to let go of.

Harriet. I shouldn't be surprised at remembering her now. Finding Harriet was a watershed, bending and focusing meaning into a pure point of understanding that altered my life forever. I can see the point glowing, welding the strands of so many events together. I grasp at it but it speeds past me as I dive much further back in my life, to where the strands had almost unravelled. It was a long time ago and death was there too.

Racing in my chest, my overworked heart has now the flutter of a captive bird that has seen the sky and is ready to leap up to blue freedom. But its fluttering brings with it the awful memory of another little captive.

# 1

## IN THE BEGINNING ALL THINGS ARE HOPEFUL

It is only a little death. A small death I try to forget. It should be significant, it should tell me to stop but there are too many raw edges to gather in, to make proper sense of it. The warning goes ignored.

I sink into the aqua sky of a July night, light enough to glow but not yet dark enough to be overtaken by that other, familiar industrial glow of molten slag. Breathing a huge sigh into the moist air, I try to make myself an empty room with quiet whitewashed walls and evening sunshine slanting on warm floors. I need to be still inside now and pull the cotton wool from out of my head. I'm trying hard to clear my mind. It feels just like the case I've tried to pack, there isn't room for one more thing. So now there is only this walking, alone, trying to break free of the manic mixture of preparation, panic and euphoria that surrounds a wedding.

My wedding.

Tomorrow.

And I'm trying really, really hard to be hopeful.

In the beginning, my Gran says, all things are hopeful.

'You've got it all there, our Mia; all possibilities are right in your hand the minute you set out on a fresh journey.' She knows stuff, my Gran does.

So I pace this scrubby, forlorn piece of waste ground I've trodden since childhood, searching for hope among the brambles, dandelions and empty bottles. The familiar clank and roar of the distant steelworks is almost a comforting background to my thoughts. It's always been there, always in my head. I've only ever known peaceful silence in the forests and hills when we go to Germany to visit Oma and Opa, my other granny and granddad.

'Am I doing the right thing?' I mutter to the sky.

A hooter sounds and the night shift begins, while a homeward stream of bicycles from the two till ten shift rushes its parched owners via the nearest pub, headlights dotting along the nearby dual carriageway. Ten o'clock. Just a small space to sink a pint or two before closing time and slake the thirst of the rolling mill floor. Urgency immediately plucks at me too, spiking and fraying the edges of the panic I've contained up until now. I think I love this man but no one has thought to tell me this isn't how it works.

'I remember.'

'What do you remember, gran?'

There's a hand on mine but I can't acknowledge it. I'm fixed on that evening more than 70 years ago, drawn tautly along the edge of its awfulness. It's 1968 and my world is the steel town of Scugton. 'Goblin's fire', in old English they said it meant at school, and I always thought it very appropriate. For even though the works had only been there about a hundred years, the livid red night skies reminded me of demons at work and I used to think that the grimy workers scurrying home were fleeing from some sort of hell. It was a frightening place to be as a child, growing up so close to a steel-work's clashing jaws.

I'm 20 now.

I'm 20, unsure and still frightened, but this has more to do with life at home than goblins or demons. Anything has to be better than where I've been until now. I've come to my limits. Marriage is my ticket out and I'm grasping at the hope that it will work out all right. Perhaps once I've started this particular journey, I'll know what to do to make it work.

The trick, Granny Rose says, is to read the signs.

'Get your nose off the ground, girl. Look around carefully enough and there will always be something there, however insignificant it may seem, that will show you what to do.'

I smile for a moment as I think of her cocking her head at me as she tries on her wedding hat over the unruly wig that covers her wispy tufts of white hair.

Our council flats loom up in front of me, grey and expressionless as always, their orange window eyes hooded promptly at sunset, no matter how beautiful the evening. Nobody around here looks at sunsets; nobody except me. I walk even more slowly. I don't want to get back yet. That would mean sitting with my mother in her growing anger and desperation, waiting to finalise tomorrow's details, while my father, pub bound, buries his increasing irritations in the ever-understanding arms of the *Open Hearth*.

His most recent gripe was the discovery that I was on the Pill. It's still a bit of a scandalous novelty in this narrow northern town where contraception has mostly been the province of blokes — if they choose to bother, that is. The expected choice for a 'good girl' is to do as my great-aunty Gertie suggests and use another pill — an aspirin clamped between my knees.

'How do you think that makes me feel, Mia? Knowing my daughter is on the Pill and couldn't wait until her wedding night?' my dad had thundered.

'Yes, and how do you think it makes me feel, everyone knowing my dad is a drunk who raises his hand to me and my mam?' I thought it but never dared say it.

'Stop it! Think!'

I stuff clenched fists deep into the pockets of my trousers and pummel my legs in frustration. I'm in clothes I loathe because tomorrow even these get left behind. A faded sugar pink hand-me-down jumper and blouse (still smelling of salami) sent from Germany by Mrs Vogel, mam's condescending friend, who reckons England is a poor and backward place; a vast pair of shapeless, blue Marks & Spencer trousers that my mother bought and wouldn't wear (and I'm too fearful to tell her that I hate them) and my favourite old jumble sale stilettos. I'm only wearing these things because there's nobody to see me and everything else is packed. There would be an argument about leaving her with washing to do even on my wedding day if I wore anything decent today.

'*Jede Tag! Jede Tag es gibt arbeite!*' ('Every day! Every day there's work!' she would say.)

Anyway, they add to a sense that I'm about to slough off an old skin and start again, so I try once more to focus on the hope that surrounds all possible futures, forcing my expanding panic back into the recesses where I've pushed everything that hurts or worries or terrifies.

'Damn!'

My stiletto sinks into the soft path and I lurch forward leaving my shoe behind. I turn, hopping backwards, trying not to put my foot on the ground. I've showered and shampooed and scrubbed at the Public Baths today because the bath in our flat has never been used and the taps no longer turn. We can't afford the hot water for it, anyway.

'Ach! Do you sink I have nozzing better to do zan clean a bassroom after you?' It wouldn't matter if I did it myself because she'd only do it again, convinced that if she could work hard enough, all things would fall into place. The bathroom sits in pristine splendour, unused towels tweaked into perfect piles. The bar of Pear's soap in the soap dish smells inviting but has a slight dusting of the steelworks grit that finds its way into every crack and crevice of living in this place. In the airing cupboard, corner squared piles of her perfect wedding present linen that would do justice to an Omo advert, all sit waiting to be used, but never will be. She dusts the cupboard now and then but that's as far as it goes. I have to get washed at the kitchen sink, with Fairy household soap, hiding my embarrassment and ignoring her jibes.

'Vot again? You shtink of fanny? Get voshed!'

A movement in a bramble patch catches my eye as I wriggle my shoe back on. It's backlit by a sky spurt of molten slag that's strangely much redder than usual. In the billowing gases and steam clouds over the works, the colours swirl and congeal to form monstrous shapes. I've seen all this before and always reasoned that it was my imagination — my childhood nights have been perpetually illuminated by such shapes looming in the redness of the ten o'clock shift. But this time it's different. I'm transfixed for a moment by the suggestion of a horrid mask with a red jag of a mouth and dark pools for eyes. Momentarily dizzy, I gasp at those menacing, sightless eye sockets. I know this from somewhere.

'Stop it. It'll go away, it always does.'

Slag clouds are ever changing, ever menacing, but they don't mean anything, except to the men who sweat over the slag tipping, I suppose. They'll watch out for the billowing clouds all right. There was a rumour when I was a child that the slag locomotives carried a long steel rod, not for rescuing men caught unawares in the tipping but for pushing them under. It was less cruel that way because there was no hope once 'old man slag' got you. I shudder as I think of a clawing hand vanishing into that treacly slurping mass and of slag pouring into burnt eye sockets and an open mouth. Then there is that eerie sensation of a connection again; a connection to somewhere, somewhen.

'Enough! This isn't getting you anywhere. You're supposed to be pulling yourself together, not frightening yourself to death. It will go. Leave it.'

Sure enough, the shape dissipates and as I turn back to the path to try and find exactly what it was that caught my eye there in the brambles, the tattered remnants of the red glow silhouettes a small bird, a sparrow. It's fluttering and not getting anywhere. It must be trapped.

'Hold on a minute, little one.'

All thoughts of faces in the clouds and clawing hands, of doubts and weddings, are pushed away as I try to reach the bird. All my life I've always rescued even the smallest living creature in trouble, carrying spiders carefully outside, feeding honey to butterflies with broken wings and ensuring that I never trod on anything that wriggled or scuttled across my path. I'm the girl with a wormery, not flowers on her bedroom windowsill.

'A life is a life,' I mutter, remembering how my dad poured boiling water down an ant hole among his broad beans and how I scooped up the forlorn stragglers returning to an empty nest.

I have to force more brambles aside to get at this little specimen of life but I still can't reach and my arms are getting scratched.

'That won't look very nice tomorrow,' I catch myself saying and realise, with a sense of sinking finality, that I've already committed myself to going through with it.

'I'm escaping tomorrow and I'll help you to do it now little birdie, if you'll just hold still.' That sounds just like one of my Gran's signs.

Taking off my pink jumper and winding it round my arm, I push my way to the centre of the bush. I can see now that the sparrow is caught by some thread that has wound round and round its legs and feet. Its beak is open and its head is lifted to the sky and freedom. It strains to escape even more as it feels me approaching. I fumble and pick at its bonds but I can't unwind the thread and this tiny soul is threshing about wildly now. I bend down and, despite the beating of wings in my face, I bite away what threads I can reach. Then, suddenly, with a whirr it's free and leaping into the twilight sky. My face, however, is bent in horror over the place where it was held. The black thread is still there, hopelessly entangled in the brambles. And caught in the thread are two tiny, clawed feet.

A fluttering, tumbling sound makes me turn and I catch sight of this desperate soul trying to find a purchase on familiar branches. Air is scooped into wings and spilled out as it falls deeper into the hawthorn. As it disappears from view I hear its voice for the first time, a single shrill call torn from its breast as it flutters, flutters, flutters. I retch violently into the brambles and begin to run along the muddy path towards the flats, my pounding footsteps and the swish of grasses against the old blue trousers drowning out that terrible sound. I don't stop until I reach my Gran's and burst through her door to stand panting in the tiny hall, the heels of my shoes digging into the green linoleum. Wretchedly, I kick them off and wipe a hand across my face, finding cold sweat there. Maybe I should go into the kitchen and wash the blood spots from my arms first.

'Is that you, Mia?'

'Just getting a drink.'

Gran lives in the flat diagonally opposite and below ours. It's a good job it isn't directly below ours or she would be subject to the continual shouting and rowing that has formed the fabric of my daily life for as long as I can remember, my mother's guttural German oaths sounding above my father's drink slurred threats. Gran knows all about it, though, from the whispered confidences shared by the neighbours and what she's seen and heard herself. One after another, the neighbours in the flat below us all left after a year or less, never saying exactly why. Now there's just Mrs White, a deaf old lady, with her handicapped son whom no one ever sees.

In the grey, cast concrete entrance hall of the flats are the stairs I hate climbing, dreading what I will find when I open the door to number 148 on the first landing. As a small child I climbed up on the outside of the iron banisters, partly because I want to feel brave and partly to take as long as I could to reach that landing. Finally, there's no choice but to stand on the coconut fibre mat that says 'Welcome' in worn orange letters. But there never is a welcome. Once, in impotent teenage rage, I wrote 'you're' and 'to this' on torn pieces of exercise book paper, placing them either side of the 'Welcome' but I didn't have the nerve to leave them there. I always listen at the door before turning the handle; sometimes retreating back down the stairs when I'm afraid of what lies inside, sneaking into Granny Rose's arms for a while to gather courage.

This is the place where I come when it gets too much, when I need comfort, or simply when I need to make sense of all that's going on in my life, although each one of these council flats has, in turn, been a bolt-hole. Mrs Revell and her poodle Topper are always glad to see me; there's a biscuit, a cup of tea and endless streams of mind-soothing chatter waiting there. Josie and Mary, two elderly Scottish spinster sisters in the flat opposite ours are a little dour but always seem to know when I need to get out of the way of my mam and dad. Except I ruin it when I teach Joey, their yellow budgie, to say 'shit'. They weren't so accommodating after a stream of 'Joey, Joey, Joey, shit, shit, shit, shit,' shocks their Presbyterian brother. The flat above ours has had as many occupants as the one below and I have no idea who lives there now.

Drying my hands on the pink jumper, I push open the door to Granny Rose's cosy, untidy living room, flinging myself down into one of her overstuffed, second-hand armchairs. I slide the snagged and bloodstained salami jumper away behind me and gather myself. Although it's summer and only just dusk, the lights are on, the worn curtains are drawn and Gran is in her nightie and green candlewick dressing gown, wig removed, sipping whisky and hot milk and seated next to her gas fire. Damn! She can see I'm upset and stares quizzically over her long nose, through thick National Health glasses, the remains of her white hair stuck out at all angles. She holds her head on one side like a bird, her scrawny neck and wattles lending to the effect.

Always alert to my moods, she sees what a state I'm in and, never one to hold back on her thoughts and feelings, puts down her china cup with a rattle and blurts out, 'You're not thinkin' of callin' it off, are you?' An arthritic knuckle on her forefinger catches in the cup handle and she shakes it free, swearing softly but never taking her eyes from me for a second. Her brows are raised in wrinkled folds high above the rim of the glasses.

'No, of course not.'

I don't suppose I'd have the courage actually to do it. Not that she would mind for one moment if I did. Her only worry would be that I was all right. She would go upstairs and stand up for me against my parents, she would go across the road to use Mrs Travers' phone and make all the necessary calls, she would find someone to buy the dress, she would get the cake portioned up and stored away for Christmas, she would tuck me up safely in her bed and tell me that things would be fine. She has been my harbour, my consolation and my hiding place for as long as I can remember. No matter what, she is always the same. She is safety.

'No Gran, don't be silly, that's the last thing I'd do. I've just had a bit of a shock, that's all.'

Haltingly, I tell her about the bird and, by the time I'm finished I've a hard lump pushing in my throat and my eyes jab with tears. I can't let them fall because if I do somewhere inside a dam will burst and the river behind will never, never stop, pouring endless grief and rage from where I have contained it as part of the rust-marked design that is now me. She stares into the gas fire for a long time, its orange light reflected in her glasses so that I can't see her eyes or what she might be thinking.

The warmth of the fire has released a fusty smell of old things into the faded room. On the sideboard, among the photos and cracked fake Toby jugs and the pile of bills that never seems to get any smaller, her wedding hat is carefully perched on her wig, ready for tomorrow. Her shoes have been cleaned and placed by the door, and handbag and gloves sit with ceremonial neatness on the crocheted doily in the middle of her big gateleg table. I know there will be at least two mothballs in that bag, as there are in every other drawer, chest or cupboard in the flat. I screw my face at the imagined smell and a tear, unbidden, squeezes out. She sees me looking at her things and although I think I have disguised the tears pretty well, she hands me a folded handkerchief from the sleeve of her dressing gown.

'I think it's a sign,' she finally pronounces.

The gas fire flickers in her glasses.

Granny Rose sees signs everywhere, a hidden hand working to tell her the paths to tread, to warn her against danger, to alert her to someone's needs. They can be anything, from the look on the face of a stranger (she believes my dead granddad smiles at her this way), to the pattern of events.

'One more crime i' the paper an' mark me words, something really nasty is goin' to 'appen soon, badness builds up, you know.' She sees signs in the shapes of washing blowing on the line, and even in the way Mrs Travers' ginger tom behaves. 'Cats pick up all sorts of things we can't see.' I feel almost relieved. I've always found her signs just a bit silly but a loveable part of her, nevertheless. I almost want to believe them but my survival tool, the relentless, fierce logic that drove me to tell my parents, when I was barely five, that there couldn't possibly be a Father Christmas, will never let me accept the presence of anything in this world that will not yield to this logic. It's how I survive.

My world is driven by cause and effect. I am unhappy, not because I fail to comply with some mysterious guiding force but because my father is an alcoholic and my mother, brought to England from Germany at the end of the war, hates this country, her life here and my father's drunken rages. I am the mutual target of their frustrations. These are simple, hard facts. Now that Granny Rose thinks the bird is a sign, its plight seems abstract and somehow less horrific. I blow my nose, ceasing to pretend unconcern, and give her a watery smile. Finally she speaks.

'Well, that bird must a' bin quite a shock. I don' think I could 'ave freed it,' and then pursing her lips, she pronounces her decision. 'I think… I think it means that if ivver you leave this marriage you'll 'ave t' tear out part o' yoursen' and leave it be'ind,' she says firmly and quietly, slipping into Lincolnshire dialect to give her thoughts emphasis.

'Oh.'

I don't probe further because I know her views on marriage. She stuck with my granddad through grinding poverty, roaring drunkenness and his countless affairs and says she would do it all again because he was the love of her life. She's spoken to me about the sacrament of marriage for as long as I can remember.

'Well, I'm not thinking about divorce before I'm even married!'

'No one ivver does.'

Her glasses glint once more as she puts on the 'well-don't-say-I-didn't-warn-you' look that she wears when I am about to do something that goes against her signs. She is silent for a long time, searching my face for some indication of dilemma or doubt but I've recovered myself now. I possess a consummate masking skill born, like my other survival skills, of dire necessity. It allows me to slip into worlds where I am not terrified, where I am calm and in control and where nothing can reach me for a while.

Now I am the eager bride, flushed with excitement, eyes filled with expectation and shyness. The part I'm playing usually takes over who I am; I sometimes wonder who I really am because my disguises fool even her every so often. Finally, satisfied there is no drama about to unfold, she cackles her wonderful laugh, slapping her thigh for emphasis.

'Well, you'd better 'elp me git this bloody wig an' 'at sorted out fer termorrer,' she cracks out, her pointed chin almost meeting her long nose as her lips suck into a mock grimace.

The task of turning the straw-like National Health wig into a suitable platform for a sugar pink confection of a wedding hat reduces us both to giggles. Granny Rose lost most of her hair in her forties when she had gold injections for severe arthritis. They didn't help much and left her head covered with a thin down of pure white wool, subdued and crimped with frequent home perms. Finally, the family doctor, for whom she cleans house, recommended her for a wig that she is too poor to afford for herself. She tolerates it until she becomes too hot and then, regardless of the company she's in, pushes it to the back of her head until she cools down.

'Now no pushing this back tomorrow, Gran.'

Granny Rose looks up at me in mock surprise and horror.

'Cross me 'eart an' 'ope to die. It will not move!'

I carefully remove hat and wig together and balance them on a tall wooden candlestick on the sideboard. I feel a little calmer now.

'Do me chin as well, duck,' she twinkles. I root around for her tweezers in one of the Toby jugs and then proceed to de-whisker her chin.

'Bugger it! That one was knotted o' th' inside,' she explodes as I remove a particularly stubborn bristle.

'There, you're done. Smooth as a moth's nose.'

'Moth's nose?'

'Yeah, Karl Shapiro, poet.' My Gran knows stuff but she likes to hear stuff I know too. Apart from my aunt Peg, she's the only one who has ever been interested in *what* I actually know.

'Any relation to Helen?' she cracks out, beginning to intone *Walking Back to Happiness*.

'Nope,' I reply, joining in with one of her favourite pop hits.

'Woopah, oh yeah, yeah!' we bellow. She's not at all square, my Gran. I dance around the cramped room with a lace antimacassar over my head, dodging furniture and making her worn fireside rug slide on the linoleum. The panic of tomorrow, the fears of yesterday, the sparrow, are all neatly parcelled up like the wedding gifts that are stacked just inside our front door, waiting for my uncle Geoff to take them to the reception in his car. I know they'll have to be opened but not today. Not today.

Fully in the role now, I switch to wedding songs.

'Here comes me Gran, hat like a frying pan,' I shriek to *Here Comes the Bride*, waving the cloth in the air. 'Here comes me dad, steaming drunk and mad.'

I pause and giggle again, remembering how he said, in an inebriated moment, that I really ought to walk down the aisle to the *Ride of the Valkyries.* He had described how the church door would crash open, thunder would roll and I'd stride in dressed in wreaths of black, accompanied by swirling storm clouds. I took it as a real compliment.

'Here comes me mam, now some doors will slam!'

Granny Rose has a finger to her lips. She gets up stiffly from her stool in front of the sideboard mirror and takes my hands in hers. For a moment I think she is going to dance with me but she folds me into her thin arms and hugs me as if I am a small child again.

'I love you, Mia,' she murmurs into the nape of my neck, her bony fingers pressing care and concern into the hard shell I wear. 'Come and see your old Gran now and then.'

She brushes my hair back from my forehead and plants a wet kiss on the scar where I fell from a chair, aged just three. She never knew how it happened and I never told on my mam. I daren't.

'Love you too, Gran. I'll come on the bus and see you whenever

I can. Just you have the kettle on ready.'

She draws back, pulling the green candlewick dressing gown around her stooped shoulders and hitching up her heavy breasts. She looks so old and fragile. My Gran.

'B' the way, I 'ope you're gitting on all right wi' the Pill,' she twinkles back. 'Good idea to git used to it afore you git married. Did it mek you sick i' the mornings like they say?'

I gape at her for a moment. She is shaking with suppressed mirth and doesn't wait for a reply.

'Now off up them stairs and git an early night.' I feel something pushed into my hand. It is a pair of pink porcelain rose-shaped earrings. Next to the cameo that auntie Alice left her, they are the only thing of any value that she possesses.

'Summats borrered,' she smiles.

And so I marry the next day, too desperate not to.

There; that is where the unravelling really began. At a point in my life when things should really have come together, they began a slow, relentless disintegration…

… I cough once more and my gaze follows the bright strands of memory twisting forward into an inevitable tangled mess.

'Talk to her, hearing is the last thing to go,' a professional voice soothes. I've heard that somewhere before.

'Gran, what are you staring at?'

'Can she see someone?'

I can but it's not what they think. It would be neat and comforting to think that the dying are visited by those who have passed on but it has never happened to me. Just this brilliance, this clarity of meanings laid out like jewels; necklaces of events, each bead a moment that can be expanded infinitely or gathered with others to view a design, a pattern to life. My mind fingers them greedily and comes to rest on not what happened next but on Harriet once more.

I can actually see her standing in her tiny back yard, bent over her washing and I don't question it. I can see her. I know it's not my imagination and yet this can't be a memory; this is a woman who died almost a hundred years ago. But here she is as clear as the rest of my intertwining memories, lodged in the tangle of my past, caught fast and held up for inspection. What *is* she doing here?

And I have hold of the strand now.

# 2

# LIFE IS SO BEAUTIFUL

I can hear her thinking.

'Life is *soooo* beautiful,' Harriet sighs to herself as she bends over her clothes steeping barrels in her tiny backyard. She has just felt the quickening of the child inside her and, with a jolt of realisation, I sense it too. I can feel her rough breathing as she rubs at a stain with cracked hands that smart and sting.

'It's got all raw bits but it's still beautiful. Sometimes you on'y see it 'cos of all the ugliness folks does. Ay, like a diamond 'gainst black. Mebbe a memory, a moment, a look or mebbe a kind word; well, it just gleams out 'gainst it all.'

My heart lurches in the heaving sea of my chest as I recognise the thick Lincolnshire dialect Granny Rose spoke. It's so long since I heard it but I pull on its familiarity like a worn and much loved coat as I run along the threads of her thoughts.

'Me numbers,' she muses, pausing to rub at a shirt collar, 'I've got some that's so beautiful, well, they light yer up inside where 'urt's carved a big 'ole. They come wi' a smile and a sigh after tears 'ave bin all cried out. Number seventeen that 'un, numbered it special, I did.'

As I am pulled along her inner conversation, there's a momentary dazzling glimpse of hundreds of carefully listed and numbered memories that is somehow at odds with a stooping washerwoman in dark, darned and mended rags.

'It's beautiful,' she smiles as she stirs, 'when you see summat real ordinary and it catches your throat, right there because of 'ow lovely it is. Yes, that's it. It sugar-melts the 'owd thorns inside, like mam's honey warmed b' the fire.'

I catch at this memory that's not mine, that could not possibly be mine. It's so real I can nearly touch it and I luxuriate in its warmth as I gaze beyond and through her life to the complex path that has brought her here.

'Bairn stirrin' inside again. That's number eight, I reckon, right next to the bird sittin' on its nest wi' eggs pressin' up close. We'd mek the same sound, me an' 'er.' In her mind I hear a low croon, like a dove. She smiles, a soft, warm light in her eyes as they fall on the dark, tousled head of her youngest child, Fred. There he sits, straggled across the back doorstep making a sticky, dribbly meal of bread and jam. A long, grubby and torn girl's dress is covered over against the February cold by a knitted jacket that's far too small and emphasises his waif-like frame. Tiny, tattered shoes are tied on to his bare feet with bits of string and, incongruously, a snow white, starched and frilled bonnet caps his long, sticky black curls. I love him instantly, or is it Harriet's feelings that surge through my old body?

'Not yet breeched but yer still my little man. Fred, my on'y son,' she murmurs to herself.

For all his ragged clothes and a filth-encrusted face that even a starched bonnet cannot offset and for all the fact that he is the tenth of the children she cares for, he is beautiful and remarkable to her, and she knows Sereton Terrace is totally and gluttonously scandalised by it. The child is a bastard and, having been got in widowhood, doubly shocking for that. As the poor relict, the lone mother, she knows she should assume modest invisibility; someone whom society can conveniently forget.

'Well they won't forget me in an 'urry!'

I feel the thought hammer insistently against her chest even as I feel the child paddling its feet inside her and we become one.

I'm Harriet.

I'm Harriet but I'm still me; an undercurrent of thought in her head muttering about logic, and how can I be remembering two lives? I haven't lived this one before, so how come?

We swat the thought away like a fly and shift our gaze to stare absently over the wash house rooftops along the single sided, long, uniform row of red brick houses that makes up Sereton Terrace. All are home to the families of iron workers, first hopeful and now resigned refugees from the surrounding countryside, just like us. Behind the houses, less than two hundred yards away, the Appleton Iron Works squats like a monstrous grey toad. The cycle of toil as its twin furnaces are fed provides a livelihood for each one of these families, their menfolk milling around its dangerous flanks. Loading the furnaces with ore, coke and limestone is a non-stop occupation.

'Ay, the beast is allus 'ungry,' she sighs, inspecting a delicate lace handkerchief for stains as she bends once more to her work.

The beast really is always hungry and never sleeps, for if the furnaces were ever allowed to cool, the resulting cut off in production while they were bored out would mean loss of earnings for everyone.

'No bread upon the table then,' we mutter.

Stoking the blasting ovens, blasting the ore mixture and forming the sand moulds or pigs for the molten iron also has to continue non-stop because every now and then, the beast is milked.

'A gret sow wi' piglets.'

The furnaces are tapped at their bases to run off the contents into the pigs before the pig iron is finally loaded into wagons for its journey across the river to various steelworks. Slag, the volatile, molten and crusted impurities, the unwanted excrement at the end of this process, has to be dumped. The grind is endless. Dig the ore, load the furnace, blast the mixture, tap off the iron, stack the pigs and dump the slag.

The men get one Sunday a month off if they're lucky. Locals sometimes call this monster the 'Irish Works', referring to its owners, others mouth oaths about it, but to most it is just 'the Works', its twin furnaces and two tall brick chimneys dominating the backyard skyline of Sereton Terrace.

'What a claggy owd place! This i'n't my Wolds!' we sigh, remembering the gently folded hills where we grew up.

We straighten up again and stare at our surroundings in distaste. Away to the fore of the Terrace is a wasteland of opencast mining and shallow tunnels as men grovel and shovel for the iron ore to fuel this monster. Their toils have inflicted long, sandy scars deep into the hillside and across the woods and fields that lead to Sereton village. It is altogether a bleak, wrecked and wretched landscape.

'Look at us all, what we're doin' for a roof and a bite to yet. Still, it's better than starvin', an' more than what we left be'ind.'

Thirty or so smaller chimneys puff out the smoke of a Sunday afternoon coal fire as the abundant and uncountable children of thirty or so families swarm around the street. Some stand stiffly and awkwardly in their Sunday best clothes, pinafores clean and starched, with cloth caps wedged uncomfortably atop scrubbed faces. Others, who have never known the need for cleanliness or Godliness, bowl hoops, skip, throw stones, fight, chalk the ends of wooden spinning tops ready for the whip, or simply run up and down shouting. Harriet can just make out her girls Mary, Edith, Gertie and Alice playing hopscotch with Will's four children. Will... Fred's father. She's mothered his four as best she can, since taking up with him but it's made ten mouths to feed with Fred, and Clara, her eldest.

'Thank God for Clara. She's a worker like 'er mam. As for them sisters of 'ers, there's nowt to mention o' me in 'em; they're all a bit nobbut,' she mutters to herself. Awkward lasses, those four, every one of them. Just like their father.

'God rest his soul!' The thought is agonising, burning and intense and surges like molten slag into our every corner and crevice. Shocked, I pull away. I thought I glimpsed a familiar face there, its jagged mouth slackening and sliding itself off into a pig mould, while a skeletal hand with fingers burned to the bone, flaps weakly in her face...

... The horror of it jolts me back into the ward, sweating into my pillow.

The distorted images that have billowed their way through the slag clouds of my childhood are in Harriet's thoughts too. But that face! It seems only moments since I glimpsed it in my own memories. Now I'm seeing it in hers. How could that be?

'What am I talking about? These aren't my memories,' the thought stamps into my mind.

This doesn't make sense but it feels so real. I'm not afraid; there's a little fever now and it's not drugs. I've stayed deliberately calm and focused, refusing everything that's been offered because I so want to experience once more the peace and absolute joy that comes at the end. Yet still there is that bright and horrible point of a memory that Harriet and I seem to have shared. I hadn't expected this. This isn't the dying process I longed for.

'Not right,' I insist to myself.

'What's not right, gran?' my granddaughter murmurs, stroking my hand.

I can't explain any of this. What would it mean to my family anyway? So I keep my eyes closed and sweat quietly into my pillow, puzzling and puzzling over what I've just seen…

… When I open them once more I'm gazing over the rooftops of Sereton Terrace again, trying to distance myself a little from Harriet's thoughts. I need to understand this. I never knew that much about her life so it's not as if I'm creating a memory from things that I knew. Yet, for a few moments, I was Harriet. I know I was.

She looks down to the house eight doors along where she used to live with her five daughters and John Henry Blanchard, her late husband. There's a crawling, pricking thought around his name that

I try to follow but she is distracted by a movement among the throng near her gate. A shawled and bonneted woman pushes through, her eyes fixed determinedly our way, her shawl clutched tightly around her shoulders. Harriet turns away and I mentally back away with her because we already know what's coming. With a cough, a rasp and the sound of a practised and expertly aimed spit, a large gob of saliva and green mucus flies her way and lands at her feet.

'Hooar! Trollops!' the woman hisses, staring at Harriet and Fred. 'An' that little bastard ought to be tekken away. Tha's 'ad more tail than 'ud retch from 'ere to the station. Wicked 'ussy!'

Ignoring the insults and quickly swilling the slime away down the yard gully with a bucket of steeping water, Harriet's face remains a blank.

'It doesn't matter what that old cow says,' I whisper fiercely into her consciousness but she can't hear me. Still, I feel no upset or shame in her, just an acceptance and a proud backbone that is her fierce love of life. It's all in our conjoined mind's eye. When knowing eyes and tongues pick at her sorrow, which they do most of the time, she thinks of her son Fred and all the beautiful things she has collected and numbered in her memory. All through the sting of words whispered behind hands as she passes by, through the disgusted looks in the street, through the pointed spitting in the scuffed sawdust at her feet when she takes her quart can to the *Blue Bell* for ale — through it all she counts her litany of beautiful things. No, there is no shame there but rather a feeling that she is as she is, for better or worse.

'You git what you git,' Harriet murmurs to herself. 'It's 'ow yer live it what counts.'

There are times, I can feel, when she is just numb, carrying on unseeing with the maze of tasks her life as a widow with nine children and another got in widowhood continually presents. And, yes, despite the consolation of her youngest and the rare, boundless beauty of the inner life that sustains her, there are times when she is angry. Then she fixes her thoughts on her numbered list and walks, head up, with a distant gaze and a fiery smile that further incenses the righteous.

A calendar nailed in the shelter of the outhouse privy pronounces the year is 1897. Its weeks are circled and marked with signs that denote Harriet's duties as a washerwoman. She is staring absently at its pages, her rough finger carefully counting the months of the year laid out at the top of the page. I can feel the deep cracks at the side of her fingernails smarting as she touches each month. She can count them but I see she can only read their names properly with real effort.

'February 1897,' she muses out loud, twisting a stray lock of hair behind her ear. 'Five months to go then, mebbbe less. Now 'ere's a pretty pickle. 'Ere I am, a widow wi' five girls, in the arms of a widower wi' 'is own four in tow. Not to mention Fred! Oh Will, whatever next?'

But it's a coy smile that plays on her tired face now as I feel her thoughts run around his sturdy shape. Her body tells me not only of her love but also of her desire for him and I can feel, on the far, white remoteness of my hospital bed, a soft moan of longing and recognition escape my lips.

The difficulties of her situation seethe and fulminate through

Harriet's mind as she puts another load of whites to steep in lye, in one of the seven half-barrels. Her hands are scorched by splashes from the caustic solution and its rankness catches at her breath. She'd only had just enough for soaking and soaping this week. The gravel-filled hardwood tub through which she strains pounded wood ash and rainwater has yielded its last from where it stands, raised up on two bricks. There's not a drop of lye in the old iron pan underneath. Nothing to boil up into that foul brew that, when mixed with pig fat, could make her enough soap to get by.

She stares at her barrels once more. Each one has a different stone tied to it by which she remembers whose linen, with its stains and secrets, belong to whom. The marks are repeated on the faded calendar at which she now glances. The Lord knows, she shouldn't be steeping on a Sunday but if she doesn't, then the washing will never be back on time.

The wisp of reddish brown hair that she tucked behind her ear falls forward as she bends to agitate each barrel. Harriet tucks it back into her neat bun and her lined, parchment coloured face shoots another smile at her youngest on the back doorstep who is eating his bread with a bare scraping of jam as though it was a feast. Her beloved Fred has been the outcome of a coming together of two souls in need and now another child is on the way; she is not dismayed but happy. Intensely happy. Our eyes gleam as she thinks of his father again.

'Med sure of that. Fred is keepin' 'is father's name.'

I catch at the memory and its ferocity. When she'd emerged after her brief lying-in to stand before old Bainton, the registrar, she looked at this tiny warmth cradled in her arms and, while stoutly declaring the father to be unknown, had given the child Will's last name, attaching her widow's name after.

'Make your mark here then,' old Bainton had sighed, still frowning slightly at the odd ring 'Fred Ogley Blanchard' had to it. Harriet remembers thankfully that he was in no mood to comment. She'd overheard him telling the secretary that he'd just registered the fifth infant death that day to which the only attributable cause of death was phythisis.

'Sheer want and poverty,' he'd rumbled, beckoning Harriet into the panelled office. 'All too common, Miss Stevens, in the streets around the iron and steelworks of this area,' he'd growled. 'The iron industry is a very mixed blessing indeed.'

Harriet had dipped the pen into his brass topped inkwell and made her mark, a cross whose two arms were joined at the top with a careful wave that made it look like a bleeding heart. Her longing is so intense that I pull away for a while again. It hurts so much to be Harriet, not because of her circumstances but because of that deep, pressing hunger for a man; a particular man. I remember that so well. It was the cause of most of my troubles too.

'If only I could write proper.'

She captures me again, the thought coming to her as she clicks her tongue over the women's stains in the Duffelen's bucket. She knows she will have to soap, scrub and boil those tomorrow. I catch the thought and feel its heaviness. Its weight almost pulls her out of focus but I hold it fast.

'Steeping Sunday, boiling, scrubbing and washing Monday — drying if I get lucky — folding and starching Tuesday, ironing and airing Wednesday, clean bundles returned on Thursday for the housekeepers to check it and the maids store to it away. It's on'y because I git the washing back a day early I 'ave so much work, thank the Lord.'

Harriet bends to examine the drawers in the Duffelen's bucket once more.

'If on'y I could write proper I would set it all down in a jou… what's the word? A journal, that's it, like the one I saw when I called back wi' the washing from the big 'ouse in Church Lane.'

I am startled by the sheer intensity of the thought and pulled tight by its longing.

A maid had knocked ink over the missus's diary when she was dusting and there she was crying and wringing her hands in a corner of the kitchen while the cook squeezed lemon juice on the stains and fussed and dabbed and squeezed and dabbed until the ink grew faint and brown. There was such a commotion on that nobody had noticed as she stood by the scullery door, waiting for her next bundle. Fascinated, she'd watched as the blue, leather bound pages were turned to reveal a delicate script, interspersed with tiny swatches of fabric, a sketch of a bridge, a ticket of some sort pasted in, a pressed flower. She inhaled a faint scent of lily of the valley (just like those that bloomed outside her childhood home for a brief week in May) as a decorated card fluttered to the floor. But it was the vigorous, looped writing that burned into her memory.

'What does it say?' she'd breathed, her narrow grey eyes and furrowed forehead for once widening with wonder. I can feel that wonder pass through her even now as she stands stock still in her tiny yard.

'Lord, what are you doing here all as quiet as a mouse? This is nothing for the likes of you. It's a journal but I doubt whether you would have much to tell about the daily goings on in your life unless it was for a penny dreadful!'

The housekeeper, a tightly corseted wasp of a woman in brown serge, had appeared from the bottom of the servant's stairs and thrust a rancid bundle of washing into her arms, pushing her towards the back door as she did so.

'And we want it back by Thursday again this week as guests will be wanting them sheets.'

'To be able to tell your doins' like that,' she says out loud, then continues to herself, 'the beauty. To set down the seasons, the flowers o' the wayside I know so well, the day yer baby quickens, a recipe I want my Clara to know, but most of all pour me heart out, say it all, empty me soul onto a white, forgivin' page and have it all clean and returned fresh like me washing'.

I feel Harriet's stomach knot as if it is my own, her mood changing abruptly. She pulls herself in until she is a dry stick, loose inside her corset for all her swelling belly, but though she yearns she will not cry. I know she will not. She has room for occasional anger but self-pity is alien to this woman who whitens both the stains and the meanness of her existence with equal vigour. Lye, boiling and scrubbing deals with the dirty washing she takes in but the litany of beautiful things she holds and recites inside her head whitens her bleak, grey daily life with a molten joy.

'Blue bound journal — two hundred and… three,' she murmurs, stroking the words as though they were silk, and stirring her soaking barrels of lye water to their rhythm. She glances up at the grey sky, hoping for rain any day but Monday and noting, with an involuntary shudder, the blood flush of slag tipping over at the Frodsby Works. For a searing instant there is that thought again; it shrieks past me almost too fast to grasp but now I'm sure I see a twisted mask of a face, before cold worry floods the forefront of our united thoughts.

'Now they're mekking this new steel ovver there, it's work seven days of the week, no time off and no more pay, hayther. They'll 'ave *us* doin' it next!' Leaden and filled with foreboding, the thought chills the fire of the brief horror I glimpsed. What is she hiding, this woman whom I sense is mostly in good spirits, despite everything? Why do we share that same uncomfortable memory and what does it mean?

Mrs Duffelen's drawers continue to occupy her attention and her mundane tasks draw me away from that unease. Her store of soft rainwater is low and Mrs Duffelen and her daughters like their drawers, petticoats and bodices gentle against their fine skins. She will have to keep the fire well stoked for fine white wood ash. It will be a good time to make bread too, as the bread they serve up in the town hurts her belly so.

'Lord knows what muck they put in it; it i'n't up to much,' she thinks as she turns to her tiny son, 'still, what else can I give the bairn?'

'Fred!' she calls as the pale-faced child lines up a little row of bread pellets he has made before eating them carefully, one by one. 'Fred, I want you to go with Clara and Alice to find me some more bits of apple and oak wood if you can; you know it's the best for lye but if you can't, any wood'll do. Down b' the beck I saw an old apple tree the other day. Claaaara!'

'Yes, she's the eldest, bless 'er,' thinks Harriet, 'but 'er job is to work here with 'er mam even though at fourteen she could 'ave bin in service for two years already and bringin' in a bit, like Gertie.'

I feel a surge of gratitude for Clara, who helps the indomitable Harriet hold her little family together in the best way she can. Clara turns the mangle, pegs washing, irons sheets and keeps the fire stoked. Quite a lot of her time is spent looking for fuel. Tarry blocks are best. Some of the high streets of the five villages around Sereton Terrace are paved with blocks of hard wood, weather-proofed with tar. When they're dug up to repair the roads, children gather from miles around to take them home.

'Writing! Why do I want such vain things?' Harriet admonishes herself, then reflects that her other four daughters can all write a beautiful hand, 'Though much good Gertie 'as for it as a scullery maid'. With a rush of determination that flails at my heart, she vows that Fred, her only son, will be well-schooled.

Fred already shows the signs that Harriet knows so well from her own childhood. He is different. A fussy and extraordinarily difficult baby, he can only be calmed with Godfrey's Cordial or Atkinson's Infant Preservative. Part of me detaches to realise with a shock that this is a laudanum derivative that Harriet resorts to in order to be able to get her laundry done. I sense that she has, unwittingly, triggered an addictive nature in Fred that will dog him for the rest of his life. Now he's growing into a little boy somewhat given to excess of behaviour, but he sees things. He sees what Harriet sees.

Her children got by the late John Henry Blanchard, however, do not rouse the feelings of love in her breast that Fred draws forth.

She has regard for them but now that they are flying the nest one by one, she often feels as little towards them as a mother blackbird finally tiring of feeding its young upon the ground, might feel.

'Want... want cuwant wood!' stammers Fred.

'What iver for, bairn? It goes on the fire back wi' the rest, for lye.' Harriet remembers only last week pulling a stolen stick of whitecurrant wood, taken from next door's scrubby bit of back garden, out of his protesting hands. She'd tried to dismiss from her mind what she now knows to be true. He sees what she sees. He sees beautiful things.

'No good fo' t' bairn, and 'im a lad an' all! It'll fill 'is 'ead when 'e should be schoolin'.'

'Boo boo,' Fred's small, barely three-year-old mouth works around the word he is seeking as he scuffs away jam from his face with his sleeve. Finally he draws an emphatic breath, 'booful,' he finally gets out, searching his mother's face for approval.

Harriet smiles down and engulfs him in a secret bond that goes far beyond the ties of mother and child. I feel her pride, warm and soft, swelling like a baby's head against my flailing heart.

''Tis. Oh yes it is; and it's number fifty-nine!' she croons.

Her gush of love overwhelms me and deposits me like driftwood upon the bleak white shore of my hospital bed once more, damp and sweat-drenched with emotions that are not mine.

'Not my memories, not my memories,' I mutter to myself again, but I am so deep down among them it's as though I have been watching my own life. I have been embedded in the consciousness of a woman who died a hundred years ago. And that shape in the slag flushed clouds — I'm sure it means something. It seemed so familiar. Was it really that forgotten shadow that I saw all those years ago on the eve of my wedding? And why would Harriet see it too?

The questions slide and drift away as death inhales the air that I'm breathing, sucking it so clean of everything that there's nothing for me to pull on. *Not yet. I won't go yet.'* I don't feel how I felt when death came before. This isn't how it should be. I want that peace.

Bright July sky forces itself back into my consciousness once more. Blue, so, so blue. I want to melt into it and vanish into my ball of light, but it isn't time yet. There's something I need to know.

# 3

# FORTY YEARS LATER

The intense July light of today dissolves into another day years ago. One acutely uncomfortable day — yes, I remember it now.

The tops of autumn beech trees restlessly finger a sleek sky of cobalt blue and my mind moves with the wind, idly through the branches. Nearby, a grove of white-armed slender birches, already undressed, dance in graceful rhythm. It is one of those rare, perfect November days when the clarity of the air polishes everything to look like a picture postcard. I stare, hypnotised by the brightness and the motion of the trees and realise, with a grimace that makes my family rush to my side to pat my hand again, that I am staring through a gymnasium window…

'Is she in pain?'

'Go and fetch a nurse.'

… I am sitting at the adductor machine, enthusiastically toning my inner thigh muscles. It's a good machine to be using because it helps maintain that youthful 'crotch gap' I am still vain enough to want to keep at sixty years of age. It also faces a window looking onto mature, manicured parkland, so you can dream away while you push. I like to think it makes the exercise a bit less painful. My iPod is playing *We Will Rock You*, as my legs pump rhythmically in time against the pads.

'*We…* eleven, twelve, can I make it to twenty pushes this round? *will rock you.*'

A bright red flame fidgets and sways among the autumnal gold, as a robin surveys the ground below.

'*You got mud on your face,* sixteen, seventeen… '

A flash of light, maybe it's a car windscreen as someone turns out of the drive, I don't know, but I think of my gran's glasses reflecting her gas fire forty years ago and I remember the sparrow all at once, his miniscule feet, the gaping beak, his call, my crawling horror. And I'm twenty again. The dreaming turns to a nightmare. My eyes prick and my throat catches savagely still after all this time. Pain surges; mine or the bird's? I'm not sure. Panic! I see it fluttering free, then cascading through the hawthorn as it tries to land, unable to find a perch. And I can't do anything for it.

I can't do anything now but what I do when this happens. I start to force lines from D H Lawrence through my recoiling mind, hauling myself back from the brink of places I don't want to go.

'I never saw a wild thing sorry for itself. I never saw a wild thing sorry for itself. A wild bird will fall frozen from its perch before feeling sorry for itself,' I jabber but I can't staunch the flow of memories today as I stop my workout and sit, transfixed.

'Why didn't I read the signs? Why? Why did I go on to wreak havoc in so many lives?' I whisper.

A low animal moan escapes my throat and I bury my face in the folds of my towel, knuckling it into my mouth to avoid further sound. Mingled grief and self-loathing writhe from deep within me where I have kept them contained, as best I can, in between moments like this.

I stare, unseeing now, as the robin twitches itself onto a low branch to sing and posture. I'm seeing instead that childhood nightmare of clutching hands vanishing beneath molten slag, and I don't know why. Was it the redness of the robin's breast? Is it me that's sinking? This is crazy.

A blank. A pause…

… My mind lurches in an untidy heap back into the ward and I'm being lifted and turned on to my side for a moment while the sheets under me are inspected. Like a bedwetting child, I think. I am aware that my nightdress has ridden up and I make to cover myself, visualising my wrinkled thighs and grey pubic hair displayed to all. Dying strips away the last vestiges of modesty but I am not there yet. I pull off my oxygen mask for a moment and mouth, 'I'm ok.'

They let me be, tucking me round in white once more. I've got to find where this is going….

… 'Are you finished on this machine?'

It's a fitness fanatic 'gym bunny' and I'm interrupting her punishing, self-imposed schedule.

'Oh, I could tell you about punishment,' I mentally flash at her but make as if to wipe the sweat from my face, recover and turn cheerfully.

The robin has gone.

'Sure! It's yours,' I beam and hop down, turning away momentarily to fight surging grief once more.

Her narrow rabbity bottom almost twitches in disdain as she leans forward to double the weight load. The gym is host to a number of these narrow hipped, breast enhanced, iron-willed women. Nowadays, I'm old enough and wise enough to know that her life has only the illusion of containment. She gets it from the strict control she exerts over her body but still I feel truly diminished by her taut fitness today. I need to get out of here. I'm a mess.

With a stranglehold on my panic, I perform stretches as an exit strategy, and then, hair smoothed, posture adjusted and the serene veneer I've polished over the years reapplied, I smile coquettishly at my reflection in the window glass to complete the counterfeit.

'Great control!' I mutter as a weak humour returns.

The gym bunny's head is bobbing up and down to an Ibiza remix that I can hear coming from her headphones and she misses the irony as I slip out of the door. She'll be in the gym all morning, only content when she's exceeded yesterday's exertions. Then she'll go and gossip to her friends about how this miserable looking old woman had the audacity to be taking up time on the machines.

Gossips find their daily bread here at the club and need no excuse to dissect the downcast. As I pass the reception and refreshment bars, I'm careful to greet everyone as chirpily as the robin that started this tumble of memories. Singing to my iPod as I go, I hold everything in until I reach the sanctuary of the changing room.

Except today it isn't a sanctuary at all. I push open the door and am engulfed by a steamy, raucous hen house. The changing room is full of the pink, naked and semi-naked bodies of young women fresh from a kick-boxing class, showering, changing or chatting loudly.

It has to be loud because they need everyone else to hear. The talk is all of how much or how little they've eaten and especially how much they've drunk, what they're making for their children's autumn fayre, whether the class really stretched them enough, the perfidy of the gymnasium scales and who is fucking whom. It's usually one of the gym instructors, those muscled up, testosterone charged young men who think these young women are fair game.

As a rule, I'm endlessly fascinated by the detail of these carelessly fecund young lives. Content to be sixty and, therefore, invisible to their eyes, I usually listen in quiet acknowledgement of this living pulse of human affairs, smiling at its self-confident immortality and knowing that the pumped up boost of youth, health and fitness will fade soon enough. They should enjoy it while they can. Today, I just want the chatter to stop.

A cubicle becomes free and I bolt the door, sitting down to bury my face in my towel once more. It's a long time since it's been this bad.

'Breathe!'

Gradually, panic is forced down until I can gain space to deal with it. I thought I'd dealt with all this many years ago. Yet here is the guilt, the pain and the anguish, and it's as fresh as ever.

Gradually the changing room empties as the occupants drift off to take coffee together, collect children from the crèche or perform other tasks in lives where journeys have hardly begun yet, and where the possibilities are endless. Finally the changing room is left to dripping showers, heaps of wet towels, forgotten t-shirts and combs, and me. I change quickly without showering and fix my mind on home.

'I've paid for your coffee.'

The veneer almost cracks.

It's Coral. Her husband died last year and she has risen with an unspoken shriek from depths of numbness and incomprehension straight into anger. She's my friend and I can see from her face that she needs to draw on that unwritten contract between women and unload her problems.

'Not now Coral. Not today!' I moan to myself, thinking of a hundred excuses to go. I'm too full of my own troubles to want to listen to hers today. I shouldn't be so uncharitable but I just need to get away. I'll have to spend time listening to her pain just when I need to find salve for my own.

Lord knows, I unloaded enough on her. We go so far back, Coral and I, and she pulled me teetering from the brink so many, many times. Oh, *she* knows *all* about my first marriage, though not how it ended. She held my hand on the morning of my wedding, sitting there at my feet in a cloud of perfume and a shocking pink brides-maid's dress, while she pulled tissues from a box as I choked out my uncertainties. She would have gone straight to my waiting parents and declared that it was all off — I know she would — had I asked her to do it. But I was too much in need of an escape route and she knew that too.

There she was again, coaxing me through my final year at teacher training college, when being evicted from the halls of residence as a newly married student made it so hard to stick the course. One bitterly cold Easter holiday she came all the way on the train from

Hertfordshire, getting hopelessly lost at Doncaster en route, travelling way beyond her comfort zone and into the arena of my already stormy marriage just to persuade me not to take the plum job I'd landed in the lab at a local chemical works.

"Mia, you've come so far. You've just about made it. Just one more term!" she'd pleaded with me as my new husband frowned from the sidelines at her intrusion.

And so I became a teacher and not a lab assistant at the steel works, moaning at her all the while that I'd lost a really well paid job with PROSPECTS. What was I thinking? Dear Coral, how did you put up with me? You even found your own teaching job in the area where I was working, just so that we could stay close friends. And we were close. Inseparable. If I'd had a sister I wish it could have been Coral. I think, in the beginning, she loved me far more than I did her, in the protective way that an older sister would. I wonder sometimes what she got from our early days together.

Later, as wives and mothers, though, we were so good for each other in the way only female friends can be. Sharing each other's babies and kitchens, painting toenails and walls, perming hair, jam making, joy and jumble sales, we practically never let a day go by without popping in to see each other. Then, as she moved away with Geoff, we gradually lost contact in the middle years.

Now reunited, we should be picking up where we left off but, and I hate to admit it, there's something missing. She's changed and probably I have too. Worst of all, she's never known my guilty secret, and I've a feeling that if she did, things really would never be the same. Her views on life, love and marriage were always so unshakeable.

I see that another new, dark, sleek outfit is draping her slender form, whose purchase would have filled her raging void only briefly. She is every inch the widow, accepting with a sad sideways incline of the head, both condolences and hugs alike. I wouldn't say she enjoys widowhood but she likes the attention. Her eyes swiftly appraise my clothes but not my face; a bad sign. She's pre-occupied.

There's no getting away and so we exchange small talk while I push the guilt and panic back to the recesses from which they came. Her new outfits, the sales, her health, finding the perfect pair of jeans, a missing child in the papers, they all gloss over the real business in hand. Outside the lounge windows the robin reappears on the path close to the glass and turns its head as though listening, its eyes black with interest.

Finally I ask the question Coral needs, in order to prompt the catharsis of real talk.

'How are you coping this week?'

I feel her rage shroud me, beating impotent fists against the injustice of it all and I wonder how I would manage in her circumstances. Stories fixed in the amber of telling and retelling, moments of life frozen and given retrospective meaning, the freshly washed bones of existence laid out so as to make sense of it all, again and again and again. Probably I wouldn't cope any better than her. I shudder involuntarily and she takes it as confirmation of shared outrage and pushes on, cataloguing the reasons why he shouldn't have died.

Inevitably the urge to tell begins to bubble up in me too, but I can't. I would not have the high moral ground of bereavement to stand upon and so I keep quiet, just breaking her halting monologue with the occasional murmur of support. Finally I sense that she has vented enough and, scanning her face, see her eyes brimming with tears. She swallows it down.

Covert and swift sideways glances indicate that she is about to enter the door of the confessional and she pauses with a spoonful of milky foam from her coffee mug halfway to her lips, staring into the distance.

'I was once unfaithful to him, you know.' Sleek hair swings forward as she bends her head in a show of shame. Or is it denial still?

Outside the robin has moved to the trunk of a fallen tree and is excavating its rotting crevices. It flies off suddenly as if it has heard and wants no part of this.

'Listen, you mustn't start blaming yourself now. What happened, happened.'

These lines slip honeyed from my tongue but I know with abrupt clarity that she will never stop beating herself with this stick. I know because my own brutal briar bundle is never really far away.

'He...'

'I don't want to know. What's done is done.' I place a hand gently on her arm and squeeze to urge a reflective silence. I want to cry out that, long ago, I was unfaithful to the young man I first married but I can't because I would have to tell the rest too, drawing it out from my body like a spear that stops an artery. Instead I reach over and hug her, wordlessly, and we take comfort from each other.

Over her shoulder I notice a flash of scarlet once more as the robin returns to continue his foraging, his impossibly thin legs straining backwards as he leans to extract some kind of insect from the log. There! He has it and is gone, his scarlet flutter blurring the space where he's been.

Time, too, becomes blurred and muddled for a moment and, through swimming senses, I feel I'm in an infinity loop. There's that strange sense of many threads connecting, of memories that aren't mine and the certainty that I'm a child — somehow outside all of this and looking in. I *am* a child, watching the robin and cataloguing what I see. Number seventeen I've labelled it.

My pneumonia fuddled brain surfaces briefly to realise, all these years later, that perhaps Harriet had a connection to me even then. Yet how could I have known back then what it all meant? There was no peg to hang it on, no connecting threads. Not until some time later in my life did I suspect that I did, indeed, have a very real door open to a woman from the past.

A piece of a puzzle almost fits as the sun glints from a window opening in an adjacent building and it is my Gran again, staring into the gas fire the night before my wedding, predicting my path from the fate of a tiny bird. I rub my forehead in frustration, but smile at Coral as though I'm bemused by her predicament, because something has clicked into place in my brain. A circle has been completed but I can't quite bring it into focus and I grasp at the fleeting tail of understanding.

It's gone. Threads snap as she gets up to go, with promises to mail me later, maybe even chat online, where words will flow from fingers for easier relief. I sit for a while puzzling over what it was that I suddenly understood. The post-menopausal brain does this a lot, letting things slip through the net of understanding but this seemed to be different; almost from another time and place. Anyhow, by the time I finally gather my things once more and get up to leave, I've made a decision. Hiding away my memories won't work any more. The time has to come to pick at my own dead and rotten parts, removing whatever is there before, forty years on, I can find peace.

Shaking my head as I turn the car key in the ignition, I turn to Granny Rose, still there, warm in my mind, long years after her death.

'The robin isn't a sign, you know, Gran,' I say into her quizzical gaze. 'It's just that watching it has made me analyse myself.'

'Hmmmm,' she chuckles, an expression of amusement and knowing disbelief on her face.

By the time the tyres crunch in the gravel at the end of the wooded drive that leads homewards I've slid once more, with practised and consummate skill, into a life that is fulfilled and happy.

And it is nearly true.

# 4

## A STARLING'S THROAT

Yes, that's the point where I first began to make sense of it all; that's where I began looking for myself and found Harriet instead. That's when I seriously began to face up to the past instead of insulating it from close inspection under layers of living. In my own way, I suppose, like my friend Coral, I'd never moved on but had just sidestepped into another life, leaving one journey unfinished. Harriet helped me finish that journey many years ago, I know, so why has she been in my thoughts now? Why now and so — almost — me? We were seamless. And these two particular memories from my own past; two occasions when time seemed to slip sideways, a couple of infinitesimal moments of life that I'd totally forgotten. What do they mean?...

... 'No I'm definitely not ready!' I croak, sucking life back into my failing lungs.

'I hope you're not, gran! You *can* fight this,' my granddaughter pleads at my side, grasping my hand once more. 'Take those drugs, *please* gran.'

I wish she understood what all this is about. She just sees her dying granny, not the complex vortex of experiences that whirl around me now.

I shift painfully, plucking the sheets. Pneumonia necessitates that you sit up in bed to relieve pressure on failing lungs. After a while in this position, old bones and thin skin start to protest a bit. I try to shuffle some feeling back into my own ancient and now very rabbity bottom, wishing I had a bit more padding there. There's a turnabout! I always had such a voluptuous rear and desperately wanted it to be smaller for most of my life. I remember bending to take shopping from the car boot one day and a passing motorist calling out, 'What a magnificent arse!'

Now it is all bones and wasted muscle. Such a pity how age strips away our physical strength, taking us down to the core of what we are. If I can just move off that crease an inch or two…

… The sheets against my skin are rough and uncomfortable but it's not the hospital bed that presses so hard against my back, it's Harriet's straw mattress. I'm pulled along by another memory that isn't mine, to find myself staring into the night alongside a small child, bright eyed and wide awake, reciting her lists. She gives out 'different' like a radio beacon — she's quite unlike any of the thousands of children I've ever known. And I've known so, so many.

Harriet is the one who causes the most bother in this house. A prickle of hostility fills this mud and stud Ellenby cottage. It's a happy enough home for her brothers and sisters but 'beneath' Harriet, her mother always says, adding meaningfully, 'as is doing honest work'. Harriet doesn't quite know what that means only that, as usual, she's in trouble.

'I can relate to that, Harriet,' I agree. 'Most times I never knew what that stinging blow to the side of my head was about. I just learned to lay low for a while.'

Harriet loves her home and family, it's just that she sees things — seemingly bigger to her — that no one else thinks of as important even if they see them too. I see her momentarily as a tiny child standing, staring, into an unknowable distance, neglecting the simple practical tasks she's given. I catch at the memory that can't be a memory as the bulk of Ann, her formidable mother, looms over me.

'Huskin' broad beans — now theer's a job as any little'un 'd be glad of,' her mother tells Shiloh one evening in exasperation. 'Yet a few, pop a few, why there's nowt to it. But what did I 'appen on 'er doing again? I ask you. There she was a gawpin' and a starin' at nowt at all. And I says, Harriet I says, what are you a starin' at girl? An' she says, "Them feathers o' that starlin's throttle, mam. How they stick out when 'e rattles and a-rattles his song. It's so beautiful, mam."'

'Well, cheeky madam! I fetched 'er a gret scutch at the side of th' 'ead. Beautiful indeed, when starlin's dun't even sing! And they wasn't but a bean or two shelled, hayther.'

Harriet cries bitterly and adds the throat feathers to her litany of beautiful things.

Tonight she is engrossed once more in her list, snug between Alice and Ann, both older sisters turned inwards in deep sleep with an arm curling protectively around Harriet. I snuggle into their warmth too, but I'm cautious now. The taut reality of that last encounter with her mind has left me mentally bruised and wary. I needn't have worried though; here in her childhood, I'm not quite as one with her as I was before. Even so, I feel Harriet's intense joy swell my chest with joy too, as she examines more items.

'Cherry blossom melting 'gainst a blue sky.' The whisper hangs between us, caressing the night. It is a simple love song.

'Winter night branches curvin' an 'alo round the light o' the lantern, like babby Jesus i' the church.'

'Stars in a winter dark sky. So, so many sprayed there like drops of rain on me mam's black Sunday bonnet, mekking the blackness glow.'

I am breathless with it all; her memories are so powerful, so exquisitely and intricately painted that I could reach out and touch them.

'Evenin' sun polishin' a spider's web. Wonder if spiders see it too, if they stop just to admire it all? What a wonderful web I've done all a-shinin' in the sunset.

'Silent croon of a bird settlin' 'pon its eggs. Reckon they must feel so good pressin' theere.' (She had once tucked the blue speckled egg of a blackbird against her own bare skin and tried to voice that silent note.)

'Soughing dance of pine branches i' the wind.' Old Shiloh says it's a lonely sound when she tells him about it, dancing back from the Ellenby estate with him one evening but it connects Harriet by invisible stitching to the sky and beyond, binding her fast to a world no one else around even glimpses.

'Low sun through long gress, shinin' copper, gold an' blue. Why blue? Gress ain't blue,' she puzzles.

'Feel of a babby's head 'gainst your cheek.' Each time Hellen gives her another cousin, she can't wait to press that silky warmth to her face. I remember it as eagerly as she does; the gentle trap that pulls us women willingly into its folds.

'Secret 'ello.' Old Barney Robbins can flash his eyebrows as he 'obbles by me down the lane and it says 'ello, just like that. Wind ripplin' o'er barley and rye'. Up by the sheep pen on the hill, the Wolds undulate and swell, vast seas rolling to some faraway shore.

And still her list of numbered memories unfolds. 'Perfect space 'tween two lovers.' When John and his Katy sit by the wall, silhouetted against the glowing evening, they make a heart shape when their heads touch and he reaches for her hand. Harriet smirks knowingly into the darkness.

'Skylark singin' so 'ard as a dancin' 'awk chases 'im. CAN'T CATCH ME!'

'Sun so 'ot you can hear it crackle.'

'Puff on a robin's breath as he pipes a song of a frosty mornin'.'

And my old heart finally breaks with Harriet's at the sight of a robin, tiny feet clasped upon his perch, opening his beak to sing; a faint wisp of the warm, moist air that sustains him dissipating into the crisp morning with each note and trill.

'Yes!'

She did catalogue a robin and I was here, too, thirty-seven years ago, that day at the gym. But in my pale cocoon, here in the ward, struggling to come to terms with my life, I find the thought too much to hold, and like a hot coal it slips from my grasp to glow ever more dimly. Yet still it leaves an imprint. This is important. There have been things going on in my life that are only now, here at its ending, beginning to surface.

Harriet recites long into the night, tears streaming down her cheeks with the wonder of it all, each picture shooting fierce joy through her thin body and into mine, as if I really am laid next to her. When she finally sleeps, it is nearly dawn and the cottage below is already stirring. Her father Shiloh rises first, coughs and spits and puts on his milking coat; then her mother begins to make a fire next to the oven for the morning's bread, stirring the embers with the poker in a marked manner designed to rouse the household. Harriet sleeps on while each member of the crowded cottage wakes in turn and goes about their allotted tasks.

'Git up dozzen 'ead! Liggin in bed all day!'

A well-aimed kick from her brother John sends Harriet from the warm fuzziness of sleep to abrupt cold floorboards. Too practised to cry, she stands up stiffly, turns her crumpling face away from him and reaches under the bed for the chamber-lees. She's never able to carry the bucket down to the vegetable rows without splashing and so she has an old cloth folded under the bed to cover it as she lugs it, with both hands, down the stairs.

'Let go!' Harriet jags out the breath she has sucked in so tightly a moment ago, struggling as John puts his boot on the cloth.

'Let go, John! Mam!'

A shriek from their mother and John clatters down the stairs and out through the cottage door to chop wood, though not before he's thrown her cloth out of the window. Harriet shuffles into her wooden clogs and follows him down, heaving the bucket with her, pausing to pick up her cloth and grimacing as she drops it over the bucket. She always does this job in her nightdress, despite the early damp cold of the morning, as she hates her pinafore getting fouled by the bucket's contents. Halfway down the cinder path to the vegetable patch her mother calls after her. 'There's some apple branches blown down in th'orchard. Gither 'em up quick now while there's a good fire on. I need to mek lye.'

'Carrots today,' thinks Harriet and, having emptied the bucket along the appropriate row, sets it down on the path with its cloth neatly folded next to it. Astride the newly sooted rows of carrot seed she adds her own morning contribution, clicking her tongue with annoyance at the sooty splashes on her ankles and then, pulling the back hem of her nightdress through her legs, she bundles it up and shuffles off through the long grass to the orchard. The low early sun lights the apple branches as she wanders through the dew, her thin legs growing goose pimples, her teeth chattering.

'Dd, dddddd, dd,' she chatters into the cold air. 'Dddddddd, ddddd!'

I'm so cold too, and there's a shaking and a rattling but it's me, not Harriet. The metal sides of my bed vibrate while a disembodied voice pronounces, 'Her blood pressure's dropping.'

I'm so cold.

The orchard is cold. Harriet's breath hangs about her as she lifts her head for a moment to squint at the sun. Heading for a corner of the orchard where sunlight already dapples the grass, she enjoys the warmth on her back for a moment before turning to look for apple wood. She freezes, suddenly, and stares.

'Jewels!' she breathes, a plume of steam hanging about her head.

There, backlit by the low early morning sun, stands an elderly whitecurrant bush, its branches bare and hardly a knobble to show where the spring flowers will soon dangle, damp and new. Last year's growth is a dull grey but the old stems, the ones that have yielded the heavy strings of glass-like fruit for year upon year, have partially shelled their bark which now glows a brilliant transparent red, shot through with gold. It takes Harriet's breath clean away.

She walks around the bush but the glow disappears as her shadow falls on it. Harriet walks back again and squats down next to it, hauling up her nightdress to keep it dry, and committing the colour, the glow, the shapes, the gold fringing of the sun, to her memory.

She is in rapt attention like this for some time when a sharp blow across her shoulders sends her face down into the middle of the whitecurrant stems.

'Lazy, uneppen, and dozzen 'eaded child!' her mother shrieks, applying her stick about the girl's shoulders once more. 'Yah'll catch cowd if ya sits o' that wet gress. Now where's… my… apple wood?' Each word is emphasised with a further blow and then, with a snort of exasperation, Ann Parsons grabs her daughter by the arm and pulls her upright.

'It's Monday mornin' bairn! Washday! I've got lye to mek and no apple wood to start it. The fire's roarin'; now git back in th'ouse wi' some wood!' Turning on her heels, she stalks back through the orchard to the cinder path, landing a well-aimed kick at a hen unfortunate enough to be scratching along its edge.

'You needn't think I'm washin' that nightie, hayther!' is her parting shot.

The words drift towards a shaking Harriet on the still morning air and she tosses her head as if to avoid them. My cheeks and shoulders sting from the scratches and blows too, but it is not tears that shake her from her sleep-straggled hair down to the tips of her cold toes. It is anger. Anger, and a slow dawning that no one else in

Shiloh's cottage sees what she sees, hears what she hears and feels what she feels or, if they do, they think it mean and unimportant. She turns for a last look at her newly discovered treasure but the sun that has wrought the original magic is now too high in the sky. Harriet paddles her six-year-old clogged feet up and down and finally lets forth a howl of impotent rage. It shakes my whole body.

I can feel its heat like I felt the later warmth of her pride over Fred. It spreads like fire through my old body and my own shaking finally stops.

'We'll keep the blower on for a while longer but if her blood pressure drops again, there's not much more we can do. She doesn't want any fluids giving, so we can't put a line in.'

'Not yet! Not yet! I'm not ready. I have to see where this is going.' An involuntary groan escapes my lips.

'An' you can stop that roarin'!' is Ann Parson's final shot.

Harriet gathers her apple sticks and piles them in the night soil bucket, as she can't carry both separately and fears further retribution if she leaves one or the other behind. She continues her angry howling, sucking in great lungfuls of cold air and releasing it in billowing clouds of vapour. All thoughts of keeping her nightdress clean have been evaporated by the heat of her rage and she lets loose its hem, only to then catch its folds between her heel and clog. She stumbles forwards and the sticks shoot from the bucket. Misery complete, she spread-eagles herself on the path and screams in full-throated rage.

'Na then lass, up yer comes. Kelchin' thasen i' the floor is a bit daft.'

Shiloh, returned from milking and ready to breakfast, sets her on her feet and gathers up the strewn apple wood. 'Yah'll be all squad an' blather liggin' there and mam'll be even more ugly.'

He always finds it best not to enter into discussion about his strange, thin faced youngest daughter and diverts attention away from Harriet's distress as he leads her sobbing form, towing her by her small cold hand, into the cottage.

'I'm a bit sharp set, Mrs Parsons!' he announces loudly to Harriet's mother, whose composure is recovered upon seeing the wood. With the wood set to char, Ann reaches above her head to a hook in the low, beamed ceiling to fetch down a glistening pink, white and yellow mass.

'Fat bacon?' she enquires of her husband.

'Ay, I should like nowt better!' Shiloh enthuses, pleased that the subject of Harriet has been avoided. He lays a broad, dung-soiled hand across the slab of marbled fat and hacks into the bacon with a knife.

'Yah'll not have it fried today,' Ann remarks, assuming her wash-day face once more. 'I need the fire for boilin', as well as the copper. Ya'll yet it cowd, swath an' all.'

Shiloh nods silently, already halfway down his slice of cold fat but chewing carefully for all that to avoid a painful tooth. A sniff behind him catches his attention and he turns, habitually, to offer Harriet the last sliver on the back of his knife, knowing her reaction and waiting for it. She backs away grimacing; the taste of fat always makes her retch.

'I allus 'ave milk for breakfast,' she whispers to her father, looking meaningfully at the bulging pocket of his milking coat and hiccoughing back a last lingering sob. Smiling, Shiloh reaches into his pocket and pulls out a small, white enamel lidded canister by its wood and metal handle.

'Tha wain't boak o'er this, though,' he laughs, dangling it in front of Harriet. She takes the can wordlessly.

'There'll be besling's milk soon,' he says, staring thoughtfully at the ample hindquarters of his wife as she bends to tend the fire. 'There's a four on 'em in calf.'

'Ya'll spoil that bairn, you should tek a stick to 'er,' grumbles Ann into the glowing embers and, turning eventually to add more invective about Harriet's uselessness, she's in time to see Shiloh vanishing in the direction of the estate once more. Harriet, meanwhile, has swiftly drained her milk canister and is wobbling on a stool trying to wash her dirtied face, hands and nightdress hem at the pump.

'Git that muck from down yer wikins!' snaps Ann at the child, then mutters, 'Tha's a queer one. Can't bear a speck o' muck, can you? Well you can 'elp me with the washin' today. Go get your frock and pinny on an' I'll brush them rat-tails.'

By the time Harriet presents herself to have her back buttons fastened and lank red hair brushed, the tub is in the yard already half full of steaming water. A family-sized cold lunch of cheese, dry bread and pickle and jam has been set out on the table by the back door.

'Now you can knock them chickens off if they git up the-ar,' her mother chuckles. 'Give 'em the stick.'

I listen to Ann's thoughts but remain strangely separate from them. It's not at all like my connection with Harriet. More like an insistent fat fly buzzing around my head. She mutters and mutters and knows it's useless asking much else of Harriet for the moment.

Once crossed, she remains stubborn and uncooperative, no matter how soundly she's beaten or how long she's punished. Better to let her be quiet a while, then she'll be biddable again and might be put to work. Hardly daring to visualise a future for such a difficult, plain and altogether unpromising child, Ann has already dismissed the notion of schooling as a remedy. There has been heated talk of the unaffordable cost, and even when the Reverend Davies offers to tutor her and the other village children in reading, writing and simple arithmetic, Ann feels that Harriet is unschoolable. Besides, none of her children can read or write. Of what use is such stuff in the day-to-day goings on of the countryside?

Harriet, I sense, always had other ideas. I catch a memory in that, in trying to number and order her lists, she'd firmly discarded Shiloh's country adding methods.

'Ran, tan, tethera, pethera, fethera, and it on'y goes up to bum-fits,' she'd muttered, beseeching her only village friend, Betsey Grassby, to teach her numbers that went on and on for as long as you could count them. Had Ann known that Harriet had already counted the wheat grains she'd spilled across the floor the other day, numbering them beyond a thousand as she gathered up each one, she still would not have changed her mind about her challenging daughter.

'No. Raise 'er, work 'er and mebbe, God willin', marry her, is all that can be reckoned for such a queer 'un,' Ann mutters again to the fire.

Brushed, buttoned and pinafored, Harriet stands by the back door, absorbing the washday smells and watching her mother's methodical approach to the week's laundry. Taking another pair of drawers from the steeping barrel, Ann puts her hand up through the open crotch and pulls them over the top of the washboard. A little soap is then grated on to an area that requires the attentions of her plump, meaty hands and she begins to rub the fabric vigorously up and down the board, grunting with effort and satisfaction as she does so. After a while she turns the drawers and repeats the process on the other side, finally freeing them from the board to pump them up and down in the washtub. Next they're wrung until her knuckles turn white and the tendons stand out on her wrists, shaken out with a sharp crack like a wet sail and dropped into the clear water of the wrenching tub.

'Alice bain't be wantin' these for a month o' two once she's wed,' she chuckles to herself, reaching for another pair.

'Why wain't Alice be wearing drawers after she's wed?' Harriet wants to know. Ann looks up sharply from her tub.

'Never you mind, girl,' she smiles to herself and, bending her head once more, remembers the early days of her marriage to Shiloh and his rough, urgent clumsiness. Goin' without drawers was the only way to avoid the scalding piss that followed a honeymoon. She sighs and smiles once more, thinking of a suitable rebuff to the inevitable next question. Harriet never pays heed, yet contrarywise is always listening, always there behind you when you least expect it, never there when you need her.

'Yah'll a' ter ton the mangle,' Ann continues in a hopeful attempt to deflect her troublesome daughter. Harriet loves that mangle and the way it squeezes clothes so they dance themselves dry in no time at all on the line.

Harriet's attention, however, has now wandered, drawn by a

starling fizzing and rattling its morning song in the hedgerow, throat feathers stuck out as though tarred. Its iridescent back catches the sun, its wings and tail feathers twitching to add emphasis as it adds a final 'peeeeeoooh' to its song. It then launches itself to join a number of others swooping by and leaves Harriet's plain face lit with happiness.

Her anger has now subsided and she feels a strange and comforting warmth where it has been, like the imprint of the oven shelf in her cold bed. Then she remembers the whitecurrant bush with a surge of pleasure. Waving her mother's stick sideways at a hen eying the bread on the table, she adds the bush's glowing stems to her list of beautiful things which now number more than three hundred, tirelessly ordered, ranked and then re-ordered.

'Eighty-three,' she thinks with satisfaction, 'for my beautiful starling, an' whitecurrant stems, mebbbe fifty-nine.

'Misfit,' thinks her mother, sighing at how nothing fits Harriet properly; not her clothes, not her place in the Ellenby cottage, not the way she goes at even the simplest of tasks. Nothing. She doesn't belong anywhere.

# 5

## MISFIT

The hospital ward is quieter than usual. I open my eyes expecting the anxious faces of my family after my episode of violent shaking but the nurse, who's just removing the blood pressure monitor from my arm, says they're away making arrangements for lunch. You have to eat, even when you're sitting with the dying. It reminds you, thankfully, that you're alive but also makes you feel guilty. I don't care about that. Harriet's list is still with me, each item leaving firework tracery in my head. She painted her young world with colours so vastly different from my own, choosing her palette from blazing patterns that I had my head too far down to see. I don't even wonder any more how I can possibly be reliving her memories as well as my own, or how it was that, twice before in my life, we were almost connected. I just accept, with certainty, that this is part of the dying process too.

Well, whatever else, this is it; the end game, the final journey, and I *am* on my way. My chest feels as though it is full of water. It will be today, I know, I just don't want to go until I understand.

'Harriet, nobody ever got what I was all about, either,' I sigh to myself. But that's too obvious. There's something else hiding in there, something that's eluding me.

A curtain lifted in a breeze wafts the sound of church bells in on warm, sleepy morning air and my chest suddenly rises with sorrow as well as with the effort to breathe. Is it Sunday today? Maybe it's Sunday. I can't remember.

Church bells have threaded their way around and through my life in a continuous chain for as far back as I can remember. Like lights wound around a Christmas tree, they flash the same pattern over and over; a long peal of memories that repeats a message, except that it's not any message that I was able to put into words, not in the beginning. It's only much later that it becomes clear what they mean to me.

I remember the first time they moved me. Now here's a darker strand of my life that I'd rather not follow, but I can't help but be drawn along its glistening length to other, earlier journeys still...

... My mother and I have just stepped from a taxi to stare at the smoke-blackened bricks of Lincoln railway station. It's the first car I've ever been in and I screamed because it was strange and because the deep, sonorous cathedral bells started to chime just as the man lifted me inside. It made me unhappy. As we set off, it sounded as though they were chasing the car. My dad might chase us, she says, and we have to go on a train so that he can't catch us.

'Ve are going on ze boat train,' she says encouragingly as she hauls me and the brown cardboard suitcase on to the station plat-form.

I peer suspiciously from under my woollen bonnet, whose peak has settled over my eyebrows, at my mother and a world of roaring noise, confusion and strange smells that break another hot wave of fear into my two-year-old senses.

'Look, oooh look, zere's a big train ofer zere!'

Sharp metallic whiffs of grime and soot immediately envelope us, hovering tangibly among the crowds of people and making my teeth feel tingly. I don't know what I'm looking at. The trains in my books all have faces but I don't like these. I stiffen and drag the toes of my new brown Start-rite shoes as her grip on my hand gets tighter and we make our way towards a wooden bridge with a roof.

'Now shtop zat mit your new shoos! Chust look at zat train — isn't it exciting?'

She sounds tight and dry as if she might crack or break and I get even more nervous because I can still hear the bells. I don't know why a bridge should have a roof or what a boat train is or why everything smells so. Legs and feet swish and stride by. 'Climp, climp', the metal bits on the heavy soles of a pair of cracked boots with thick-knotted laces, march smartly by. 'Leggett, leggett, leggett', a lady and three big boys matching their strides together, push past. My new shoes just trip each other up as I hang back. Everyone knows where they're going but I don't and the bells won't get out of my head.

'Vould you like to valk up the shteps?'

She means up the bridge with a roof and I don't like the way the sides are all criss-crossed and wooden. Maybe I might fall through. Maybe a train might look up at me. I pull back and start to cry and try to struggle free from her grasp.

'Ach du Lieber, I'll carry you, zen,' she sighs, bending down as I gratefully lift my arms.

I put my arms around her neck and bury my face in the soft hair that smells of flowers. She sits me in that safe place on her hip and heaves up the case with her other hand.

'Don't do zat, you'f got a runny nose!'

She resites me on her hip, shaking her hair down her back, trying to carry me and the case along the platform. Her grasp tightens on the case, holding it away from her to stop it banging on her legs. I can see that she's looking around for someone to help but all the porters are busy fussing around ladies with elaborate hats, shiny shoes and smart, light tan coloured luggage. She just has an old brown case and a child on her hip. Platform Three is where the boat train is due any minute and it's on the other side of the bridge, a long haul away.

I don't, I don't, I don't want to go on the bridge. The paint is flaking green bits on to the steps and pigeons are doing dirt all over it. I struggle some more, straightening my body and leaning back in a bid to slide down. Her coat and dress get dragged up as she heaves me back and the metal edges of the suitcase bang sharply against her legs. She puts me down suddenly and stands back as if I am an armful of something menacing. I scream and cling to her skirt, trying to climb back on to her hip again as smoke and steam billow up through the gaps in the bridge and something awful I don't quite see passes underneath it.

Now I hear another hissing. It's the sigh that means trouble and I see the lips tighten to hold in the rage and frustration that are trying to force their way out. I can only wail all the louder in my misery. I know what's coming, and sure enough a stinging slap rattles across my cheek, making the peak of my bonnet slide further over my face. I pump my legs up and down. Snot bubbles out of my nose and then I suck in hard on my breath and make a sound like Mrs Abbot's Alfie, who has whooping cough.

I open my eyes for a moment and, suddenly, all I can see is another little girl in a long nightie and trees and bushes and grass all around me. She's screaming too. I don't know where I am and so I scream even louder, making a man walking behind us look sharply at my mother.

Surely not! My forehead breaks into a cold sweat at the realisation. Not at such a young age. Was I connected to Harriet even then? This memory is so perfect, so detailed and so real that I don't doubt it for a minute. How many more instances have I forgotten along the way, dismissed as illogical?

She picks me up again and I sit limply against her side pulling in great gasps of air. The trees and the girl are gone.

'Now chust shtop!' she says, her pretty lips getting thinner and whiter, her shoulders squaring themselves against the task of getting both me and the case up the steps; they square against me, against the people who push unseeing past us, against the whole world. I heave a great shuddering sigh and feel my cheek red and hot from the slap. Its sharpness and the clamour of the bells fill my mind, my bonnet hooding my eyes so I don't see the bridge after all. I just hang over her shoulder and squeeze tears down her back.

At the top of the steps down to the other side, she sets me down smartly on the wooden planks of the bridge, yanking up my hand into hers so that my fingers begin to slide out of my woollen mitten, now sodden from where I've wiped it around my nose and chewed its fuzzy, stringiness for comfort in our halting progress.

'You'll haf to valk down the shteps. Be careful!' she snaps.

I can see the platform at the bottom and it looks safe. I like steps because my Granny Rose sings a song when we go up or down them. I forget all about the bridge and the bells and the slap and the other girl, and take one step at a time downwards, crooning, 'Down, down, we go, down the dairs we go, melly, melly, melly, melly, down the dairs we go!' Except in the middle I have to catch my breath, and stop singing and stepping for a moment. She pulls me onwards and my hand slides out of my slimy mitten.

'It's 'shtairs, say sht… airs,' she intones, tucking my mitten into her coat pocket and staring ahead at the platform.

'Stairs,' I say obligingly. Here's something I'm good at and I want her to say 'good girl!' but she doesn't. 'Stairs!' I say more loudly and firmly, just as the soggy mitten drops out of her pocket. I hang back to pick it up. She turns, her face twisted in anger, her hand pulling fiercely on mine, her chest rising to the shout she's been holding back all day.

But it doesn't come.

She sees the mitten and bends to pick it up herself. Her face is close to mine and even though her soft hair hangs forwards I notice, uncomprehendingly, that her eyes are wet.

We reach the bottom of the steps and she stops to jam my wet mitten back on to my hand. I don't want it on but I don't protest and merely curl my fingers into a tight fist away from its cold tip. This means she can't hold my hand but she seems not to notice and pulls me along the platform by my wrist. There are a lot of people standing with their bags and cases, and we thread our way among them to find a space for us to stand. At last she puts the case down and her neck arches backwards as her hand goes to the small of her back.

'You mustn't go near ze edge off ze platform,' her voice snaps out, cold and brittle. She rubs the back of her neck. She gets tired a lot and I wonder why. Why I would want to go near the edge? It's obvious that it's a big hole and nobody is standing anywhere near it. Suddenly, her grip on my wrist tightens and the people standing all around turn to face in the same direction. I turn too, but I can only see the backs of coats.

'BOAT TRAIN FOR HARWICH!' a voice booms and everyone shuffles their feet and picks up their bags and cases.

Now I remember the trains. I hear a strange noise like a monster blowing sharp, hot breaths, and between the legs of a tall boy next to us, I see it. As it comes around a bend it looks like a long caterpillar squirting out greyness at its head and feet, huffing dangerous things, hissing that sigh like my mother when she's at the end of her patience. It comes closer and there's no getting away. My wrist burns, she's holding it so tightly. It's almost up to us now and people are stepping backwards as it groans and breathes its way past them along the platform, a wheezing monster pushing air in front of it.

Suddenly, from nowhere, I feel angry. All my misery has balled up into rage. I can still hear the bells and now they fill me up and push at the anger. You shout at things when you are angry and, like my mother does, I shout and shout. I shout and shout at the monster. I kick out too. 'Goway, goway, goWAY!' I should be frightened but I'm not. I feel warm inside now and big. Hot air rushes past us and blows my mother's hair across her face, and I jump up and down with excitement and scream.

'Don't shtart zat again!' the knife-voice hurls at me automatically, then, relenting as she looks down, and in a softer tone, 'It's all right. It's only a train. Look! Ve are going for a ride on it.' I feel even warmer because she's nice, and I'm happy when she's nice so I pull in my stomach and hold everything inside. I stay still and quiet but my chest is full and tight with bigness and warmth.

A wooden door with a funny leather strap on it swings open with a clatter and all along the train, 'clack, clack, clack, clack', more doors open. 'Clack, clack, clack, clack.' A man gets down from the train and walks away. It's a long way up to that door and there's a hole under the step but I'm not afraid of this thing any more because I'm so full of excitement now. My mother scoops me up and drags the case behind her, up the high step and into a place where there are two long seats facing each other.

'See? It's all right. Oh, sank you wery much!' More people get in and a man in a flat grey hat like my father's picks up our case. He puts it in a string net up above our heads just as my mother lifts me onto the seat. The seat feels furry like my teddy and has twirly green and brown patterns on it.

'Teddy!' I say. 'Ted…dy!' A look of horror crosses my mother's face.

'Vere's your teddy?' she demands. '*Oh nein… ach du liebe Gott!*' (Oh my God, no!)

I don't know where my teddy is; it's just that he's always there when I need him. I can't see him now. Why hasn't my mother got him? I suddenly catch her panic and wail.

'Teedddy!' Loss and longing and burst in a great bubble into the space that was so big and warm, and it hurts so much. 'Teddeyey-eyey!'

'Vat haf you done viz him?'

How do I know? Grown-ups give me teddy when I want him. I want him now. I go straight and slide off the seat on to the floor making a silent open-mouthed cry and not stopping to breathe. I am across the shoes of a man who has just climbed in behind us and I go straighter still as he tries to pick me up, throwing myself back. Nothing works without teddy. Teddy is there when it's dark and nobody comes. Teddy helps me when they're shouting. Teddy doesn't say 'stop it!' when I fall down and cry. Teddy makes me better when she's angry.

I hear talking above my head as a sharp slap stings my thigh. I let go of my breath and wail again. More talking and a loud shout. 'The porter's gone to look!' I hear sounds like a fast wooden drum as someone runs across the footbridge. My legs beat time, scraping the heels of my new shoes on the floor so that one comes halfway off.

'He's running back over the bridge, ducky! Maybe she dropped it on the way over.'

'You really shouldn't bother. Ze train is going in a minute. She'll chust haff to get ofer it.'

Clack, clack. Doors shut. A whistle. A loud huff from the train. A lurch and then faster huffs.

Suddenly a red face appears at the train window. It's the porter.

'Is this it, darlin'?' he puffs, and there's my teddy, flying through the air towards me as the red face disappears rapidly down the platform. I recognise it briefly as the face of one of the men who had ignored us early on... or had my mother simply not wanted help?

'Ach, I didn't gif him any money.'

'Don't worry love, he won't mind — it was for your little girl. Don't upset yourself now, it really doesn't matter. There you are, ducky, there's your teddy.'

Consoled by my teddy and soothed by the rhythm of the train, I'm quiet now. Arms stand me up and push my shoe back on my foot. Teddy is on the seat and I want to cuddle him. I rub my other mitten into my face until it's as soggy and slimy as its partner, with long woollen points where I've sucked and chewed. Waving their Fairisle patterns around in front of her, and clenching and unclenching my fists, I hold up my hands for my mother to take them off but she isn't looking at me. I look up at her and wonder, uncomprehendingly again, why she is crying. Is this a good thing or a bad thing? I try and climb on her knee to find out.

'Not on my new coat!' She plants me so firmly on the seat at the side of her that my teeth rattle. She drags off my mittens and my woollen bonnet, clenching them, white-knuckled, in her lap along with her shoulder bag. I content myself by chewing on teddy's nose, stroking his silky label with my forefinger and peeping over his fuzzy head at the other people in the carriage.

On the seat opposite there's a lady in a small, shiny green feather hat with a bit of net that comes down over her face. She has on very red lipstick and red shoes and she keeps smiling at me. People smile at me a lot but my mother doesn't smile at me so I just stare hard because I don't know if it's all right to smile or not.

'She's a serious one!'

She's talking to my mother and nodding at me. My mother blows her nose on a clean rag from her pocket because she doesn't like washing hankies and won't have them, but she doesn't say anything. She doesn't like people or talking to them because if anybody comes to visit us we have to hide under the table and be very quiet and pretend to be out. We do this even when her best friend from Germany comes. We're going to Germany now, on the boat train.

'Look, ducky, out the window — there's Lincoln Cathedral,' the red lipstick says. But I don't look. I just suck teddy's nose and think about the bells and wonder if we're being chased. The bells make me want to cry…

… Adjusting my oxygen mask, I try and wipe away tears that have escaped from my rheumy old eyes. It was so long ago and I didn't realise how bad things were at the time. You just accept it as normal when you're little. That's also the first time that I remember how my mother and I ran away so often and how church bells made me feel. I felt a lot of awful things as a child but learned never to show them — it was more peaceful that way. Ah, but if I heard church bells, it broke down my walls, no matter how well I'd barricaded myself in.

Yes, it must be Sunday, the bells are still ringing and I can already catch the rattle of the trolley as it bears its load of roast dinners to the ward. I wish I could smell that. My sense of smell, once so sharp, doesn't pick up much these days. Just listen to those bells… listen… listen…

… Faint, English village church bells sounding across drowsy summer cornfields find me in a place that I'm supposed to call home but by now I've been in so many places with my mother, pulled by the hand in a headlong rush to escape, that nowhere feels like home. I don't seem to fit here but now I know that I'm not German, either. At least we don't run any more, though. She just stays in the house and cries.

Along the footpath from Scugton to Mottesford, where the town ends and wide open spaces begin, my dad takes me for an evening walk to get away from the tears and seething anger that claw the walls of our cottage flat in Grange Lane South. We walk to where the lane peters out into a brown footpath and weeds, then we stare out across the fields. Sometimes when it's dry, we walk along the path but we can't go if it's muddy, in case I get dirty and she has to get out the dolly legs and washtub.

She hates washing.

I'm glad to go with him and hold on to the little finger of his broad, calloused hand, chattering incessantly. At five years of age, I have a million questions about everything we see, and I learn, wide-eyed, about skylarks and their bold songs, corn stooks and how to stack them in eights, field mice nests and why a harvest moon is so big but, eventually, I always come back to the bells. Why do they make me feel sad, I want to know. I know that I'm sad. I'm sad because everything is angry at home and because I don't fit in to the tight, thin-lipped spaces between the anger. That I do know, but what I don't know is why the bells touch my sadness and make it bubble out. He can't answer this question and tells me that I should ignore the way things make me feel. It's better that way, he says. Feelings deceive us. My fierce, logical brain believes him but my child's heart, searching for comfort, does not. Then he recites a poem about islands, finishing with a booming: 'Send not to ask for whom the bell tolls, It tolls for thee.'

He likes reciting poems and I listen but I still wonder why the bells should be ringing for me and what it has to do with islands...

... The sharp, metallic clatter of a knife dropped to the floor by the lady in the next bed brings me back sharply into the ward. I'd rather be here than on this train of thought, but drowsiness and the sheer effort of breathing overwhelm me once more. Oh, I remember Sunday lunches...

... I'm seven and back at last in Germany, a place I've missed so much since we had to go back to England when my dad came to fetch us.

'*Ich bin wie ein Mann mit ohne Arme*,' he said and my mum laughed because it means, 'I'm like a man with, without arms.' She kissed him and we got on a train for England.

Now I'm standing in Oma's loft in the tall apartment house on Willhelmstrasse, surrounded by drying washing and strings of onions, peering on tiptoe through the open loft doors at a jumble of ancient rooftops and the sky. I am listening in rapt attention to the jangly, discordant chimes of continental bells, trying to find a pattern, failing, and yet still mesmerised, carried along in that chaotic sound.

Fat Frau Vogel startles me when she puffs up the stairs to get some onions and flaps pinkly down again to tell Oma that I'm crying once more. Then there's a commotion because I cannot say, in German, just why I'm crying or how the bells make me feel. The words won't come, cleaving my tongue to the roof of my mouth as if I had eaten sour rhubarb. Of course, she thinks there's something sinister going on that I simply won't tell her.

'*Was ist los, Kind?*' (What's the matter, child?) she keeps repeating, pressing me to the bosom of her faded pinafore and stroking my head. I inhale on the familiar, loved scent of old lady, rye bread and salami, and stay silent. How can I explain to her that the bells toll out the confusion I feel whenever my parents start yet another argument? How can I tell her about clinging, screaming, to my mother while my drink-sodden father hurls his Sunday lunch at the wall yet again, and then sets about her with his fists? The words won't come, just as they won't when Granny Rose tries her best to prise open my clenched heart. Only the bells can do that. Oma finally throws up her hands and rolls her eyes just like my mum does.

'*Ach Du Lieber Gott!*' (Oh dear God!)

She pats me on the bottom and urges me to go along the street and play with my cousin, Anne-Marie, but I make an excuse about wanting to take Opa's dog, Trolley, for a walk, instead. Trolley lifts an ear and one grizzled lip, growling from his blanket by the porcelain-tiled stove.

'*Tröllchen, kommst Du mit?*' (Are you coming with me, little Trolley?) I wheedle, patting my leg, but his throaty growl turns to a snap as I reach for his collar and his eyes roll whitely.

'*Schrekliche Hündchen!*' (Terrible doggie!) I chide.

I really don't want to play with Anne-Marie because she hates me. The two of us have to sleep together at her house when we come to Germany now. My dad comes with us these days so there isn't a bed for me in Oma's tiny apartment house any more. Anne-Marie bites, scratches and sticks pins in me if I roll anywhere near her in bed. One night she even stuck a hair slide up my bum. I told her that her hair would smell and laughed so she couldn't see how upset I was.

She says I don't belong here in Germany but I think that maybe I do, after all. I feel at more at home here than in England where girls poke fun at me because I wear warm, woollen trousers instead of skirts in winter and carry my satchel on my back like they do here, and not over my shoulder. Here no one points and whispers, 'Don't talk to her. Her mother is German!' The war was ten years ago but it doesn't seem to make any difference to them.

I drag my feet down the wooden stairs and go out into the street. The bells are still jangling out their tunes. '*Tag Dummkopf*,' (Hello stupid) sneers Anne-Marie.

\* \* \*

Now I'm nine and those bells are wrapped tightly around my heart once more, squeezing out the tears I've saved up for most of the year. I'm in Tante Kathe's bedroom and Anne-Marie is out shopping with her. I didn't want to go; my cousin always finds an excuse to get me into trouble with her mum when we're together, so I said I'd stay behind and read a book. I shouldn't be in this bedroom but there's a big attraction; I can hear the bells best from here.

The sun's rays stream through the open widow where a fluffy white *Bettdecke* (duvet) is carefully laid out to catch the fresh air. They don't have Bettdeckes in England, so they don't know about hanging them outside for a bit every day to keep them fresh. All my friends sleep under heavy sheets and tickly blankets, moaning about cold feet in the winter but I have my very own real eider duck down

Bettdecke and I'm never cold.

'Germany one, England nil,' I mutter defiantly through my tears.

There's a large mirror on Tante Kathe's wardrobe and on the wall above the low window opposite is another smaller mirror she uses to check that her bun is neatly in place. If you stand in just the right spot, you can see yourself reflected over and over on into infinity in the mirror on the wardrobe. *'Spiegel im Spiegel'*, my aunt calls it — mirrors in a mirror. I've never actually seen myself cry before and it's horribly fascinating.

Looking at myself now, turning this way and that, I try to count the long corridor of mirror images of my misery that stretch off into infinity. I blink abruptly with disbelief and then freeze as I catch sight of something that can't logically be there at all. Way back in the distance where my face repeats on and on, is a solitary, unmirrored caricature of a face. It's hard to tell but it seems something like a red mask with empty eye sockets and a jag of a mouth that is reflecting wickedly over my shoulder. And, very tiny but sinister and unexpected enough to burn its shape into my mind, a skeletal hand creeps around the mirror frame and beckons me towards that face, pointing, pointing.

Utterly terrified, I spin around, trip over the Bettdecke and fall backwards out of the low window into a bush, taking the feathery white mass with me in a tangled heap as I scrabble at the window ledge. That's the moment when my cousin and my aunt arrive back to find me spread-eagled on my back, struggling to get down from the massive blue hydrangea that has broken my fall. They see my red, blotchy, tearful face and assume the worst. In between reassuring her that I'm not hurt, trying to explain why I was in the bedroom in the first place and excusing the filthy state of her pristine white Bettdecke, I forget the mask and the beckoning hand entirely. Anne-Marie doesn't let me forget my accident so easily, though, and makes the rest of my holiday that year an absolute misery.

* * *

I'm ten and we're here again. We can never afford the trip ourselves on the eleven pounds, eleven shillings and ninepence a week my dad gets for being an iron moulder. I don't even get any pocket money from him. So Oma sends the money to get my mother home for the three weeks in a year when she smiles. You can't send money out of Germany — because of what they did in the war, I think — so a letter in my grandmother's precise Gothic hand arrives first to say where the money will be. Then a string and sealing wax parcel is delivered with a tight roll of notes hidden in a salami or a soup packet. My dad goes to Martin's, the travel agency on Oswald Road, and a complicated journey across Europe is organised for us. We take buses, trains, boats, trains and more trains before arriving at our Bahnhof, Letmathe Station, two days later.

Opa waits, as always, to fling his arms around us and burst into tears. He is the only man that I've ever seen cry and he hoists me on to his shoulders, still sniffling, to catch a Strassenbahn to the house on Wilhelmstrasse, blowing his nose all the while and telling everyone on the rattling wooden seats that I'm his granddaughter from England and that I can speak both English and German.

'*Tag Zusammen,*' (Hello everyone) I beam around on cue, standing on the seat, hanging on to the leather strap and counting the streets until I can see the bell tower and the ornate roof of Oma's apartment house again.

I love this place because it's so old and beautiful. I wonder how Letmathe can be so pretty when my bit of Scugton is so grey and ugly. Not many bombs dropped here in the war, my mam says, even though it's close to Germany's industrial heart. I always think of an iron heart with a swastika scorched into it when she says this. Then she shakes her head and remembers Dortmund, and her brother Willie who died there in a bombed out factory, leaving parts of himself for my mother to go and identify, all over the factory floor.

I love this place because everyone here, apart from Anne-Marie, loves me and I'm never in the way or shouted at. Now I'm walking down Kirkestrasse on my way to my grandmother's house, singing along to the clang of Sunday morning bells.

'Jangle, jangle-ja! Ja, ja. Jangle ja!' I mimic.

If I listen to them long enough, they will take the lid off all my troubles and, although I'll cry, it will be strange tears that turn into a swelling joy that I can hardly contain. It's as if the sadder I am, the happier the bells will make me. Granny Rose says so too. She says the bells are the key to my soul but I haven't a clue what she means. She talks in riddles about her signs sometimes.

Plane trees line the street, dappling sunshine on worn cobbles, while on either side tall, graceful houses with impossible roofs breathe out smells of fresh coffee, poppy seed rolls, cinnamon and Apfelküchen. Great white puffs of Bettdeckes hang out of every bedroom window and a Hausfrau is sweeping her steps. The houses on Kirkestrasse all have at least six steps up to the front doors, which are large with heavy iron knobs but no letterboxes. The post goes in a box at the side. I'm singing and looking at a box with a little pointed roof and a fox and a rabbit chasing along the top, when a fist rams into the side of my head and two large hands push me to the ground.

Rolling over, winded and dazed, I see a blonde youth of about sixteen. He is wearing Lederhosen and has a green felt hat with a feather in it in his hand. The sun is behind him, making his yellow curls look like a halo but his face is white and angry and his other hand is raised in a fist once more.

'*Mensch! Sind Sie verrückt?*' I shout at him. 'Hey, are you mad?' and it doesn't help matters at all. He carefully sets the green hat on a step as if he doesn't want it to get damaged, takes a pace back and lowers his fist.

'*Englische Schweinhund!*' he spits at me and lands a kick in my ribs as I struggle to my feet. There follows a rain of slaps and punches as I back away, trying to shield my head from his blows. I'm crying and half hysterical now. I haven't a clue why this is happening and a detached part of me is hearing the creak of his Lederhosen as he works away. There are tiny bells on the braces and they jingle with each slap. I wonder why there is foamy white spittle at the corners of his mouth and why the sunshine is so bright at this awful time. My head is jerked back against a house wall by one of his blows and I snap suddenly to attention, fill my lungs and shout, '*Zu Hilfe rufen! HILFE!!*' (Help, Help!)

He grabs my hair and pulls me towards him but my shout has brought the Hausfrau with her sweeping brush out on to the street again. I think she is going to help me but she beats at both of us with her brush and tells us to go or she will fetch the police.

*'Alte Schaf Nase!'* (Old busybody!) the youth hisses at her and he picks up his hat and turns on his heel whistling *Oh Du Schöne Westerwald,* just like he was on a Sunday stroll.

I expect the old lady to comfort me as he vanishes, cheerfully, down the street but she just turns away too, and waddles back into her house. I'm distraught. Dropping to my knees on the pavement I don't know what to do for a moment and watch snot, saliva and tears drip into the dust. All around me the bells are still ringing and, although I think I've been quite brave up until now, I finally break down. It's apparent that no one is coming to help; no one in this place I love cares at all, so I just get up and run, gasping huge shuddering sobs, all the way to Oma's house. I bang on the door and, when she opens it, I fall into her arms and on to that warm pinafore, once more unable to find the words to tell.

I describe him exactly to my mother and father when I finally recover myself, but no one ever goes to the police or asks the Hausfrau to explain what she's seen. I hear them all whispering that even now, in 1958, there are still Nazis in the town who sometimes take the law into their own hands, unable to accept the shame of defeat and believing still that they will be able to rise up and wrest Germany from the hands of democracy. I don't quite know what this all means, except that the youth will go unpunished even though Opa knows his name.

'Life isn't fair!' my father snaps, when I complain. So I learn that beautiful places can hide great ugliness, that even adults are afraid of monsters and that I just don't fit in.

Anywhere.

\* \* \*

Now I'm back in England, a few months later, hanging out of the bedroom window of our bleak council flat on Warley Road, flicking pebbledash off the wall and trying to soak up the Wednesday night bell practice as it drifts and dreams its way over sooty chimney pots. It's getting dark and the ragged clouds flush suddenly blood red and menacing, spreading a stain of dirty glowing slag across the eastern sky. Straining further out of the window I think I can almost see a face in its whorls and squint through half-closed eyes to take it in. It's like a mask with empty eye sockets and a jag of an open mouth hanging free. It's suddenly very familiar and I remember the mirrors at Tante Kathe's. This makes me feel so dizzy that I think I might fall out of this window as well and on to the concrete below.

'Shut ze vindow, you'll let ze vorks dust blow in, your fazzer has TB,' my mother snaps out all in one breath, as if the three are con-nected.

I take a moment to clear the bells and the mask from my head and think about what she's just said. Pulling on the window latch, I turn anxiously to scan her face. I've learned to read that beautiful face very well and watched in terror a thousand times as its porce-lain fragility hardens to fury-etched marble. But for once, her lovely mouth is not set, and she looks at me with a strange softness, her wide sapphire eyes swimming with something I can't identify at all. The only bit I know about tuberculosis is that Granny Rose told me how she'd had it before the war and had had to go away to a place in the countryside. My size eight Start-rites become clumsy as boxes and I nervously scuff the linoleum as I stare into those eyes and brave a question.

'Is he going away?' I ask.

'How do you know zat?' she whispers, reaching forward to put her arms around me and pull me close.

Totally off guard, I jump as somewhere on the steelworks a machine gives a ferocious industrial roar that makes the window glass vibrate. Then I don't know what else to do but relax onto her shoulder. This is such a rare thing, this embrace. So rare that I have marked, counted, treasured and re-lived each one many times. In my memory they have not even numbered above my years. I am eleven now and as tall as she is, so this seems incongruous to my embarrassed, emerging adulthood, yet I still savour it, leech on it greedily and, finally, hesitantly, begin to return its unaccustomed feel. It is the beginning of a time of calm.

'TB is an opportunistic bug,' the white-coated specialist tells my mother, who has taken me for a test. 'Always gets you when you're down. It must be his time as a POW that has caused it to return.'

'Fourteen years ago?' I think. 'More likely the drink.'

My mother says nothing and he continues to chat as he does the skin test between my shoulder blades where I can't reach, about how antibiotics were invented in 1947 and in ten more years everyone thinks that TB will be history.

My father has to go to Mumby TB Isolation Hospital for six months. It turns out that I'm carrying antibodies to the disease, through my having caught and fought it as a baby but I'm still not allowed to visit and I wonder if I should feel guilty that I just don't care. Everyone is so nice to me. I'm the only one not going on the school trip to Derbyshire because my mother can't afford it now dad isn't working. Then one day, Mr Rotherham — who like every other teacher I've ever had, is convinced I'm from Mars and actually calls me a 'misfit' — smiles at me, pats my head and says what a lucky girly I am to be going on the school trip after all, with the other children. I think so too. My mother, if not exactly sweet, is far more even tempered, Granny Rose keeps pressing threepenny bits into my hand with a big fat wink, her finger pressed to her lips, and even the lady in the grocer's shop opposite our school regularly gives me an apple when the other children aren't looking.

This is a good time, a peaceful time, a time when I can listen to the bells and not feel sad. My mother, however, says that all things, no matter how bad or good they are, come to an end.

And they do.

I have finally given my heart to my mother and when my dad comes out of hospital, she tosses it back again.

# 6

# A PROCESS OF SHAPING

Abruptly my chain of memories snaps as, once again, a blur of daylight comes into focus. I can feel my hands plucking at the sheets and I try to still them. The hiss of my oxygen mask mingles, soporifically, with the Sunday bells that are still drifting their summer sound across the hospital grounds.

I suppose I should have known.

In my job I always used say that there was a key to every child. It seems the bells were mine. They were the only thing that ever released my pent up sorrows, fears and frustrations, prising a salve of tears from the place where all the dark things hid. Harriet had her lists, I had my bells. Harriet and I — two total misfits born nearly a century apart.

No. For now I know for sure that it's more than that. My mind returns uneasily to the mask-like face that has been floating like crusted slag scum over my memories. I *do* remember that now. I know I haven't, in the retrospective adjustments of old age, added that detail but it never assumed any real importance at the time.

Red flushed skies magnified the shadowy, fear filled corners of each and every one of my childhood nights. Every night was terrifying; I don't remember the mask as being any more frightening than the wardrobe that sidled towards my bed or the slanting faces in the lampshade, yet now it seems far more sinister.

And Harriet — I know she glimpsed it too. Then there was that skeletal hand once more. Fingering my long forgotten memory of that hand and the fleeting horror Harriet felt at her memory of the mask, I shudder.

The growing certainty that there's something really important I have to do presses down on my weakened lungs, stifling me with its awful weight. This is all wrong. I'm dying. I'm so tired, so why can't I sink into that sense of peace I know so well? Why won't it come? My every fibre yearns for it, that glowing ball of light that will bear me away.

What process is this? Why did death, with all his little intimacies, never reveal this to me before? I shift uneasily and yet again flinch at paper-thin skin grazing against sheets. This should be a slow disconnection from life, a welcome gathering up and then unseaming of all that I was, but now there's Harriet, that mask and the grasping hand. A pattern, a story, a meaning I never saw until now is being cast and moulded from the mess of my earlier life.

'There's something I should know.'

The thought won't go away. This dying is turning out to be a knowing, a growing, almost a process of ordering and shaping of all that I was. It's taking everything I was, melting it down and showing it to me differently.

'Perhaps death is the final shaping.'

I try to move once more but my unwilling frame stays stubbornly stuck to the sheets. I'm so tired now but grateful for this revelation. A final shaping! I do so want to be properly ready, finished and fettled for the end when it comes. I want it all set straight.

Beyond the glass womb wall of the hospital window a blackbird lapses suddenly from song into a prolonged alarm call, and at that familiar sound I hurtle to a point in the tangled filaments of my life where the loose ends began to gather.

'Fettled. Now there's a word.' I can feel it plucking at another strand of memory…

… A grey and cheerless late November day. Outside in the garden everything is wet, dripping, decaying, chill. A droop-winged blackbird shelters miserably under the jasmine arch, eyeing the last blackberry which is just beyond reach, dangling from its frame on the garage wall. Prised from under a plant pot rim, the flesh teased by a foraging thrush out of a short stack of snail shells, echoes the almost gristly quality to the light.

It is a day for being indoors.

Inside, in the bright yellow lights of the pottery studio above the garage, an iron pot-bellied stove is chugging away, sending whorls of grey smoke to join the greyness above. Windows are steamy with moisture evaporating from the clay and the plumes of a kettle whistling low and insistently, just on the boil. The only other sound is the hum of the potter's wheel as John bends over the shape emerging from beneath his hands.

'Cup of tea?' I ask.

I break into the companiable warm fug, looking for an excuse to leave the model I am working on. It's a starling, its beak in the air, rattling and fizzing with that cheerful sound that punctuates even the darkest autumn day. It's not going well, something isn't quite right. I wash my hands and take a cloth to the handle of the kettle.

'Mmmm?'

'Yes darling, I would love a cuppa,' I chide at his absorbed form, body and spirit at one with the yielding clay.

His hands are beautiful, sensitive, delicate, not at all like anyone would imagine the hands of a potter to be. With a tiny wet sponge he rounds the rim of a tall vase-like shape. Putting two fingers of his left hand underneath the rim and one finger of his right hand inside, he rolls the rim outwards to flute the neck in one smooth, sensuous motion.

'What?'

A wet sponge on a stick removes all the water from inside the pot. Then he picks up an old credit card to skim its surface, wiping the slurry with rapid practised fingers on the bowl of the wheel. I hear that satisfied catch in his breath as he undercuts the base of the vase slightly with a pointed tool I can't quite identify. Probably yet another gadget of his own making, like the crazy razor handle he fashioned from olive wood on a Greek island holiday, too stubborn to buy a complete new razor. I know he's now going to leave the vase on the wheel until it's leather-hard and can be further turned and finished. It's safe to repeat my question.

'I said, do you want a cuppa?' and wave the kettle at him.

*The Anvil Chorus* plays on the old dusty transistor radio he has hung up by a nail on the studio wall — along with whisks, sieves, jugs and various other implements removed from my kitchen because they're useful to his craft. We laugh and exchange looks. It's what I call his 'busy' tune, reminding me of the days when he'd disappear to hammer and crash and saw in the depths of the garage or the studio. Even now he pauses in his work only long enough to take a mouthful of tea before taking a cheese wire to slice a chunk from a bag of clay.

I'm still reluctant to get back to my modelling. I sit instead and watch him knock up this lump for further throwing on an old paving slab that sucks out just enough moisture from the clay to stop it sticking. The heel of his hand kneads a spiral into the supple mass, making possible a smooth, circular flow of microscopic clay platelets on the wheel. He then forms six 200 gram balls, weighing them out on a pair of old potato scales in order to test one identical shape against another in the throwing. The radio plays Bizet's *Habanera* from *Carmen* and I feel an habitual lurch inside. I've been able to hum this tune, pitch perfect, since I was five, when I went to the Scugton Essoldo on Cole Street with my mum and dad to see *Carmen Jones*. The line, 'If you love me then you'd better watch out,' always seemed to sum up my life. I even used to call my every misfortune 'the Carmen syndrome', thinking I was doomed to misery — until I met John, that is.

Outside in the garden, a blackbird sets up another alarm.

'Hysteria in the blackbird world,' he quips, returning to his wheel and, taking a dry, circular wooden throwing bat from the wall, fixes it to the wheel head.

I love to watch this man throw. My husband, the potter.

As he sits astride the wheel, the yellow fisherman's *vareuse* that he wears to protect his clothes tautens across his broad back. Forearms locked on the wheel bowl to stop his hands wobbling, he starts the hardest part, centering the clay. Art students take months to learn this one simple task, repeating it hour after hour, day after day. This tall, elegant man, more headmaster than artisan, makes it look simple.

Setting the ball of clay on the bat, he scoops water and cups it with his right hand, the other holding the clay in, thumbs acting as restrainers to this slippery mass. As he pushes down, concentrating on this smooth, steady movement, a splash of watery clay catches in the curls at his tanned nape. He works the clay, stretching and compressing it as the wheel turns at high speed. First a tower, then a squat mushroom and then a tower once more. Sitting back, he slides his hands slowly, so suggestively, up the column of clay, taking them off at the top so as not to create a wobble. Finally he pushes down once more, satisfied that it is centred.

In the beginning, all shapes are possible but now he must restrict his choices to a cylinder or a bowl. I know he has another vase in mind, like the one he's just made, and a cylinder will emerge from this truncated cone of clay. He holds his wrist with his left hand and puts two wet, probing fingers on its top, feeling them run automatically towards the middle of the cavity he's about to create. He can feel the centre as his fingers drop into it. Pressing down with both fingers, he reaches down to where he thinks the base should be. I can feel my body tighten inside as I flush with pleasure. Now, putting two fingers into the cavity with his thumb at the back pointing down, he cups the front of the pot with his other hand and pulls towards his body, horizontally across the wheel head. This is the base.

When the base is wide enough, his hands lift away smoothly

once more to scoop water. With his left hand still cupping the clay, two fingers search inside the pot to compress the clay in its base and prevent cracking. The pot has fanned out a lot at the base now and he momentarily removes his hands. Here comes the moment that transfixes me every time and I focus all my attention upon it.

With two hands he now pushes the clay inwards to get a strong, short vertical shape. The clay rises magically, phallically. His left hand disappears inside the pot while the other opposes it outside, knuckling the pot upwards. This is the first lift and he slides his hands gently away to cup more water as the clay loses its slipperiness. Leaning back to check he still has a strong shape, he turns to mouth a kiss at me, knowing I'm watching. Knuckling up and down for a couple of inches, he gets the pot wall right-angled at the base. It doesn't matter about the thickness of a bowl base but a cylinder has to be evenly formed. Now comes the third lift and the cylinder is strong and ready to take on his imagined shape.

The wheel spins more slowly now. Inside the cylinder, the fingers of his left hand push and roll into the palm of his right hand, and a belly swells and rises beneath his touch. A slender neck turning above is stroked with firm but supple fingers, drawing the clay in and upwards until his hands slide from the pot once more. The wheel turns one final time as he knifes a small ring of clay from the mouth. A vase has been eased and caressed once more from the raw clay. He turns to drink his cold tea before performing the ritual of finishing. The base of the pot must be cut away from the wheel and spare clay fettled away with a knife to smoothness.

I am always totally fascinated by the way the nature of the clay has combined with his vision, imagination and skill to produce a beautiful artifact from what is basically water and fine rock particles.

Frowning and squinting a little, I try to see the starling in my mind's eye. I'm working at the very limits of what clay can do as it dries and crumbles beneath my fingers. It's a balancing act between two forces, this process of making.

'I know what's wrong,' I call across the studio.

'Mmmm?'

'I can't get the way that the feathers stick out on a starling's throat when it sings.'

The moment the words are out of my mouth I have that uncanny feeling I felt at the gym the other day, a feeling that there's a door opening up in my head, linking me to something complete; a wholeness. I can feel the excitement of a child bubbling up once more and I know this is really important but, again, I just can't grasp it and the thought is interrupted by the dearly beloved.

'Trust you to think of something as difficult as that — and anyway, they'd be terribly fragile,' he observes, 'probably come off in the firing.'

The door has closed again and I dismiss it. I know he's right and I reluctantly settle for a suggestion of throat feathers, raking and roughing the clay with a fork.

'There.'

'Put it on the right shelf, then, if it's finished.'

I smile to myself. He's totally chaotic in matters of storage in his daily life. Objects are stowed randomly around the house, often because it was the nearest place to hand. Until anything new acquires a permanent position, it could turn up anywhere, but here in the pottery, each tool, each glaze, each half finished pot has a place. He creates beauty and order from dust, chaos and disorder, carefully writing each firing, each glaze trial, each chemical combination, in an old, worn log book so that it can be replicated if he likes the effect. With my chin resting on grey, clay cracked hands, I watch as he takes another ball from the line in front of him.

'People are like pots,' I think, 'their shape can only be formed as their clay and their circumstances will allow until, finally, they harden for good'.

That awful day at the gym last week drops back into my mind. What about my own shaping? I rub the clay from my chin. So many rough, thoughtless acts wrought their effect upon the raw clay that was me and I really wasn't too nice a person when John and I met. But this man, with the potter's skill, has moulded my unwilling form with hands that sought out promise. He has taken my possibilities and turned them in his hands until they became the best that I could be. I have been a vessel that has held so much joy. I owe it to him that the lingering dead wood of my past was cleared away. How can I be with the man I love and still be haunted by it? Enough is enough.

'I'm going up to the house now.'

'Mmmm? Ok, I won't be long.'

I know that this means I will have at least an hour before he appears and, back in the yellow warmth of the house, my hands washed and clay brushed from my clothes and shoes, I switch on the computer. Behind me the Godin stove clicks and rustles companionably on its load of wood, radiating glowing warmth through the room. A pale, elongated creature stretches up tall in front of it, eyes almost closed in pleasure.

'Heat seeker,' I chide at his inscrutable back. Bony chest warmed, the Siamese cat barely flicks his tail in assent before attempting to coil into a neat ball. No, that's not quite what he has in mind. With infinitely honed precision, the cat uncoils himself again to measure the heat output of my knee and, calibrating that will be warmer than his place in front of the stove, he jumps up. Juggling him into place, I turn to my emails.

Strange how important and useful receiving mail can make you feel when you no longer work. It's cruelly sobering, to begin with, on leaving a school, to have to accept that I've left a large group of people whom I loved dearly but to whom I no longer have any significance. The losses are acute. No tiny children to fling their arms around my knees in the playground, no secretary to gauge my mood, no sea of faces each morning as the children wait for my story, breath tensed in expectation, their minds vibrant in the palm of my hand; no parents to guide or comfort with practised words, no visitors to show proudly around the beating heart that is a school. I no longer exist to any of them.

The first six months was easy. I walked through a gentle rolling landscape of relief at the end of a long and, at times, exhausting working life before I began to flail, wounded and thirsty, in a bleak desert of doubt.

'So what was it all about, then? Here I am, a formed vessel. How can I take on another shape?' was my mournful mantra for what seemed quite a long time. Now I've moved on, as most retired folks do, to the stage of trying to make sense of my place in the world. I'm not really a Facebook, Twitter or Friends Reunited person; apart

from one or two close friends, I've mostly been the 'cat who walked by himself' and quite content to be so. Instead, I'm putting my life into some sort of perspective by looking at my ancestry, at the past. For me, though, it's not just a hobby, it's critical — a gnawing, driving need. I'm hoping to find that I'm not the awful monster I think I am.

'Ouch! Don't do that! Put your mittens on in polite society.' Unpicking the cat's claws from my jeans where he's firmly anchored, I stroke his silky length and listen to his rumbling purr as I pause to think. Stroking the cat lines up each thought and idea for me in a calm and logical way, and I need to collect my thoughts. Finding out about your family is like placing a stamp in a collection. It tells a story — your story. It gives perspective to who you are and where you come from. The time before you were born which was once a dim, featureless void, becomes a continuum of which you are part. Names you've only heard take on a life and a personality as you attach them to old photographs, certificates and letters. Marriage certificates are best, so many clues on one piece of paper. Maiden names, fathers' names and occupations, addresses if you're lucky, ages, witnesses, they all give you starting points for the next hungry search.

With the protesting Siamese calmed and readjusted, I click on to my family tree and settle down to trawling the data for family members whose names I can as yet only guess at. Will there be meaning there? An explanation, maybe, of who I am and why I did what I did?

'I bet there's no one there who did such an appalling thing as me,' I tell the cat, who looks up with a mournful 'wooow' that

seems to concur.

'Well you didn't have to agree with me. Just remember where your fish comes from.'

Down in the pottery, a row of vases stand drying, yielding up the moisture that has been locked into them from the clay of the earth, slowly changing their nature to become leather-hard, then dry and brittle before their form is finally locked in by the heat of the kiln.

Like a pot, it seems, the closer I come to completion, the harder and more definite my form becomes; my possibilities become fewer. In a couple of decades the full impact of what I am will be all that there is. I don't want to fossilise in old age, I want to continue to change and grow right up to my deathbed. I want my form then to be as finished and fettled at the end as I can make it, and there's so much more to do…

… My eyes flick briefly open. Was it really 37 years ago that I first said this? Lord, I'm old!

# 7

# AT THE CREMATORIUM

The soft slow mutter of several pairs of feet approaching, the pause at the reception desk, my name spoken in a low, reverential whisper; all these sounds tell me that visitors are on the way. They've heard I'm dying.

I don't want to see anyone, really. I need to sort this stuff in my head. Why did I totally disregard all those odd time slip moments from my life? I always had to be so damn logical! Well, they're certainly all coming together now, thick and fast. It seems as though death is picking over the bones of every single moment from my past. Maybe he's been waiting to catch me unawares when my defences are down. These are connected things, important things, so this really is my final shaping, something I should put together before I go. But I still can't connect it all in my fuddled brain and, right now, I'm not sure I want to.

Thoughts of a line of pots linger as I shift restlessly and feel my tongue wobble; sucking, sucking in the retrogression of this old body as it lurches on towards its end. I hear more footsteps and the sound of the television. I catch the echo of an old song from many years ago drifting by the end of my bed, 'My big, bad, handsome man, he's got me in the palm of his hands…'

He had such beautiful hands. I would like to feel them on me now, caressing me like the clay that rose and folded and bellied beneath his touch, but the shapes of the pots dissolve and become blurry faces bobbing at the foot of my bed.

'Now then, look at you all dolled up in a pretty nightie!'

It's three friends who have come to make their farewell. I wish it was Coral. She died long before I could tell her of my regrets, give her my thanks and hold out a hand to her one more time. Why, oh why don't we tell the people we've loved how we feel when they're alive, instead of regretting our silence after they've gone?

Prising open my eyes again, I manage a feeble wave, holding on to that thought. I'm so, so tired. The attempt at anything physical is all-consuming. Crystal bright, I can see those potter's hands briefly reflected before my thoughts are interrupted.

'What are you doing with pneumonia? And you such a tough old bird.' 'Just look at those pink roses; they were always your favourite.' 'Ooooh! You lucky thing! Have you seen that dishy doctor?'

Brittle voices and forced bright smiles tell me how brilliantly they think I'm doing, how lovely my cards and flowers are, and how they just popped in to see that I was ok. It's a well-intentioned gambit uncomfortable visitors use, as much to ease their own suffering as that of the patient. I watched it all with the lady in the bed opposite who died last week. Next follows the inevitable recounting of what's going on in the world out there. My friends find it hard to speak of their affection, for to do it would be *la chamade* for them; a roll on the drums to announce defeat. They don't yet know that there is no defeat, only this unfolding and tidying up of a life.

Long past the point of conversation, I manage to squeeze their hands, lift my mask a little and mouth, 'Goodbye,' and after a painful pause to capture a little more breath, a 'thank you'. There, I've said it. It needed saying but the exertion has exhausted me utterly. Closing my eyes again, I let their voices become a pleasant bumble. I don't want their sorrow, I don't want Coral, I don't want Harriet or her mysteries. I want to think of pots, of making, of beautiful hands easing the clay into its hidden shape.

But I think of sorrow, which has crept into the ward at their heels and has now wreathed itself around the metalwork of my bed. Like a pot shaped upon the wheel, I think how the deeper that sorrow carves into some people, the more happiness they seem able to hold, becoming a vessel for limitless joy and taking on an almost luminous quality. They glow with life and are at peace with whatever life throws at them, finding a gift in the centre of each trauma and tragedy.

Granny Rose was like that.

'Now you listen to me, our Mia,' she would say, wagging her finger at me as I came to her with yet another sob story, 'wrapped up in every problem there's a gift. Find it!'

My mother, on the other hand, was bowed, crabbed, withered and diminished by her life and the materials of her being. An unsuccessful attempt at a vessel, her shape shrank and wobbled on the wheel. Each household task, each failed effort at bringing my father to heel, each journey home to Germany, each post-war insult spat at her retreating back, reduced and condensed her ailing spirit so that she became unbearably hard and impervious to joy.

She was a shape fired to permanence long before the end, eventually rejecting every helping hand offered by friends or family, repulsing every gift I or anyone else ever gave her, and any attempt on anyone's part to make her life easier. On her own deathbed just twelve years after my father's re-acquaintance with TB she even rejected the comfort I tried to offer, snarling at me in derision.

That snarl is my last memory of her. That and the grey January day at the crematorium when I realised, with that sense of sinking finality that comes when you experience your first real death, that I would never see her again. I was only twenty-two years old, numbed by my marriage and the effort of looking after a difficult first baby. I forgave her then as I followed her small coffin into the chapel at the crematorium. How could I not? She was my mother but I was too full of my own troubles to grieve. I thought I had no grief for her in any corner of me. Until now, that is.

I stretch out a hand in panic as a wave of sorrow for my long departed mother hits me in the stomach, washes through me and fetches me up, gasping, on the strandline of my hospital bed. I want someone to grab this hand and anchor me to their heart before I am swept away, together with all this driftwood of my life. I want to be remembered with a smile, not the numb indifference I felt then. How will my children remember me? What I did was as hard on them as my mother's unkindnesses were to me.

My three friends crowd round and cherish my searching hand in theirs, taking tissues from their sleeves to blow their noses and sniff loudly. My fingers clasp theirs gratefully but my mind is grasping at a memory which whirls its bright loops about me and I follow it willingly. Too many people, too much effort. I need peace. I let go of my friends' hands and dive into another time and place.

Yes, it was a crematorium; that's how I first located Harriet and began another process of shaping my life. During my last thirty or so years I've been far better fettled than in my earlier days. Harriet helped me to move on and as I did so, I became part of a great sequence of lives stretching from the past into the future; a purpose, a small story, a chapter among many. Finding Harriet remade my life thirty-seven years ago; now she's remaking me once more in death. I must let her get on with it.

Across the ward, cups rattle as the after lunch trolley makes its round. 'Coffee love?' a kindly voice enquires of a nearby bed…

… 'It's Geoff's anniversary tomorrow,' sniffs Coral, hunching her shoulders and cupping her hands around her coffee cup.

Yes, the crematorium was, paradoxically, the beginning of a new me.

We'd found a quiet corner in the health club lounge to enjoy the best part of any workout, the relaxation in good company afterwards.

'Is this about you, or about Geoff?' I murmur, wincing inwardly at the thought of another dissection of his character.

That was unkind. It's about Coral and her grief and guilt, of course, and about a public demonstration of remembering her husband but, thankfully, she misinterprets my question.

'Oh that!' she grimaces, remembering her confession of a few months ago, and she pushes her hair back from her forehead in irritation. 'I was going to tell you how it all happened. It was inevitable that I would be unfaithful, you know, given how he was. But no, I was just thinking of going to the crematorium and wondered whether you'd come with me. There's a garden of remembrance where they put all the ashes and I thought I should take some flowers and go. It's been a year.'

'Only if we can sit and say nice things about him,' I mutter to myself through crumbs, offering Coral a piece of my lemon drizzle cake. I have a vain hope that the cake might cheer her up and temporarily overcome the vicious diet that she's enforced upon herself. It's a familiar pattern at the health club; women who've become painfully thin through illness, family problems or bereavement and who then choose to starve themselves or exercise to destruction to remain that way. I can control this one thing in my life, seems to be their reaction to trauma.

For my mother, it was her housework that gave her control. If only she could just complete each task perfectly, if only the house could look just so, there would be some satisfaction and things might fall into place. For Coral, it is her weight, the dieting and exercise help her with her mental ordering of things. She can control the turmoil of her mind by the counting of calories. As for me, I took control of my chaotic early life by escaping into marriage and, of course, I still have my logic.

'It would be really good to go,' she smiles, declining the lemon cake with a wave of her manicured hand.

'It's the new shellac polish,' she smiles, noticing as I follow her gesture. 'Lasts a fortnight, doesn't chip; what do you think?' 'Nice.'

I stare at her face while she sips her coffee and performs an elegant nail display around her cup, pretending to be engrossed in a child wriggling at the next table. I do love her and I understand totally why she acts as she does but it doesn't make dealing with her any easier.

Hers was once a pretty face but the mental habits of years have given it lines that mark the progress of a life.

'There's that woman who was so rude to me the other day,' she gestures suddenly towards a figure in the pool. 'She pushed right past me in the changing room and gave me a really funny look.' Coral thinks everyone gives her funny looks. It's pointless me saying anything, for her deep insecurity and lack of feeling loved has put Coral constantly on the defensive, always seeing insult where none is intended. And she can never be persuaded otherwise.

Always alert to possible attack, Coral decided long ago that attack is her own best form of defence. She calls this 'being a fighter' but other people, regrettably, see it as plain rudeness. Consequently she has few real friends, even though she tries to dull the edge of her aggressiveness with humour.

Her mouth has deep lines etched around it and, in constantly pulling the corners down in open-mouthed anger and disbelief at the blows life seemingly doles out to her, it has taken on a letterbox-shaped quality. I watch for the customary expression and she produces it on cue. Watching her smooth down yet another new outfit, I think to myself that of all the things we wear, our expression is the most important. We truly do end up with the faces we wear over the years; just as the hand of the potter finds the shape that suits the clay.

I attempt to deflect her outrage at this latest perceived slight with a sympathetic remark about her late husband but realise too late that I have ignited the fires of real fury. A cold light glints in her eyes as talk of her husband leads her on to his faults, how hard he made life for her and how he was just like his mother. This has been told and retold a thousand times, each telling adding another layer of anger and a little more veracity.

'I worked my fingers to bone for that man.'

The story is written in stone and cannot be changed, eased or softened by time or memory. No reminders of her husband's good points will be countenanced. She hears what she wants to hear and disregards the rest. Oh Coral, write in sand and not stone, then the passing years can blow all your grudges and hatred away. Don't be so blinkered and fixed, I think. But I know she won't soften her story to allow love in.

'Well, I realised that if I was ever going to have a life, I'd have to go out and do things without him. He was no good around the house either, and he never looked after the car. I stayed with him and brought the girls up but he just turned them against me.'

The hard, etched words prevent her from ever moving on. She is the injured party who will never forget and certainly never forgive. The burden of life's insults that she carries around with her now somehow seems to justify her sorrow...

... As I shift myself once more on the rippling mattress, trying to ease the folds of my nightdress from the red grooves they've worn into my thin old skin, two thoughts come together. Coral and my mother saw the world in much the same way — as a constant threat to be dealt with by anger and hostility. Two souls whose clay was never softened by love, they couldn't accept and absorb the sorrows that carved at them, so that neither could ever hope to hold enough love for their own sustenance, let alone to share with others...

… 'You will come then?' Coral persists with her original train of thought, her bile temporarily spent once more.

'Yes, as long as you can list at least five good things about Geoff to me,' I smile back. 'There are always two stories to a marriage and I'd really like to hear some of his story. Since we met up again you've never got round to telling me that.' Her immaculately groomed head jerks back in annoyance, and I sense a defensive spear being hurled my way.

'Can you list five good things about your mother?'

'I don't know, Coral, she died so long ago. There's an awful lot of bad things I remember about her, but there has to be some good stuff in there. You can help me find it and I'll help you find some of Geoff's good points. Forgiving him will make you feel a lot better, you know. Now, whose car are we going in?'

Coral's car is an exact expression of her personality. Outwardly dark and sleek, inside an absolute mess of half finished tasks and aspirations. I move a pile of rock music CDs without cases into the glove compartment, stuff chewing gum wrappers into the ashtray and climb in. She drives us to the crematorium in relative silence, apart from the odd rail at passing traffic.

Mostly, however, she's concentrating too hard to talk much and I seize my opportunity to tell her the things that have been happening to me. I need, so much, to share my thoughts and discoveries.

'There I was, it was last November, I think, adverts popping up onto my web mail page as I clicked through my emails. You know how it is, with a practised eye you can avoid them but the cat jumps on my knee and, by one of those infuriating pieces of electronic sleight of hand that computers perform so well, there I am being invited to join a genealogy research site.'

'I got a strange email the other day.'

I'm not to be deflected.

'On an impulse I did it. A few clicks and I was away.'

'I hate the past or anything old — anyway, don't you have to pay?' she queries as she turns her head, the letterbox mouth dropping into its customary whaaaaat? expression.

Coral doesn't like paying good money for anything she can get in a sale or a lot cheaper. She's a true latter day huntress, the hunting filling so many gaps in her life. Since Geoff died, her passion for bargains has turned into an obsession to find the one object, the perfect purchase that will take away all the pain.

'Yes, but I've been feeling for a few months now that I really need to know who I am. I desperately want to find out who were the people, you know — the raw materials that made me what I am.'

'So?'

Perhaps there will be clues there to that unforgivable thing I did, I think. I know so little about any of my family and they were so far removed from the place where I struggled that I never thought to ask.

'I sorted through ideas for the requested password and settled on 'starling'; I love starlings. Do you remember that flock we saw last winter, swirling and displaying over the beach?'

There it is again. A giddy feeling that yet another piece of a jigsaw is being manoeuvred into place; a connection to another place, another time. I hold my breath, mentally grasping at what it was that I glimpsed, running the thought sequence again and again but it's gone. With no indication that Coral is paying attention, I press on, hopeful for any release from my discomfort.

'My aunt remembered the maiden name of Granny Rose's mum, Emma Holland. She knew how old Emma was when she died, so I put her name in the ancestry search engine, looked through all the Emma Hollands in our area who had died in that year and there was only one for the Scugton area, so it had to be her. That's how I began. That's all I had, just one name. All the records are online and if you look in the original census records, you get the parents and the siblings, as well as their occupations and where they lived. It's amazing!'

'Yes, but they're all dead and gone. You can't talk to them, they can't listen to you. What's the point?'

I can see how this would be a pointless exercise for Coral. The past, for her, is not open to ongoing interpretation, and once she's made up her mind about someone or something, nothing will change it. I try a different tack.

'Wouldn't you like someone to tell your story or realise that they'd inherited your gorgeous hair?'

'I couldn't be bothered to trawl through all those dead lives and I certainly don't want to think about dying. I can't imagine not being here and when I'm dead I won't know, so what's the point? Geoff spent hours doing that sort of research, though. Do you know, he once came towards me with his fist raised when I complained about him clicking away on his laptop? I was sure he was going to hit me.'

I sympathise but as we wait at a red light, I realise the chance to share this burden has slipped away again. At a time when I finally need to bring things out in the open, she's too self- absorbed to notice and I'm afraid to tell her.

'I didn't think he was a violent man, what had you done to get him wound up?'

'I don't know!' snorts Coral, as she steers the car through the gates of the crematorium.

The crematorium is a bland brick edifice; a post-war display of modernity surmounted by a furnace tower that tries to give the building the appearance of a church but, to those with memories long enough, must look a little like Dachau, the continual dull background roar only serving to bolster the impression. It does its best, however, to be a place of solemnity, its saving grace the beautiful mature grounds within which it is set.

We find a seat by the lawned rectangle where wreaths and floral tributes are laid following a service. An undertaker glides by, the long black ribbons of his top hat blowing in the icy wind as he rearranges the metal stands that bear the names of the departed, in order to make space on the grass for further flowers. Coral turns to me, her face twisted in what is meant to be grief, but to me it looks more like panic. She doesn't really know why she's here.

'You know, I think I really would like a little bit of time on my own after all,' she sniffs, fiddling with the cellophane wrapping that shrouds the flowers in her lap.

Even though I recognise this as an invitation for me to stay and comfort her and listen to another rant about her late husband, I move away.

I've had an idea.

My ancestry research has hit a dead end with my English grand-dad, Granny Rose's husband. He's quite a mystery, apart from some faded photos, his gravestone and a stainless steel plaque that marks 40 years of continuous service at Scugton Steelworks. Even his name is an enigma. None of the Frederick Blanchards I've turned up are him, I don't have his birth certificate and when I wrote a speculative letter to the Register Office, I obviously didn't have his proper name because they couldn't find him either and returned my cheque. So there's no hope of finding his parents.

Birth certificates always give the mother's maiden name and that would have been a start to researching his side of the family. I'd like to know if they, too, were forged in the wicked goblin's fire of the steelworks, or if they did other things. It's frustrating to run into a dead end so soon. Yet I do remember Granny Rose telling me where his mother was buried. Making my way to the crematorium office, I hope I don't need an appointment, and I ring the bell tentatively.

Half an hour later, in incredulous elation, I burst through the door into the gardens again.

'Coral! Guess what?' Breaking in on her reverie, I've quite forgotten the true purpose of our visit.

'You've been a long time!' she flashes as I sit down.

'I thought you needed time; sorry I was so long.'

'So where were you, then?'

'I popped into the office. It turns out that crematoria keep cemetery records too, and a phone call found my family surnames on file. If I can just work out the possibilities from the few details I have, I'll have a new line of research. I just need to write in with more information and they'll send me a plan of possible grave plots with names and dates. Maybe I can find my great grandmother — you know, the one nobody ever talked about.'

'Well, I've been sitting here thinking what a waste of time my life with Geoff was.'

In the nearby cedar trees, a magpie's coarse rattle is followed by the clatter of pigeon wings and a general commotion. The magpie emerges from the branches bearing a tiny squab in its beak, carrying it away to feed its own young. I remember when Coral lost her first baby, a boy, how we clung to each other then; me in the misery of a failing marriage and Coral in the anguish of a miscarriage. She needs my sympathy and understanding now, just as she did then.

'Did you ever show each other love?' I query gently. Sitting down beside her, I reach out my arm and give her a hug, hoping to prise some joy from her memories. She stiffens as she answers.

'Yes, but that was in the early days…'

'No act of love is ever wasted.'

'Mine were; I worked my fingers to the bone looking after him and bringing up his children. He was idle, just like his mother,' she says again. I realise how tightly wound up she is and that I have just released the key. All she needs is what anyone wants — my love and undivided attention while she talks. May be that will help move her on.

Nodding and smiling, I gaze across the chill ranks of flowers set in their conical metal vases, placed there in memory of some loved one long gone.

'You should put your flowers in water.'

I try to absorb a little warmth from the late morning sun that peers briefly through the greyness while Coral arranges the bouquet of red roses she's brought. It is no tribute and it will bring no sense of peace.

'You two were totally incompatible, you know,' I venture as she stuffs the last stem vehemently into the arrangement. That doesn't make him a bad person. You just couldn't understand each other's needs.'

'It's getting really cold. We should go.' She gathers her belongings and crumples the cellophane into a nearby bin, effectively terminating this line of thought.

Later in the car, with the heater blasting warmth on our cold hands and feet and her favourite rock tracks drowning all conversation, I silently turn over the information I've gleaned today.

Half an hour after arriving home, the letter is already in my hand, written in time to catch the teatime post. Pushing it through the chipped façade of our ancient VR postbox, I'm still turning my discovery over like a freshly discovered treasure in the earth as I walk up the steps to our front door.

That afternoon, I shrug on a huge, comfy old red cardigan and worn boots and resolve to do some early spring tidying in my garden. Far away from childhood memories and the belching furnaces of Scugton, it has always been the place where I go to unravel problems, or simply just be. Twenty years in the making, it has allowed my own roots to go down deep here, intertwining with those of shrub, tree, bulb and creeper. Digging out half-buried outbuildings, heaving up walled terraces on steep slopes, finding plants that would thrive in all its unforgiving aspects, and creating intimate spaces — each a little island of peace — has been my solace and joy. At the end of a working day I would kick off my shoes and walk barefoot here until the Babel of chatter that is a school receded and I could expand the moment of an opening bud or the air-dangling antics of a hoverfly until it entirely filled my head.

I need to fill it now. I always feel so helpless and mentally bruised after Coral has launched off down her well-trodden path to self-destruction, as echoes of my parents' own mutually caustic and destructive lives are mirrored in hers.

A cold wind kicks at the pile of debris I'm gathering and stirs the metallic smell of last autumn's decaying copper beech leaves. I meander aimlessly among uneasy memories and half formed ideas, driven like the leaves, round and back again until I stick fast into a corner. I can't clear my mind of that strange feeling I had in the car. This sense of memories half recollected, of a picture glimpsed that, if I only could see it, would be the completion of one part of my life. This weird grasping at a hidden meaning has been happening a lot lately. These odd ideas feel as though they're really important but I only ever catch them by the tail and then they're gone.

'Try this!'

There's a muffled roar and my husband appears with the leaf blower, cheerfully blasting aside mouldering leaves and stems. He always catches me unawares, sliding humour under my resisting feet until I overbalance and topple into mirth. I laugh and twirl with the brightly coloured leaves and something almost tangible is swept out of my head into the chill air.

The leaf blower sputters and stops.

'Are you paralysed or Church of England?' I'm jolted from my reverie. 'You were staring into space for at least five minutes.' I recover and smile.

'That was one of Granny Rose's favourite sayings, you know. She used to say that to granddad; she was Catholic and he was Church of England.'

'She's been on your mind a lot recently. Have you been walking on her grave?' A playful hand sneaks around my waist and under my cardigan. I manage to grab it before his cold fingers make contact with my warm flesh.

'I said, have you been treading over her graaaaaave,' he breathes into the nape of my neck, in an attempt at a ghostly voice.

I picture her and my granddad's grave among the long lines of headstones in Cemetery Road. At least I know where he's buried. Few of the graves have been visited in recent years, though. I should really go, despite that fierce, logical voice inside me that says there's nothing there to visit. She knew so much, saw patterns in the world that made it make sense to her. They were only patterns and yet…

The hand finally makes contact with my stomach and I shriek at the icy shock, then melt at the gentle nuzzles around my neck and face. This is what has sustained me all these years after I wrecked those lives; this man and his gentle humour and love. I have lost and hidden myself in it, losing sight of the world of pain I left behind but now I have to reach beyond its shield and continue my shaping. He inclines his head towards the leaf blower and reverses it to 'vacuum'.

'Do you want anything sucking, madam?'

We explode into laughter, and tussle and scuffle in the leaves. I can see my good intentions fading for today. I want to lose myself again… just for now.

As the garden settles back beneath its grey mantle, I glimpse a robin from our bedroom window as it snips up a thin red worm from where it has lain, stripped of its blanket of leaf mould. It tosses aside more debris, encouraged by the find, and pauses to deliver its shrill call to the frozen air. Can you see a robin's breath piping in the cold air? I wonder, then stand, mesmerised for a moment at the wonderful thought of this tiny scrap of life giving up its warmth in a song. And there is that feeling again! I know I've seen this before.

'Ok, it's a sign, Gran,' I murmur. 'I really am going to start digging, just like that robin. I'm going to set my life straight once and for all'…

… 'Not logical,' I mutter into my oxygen mask.

But I yielded to something deeper than logic that day. I had a glimpse of forces weaving me into a fabric from another time and place, something that wouldn't fall under the mantle of reason. How could I have forgotten that yet again? Perhaps I figured that when I'd found Harriet everything was solved. The moment glows and begins to focus into a meaning but then I'm overtaken by pain before I can really begin to home in on it.

'She's opening her eyes again.'

'The mattress isn't working properly.'

Voices, clicks and fiddles before my bed begins to ripple under me once more, distributing pressure evenly over the skin that barely covers my old bones.

# 8

# A SPRING WEDDING

Comfortable again, I try to focus once more on the man who made me so happy for so much of my life, my husband, the potter. Now there are some memories I'd like to revisit! I try once more to think of the silken hands that, even when we were quite old, could turn me, trembling and pliant to his every intent. Younger folk think they have the monopoly on sex and never even glimpse the power of intimacy that far exceeds anything you could imagine as you grow old together.

Those are some of the memories I want now.

But death takes away so much of one's willpower, and now that my defences are down, he's here, pushing, scraping and scooping up all the forgotten moments I seem to have conveniently pushed from my mind, all the things I should have tied together and made some sense of. I can't ignore them any longer.

'You've had to wait a long time for this, old man death!' I almost cackle into my oxygen mask. 'Sorry I took so long.'

Sorrow. It's about sorrow, but whose? Not mine, that's for sure.

I haven't got to ninety-seven to feel miserable about my lot.

Yet the deeper sorrow carves into some people, the more happiness they seem able to hold. Again I turn this thought in my mind, recalling how the post returned an answer a few days later and how I began to catch little glimpses of the sorrows carved into Harriet; glimpses that turned into an obsession, and which eventually cost me a friend.

*There are only two female Blanchards from that period buried in Scugton Cemetery. Here are their details with the grave plots marked.* A photocopied sheet highlighted with green was my first glimpse of her. My father had never intimated that she'd even existed, let alone was buried somewhere close. Granny Rose never mentioned her by name. My granddad, whose mother she was, never mentioned her name either. My great aunts, her daughters, never spoke of her, and my wonderful aunt Peg, her granddaughter, didn't even know her name. She knew only that she'd done something terrible and was talked about behind closed doors, in whispers. The only definite thing she did know was that she was buried by the back wall of Scugton Cemetery, in the corner, and that when she died the family said that she'd got her comeuppance at last. And there it was. Plot 236, in the corner, Harriet Blanchard. She was suddenly a real person, my great grandmother; the woman whose life would change mine so much.

I'd sent for a copy of her death certificate from the Register Office then, and she'd leapt from the stark formal print straight into my heart; my unknown, deleted but now restored great grandmother who ended her days dying from bowel cancer in a workhouse infirmary.

Harriet. The woman whose very thoughts seem to be finding their way to my deathbed. With that piece of paper began a feverish search for the details of her life. What had she done? Why was it so awful? Was it worse than the terrible thing I'd done? I needed to know but the more I discovered, the more I realised she was a remarkable, and not a terrible, woman at all.

Even though I now had her name, she was still hard to pin down — a shadowy, elusive figure slipping through the pages of my family history, seemingly receding at every turn. She didn't seem to want to be found. I first prised her from hiding by making a stab at my granddad's birth year and patiently trawling the 1901 census. There she was, living in Derby, declaring herself to be a widow and a washerwoman. Of my granddad's sisters, my four madcap great aunts, there was only the young Alice and Mary living with her, as well as a fifth, hitherto unknown, much older girl, Clara, who should have been out working but who, the census declared, stayed at home helping Harriet with the washing.

The thought of Harriet's lonely unmarked grave did its work, too. The following week, after years of absence, I finally made myself visit Scugton and Granny Rose's grave, driving through the streets of my childhood with an involuntary shudder, before parking outside the cemetery's side entrance on Bushfield Road and counting my way down the pale ranks and rows to where I knew she rested. At least she had a stone, not just an unnumbered plot like Harriet. The white marble was green with algae, and ivy had begun to obscure hers and granddad's names. I remember how, kneeling down to clear it away as best I could, I'd stared in amazement at his name carved above hers. Fred Ogley Blanchard. How could I have forgotten? I remembered his name then as clearly as I remembered his antics.

'That's my real and only name,' he had once told the five-year-old me, dandled upon his grimy knee. He was showing me a sunflower head from his allotment and tracing the seed spirals with a dirt-encrusted fingernail. He grew the flowers just for me from seed kernels gleaned from a mate's parrot food.

'Three beautiful things. There. This great fat, yellow flower, your name and my name — Fred Ogley Blanchard. Now Mia Pia, what do you know that's beautiful? There's so many things. If you're good, I'll tell you me list and then you can start your own.'

I didn't know anything beautiful. I was too scared of life, too busy surviving to go around looking for beauty but I filed that sunflower away in my head and brought it out many times, its precise yellowness shining through the dark. Then I remember how that, when he lifted me from his knee, he always pretended to fart, giggling in mock horror.

'Was that you, Mia Pia?'

Standing there in front of his grave I remember how I'd laughed and laughed. And I can hear him singing now as my mind is pulled, giggling too, down along another thread of my life.

I'm standing in Granny Rose's living room, my twelve-year-old self smothering laughter as granddad pulls a threepenny bit from behind my ear and whispers for me to go and get him ten Woodbines from the shop. He shouldn't smoke; I've heard Gran say he has cardiac asthma, which means he gets breathless but I love him a lot, and so I take the money, slyly, and kiss him on the cheek. His cheeks are purple and red veined just like my dad's and he says it's the blast furnaces that have made them that way but I'm old enough now to think it's the drink as well. He wears an ancient, jumble sale Harris Tweed jacket that's far too small for him, and the dirty leather apron and flat cap that mark him as an iron and steel worker.

He's also slightly drunk, having called at the *Talbot* on the way home. He doesn't go to the *Open Hearth*; he likes the cosiness of that tiny pub in the middle of a works terrace. And, unlike my dad, he's usually really happy and very silly when he's drunk, so I know I'm in for a treat.

'Get your mucky self changed, Fred,' clucks my Gran in annoyance from the kitchen.

After an extraordinarily long and noisy pee, (my Gran calls it his exhibition pee) which indicates just how much he's drunk, he disappears into the bedroom of the flat and reappears in his shirt tails and grubby long coms. Picking up his shirt tails, he begins to do a Highland Fling, lifting his knee and waggling his foot in time to his singing.

'… Iiiiiiif any young lady wants a baby, give her the cock of the north,' he warbles to the tune of *Chase Me Charlie*, the only tune he knows when he's drunk.

'Fred! Not in front of Mia!' Gran calls, trying to sound menacing.

Unbowed he continues to the same tune, 'Aunty Mary had a canary, up the leg of her drawers. Iiiiiiif you find it, never you mind it but just watch out for the claws!'

I giggle and think of my great aunty Mary, one of his sisters.

'Fred!'

My Gran stomps into the living room with a bowl of sugar for the table in one hand and the coal bucket in the other. Suddenly granddad manages to pluck another melody from his fuddled brain.

'Once upon a time when the birds shit lime, and the monkeys chewed tobacco, the little piggies ran with their fingers up their bums, to see what was the matter. Oooooh, the pissin' in the breeze...' he croons to a corrupted Burl Ives hit.

'Fred!'

Granny Rose's voice rises to a crescendo and she lurches towards him, putting the coal bucket on the table and throwing the sugar on the fire in a confused ecstasy of rage and embarrassment. I collapse onto the settee in helpless mirth and granddad falls like a sack of coal beside me, hooting and pointing speechlessly at his beloved Rose, who is staring at the fire and the half pound of sugar crackling away in the flames. A smell of burnt caramel fills the room and I vaguely notice that granddad's lips are bluish tinged but I don't think anything of it because I'm young and my world is indestructible. I throw my arms around Gran, who has also collapsed, shrieking with mirth, upon the settee. Kissing her whiskery cheeks, I hug them both in turn and we laugh until I have to wipe the tears away with my Gran's apron. Granddad blows his nose on his shirt tails and puffs loudly.

'I'm a bastard, mate,' he giggles.

'Freeeed!' Granny Rose chides weakly...

... I remember, as I turn on my sweat damp hospital pillow, that later that year he retired and two years on, he died of a bad heart without ever mentioning again the fact that he was, indeed, a bastard. He never revealed his list and I never knew what he meant about his name until that day at his graveside. Harriet, he was like you. I'm so glad you made me remember that. He must have been so special to you.

'Has she been laughing or crying?' Is it my granddaughter once more, or my friends who just won't go and leave me be?

'It's hard to tell. I think she was laughing. Mia, Mia — are you ok? Who's Fred?'

'They sometimes see people from their past lives; it's nothing to worry about,' the voice of a nurse reassures. 'But maybe it's time for you to say your goodbyes now.'

Hands pat mine and someone strokes my face. A voice croaks a tearful goodbye, pretence abandoned at last. I nod; it's all I can do. Strange how my friends are more upset than I am. I hear more tears accompanying their fading footsteps down the corridor and, incongruously, I feel sorry for their loss. It's always harder for those left behind. I wish I'd had the strength to say something to them.

There was something I was excited about, I think, as the last footstep fades away and I can turn once more to my own thoughts. Fred Ogley Blanchard. That was it! I finger the delight I felt at finding granddad's full name. That was it, yes! The real start of unravelling the mystery surrounding Harriet, was granddad's birth certificate.

I'd sent my cheque for seven pounds to the Register Office the day after reading his proper name on that gravestone. Now I would know the name of my great grandfather as well as Harriet's maiden name; a new branch of the family tree awaited discovery. But opening the return envelope had only deepened the mystery around her as, yet again, she fled further from my grasp down the corridors of a convoluted past.

The certificate had said she was a widow at the time of grand-dad's birth and that the father was unknown. The only other scrap of information was that granddad had been born in Sereton Terrace, a row of works houses that had disappeared into the giant maw of the main Scugton Steelworks site over 50 years ago. And yes, she was illiterate, making her mark in the shape of a cross, joined with a wave at the top, making it look like a heart upon the paper. I'm filled with a sudden glow at those twin memories, hers and mine; two hearts now becoming one. My own heart had gone out to her once more, then, as I mentally tried to fold her up in my arms, needing to tell her that she wasn't forgotten; I'd found her and would make sure no one buried her memory again. This new liaison that had produced my illegitimate granddad was still part of my heritage and I wanted to let her know that I was grateful. Whatever else she had done surely couldn't be that bad. That day I visited another grave. Standing by the plain, unmarked grass mound in the far corner of Scugton Cemetery I wept, marking her passing with a single pink rose.

'And why Fred Ogley?' Coral asks, in a not too convincing attempt to appear interested in my new obsession. She's fingering the bunch of pink roses that were an anniversary gift from my husband.

'I never really liked pink flowers. They've no style about them; too girly for me!'

I ignore her irritation at the roses because I know that Geoff never remembered her anniversary and it jars her to see my bouquet. It's been one of a series of little digs lately, almost as if she's jealous. But no, we're such old friends that it doesn't make sense.

'Well, Ogley's a Yorkshire surname, not a Christian name. It's not a name that a working class Victorian mother would have put on a birth certificate unless it meant something. That made me suspicious, especially since I'd turned up her marriage certificate, quite late on in years in Victorian terms, to a John Henry Blanchard.'

'So what? Blanchard's your maiden name isn't it, not Ogley Blanchard? You were just Blanchard when we were at college. So isn't John Henry Blanchard your grandfather then? Is that what you mean?'

'He can't be. I know Harriet married him and had my four aunts plus a fifth whom I never met, but my granddad was illegitimate, born when Harriet was a widow.'

'That's easy — she had a fancy man! She didn't have to marry him, did she?' Coral's words are glib, lacking any understanding of what's perplexing me. How come granddad was born in Sereton Terrace? As a widow, Harriet shouldn't have been there at all.

We're sitting by the warm glow of the stove on an achingly bright but chill spring evening. I've laid out all my accumulated certificates on the dining room table, ready for an evening's research at the computer, but she's called in, bristling with a volatile mixture of irritation and indignation to tell me the red-hot news of her daughter's wedding in May. The mention of marriage sets her off again.

'Fancy getting married in a bluebell wood!' she snorts for at least the fifth time, 'and the reception in a barn!'

'Oh, it'll be lovely,' I soothe once more.

'Yes but how are all those elderly aunts going to manage it, traipsing through the woods?'

'I'm sure Maddy has it all in hand. You know what a methodical creature she is. And, speaking of elderly aunts, there was no Ogley in my great aunts' names.' I prod my collection of certificates and wave great aunty Mary's certificate at her.

'What?'

I know I'm losing her interest now and she has, after all, come to tell me all about the wedding, so I steer things back to the forth-coming event, shuffle all my documents into a heap at the end of the table and make resignedly for the kitchen.

'Cuppa? Do you think they're right for each other, by the way? She hasn't been going out with him very long,' I call through the serving hatch.

Maybe that wasn't what I should have asked. I flinch involun-tarily at the thought of the coals of Coral's marriage being raked over yet again but she takes me by surprise.

'Well, she knows how to keep a man, that's for sure. She knows that as long as you're prepared to treat a man like a king, he'll do absolutely anything for you, including getting married in a bluebell wood! She has him right around her little finger! Her head goes down, her eyes go up, the classic female submission posture and then it's, Sean, what do you think to this? Sean, you're so strong, Sean you're so clever, Sean, what would you like me to cook for you? Yeeeeakkk!'

'Where did she learn that from then?' I shout humorously over the bubble of the kettle. Coral gets my drift and smirks through the hatch.

'Not from me, that's for sure! Passion fell out of my knickers and on to the floor somewhere between having the girls and my early menopause. I suppose Geoff must have found it difficult but he didn't help matters by telling me to go and read a book on the subject.'

I push two teas through the hatch and cock my head expectantly, waiting for the tirade. But it doesn't come; just more hand wringing over the bluebell wood. I make a real effort to sympathise, nodding in time to the flood of objections and attempting to think of something positive about this spring wedding. Personally, I'd be so excited about it all but Coral clearly isn't. She'd been expecting something conventional that she could dress up for, to organise and reign supreme over as the mother of the bride.

'They'll have to clear a path… What about music? Who'll do the ceremony in the woods? There'll have to be a civil service, too. Terrible old barn when there's a nice hall nearby. And what if it rains? And she was living with that married man not so long ago. What if Sean finds out?' I nod and listen, and listen and soothe for what seems like an age, warming my hands by the stove, but a phrase nags around the edges of my mind, unpicking my attention and sending me off at a tangent.

That's it! Harriet must have been living with a married man in Sereton Terrace when she produced my granddad. She couldn't have been living in a works house on her own because all the houses belonged to the Appleton Works, who let them to workers' families. Widows moved on and single men lodged with families already living there, so she must have been with another iron worker, and maybe even his family too. Maybe Ogley was the father's name. My fingers itch to get back to the computer but I make myself focus on Coral. This is the second telling, so she's bound to run out of steam soon.

'It could be absolutely wonderful, you know,' I sigh making a good shot at sounding wistfully envious, 'and anyway, you'll have to buy two outfits, won't you? You'll have to have one for the civil ceremony and something lovely for the woods.' I proffer the thought of clothes buying as a sweetener.

'Well, I just don't think she's thought it through.' A pause at last. 'Will you come with me to look for outfits?' Her eyes have softened a little now.

I know Coral hunts alone, so this is a bit unexpected and really lovely. Perhaps she's making an effort to be a bit more inclusive. We make a tentative diary date for a couple of weeks' time and she leaves with names of a few internet made-to-measure dress sites clutched in her hand as well. For the first time since we met up again after all these years, I feel that I'm really needed for something other than simply being an uncritical ear into which she can pour all the sorrows of widowhood, and the bile and vitriol of her marriage.

Once she's gone, I grab at the tantalising thought that's been dancing around in my mind. I want to pin it to the table among all my certificates and make it real and valid. Just to check once more, I pick out the papers of the four great aunts who were all older than my granddad.

I was right. Father, John Henry Blanchard; no Ogley there. What if Ogley was the surname of granddad's father? It takes me a while to trawl, house by house, though the 1891 census of Sereton Terrace, where he'd been born only a few short years later in 1895.

Peering through the ink blots and alterations at the spidery, handwritten lists, I read the words that marked out the lives of the iron workers. Sanders, removing the overburden in the open cast mines; ironstone chuckers hurling raw ore into wagons; barrow men, hand charging the furnaces; shunters operating the ore and the slag wagon locomotives; foremen, labourers, tappers, pig iron carriers; all the men and many of the boys who were employed in the iron industry lived in houses that stood just yards from their place of employment, the Appleton Iron Works. I wonder at the lives they must have led, coming in from the villages and the countryside for the promise of employment and housing, to find themselves on the doorstep of a smouldering, molten hell.

With frustrating difficulty, I continue to scroll through the facsimiles of the faint, cursive-written sheets. Some names are illegible, most are irrelevant to my search and still others I recognise, with a smile, as family names I knew as a child; Maw, Piggott, Stamp… but there! There it is!

As I push my chair back in the flush of discovery, the slope of the floor in this old house sends it skittering sideways on its casters across the room, and I catch the edge of the pile of certificates on the table which cascade to the floor in a messy heap. Leaping out of the chair, I don't even pause to pick them up but return to stand, mesmerised, in front of the computer, bent low and peering at an unmistakable name.

It's a furnace worker, William Henry Ogley and his wife and family.

Like a present I'm afraid to open, I almost daren't continue, resisting the lure of the keyboard for a few minutes and pacing up and down the room. Could this be him? Ancestry research is full of dashed hopes, false starts and mistaken identities. It's human nature to want to claim someone as your own, and people make mistakes all the time. Anxious not to leap to conclusions, I should now ask myself how many more Ogleys were there living in that area in 1891 and, in particular, how many were there on Sereton Terrace? But I have to go and make a cup of tea first, putting off the disappointment that I'm expecting in this detective story.

'Come on, do it!' I have to know.

Putting my mug on the desk and dragging my chair roughly back over piles of paper that have cost me £7 a sheet from various Register Offices, I finally have to look. I'm off on an impatient romp through several censuses before I have the answer I had hoped for. They lived mostly in Yorkshire so this Ogley must be him. I jiggle on my seat, animated, pushing my long red hair out of my face and drinking down tea in great gulps. This is amazing! I suddenly have a hitherto totally unknown great grandfather and, with him, a whole new past! But I need to know for sure. If he's still with his family at the 1901 census, then my theory still might not be correct. If Harriet was in Derby in 1901, where was William Ogley?

A little more digging, ten years on, through the pages of the 1901 census and I'm no nearer an answer. It's disappointing. There's no trace of him or his wife Betsey, not on Sereton Terrace, not anywhere in the country, not on any emigration list. They've disappeared. In 1901 his children are either in service or living with their grandparents. Something happened to this family. Was it to do with Harriet? Did she split them apart? Finally I have to stop in frustration because I can't find William or Betsey's deaths at all. It's a temporary dead end. John Henry Blanchard has vanished into thin air, too, after the 1891 census, but he's suddenly become less important to me, now that I know he's no real relation.

In the gathering dusk, I stand up and stretch, full of my discovery. It takes a while to digest it as, for the past few months, I've looked at my granddad's birth certificate with little hope of tracing my great grandfather. It could have been anyone. I wonder how people will go on in the future now that unmarried parents and split families are the norm rather than the exception? How will these people ever find their past?

Caught for a moment by the flamingo flush of a spring sunset, I decide to leave the curtains open tonight. I'm full of anticipation at new finds and my heart gives a momentary skitter at the thought of long summer days; another month and it will be light until nine o'clock at night and I can enjoy the long English twilight out under the heater in the garden. I can sit beneath beautiful red skies that have nothing to do with slag or steel or Scugton. No one ever sat out then. On a bad day even my mother's nylons hung out on the washing line developed holes in them from the acrid smoke.

As the light fades, the clouds behind the old willow tree move in lengthy crimson streaks, momentarily forming themselves into islands in an azure ocean. I spent hours as a child staring at skies like that, dreading the moments when the glow of sunset would be overtaken by the horrid glow of molten slag.

'Now that one's definitely out of place,' I murmur to myself, peering at the sky again, the curtains still in my hands.

The semblance of a tattered red mask with gaping eyeholes and a drooped jag of a mouth is rearranged and reformed momentarily by the brisk March winds. I incline my head to see it better before the pattern drifts away.

'Wait. I should know this. I've seen it before. Somewhere, some-time but when?'

Time twists and bends in on itself and, feeling slightly sick, I drop into my old blue chair by the window, my back to the sky, trying to pluck the meaning of that shape from memories that are only half formed and as elusive as smoke. I've seen it before, I know I have.

On the screen, across the room, John Henry Blanchard's name flickers momentarily and then disappears as my screensaver slides on…

… Sliding suddenly and violently back into the ward I am, for a second time, filled with that prickling feeling of utter horror that surrounded his name in Harriet's mind. It swamps the hushed hiss of my mask, my bubbling chest and my feebly plucking hands, to ooze, hot and stickily, over my bed and on to the polished floor. A slag red, dread red mist, I can vaguely see its glow pooling around the feet of the nurse who comes to pull a curtain to protect my eyes from the bright July sunlight. And another light somewhere flickers off.

It's gone. The redness, the understanding, the meaning of this day of days…

… Back in my old blue chair, as I rise and turn to close the cur-tains, the light fading fast, again I'm forced to dismiss the moment as menopausal confusion. It was nothing. All I was doing was remembering my childhood with that sickening lurch I still get whenever I think about home. Two hours have passed in the wink of an eye. The stove has gone out, I'm cold and hungry, the cat is attempting to dance on the keyboard to gain my attention and there's a heap of paper on the floor. Enough of this obsession for tonight. Bending to scoop my certificates into some sort of order before I embark on the most pressing matter of feeding a persistent Siamese, I find myself staring once more at my granddad's birth certificate.

'Maybe there are more Ogleys.'

Returning to the computer, I move the protesting creature on to my knee with murmured promises of fish. I tickle under his chin until he's distracted and begins to purr, food momentarily forgotten in the ecstasy of a scratch in just the right place.

An unusual name, Ogley, even today, Ogley Blanchard even more so. So unusual, in fact, that I enter simply 'Ogley Blanchard' into the ancestry site search engine just to see what comes up. I wasn't expecting anything but there they were. Just two names, out of the millions of UK names on record there were just two more bearing my grandfather's strange identity. I'm stunned by my discovery.

Edward Ogley Blanchard, born 1898. Mother, Harriet Blanchard, née Parsons. And there it was once more, Kate Ogley Blanchard, a little girl born to her a year later. Elated, I press on through the births, marriages and deaths to find one more entry. Edward had died shortly after birth. Of Kate, there is no further mention. So Harriet had three children by the mysterious Mr Ogley, including my granddad.

'Well,' I announce to the cat, who is yowling in encouragement as I retrieve a plate of fish from the fridge, 'the enigmatic Harriet has stepped out of hiding at last'.

But, in catching hold of her, it seems again that while one mystery has been solved, more have been created. What had happened to Kate, who was clearly my great aunt and my granddad's true sister? There was never a great aunt Kate that I remember. What's more, the madcap great aunts of my childhood, Mad aunt Mary, stuffy aunty Gertie, waspish aunty Edith and sweet, gentle aunt Alice were only my granddad's half sisters. It's all a bit of a shock. I'm not who I thought I was.

Three mysteries have sprouted from the place where one was solved.

What happened to my newly discovered great grandfather, William Henry Ogley? What happened to his wife, Betsey, and what happened to John Henry Blanchard, the man whom I thought was my great grandfather?

'You're a shady lady, Harriet,' I announce to the cat. 'Do you know, I'm not really a Blanchard at all, genetically speaking,' I conclude, stroking his long black silky tail.

Nevertheless, I still love this woman who is beginning to dominate my every waking thought. Was this what the family scandal was all about? The cat looks up from wolfing his fish and gives me that grateful slitty eyed look before returning to nap his jaws together over the last of his meal which hasn't even touched the sides on its way down. Genetics don't rank very highly next to a plate of salmon…

… I surface once more but, this time, a little more happily. The memory of those astonishing discoveries that evening makes me chuckle and I rasp an attempt at laughter beneath my oxygen mask. I'd sent for Edward's and Kate's birth certificates the very next day.

They were both born on Sereton Terrace and their father, as with my granddad, was declared to be unknown. Harriet, in her widowhood had borne three illegitimate children to a Mr Ogley of Sereton Terrace and I was the descendant of one of them.

The effort of trying to laugh produces rising bubbles of mucus and a wet cough and there's a tangible wave of concern around my bedside. I should try and show some recognition; reassure them I'm in no real pain. Prising my eyes open is like trying to push a boulder uphill but I do it and, with enormous effort, find my granddaughter is here once more. Bless her heart, I love her so. I motion for her hand to give it a squeeze. Her flesh is warm, plump and alive against my cold, thin hand. At forty-two, she's still a young woman. Time has hardly marked her striking features at all. I don't want her to see me like this. I'd like her to remember me when I was a bit younger or even as I was when she was a child and we had such wicked times together. It's funny. When relatives do an order of service sheet for the funeral, they always choose a picture of the departed from much earlier in their lives, not from when they were wrecked upon the shores of death. Obituaries are the same. It's as if we want to remember a different, more wholesome and vigorous person. And yet I know I couldn't be more whole than I am becoming now, seeing my story again this way.

Or is it Harriet's story?

One thing I know, there's something really important that I'm about to discover. I can feel it growing large inside, just as the rest of me is shrinking and withering away.

# 9

# THE SACRAMENT
# OF MARRIAGE

*What day is it?*

It's a Sunday; I remember now. It's odd how hard it is to keep track of the days as you get really old and then sick. Now that I've shrunk even further to the thing that lies upon this bed it's even harder to locate myself, but there's still this sense of something about to emerge; a pattern, a path and a purpose that death is beckoning me to follow. This isn't a trip down memory lane, it's a voyage of discovery, and how amazing that it should come right at the end.

What day is it?

Yes, Sunday. I was born on a Sunday. It's a nice day to die, too.

In the early afternoon light, the ward is shadow-dappled blue-grey and I turn my head to try and see the branches that soften the hospital walls with their silhouettes. I would like to sit in the shade of a tree just once more, so that I may sort through this forest tangle of memories that has come as I fall, in slow motion, towards death.

I so want to understand this final growth process, this jumble of ideas, recollections, feelings and memories that aren't even mine. I need to be still.

There was another spring wedding, I know there was. But I can't pull out its significance. I know it was important to me. I try my old trick of expanding the moment, a mind game that often brought ease and clarity in my own garden years ago. The leaves tremble and I climb on to one of them, imagining a beetle's eye view of life. Nothing matters but the green and the here and now as I sway, soothed by a warm July breeze, on a leaf; its hairs prickle as I walk over them, headed for its underside. A hand reaches out and I scuttle over one of its fingers. It is Harriet…

… Privy to her innermost thoughts once more, I find her, skirts hitched up, perching on a low branch of an ancient gnarled ash that is just coming into leaf. Her head is bent low, studying a tiny beetle. I know instantly that she spends her monthly free Sunday afternoon here where she sat as a child, ordering her lists. Her hands caress the familiar wood. Too fibrous for the logger to saw, too twisted to suit a carpenter's eye, it has lasted out the other straighter, more comely trees.

'Like folk,' she thinks. 'If you're comely, everyone flatters you for yer attention. If you're too plain, or just nobbut then you survive. You can be as you want and live t' yer own recknin'.'

I feel that this is exactly what Harriet intends to do despite her impending marriage. She is her own person, yet still she knows that she must take a husband. She is twenty-seven, an old maid, far too old to be single and, if she wants to be her own mistress and not spend her days in service, she must marry the only man who has asked, roughly, for her hand.

Harriet knows she's not pretty by any standards. At her age, only a faint remaining flush of youth gives her anything of a pleasing appearance. She has known she will find it almost impossible to find someone who will marry her ever since she worked for Sam Sowerby; and she was warned. An eager young entrepreneur making his fortune on the back of the rising iron industry, Sam had seen the opportunity for an ironmonger's shop, selling household wares to families moving by the hundreds to the areas around the works. An arrangement with a couple of craftsman iron moulders who cast him shovels, pokers and flat irons down on their knees in the fine, black moulding sand of the foundry floor provides him with cheap wares. He is a fresh-faced, cocky, brash young man, full of the confidence endowed by being a big fish in the small pool that is the growing town of Scugton.

Harriet keeps house for him; he sets his hat at her and then takes advantage when Harriet shows a grateful response to someone who doesn't seem to think her strange and aloof. His interest quickly evaporates, however, when she mentions marriage, spitting into her white face that he has no intention of marrying anyone as plain or mad as Harriet; and what would a self-made man be wanting with a country girl like her? His face colours up and he stops by the mirror Harriet has just polished, to smooth back his fine blonde hair, giving her a good view of the disdain and disgust flashing in his eyes.

I recoil at the memory; mine or Harriet's, it doesn't matter any more.

She would sooner not have married Sam Sowerby anyway. She

likes being beholden to no one, being free to explore her own private and beautiful world as she wishes, but her brief liaison with him leaves her pregnant with his child.

'Telling me mam was bad enough.' We think the thought in unison.

Ann Parsons slaps her cheek many times shrieking, 'Whoaar!' as she upturns Harriet's face to her own, holding her fast by a coil of hair. Harriet can see the whites of her small, shrewish eyes rolling wildly in an ecstasy of rage. None of her daughters has brought this disgrace to the house. None of her daughters has had any trouble marrying and none of her daughters is such a dozzen 'eaded fool. Ann finally flings her into a corner of the cottage kitchen and hurls on a shawl before vanishing up the lane. Shiloh, as usual in times of trouble, is absent and lets his wife deal with the crisis, fading quietly into the orchard to whittle a stick as he hears the commotion from the cottage.

'Losing my independence was worse.'

I grasp hold of the memory as Harriet picks at the bark of the ash tree, hot with the injustice of it all. She has had to leave a good job in service but her home is no refuge either. The small Ellenby cottage of her childhood fades into the distance as she walks the long ridge road northwards to Barton on the Aumber with her small bundle of belongings. Even with the June sun on her back, her heart is as heavy and grey as the vast Aumber Estuary before her and she wishes she could be spirited over the waters and far away.

After a night with her mother's family in Barton, who are very curious about *just* what new job she's going to, she walks on to her sister Mary Ann's remote cottage at East Hawton. She is to take up residence with the family until after the birth, so no one will see the error of her ways. We — Harriet and I — think matters can't be any worse during the remaining five months of carrying, but we were wrong.

Harriet's unfolding thoughts roil and fulminate over the indignity of having to hide or pretend to be a widow if anyone calls, which is hard enough but, worst of all, her sister's husband also regards her as soiled goods and loses no opportunity to try and sully her even further, regardless of the fact that she is big with child. Her condition has classified her as a whore and fair game for anyone.

Mary Ann, always given to the vapours if she has to work too hard, lets Harriet shoulder much of the cooking and washing and gives herself over to making dresses and shirts. Rocking in her corner by the window, snipping away at calico and muslin, she occasionally receives their mother Ann for a visit in a borrowed pony and trap, and the two pointedly ignore Harriet, swatting her away like an irksome fly if she trespasses too close. She's a fallen woman, a harridan, a whore. We shudder at the memory of those months.

But as her term nears and autumn creeps through the Wolds, down towards the Aumber and to the villages that trickle haphazardly along its shores, a kind of peace drifts in with the morning mists. Like the fruits of her childhood orchard and the reddening hedgerows, Harriet feels that she too is ripening. She turns her face to the weakening sun and, as she takes in the washing laid across a hawthorn hedge, she throws back her head and opens her arms to the wind. Spinning and turning giddily, she calls to a passing smoke cloud of starlings parading the evening skies.

'Three, surely number three!'

The crack of a heron flying inland after his day's fishing seems to echo our counting as I slide into her completely, content and full and wild with life. Cradling our swollen belly, we stare far to the west where, at night, clouds beyond the horizon will be flushed by strange incomprehensible labours that release fire to reflect in the skies. It seems that, when all this is over, the streets near to the new iron works that are springing up around Scugton might offer fresh opportunities, maybe even a little anonymity; an escape. What exactly we are going to do, we can only guess at but anything would be preferable to our current predicament. We turn to carry the wash basket back to the house, head held high once more, a distant smile dancing around our eyes and the number three upon our lips.

The birth is hard but, caught fast once more in the thorns of Harriet's thoughts, I know it was strangely fulfilling for her, despite everything she has endured. As she twists at a velvet ribbon on her Sunday dress, caressing its softness, I catch an echo of a feeling that she is part of the world and its stream of life at last, no longer a misfit now but flowing along a vibrant pulse where she is just and only as she should be.

'Soft as a mouldywarp, 'e was,' she murmurs.

Mary Ann runs in, flapping and shouting and shooing the children from the cottage at the sound of Harriet's gasps and moans.

''Ave yer waters broke?' She answers her own question and fetches a pail and cloth.

And now come the pains that are familiar to me from so long ago and I gasp and writhe upon my bed with the shock of it, even though it is a memory of a memory…

… No! Not here! Not in the ward again. I don't want it. The

memory of Harriet's cry is so intense I want it to hold me bound in its joy and lust for living. In the middle of dying I feel hot with life! I need to be back with her, not stuck, insubstantial and sore, to my mattress. My mind flails out, seizing the tail end of the memory before it dissipates into breathlessness, a rising panic and a chest full of bubbles.

'Gran! Gran! Are you all right?'

My granddaughter rings for the nurse but I return to Harriet, keeping my distance to avoid those pains…

… Harriet is too intent on pushing her child into the world as Mary Ann belatedly tries to help, urging her to take to her bed. She delivers on all fours in the kitchen, like a beast of the field, grunting with both effort and satisfaction as she grasps the legs of a stool, feeling completely and utterly alive. She gathers up the boy from the folds of her dress and props her back against the wall while Mary Ann deals with the cord. Wiping the blood from his blonde hair with her petticoat, Harriet gives her firstborn son the name Charles and the middle name of Sowerby after his father.

Charles Sowerby Parsons…

… Forehead damp with the remembered pains of childbirth, my eyes open to the dappled shadows upon the ward walls once more as I recall how I found him. I'd forgotten this precious secret of Harriet's; a secret that illuminated so much of her mystery and how she came to name my granddad in the way that she did. I just couldn't trace her whereabouts on the 1881 census until I checked up on sister Alice. There she was. Harriet was visiting Alice on the day of the census along with another smaller visitor, Charles Sowerby Parsons.

It didn't take long to obtain the boy's birth certificate and read the familiar words 'father unknown'. His forenames were recorded as Charles Sowerby and, by the time Harriet had registered his birth, she was working again. Harriet Parsons, Spinster and Domestic Servant. Harriet Parsons, mother of a child she would never get to bring up herself. I'd followed his progress under Mary Ann's roof until the 1901 census and after that he disappeared; another unfinished chapter of Harriet's story.

It was after this point that finding Harriet became such a burning obsession. One child before marriage, five as a wife and three as a widow — I had to know more. I had to know it all. I dive through layers of consciousness back to her side. She's telling me things even now…

… Scuffing at pricking tears, Harriet remembers the baby's perfectly shaped head and searching mouth. Mary Ann doesn't even let her feed him and puts him straight to her own, constantly milk-charged and ample breasts.

'No good startin' yer milk. Ya'll niver git rid. Let 'im fill issen on my titties.'

When he has been fed and cleaned, Harriet takes the bundled baby from her at last, folding his tiny manhood in muslin and dressing him in a gown cut from remnants of Mary Ann's sewing. She has smocked it with threads pulled from her own Sunday best shawl and crocheted a delicate lace collar of fine white mending twine gathered up from her sister's leavings.

'Waste o' time that is. Plenty o' babby gowns here,' Mary Ann had sneered.

We remember holding the boy close to us through the night,

marvelling at every snuffle and mew, counting tiny fingers over and over and stroking the soft velvet of his head.

Harriet twists the Sunday best ribbon once more and holds it to her cheek, lost in her memories this bright spring morning.

'One, one, one,' we murmur over and over into his hair, each murmur followed by a kiss.

His soft head on her cheek dulls the pain of aching breasts for a while, until the next week when Shiloh fetches her home on a cart. Then there is no dulling any of the pain, ever. She howls her loss into the autumn winds and grey waters of the Aumber as Shiloh plods the horse along the ridge road back to Ellenby.

Charles is three years old now, red-haired and sturdy but he calls her aunty Harriet and she cannot bear it. It is all round Ellenby now, despite Ann Parson's precautions and if a man would not give her a second look before, there is even less chance now. That is what makes John Henry's attentions so surprising.

She frowns as she thinks of John Henry Blanchard's proposal. He'd snuck his arm around her waist under the lychgate after church one cold February day and said slyly, 'When the bod has two tails we shall be wed,' referring to the swifts' arrival in early May. Then he'd given her cheek a little peck. She'd nodded and there it was. The next thing she knew he'd been to see old Shiloh, who fetches her a long and questioning look but her mam leaps in and cries, 'Well, I'll be jiggered! A spring weddin' fer our 'arriet!'

'Doggerybaw! I ain't 'eard nowt good about the bugger,' mutters Shiloh into his clay pipe, clamping it fast in the gap where his two middle bottom teeth used to be. 'I 'eard he likes 'is beer ovver much, an' 'ard work a lot less. There's talk 'e's far weltered wi' on'y afe a day be'ind a plough. That's why 'e buggered off to Scugton. Mebbe thowt it were easier the-ar!' And as if to emphasise matters he stands up, spits systematically three times into the fire and heads for the cottage door, ramming his milking hat on to his head.

Despite Shiloh's misgivings, the wedding suits Harriet's purpose. Like most women, she is hostage to the simple need to breed. Despite her independent streak, she longs to be a mother again and yearns for a child whom she can finally call her own; quite apart from the fact that anything is better than working at Ellenby Hall where she is currently employed, and living here in the village with her mam and dozens of gossiping tongues.

'She was rare and ugly this morning,' thinks Harriet, and recollects Ann's shriek as we had fled the cottage, late up on our day off.

'If ya spang the dooer like that yah'll fetch it off its 'inges!' Then her mother had muttered, to herself, but loudly so Harriet can still hear, 'I can reckon what that dowter gits up to out on her own and it's nowt very good judgin' by past performance! 'Ussy! An' that owd parson's a bit of a nowter, givin' her ideas she can't do nothing with! Goin' to live in Scugton! What's wrong wi' Ellenby, I might hask?'

Sitting here now, on her favourite branch once more, scuffing her boot against the place where she rests her foot, Harriet remembers the old parson's kindly face the Sunday afternoon she went with Shiloh, to see him about having the banns read — John Henry being away in lodgings in Sereton village where he lives due to his employment at the Appleton Iron Works. Shiloh is wandering around out the back, admiring the rectory garden and pulling up some promised early rhubarb from under the forcing pots, leaving her, head bowed and awkward, to speak to Parson Edwards in his study.

He had spoken words about the solemnity and sacrament of marriage to her and tears had begun to trickle down Harriet's face on to her clean pinafore. She just couldn't help it. Her shoulders had shaken with sobs as she had tried to stem her misery and frustration as she pleated and re-pleated the white fabric in her hands.

She remembers how long it had taken for her to tell him, sniffing and hiccoughing, that she already had a child and yearned for another; and yes, she did like John Henry, he was a good man at heart and, yes, he would take her away from Ellenby and her mother which she dearly wanted, but what she really felt was that she wanted to learn things. Things you found in books. She wanted to find out if other people had written about what she saw. She wanted to write down all the beautiful things she had seen. Lifting her head for a moment, she had looked beseechingly at the old gentleman.

''Ave yer seen 'em, sir? I can tell you of skies an' flowin' fields an' leapin' fumad kits an' stars, an' the puff on a robin's winter breath.'

I see the parson in Harriet's mind's eye making much of shuffling the papers on his desk and heaving a long, helpless sigh as he tries to fathom the reasoning and ideas behind her thick country dialect, quite taken aback by her grief.

Harriet's ideas spill into his ears like seed on stony ground and he speaks to her the words that he has long practised, telling her God has ordained that a woman's place is in the home, not with books and learning and that she can, after all, teach her children the things she knows if she has sons.

'The sacrament of marriage, my dear, requires that you give your life to the needs of your husband and children. Forget these fanciful ideas.'

With another shuffle of his papers he explains how the iron industry and the new railway coming to the expanding collection of villages around Scugton means there is good work to be had. Harriet and John would have a works house in the newly built Sereton Terrace and she will be her own mistress.

'My own mistress,' thinks Harriet.

The wedding is next month, and she has given notice to the Hall that she will be moving away. I can feel in her a mixture of excited anticipation at the freedom of having her own life, and a worry that something is not quite as it should be; that there should be more than this, but desperation is driving her on…

… I swim to the surface once more from a long, long way down, in time to see the retreating back of a nurse and my granddaughter following her out of the ward. I'm alone and so I sneak a wry smile under my oxygen mask recalling my own similar dilemma. Harriet, my great grandmother, has trodden my path long before I did. Perhaps we all tread the same paths, over and over again, echoing our human weaknesses, mistakes and misdemeanours down through history. *Spiegel im Spiegel.* Mirrors in a mirror.

And then I am suddenly rocked by another discovery.

'Harriet, I know I've been here once before in my life.'

Somewhere down that long corridor of images reflected over and over, I was there. I saw the old ash tree, I remember the cracked boots and the velvet ribbon. I was there.

A heave of the chest, though little happens to relieve its struggles. I'm so out of breath now but much closer, I sense, to my final shaping. I hope I can drift off again before the rest of my family return. I hate it that they can see me like this; I was always so independent once I found the love of my life. He stopped the sky from falling down but he also knew that if you love something or someone enough, you have to let it fly wild and free — and I did. I was very much my own mistress. But then I lived at a time in history when I could be. It wasn't the same for Harriet. Someone rattles the medicine locker above my bed and the sound immediately shunts me off along another intense and twisted filament of memory…

… 'The door was unlocked, so I came in.'

Coral gives me a start as I sit, mesmerised by what I've found, at the computer.

'That's ok — put the kettle on and I'll be with you in a minute.'

It is another July day, two months after Maddy's fabled wedding in the bluebell wood. Guiltily I realise that I've forgotten that Coral and I were supposed to be looking at the wedding album and I've launched once more into finding Harriet instead of preparing tea and cakes for my friend.

My dear friend. Yet things continue to be difficult and uneasy between us. I've seen a side to her I never saw when we were college room mates and later young wives together. Every time I try to speak of what is bothering me, to reveal that broken arrowhead of pain that lies festering under my ribs, I see a distant, disinterested look come into her eyes and the talk turns, as always, to Geoff and his faults. Stupidly, I'm looking for forgiveness, I think, where there can be none — not from her, not from anyone. I should sort this out myself.

'Would you like to go down to the garden and pick some fruit, then we can have strawberries with our tea?' I deflect, hopefully.

Down in the fruit bed an hour or so later, with the afternoon sun warmly massaging our backs and shoulders, strawberry baskets full to overflowing with glistening fruit, we're now bent over blackcurrant bushes, delicately picking the luminous purple globes one by one, bagging them as we go, ready for the freezer. As we brush against them, the smell is vaguely reminiscent of cats and I chide the Siamese languidly sunning himself nearby in the apple tree arbour.

'Don't you think currant bushes always smell of cat pee, Coral?' I grimace over my shoulder and stare meaningfully towards the arbour. A tail flicks. Normally loud and loquacious, he's not to be drawn into conversation today. His world is entirely focused on a patch of sunlight and he extends the drape of his long body even further to soak up every inch.

'They do, especially the ornamental currants in spring. What's that bush over there? There's a few unripe currants left on it.'

Coral's sleek hair swings forward as she reaches to examine a nearby plant. I notice that she's wearing another pair of new sandals that show off her elegant and polished toe nails to perfection. The sight prompts a surge of helpless pity. One more purchase to stop a hole that can never be filled.

'Oh that's a whitecurrant. It's so productive we always leave a few berries on it for the birds. That's why the cat's here in the arbour; he knows where the action is.'

On cue, a young blackbird lands on the garden wall and, stubby tail feathers held high, he begins an immature shrieking as he spots us among his dinner.

'Yeakhh!' Coral spits, depositing the offending fruit she's just tasted some metres away. The young blackbird eyes the glistening berries on the ground but stays put, adjusting its tail and quietening down. 'It's sour and peppery!'

'I love them; they make great jelly if you flavour them with whisky and honey, and the bushes are so beautiful.' I stuff a handful of blackcurrants into my plastic bag and squeeze around to where Coral's standing, her face puckered in disgust.

'Beautiful? How? It's just a bush.'

'Well, it's the wrong time of year now but in spring the bark peels, and when the light is just right, the flakes look like flaming red glass.'

Bending to show her a few remaining shards of bark, I'm not sure whether it's vertigo or the drawing whirlpool forces of the odd sensations I've been experiencing lately that makes me topple forwards, head first into the bush. Swearing loudly, I back out and plonk down upon the ground, pulling leaves from my long red hair.

No, it's not *déjà vu*; more like what the French call *presque vu*, 'almost seen'. I seem to be on the brink of an epiphany, a sudden comprehension of the larger meaning of something that has been bothering me my entire life. But I also know I've been here before, headfirst in the middle of a whitecurrant bush. My head swims for a minute and there is that sense again of a long continuum where I fit, many, many times over as in parallel plane mirrors.

'*Spiegel im Spiegel,*' I mutter to myself. Mirrors in the mirror.

'Are you ok?' Coral queries, peering anxiously into my face, and the feeling evaporates as she helps me to my feet, circling my waist with a protective arm.

'This is how we used to be. Why can't we be like this again?' I complain to myself.

'Shall we put that down as your first fall, you silly old bat?' This is more like the Coral I used to know.

She sits on a low wall beside me now, out of the eyeline of the young blackbird. We both watch through the branches of the bush as he picks up courage to flutter down and inspect the remaining fruits, clucking to himself as he goes. He hasn't seen the cat yet.

'I'm fine, you know me. Un'eppen creature, I'd fall over my own shadow.' Strange how I feel so close to tears. I could throw myself spread-eagled on the ground and howl, for no reason that I can think of.

'Do you think he's learned to do that, or does he just know what to do?' Coral chuckles, nodding towards the bird.

'Oh, I think we all instinctively know what to do when the moment is right.'

My mind is on something else as I join her on the low wall, brushing the bark chippings that mulch the spaces between the fruit bushes from my skirt. The blackbird sees us but decides to stay and tug at a whitecurrant dangling temptingly over his head.

'Oh, the secrets I've kept!' I murmur under my breath, encouraged by her kindness to think that today might be the day I tell her.

'Mmm?' Coral picks a whitecurrant seed from her teeth.

'Well, I was thinking about Harriet really. I've found some incredibly interesting stuff about how things were when she was alive. It makes what she did all the more remarkable, but I think I can understand why she did it as well.'

'Oh, you're not on about that ancestry stuff again are you? It bores me rigid. I don't know how you can sit there all those hours.'

She says it with a laugh and thinks that will excuse whatever she says. Ever blunt, to the point of rudeness, Coral switches from kindness to dismissing the obsession of my life with a wave of her finely manicured hand. Her complete disinterest in my affairs of late evaporates the warm glow I was feeling but I ignore the comment and carry on, reaching into my bag of blackcurrants for a taste. I've been plotting my course carefully and I will tell her today.

'Well, you know how you always say that you could never have left your two girls, no matter how bad things were? Harriet did leave a child. She had a son before she was married and had to let her sister bring him up. I don't suppose he ever knew she was his mother. You know what a big deal illegitimacy was back then.'

'Those self-righteous Victorians! Now I know why I hate history.'

Eye cocked in interest, the young bird has spotted the glossy blackcurrants. I can see a spark of interest in Coral's eyes too, despite her protest, and so I press on.

'Well, from what I found out, it seems that righteousness had been affronted for quite some time in early Victorian England; Harriet never had a chance. I found this bit where, on February 25, 1834; the London *Times* really caught the whole mood of the emerging age.'

'That's before Harriet, isn't it?' So she has been taking in some of it.

'I know but listen.' I fish a computer printout from my pocket, where I'd consigned it when Coral arrived, and I read it to her:

'... *Poor Relief for illegitimate children had reached a pitch extremely oppressive to the parishes, and grievously detrimental to female morals throughout England.'* I try and put the pomposity and aggravation in my voice that the statement echoes.

'Poor Relief?'

'Yes, listen to this. Up to the early 1800s, local parishes paid for the upkeep of illegitimate children and it wasn't really such a big deal — more of a natural occurrence without too much scandal attached, from what I can gather. Then I found a bit in the papers where Thomas Carlyle really slammed this Poor Law of 1733 for putting a bounty on unthrift, idleness, bastardy and beer drinking. The Victorians had a real sea change in attitude.'

'Wow! He must have been a bit uptight!'

For once I've stimulated Coral's interest in the area of matters historical. Finding someone or something to be angry at always allows her to give vent to her own simmering rage, so I continue to read her Carlyle's rantings.

'Do you know what he said? It was really awful. They made a Poor Law Amendment which, he said, would properly place *'the responsibility for the support of the bastard on the vicious mother, thus relieving parish funds'.'*

'"The vicious mother" — that was a bit steep putting all the blame for getting pregnant on to women!'

'Well that's what he said and, in a male dominated society, frightened by the excesses of the previous century, it was music to their ears. Absolved men of all blame. Then they really started to put their women on pedestals and promote the idea of chivalry and the unsullied maiden, while all the time visiting whorehouses, of course.'

I think that Coral will latch on to Victorian hypocrisy but

instead she has hold of another idea.

'You mean there was no money anywhere for a mother and her illegitimate baby? Well, that might halt the teenage pregnancy rate in its tracks if they did it today. What a good idea!' Coral chortles.

I know Coral's views on these matters and it's useless to try and explain the moral cycles of history to her. She possesses all the inconsistent thought processes of a bigot these days which drives me mad, even though she's been such a good friend. Still wanting to share my discovery and scenting ignorance, the teacher in me is rearing up.

'It wasn't just that. In order to justify withdrawing financial support, they had to attach enormous moral outrage and stigma to having children outside marriage. Carlyle got up on his hind legs and positively roared at Parliament that the Amendment would end the great offence against the sacrament of marriage. He really roared out loud, the paper says. The Lord Chancellor in the House of Lords joined in and denounced — and I read from the printout again — the '*lazy, worthless and ignominious class who pursue their self-gratification at the expense of the earnings of the industrious part of the community*'.

I'm on a roll now, so I carry on, 'It was all about anger and fear, not morals, really — a bit like the outraged shrieking you get in some newspapers today'. (I know Coral reads one of them, so this is a bit naughty.)

'It wasn't just the money, either, it was a kind of reaction to the licentiousness of the century before. That's how history goes, from one extreme of the moral compass to another. All it takes is for someone to shout loudly enough and the idea will take hold if the time is right, whether it's founded on accuracy or not.'

'Morals or money, I only know we're far too soft on them today!'

'Think, Coral. Think!' I mutter under my breath. The echoes of these same attitudes, heaped up by the law and the Church into a high, insurmountable moral ground were still on the go 150 years later when you and I both married, and even when I left my husband. I grimace to myself, sucking on another blackcurrant and scuffing my feet in wood bark chippings.

Today I *will* tell her about how I left my husband; I've been trying for months. She's always assumed we just split up. I need to tell her the real story. This is it; time to get started. My point about attitudes has prepared the ground nicely.

'Yes, but don't you see, it's circular. One follows the other. What you feel strongly about you put up money for and make laws about. Those attitudes of Carlyle's were still with us when we were young. Why do you think it was most young women's aim in life to get married? No thought of a career. You worked only until you got married. Why do you think sex outside marriage was such a no-no then? Why did blokes have to marry you if you got pregnant? If they didn't, why did you have the baby secretly adopted? Why were you a virgin on your wedding night? Was it fear, religion, money — what?'

I can see that I've struck a chord but hope that I've not opened a floodgate.

'I'd never have married Geoff if it had been ok to live with him first, I suppose,' Coral admits reluctantly. 'There was no really reliable contraception unless you could get your hands on the Pill, so if you were sensible you just didn't do it. Wish I had, though, I'd have known he just wasn't right for me.' Anticipating what's to come, I push in swiftly before she can get started. But my intentions now are not just to tell all. I'm rattled and my feelings are as sour as the fruit in my mouth.

'Well anyway, the social and economic ostracism of 'fallen' women became enshrined in law, and attitudes just got worse and worse. By Harriet's time, "bastardy", as they called it, had been demonised by the new law to such an extent that you couldn't even depend on your family and friends to offer help and comfort if you got pregnant outside of marriage. As for women divorcing men — you were scorned by everybody!

Just think how dreadful it must have been for Harriet when she got pregnant. Just think how impossible it was even when we were young to leave your husband. Add to all that, the pain of leaving a child.'

I'm silent for a few moments. This is it.

She interrupts my jump from the cliff with a question and shatters the opportunity. Coral — *I was nearly there!* I just want from you what you want from me! I need the opportunity to rant and I need the confessional.

What did the mothers do, then?'

I compose myself and pull another piece of paper from my pocket. I'll try again in a minute. I've prepared this ground so well that I'm not going to give up now.

'Well, that's the awful thing. What could they do? They either persuaded the man to marry them or, very rarely, went to some old woman who performed abortions. The only other alternative was to give the baby away because if they kept it they were on their own, and they had to turn to baby farmers in order to keep working and supporting themselves.'

'Baby farmers?'

Coral's letterbox mouth drops open in her characteristic expression of disbelief and the sound of her incredulity provokes a yawn and a stretch on the arbour seat. The Siamese's half-open eyes and hunter's sharp hearing detect the bird scratching for fallen fruit and, in a sinuous, fluid movement, the cat is off the seat and crawling on its belly in ambush. I clap my hands loudly and the young blackbird takes flight at the explosion, a blackcurrant in its beak. In starting up its alarm call, the blackcurrant is lost and it bounces along the path with a soft, barely audible 'plip'. But it isn't the cat who's stalking now, it's me, creeping up on Coral's unwillingness to let go of her misconceptions so that she can understand that where we are now is built upon the past — a past which affected all of us, especially me.

'Yes, Baby farmers. Child minders. The majority of them were women themselves, who ran advertisements aimed at working class women, in national and local newspapers. On any given day a desperate new mother could find at least a dozen in the *Daily Telegraph* or the *Christian Times*, of all things. They advertised the daily, weekly or monthly care of infants.'

'Well that's not so bad, we have childcare today. I was just wondering how they managed.' Coral sounds relieved, swatting at a hoverfly that is hanging in the air in front of her face. She turns to me, about to rise, smiling complacently.

'See? I told you it's a better way of going on,' she says shoving me gently in an act meant to show humour and affection. I'm not receptive.

She stands up, and then stretches widely. Learning favours the prepared mind, and Coral's act of standing up and stretching means the barriers are being erected. She's not open to persuasion. There will be no enlightenment today and the foundations and first few building blocks of my much-needed confession have been tumbled. Putting on her sunglasses, she makes towards the blackcurrant bushes again, interest in the past waning quickly.

I should shut up now but I carry on teaching; this was always my mistake with her. She was a formed vessel with no room for any more than that which was already there.

'Mm, well it wasn't quite like that. People's attitudes to children were much different then.' I smooth out the computer printout. 'There was this bit in the newspapers of July 1870 about this woman, a Mrs Waters of Brixton, I think it was. She was a baby farmer and the law caught up with her when, it says, in a matter of a few weeks, she'd drugged and starved approximately sixteen infants to death, wrapped their bodies in old rags and newspapers, then dumped them on the streets. The papers said that nine babies were removed from her home and taken to the Lambeth Work-house, the majority dying from thrush and fluid on the brain shortly after.'

Coral is scandalised, as I knew she would be, but my plan has changed.

'Well, what did the mothers do about it? That's awful. I can't bear to think about it; I always said no mother should ever leave her children,' she mutters from the depths of a bush.

'What could they do? Catch 22; if they went to the law it would become known they were unmarried mothers and nobody, not even employers, would have anything to do with them.'

Coral is silent. I know I've run up against the brick wall of her well worn thought processes and that she'll shortly change the subject. This doesn't fit with her view of matters. On all matters of reason Coral runs along accustomed grooves and is not to be swayed. Like the blackbird, she flees from anything that unsettles her, dropping whatever she might have gained along the way. It's the survival instinct of a woman who has written her story and wants no further input. Telling her the secrets I've kept seems impossible now. It runs against the way she thinks about things and, friendship or not, I finally know now beyond all doubt that this is the one place I should not go with her.

'Let's have a look at your roses; you've got so many different sorts,' she says, depositing her bag of blackcurrants on the garden table. The subject is definitely closed.

'Show me your roses, then we'll get the wedding album out and have that cream tea while we look at it. There's a lovely picture of me in my blue and green outfit. I quite matched the woods.'

Inwardly in turmoil, I take her to my favourite, a peachy yellow, heavily scented rose called 'Jude the Obscure'. She bends to sniff the cabbage-like blooms and, for a moment, uncrumples and softens as the dense perfume does its work. That's where I should have stopped.

'It needs a lot of hard pruning in the spring because the blossoms are so heavy. The stalks get too spindly to hold them if you don't prune it back really hard,' I say, preparing my salvo.

'Strange thing, that.' Her manicured nails finger a bloom. 'The harder you are with them, the better they grow.'

Got you!

Coral absently deadheads spent flowers as she moves to another magnificent bloom in my collection, a tiny orange and brown striped floribunda, 'Tawny Tiger'. I am the tiger now, though, and she's within reach of my claws.

'My Gran always used to say that love is like that,' I say lightly, knowing I shouldn't start on this tack but I do. I'm hell bent on educating her in at least some small way now. I have so much burning inside me that I need to share, but a lesson in life will just have to do instead.

Coral's face flashes a slight frown. When I tell her about my wise old Granny she knows there's a story coming, and one which will be contrary to everything she's come to believe about life. Where my Gran always saw good, Coral sees nothing but bleak despair, bitterness and anger and is exasperated that there can be views of life that oppose hers. She says nothing but continues deadheading and I dive headlong into my explanation, determined to maul her with it until she really hears what I have to say, just for once.

'Yes,' I purr, answering an unasked query. 'Pruning was one of my Gran's signs.'

Snip. With each sentence I trim away at my roses for emphasis.

'She used to say that real love prunes you back hard so that you grow into a better person.'

Snip.

'Without pruning, without love to moderate you, you're uncontrolled, you grow any which way and become weak.'

Snip, snip.

'When you really love someone you don't want to change them at all but love changes you.'

Snip.

'It takes away all your little selfishnesses; all your petty concerns for yourself are put aside as you try to make the other person happy.'

Snip.

'You learn when it's right to speak out and when to be quiet. You put the other person first, second and last and, as you learn to restrain your 'me, me, me' voice, you become a better and stronger human being along the way.'

SNIP!

At that last snip Coral spins round, grinding the handful of spent rose petals she's just gathered into a tight ball in her fist.

'You're not saying I never loved Geoff, are you?' Coral removes her sunglasses with her free hand. Her voice is level and careless but her eyes flash with the fire of a widow protecting the sanctity of her marriage.

'You've said as much yourself, you know you have; and don't you remember your comment about passion falling out of your knickers and on to the floor?'

I try to sound level and unconcerned and reach out to put a sympathetic hand on her arm, knowing I shouldn't have said what I said, no matter how true or relevant it is. The unspoken rider — that she is not the person she could have been had she loved — hangs between us. Part of me hopes she jolly well gets it, the other half is ashamed for even suggesting such a thing to a friend.

'Anyway, shall we go and look at those wedding photos now?'

The ball of petals is scattered on the path and I watch them fall in a kind of slow motion; a sundering of something that was once whole.

'A sign of things to come,' I think and then realise it's just what Gran would have said.

'Oh, I don't know, I think I've heard enough about marriage for one day! Maybe I'll bring the album to the gym tomorrow. Anyway, I need to get off now; we've spent far too long nattering.' The voice is still careless but it has a brittle crust to it, hiding softer things underneath that I've wounded…

… I grope feebly to the surface of consciousness again. The ward clock wobbles into soft focus. Is it visiting time again already? The rest of my family will soon be back to sit, sorrowfully, by my bed, just when all my thoughts are coming together. I think of that day again, the day of a joining and a parting. It was the day I first began to understand why Harriet's life was so relevant to mine and why it had so much to say about the years of my life. It was also the day that Coral and I ceased to be really good friends. The splashback of that day tainted everything else we did together.

I wonder why that should be relevant now, apart from the regret I felt at her untimely death. What, I wonder, has Coral got to say to me after all these years, in the middle of all this stuff about Harriet?

# 10

## EDWARD

Hospital wards are never the most fragrant of places; the combined farts of the patients, lingering smells of hospital food and the sudden stench as the sick lose control of their bladders, bowels and stomachs. Even the best run ward is always faintly redolent of lavatories so I'm not at all surprised when a faint, sweet, almost fetid smell begins creep around the curtains. I'm fairly sure, even at this stage of my dying, that it can't be me, so I begin to feel really sorry for the poor woman who is probably sitting on a commode in the cubicle next to me. Your sense of smell goes when you're very old but this is incredibly strong. Poor woman.

Yet, as I turn on my pillow, I find not that most inadequate of privacy tokens, the hospital screen but a bedroom wall instead. I see that I'm with Harriet once more and all thoughts of Coral fade as I slide into her consciousness easily now, ceasing to question why her thoughts and memories are as clear as my own. I simply follow the pale yellow thread as it becomes a patch of sunlight upon a scrubbed wooden floor…

… 'If you don't mind, love, I'll have to lay him out now. I have to get to *The Oswald's* upstairs rooms some time tonight to ton a breech that's nobbut a week away. Jimmy Maw said 'e'd tek me on 'is wagon.'

Instinctively I back away from becoming totally part of her, for the atmosphere in the room is one of deep sorrow and shock.

Harriet hands the tiny inert bundle to Mrs Oliver, the midwife.

'I want it done the proper way.'

The proper way, she knows, is for the laying out to be done in absolute silence and with no one present but those actively involved in the procedure. Harriet cannot easily move from her bed as she's still waiting for the afterbirth and so she turns her head to watch, hungrily soaking up what little contact there is to be had with her tiny stillborn child.

'You'll find a clean 'anky in one of them laundry baskets down-stairs,' she says, 'an' mind you stop the mantel clock while you're down there'.

The midwife looks sharply at her and draws a questioning breath in relation to the hanky.

'I know it's not mine but laundry can go missing for a week or two, you know!' Harriet retorts, grimacing as a contraction begins to force the afterbirth from her body.

'Mek sure you fold it small and tie it well.'

Mrs Oliver returns with an embroidered lawn handkerchief and places it under the chin of the baby boy, fastening it at the top of the small blood encrusted head.

'Reckon he's stiff already,' she remarks tersely. As she lifts an arm, the baby's body turns with it as of a whole.

'No need to ask if you have coins,' she says, covering the eyes with cotton wadding instead. Harriet groans and pushes.

'I'll do you now and then get back to 'im. 'E can wait.'

Mrs Oliver is a thorough midwife and she has the membrane removed from the afterbirth and fills it with water from the bucket by the bed in no time.

'Clean as a whistle but it's very small. Poor mite must 'ave starved to death. Been dead less than a day I reckon. You ain't been looking after yoursen, 'ave you?'

'I've got to work to feed ten bairns. There's nowt for them, let alone me. And all that bending over the tubs dun't 'elp any. You know what it's like.'

'Aye.' Mrs Oliver smiles grimly.

Harriet knows she became a midwife after the last two of her children died, one from phythisis, the other from diphtheria. She's learned her trade, both from laying them out and helping her mother birth fourteen more after herself.

'Twenty-one in all and six dead 'uns my mam bore before the old bugger got 'it be a swinging chain at the coke ovens and finally laid off her.'

The midwife now begins the laying out, Harriet tautly holding in her grief and Mrs Oliver being as swift as she can while still showing the respect owed to the dead and the newly bereaved. The needless handkerchief binding the rigid jaw is removed and handed to Harriet, who holds its softness to her face. The boy's little down-turned mouth has lips the colour of ripe damsons, and his face and skin bear the customary bramble mottle of a child who has died in the womb.

'Did you 'ave an 'earse for yours?' Harriet asks as the midwife ties clean torn and folded sheets around and under her, removing the newspapers from the bed as she does so.

'On'y the fost. Me mam paid for it. Tom carried me others after that. They was only tiny mites.'

Carefully undoing the torn petticoat wrapping the tiny, blue tinged body, Mrs Oliver removes the clothes peg clipping the umbilical and hands it to Harriet. A washerwoman knows with great exactitude the number and type of her pegs but this particular one, the midwife knows, will be treasured for other reasons.

Tearing off further pieces of rag, she begins to wash off blood, vernix and faeces from the little boy with the bar of cheap scented soap she always carries with her for such occasions. It isn't much but it seems to show the proper care and she does count for it in her fees. She doesn't do the washing under a modesty sheet as is customary with adults, for she knows from long experience that mothers want to watch their dead infants being tenderly cared for. If they call for her it usually means they are unable to do the laying out themselves or something else is afoot. Few folk she deals with can routinely afford a midwife just for a birth or even a stillbirth. That puzzles Mrs Oliver. Harriet expressly sent Gertie to find her, even though she must have feared the baby to be stillborn. What's so special about this child?

After putting the used rags in the night soil bucket to be burned, with infinite gentle care, the midwife plugs the baby boy's bottom with a little of the cotton wadding that she always keeps in her pinafore pocket. She glances pointedly at the folded sheet lining a drawer bottom, ready for the child, had he lived. Harriet nods, thin-lipped and pale.

'Now I want you to say he drew breath and was born a day ago,' she says, looking meaningfully at the midwife.

Without answering, Mrs Oliver has half of the sheet quickly torn into long strips and begins binding the baby, leaving out its arms, as it gives mothers comfort to hold a tiny dead hand. Next she takes up the nightdress that Harriet has put out ready, not thinking it will be a shroud, together with a white frilled bonnet. With difficulty but great patience born of much practice, she dresses the rigid body, making a good show of arranging the ribbon of the bonnet just so. She makes the sign of the cross on the little crumpled forehead and then hands the baby once more to Harriet. She understands now. The baby cannot be named if he is declared stillborn. Harriet wants to mark the passing of this little one for all time by giving him a name. He means more to her than most.

A sound of cartwheels crunching on the clinkered road outside draws her suddenly to the window.

'It's Jimmy,' she says, pulling together the rags that do for curtains, to show the house is in mourning.

Harriet looks up, numbly nodding. 'Two week's washing, then, when I'm up and about — and he was born alive a day ago. Is it settled?'

'That will do nicely. By the by, Gertie's still downstairs. Shall I send her up?'

Harriet's face says that she cannot bear the thought of telling her sour, sallow-faced second eldest daughter at the moment and shakes her head vigorously. 'No, you tell her as you let yersen' out,' she mutters into the folds of the bonnet.

There's a careful and respectful closing of the bedroom door, where the remains of the birthing stand in two buckets, waiting to be disposed of.

A fetid sweet smell once more in the hot, July evening. Orange mottled light upon the walls, muffled voices, more curtains being closed, the front door clattering shut. A click of a tongue urging a horse forwards in its traces, wheels turning and then silence. I don't want to slide further into Harriet, but I do.

An iron girdle of self-control finally loosens as we clean blood-caked fingers on a dirty dress and delicately move aside the bonnet's goffered frill, done only last Thursday with the week's washing. Silently we suck on air, again and again as though we will never breathe out, until finally we can hold in no more grief and a thin animal wail winds its way from a rope-necked throat. A pulsing, bursting head is thrown backwards on the pillow. No, not that; no I won't go there. There's no need for that memory.

It's too much. I can't bear her sorrow and I pull away. I have felt this same animal anguish before and I do not want to remember but the memory picks viciously at the edge of my mind. The wail continues, rising in volume, her neck arching backwards so that her mouth, spittle trickling from its corners, gapes at the ceiling. The sound that now tears from her carries the same lilting, angry cadence of the newborn, finally reaching a quavering crescendo that pulls on and on and on. There is no one to lull her, no one to shush or rock her and I cannot share this. Harriet gives full, unrestrained vent to her grief, deaf to the hammering on the bedroom door.

'Mam?'

'MAM!'

Gertie stands at the bedroom door, a raven-haired thin and unattractive twelve-year-old, still in her scullery maid's uniform, the bobby having fetched her home when Mrs Bowers from next door finds her mam moaning and kneeling among the washing in the back yard.

'Get Mrs Oliver!' Harriet shrieks at Gertie, feeling the tiny body precipitating into the world beneath her skirts. The woman has been known to do miracles, blowing into the faces of babies born before their time, gently swinging them, lamb-like, by their feet until they breathe.

Now the house is empty but for Gertie and Harriet, the rest of the children being cared for on that stifling evening by Mrs Bowers, since she has no brood of her own.

'Mam, I didn't even know you were carryin'. Can I hold 'im?'

Harriet snaps back instantly into this world from the place where she has gone, alone and demented. The mask she wears comes down on haggard, hunger-hollowed cheeks and she sits up, gesturing to Gertie.

'Come here then,' she chokes out, the words rolling like marbles in her mouth through her now muffled sobs.

Gertie skirts the buckets, grimacing at their contents, and crosses the room to the bed, holding out her arms for the tiny bundle. Harriet smiles wanly and obliges, trying hard to think of the feelings of her second eldest even while drowning in her own.

Gertie pushes aside the frills and stares. It is a moment before her brain registers the still, death-marbled face. She has the baby clutched close to her, ready to press the head against her cheek and feel that downy warmth which instantly triggers the fate of most girls, urging them relentlessly towards motherhood. She shrieks at the delicate plum lips and the stiff coldness and almost throws the baby back at her mother.

'It's 'orrible!' she spits, turning on her heels and running back downstairs, her black, cracked boots clattering on the bare boards.

I know instinctively that the events of that July afternoon mark Gertie for life and alter permanently her attitude to childbearing and the human body, especially her own. The dark splashes of blood in the back yard, Mrs Bowers' hands in the crotch of Harriet's drawers, pulling out what looks like a piece of raw meat shock her to her very core. Only when her mother shouts at her to go and get Mrs Oliver the midwife does she guess it is a baby.

As I watch Gertie hurling herself down the stairs, remembering what Granny Rose told me about the poker stiff great aunt of my childhood years, I suddenly understand that chaste and prudish woman who shrank away from every touch, even mine. After many years of spinsterhood in service, Gertie finally married the master, only to reject him totally on their wedding night and subsequent honeymoon cruise. Mr Hudson publicly declared that he would rather bed a statue than this frigid, unfeeling creature he had mistakenly taken to his bosom. The marriage was quickly annulled and Gertie remained single for the rest of her life, finally having put two and two together regarding the terrible facts of procreation and birth.

The sound of the front door once more and Harriet is left alone with her sorrow to keen and rock and kiss and place her little finger repeatedly in the curled stiff fingers of the infant. He smells so sweet to her, like roses, and she buries her face in the smell, pulling in hungry lungfuls of it, on and on. I know instinctively that she will later add it to her litany of beautiful things, recalling it all through her life and smelling it once more at her own death.

Even when Mrs Bowers brings her a cup of tea and tells her as how the children, especially Fred, are asking after their mam, she does not look up or cease her rocking, as though somehow the baby is only sleeping and might wake up at any moment. At one point she puts the cold purple mouth to her breast but finds no comfort, only the bursting hotness as her bosom begins to fill with unwanted milk.

It is the early hours of the morning when she finally lays the tiny corpse in its drawer, arranging it, like a live baby, in a woollen shawl. She lights a number of candles around the room, making sure that four are on the dresser near the baby and then, after heaving the two buckets down the stairs, she stirs the kitchen fire to life ready to dispose of some of the mess of birthing.

In the middle of the flagged floor she begins to strip off her blood-soaked skirt, petticoats and bindings, and then hesitates as she remembers that it is now Sunday and she has barrels of water prepared for soaking, and more that are just fresh and clean. Gingerly she opens the back door and turns round to look at the blank, sleeping windows of the terrace. She knows she should be lying in but she needs to wash this pain from her life.

The rags and papers burnt and the afterbirth disposed of down the petty hole, she uses the bucket to swill the yard, survival automating her actions. There is washing to finish, children to feed, lye to make and coal to be found. Then there is the matter of two extra wash loads for the midwife. She will forever be scrabbling upwards, like trying to walk the grey grime of an endless slipping slag bank, if she doesn't get back to work soon. Life, not death, presses of necessity into her mind and her damp, sweat soaked head shakes from side to side as if to clear away a cloud of horse flies.

As a cool breath of air blowing upon her face soothes her momentarily, she stares down at the advancing tide of water in the yard, black in the moonlight. Harriet suddenly feels an overwhelming desire to be clean. Clean and simple with everything in its place.

The back gate clicks.

I am watching her sitting in the clear water of one of her own wrenching barrels, lit blood red by the slag tainted sky, quietly keening into the eerie glow. I don't even have to look up to know that a red mask with a jag of a mouth will be gaping down from the sky but I look up anyway and stare in incomprehension into its empty eye sockets. Harriet sees it too, and shudders. How come she knows it so well? I seem to know it too, now.

'Go away, go away. Why a' yer always there?' she moans and continues to keen into the night, oblivious to approaching footsteps.

I know that animal sound of drawn out sorrow. It almost drags me to somewhere I don't want to be but I want to see who is at the gate. She looks up and holds out her arms.

'Will!'

'Ah just got word from Tom Oliver an' came straight from t' tappin'!'

A tall, dark-haired man in filthy clothes and a scorched leather apron strides across the yard and scoops Harriet's wet form up in his arms, cradling her as if she is a baby herself.

'Come on lass, get tha'sen inside'. His accent is broader and rougher than hers, echoing from Yorkshire.

''E's in the drawer upstairs, Will. It was another lad, like you wanted.'

'Nah then, there's time enough for that. Let's get you set to rights first,' he says, brushing the tangles of wet hair from her face and lifting her gently from the barrel.

There is such an aching tenderness between them as he sets her on her feet and steers her towards the back door. Once inside, he lights a candle, though there is no need because the sky has a livid crimson glow tonight. Carefully stripping each blood-soaked layer from her thin form, he swathes her round in a newly washed and dried rag rug hanging from a chair back. Finally he sits her upon his knee and removes her wet stockings and worn shoes, placing them by the fireside.

'Tha's a good woman, our 'Arriet,' he whispers into her hair as he rocks her like a child.

'I'm not Will, I'm not; you know what I did! I deserve this! It's my punishment!'

'Tha mu'n't tek on so. What had to be done were done; no crime in that.'

For a fleeting moment I am fused to my pillow by a terrible memory, as hot and as livid as molten slag, which passes raggedly through Harriet's mind but Will's touch soothes it away.

He slips off his metal flecked flat cap and slides it to the floor without disturbing her. He smells of metal among the sweat and dirt. The hanky round his neck is pulled off with enormous cal-loused hands, to wipe his grimed face, and to staunch both Harriet's tears and his own.

I feel a sudden, semi-conscious lurch of joy and recognition. My grandson has those very same hands. *I* have them, my son has them and my dad and granddad had them. This is William Henry Ogley, Harriet's lover and my great grandfather and it is the first time I have ever seen his face. Diving down again, I scan it eagerly, greedily, almost in disbelief. Why, in death, am I seeing a face that I never saw in all my life, not even in a photograph?

What a serious face, but even featured and calm. Life has etched a stoic patience there in his wide set eyes and left no trace of bitterness on that ruddy, furnace-burnished countenance. I am transfixed as he croons and murmurs to Harriet so that gradually her keening subsides. I want to stay on this spot forever, watching the gentle iron worker who gave me these once so capable hands.

A slag surge of crimson suddenly illuminates his generous features. Outside, in the night sky, empty eye sockets and a gaping mouth leer lopsidedly on the scene below, then fade as the freshly tipped waste cools.

I want to stay but it's too late. The sound of Harriet's sorrow is taking me to that place I thought I had left behind years ago, a place where I was carved and hollowed nearly as deeply as she was. This shouldn't be part of my dying! I had laid all that grief to rest; I had come to terms with it all. What can there possibly be there to rake over now? This is a blind alley, a diversion. It is Harriet whom I want to follow.

# 11

# CHOOSING

I can no longer sidestep it or stand at its brink; I am pulled, tumbling over and over as I fall, into the pit, further and further away from Harriet. As sunshine streams through chestnut branches and dances on the grey hospital floor, I slide back to my 30th year and the sunlit floor of Wells Cathedral.

Pinks, yellows, blues and purples glass-stain the cool stone pillar against which I lean a throbbing head. A young man stands in a crowd some yards away, neck craned upwards with the rest, waiting for the chime of an ancient mechanical timepiece. High on the wall above and to the right of the inside clock face is a seated wooden figure, Jack Blandifer, holding a bell and a hammer. On the hour he strikes the bell with the hammer for the appropriate number of times. The figure turns his head as he does so, to listen to the sound.

My husband's slight frame and the sweep of his long fingers through fine blonde hair, pushed back to gain a better view of it, touch my heart with a caress that is exquisite pain. He is a kind and good man but I do not love him. In the foundry of our marriage, the force for change has not forged me into anything good. The bickering that comes when you co-exist with someone whose little imperfections grind against your very being has long taken hold, and echoes of my mother rear up daily in my shrewish voice and carping criticisms. I am neither a pleasant nor a good person in my current existence, my dissatisfactions bringing out the worst of my character. I am becoming the sum total of all that I hated in my parents…

… For a brief and blessed moment, as my blood pressure cuff tightens, the whirlpool spits me out and I focus on my right arm and cling to the here and now. There's no *need* to go there; it was resolved a long time ago. I *won't* go over it again; it's finished with and pointless. Yet, as the cuff hardens, I realise that at that particular point in my life my clay was hardening already and, if I'd done nothing about changing things, I would have gone on to become the misshapen spirit that my mother was. I think I can hear myself talking out aloud now, as I recall that unfortunate marriage of two disparate souls but only my lips are moving, protesting, protesting.

'I shouldn't have married you. I should have listened to my Gran. I was no good for you and you were no good for me. You were killing me. You were a lovely man but you were killing me. I couldn't live like you wanted to live. I couldn't pretend any more.' On and on I ramble.

And the sound of my inner frustration takes me back to the one place I do not want to go…

… My young husband is the exact antithesis of what I am and he stifles me and all that I would be, but it is not his fault. I stuff my hands deep into my mac pocket in despair and my searching fingers screw up and shred a tissue I find there. He is as he is, and I am as I am, and we are about as near a total mismatch as it is possible for two human beings to be. In my headlong flight from my parents the warning was already there and I ignored it, thinking I could grow to love his imperfections, too cramped and crabbed a character to know that when you love someone, you love them because of their imperfections, and not in spite of them. I know it now because I am in love with someone else.

For the first time in my life I understand to the innermost recesses of my being what it is to love and be loved, to be joined at the soul to another, to see my life only in terms of that person, knowing that without them there is no existence of any real consequence. Everything that has gone before has brought me to this point and it is an impossible dilemma…

… I take painful gurgling coughs try to clear out my fluid-filled lungs but I can't manage it and my chest sings and wheezes. It's getting very difficult now. I raise a hand to wipe my brow and vaguely notice my blue tinged nails and purple fingers. But at least I'm here and not there and I try to hang on to the now once more.

Why were things so difficult then? My granddaughter, sitting once more so patiently by my side, would have no concept of my dilemma or even why it should be one. No problem. Leave your husband, take the children, the benefit system will provide. Marriage today has ceased to be the serious, permanent and binding promise that centuries of practice made it for me at the time I wed. Well versed at my Gran's knee in the thinking of the Catholic Church, I saw it as a lifelong union between two people committed to each other's growth. Well, that's what she would recite to me, stroking my hair and repeating what the Church had told her, even as she had gone there to find comfort and an explanation for grand-dad's womanising and drinking.

Again I ask myself, why were things so difficult then? I'm hanging on to the thought, afraid to slip back to that period in my life once more. To begin with, in my imploding world of 1976, and in my small life, your sex was your destiny. Divorce numbers were still relatively small, even at that stage of the twentieth century, and women where I came from only left their husbands in exceptional circumstances. Women, especially schoolmistresses who were expected to be pillars of the community, most certainly did not. Men could leave but women stayed and tried to make it work. There wasn't the sturdy safety net of benefits that there was at the end of the twentieth century and what there was, was savagely means tested. Many didn't even have jobs once they married, or if they did, it was just for pin money. They were the committed ones. They pulled on tight, optimistic faces each day and turned to their friends, immersed themselves in work or children and pretended that this is how it should be. They survived, and what they survived was the affectionate but benign neglect that even the most loving of men of that era still showed towards their wives. Mutual personal growth was hardly on the agenda, despite what my Gran taught me.

Wincing at the rawness in my back and chest, I shift on my pillow, remembering how it was. Yes, a man's role was different then and a woman was trapped by her very nature. A quote from Byron slides into my thoughts. 'Man's love is of man's life a thing apart; 'tis woman's whole existence.' It was all but a woman's whole life in those days.

The idea of equal partners back then was a heady concept still some three decades away. I stood at a precipice of social isolation. Little had changed since the approbation of Harriet's day, and so-called 'free love' was a myth outside of the cities. As for the swinging sixties, they barely disturbed Scugton's steel town certainties. Where I lived, teenage girls were allowed out once a week on a Saturday night, and even then your dad always came to fetch you home at 10.30pm. And if you had a boyfriend, you were never allowed alone together. The sound of the door latch always interrupted any goodbye kiss or hopeful groping. That was usually the extent of any teenage sex. I manage yet another wry smile, though I think it must look more like an expression of pain to anyone watching.

Pain. I should not have thought of that word! I should not! The breath is knocked out of me as I begin to slip helplessly down the flume ride of emotions flowing towards that memory once more. I know where it's going and I would rather be dying and in pain here than back there, but I know I have to follow. I'm beginning to see that I must face this thing one last time before I can go. It must have some kind of relevance here at the end even though I faced it, dealt with it and laid it to rest nearly forty years ago, not long after I finally found the rest of Harriet's secrets. But I really don't want to go back there. I turn my head onto a cool part of the pillow to escape the torment that is coming…

… 'Oh God! What am I to do?' I press my temple against the stone pillar for relief from the torment but none comes. The ancient cathedral clock begins its whirring and tinkling. Figures move mechanically across its face and doors open. The crowd sucks in its breath with a collective 'Ooooooh!' and my young husband turns to me, smiling across their heads.

Jack Blandifer also turns his head and looks straight at me, counting out my guilt.

Ting! I know you.

Ting! You knew you shouldn't have married him.

Ting! You cheat.

Ting! Now what?

On the outside part of the clock, knights on horses knock off each other's heads.

My own time compresses as the clock finishes its performance. Brief murmurs and soft shuffles on stone as people drift away to other parts of the cathedral prompt me to call out again. I came to this ancient place hoping to fathom out an answer but my few moments alone here are drawing to a close.

Panic.

I wander inside now and my eyes search wildly around, pulled upwards, as those medieval architects intended, to the scissor arches, and to the top of the tree-like column against which I stand. Its long trunk leads to the ceiling of the cathedral where it sprouts a crown of masonry branches.

'What shall I do, what shall I do?'

A fierce whisper in that vaulted space can sound as loudly as a conversation, and then… I hear it, softly but quite plainly.

'You must follow your heart.'

Startled, I look round. The voice doesn't seep like a mysterious mist from between the cathedral's columns or hang in the air, insistent and pervasive. It is so small and quiet that it's hardly there, yet it's what I've been so desperate to find. It is an argument to take me forward, maybe — a suggestion given substance. It is an answer.

'You must follow your heart.'

There it is once more; a kind, compassionate and matter-of-fact voice that speaks as though the owner has an arm round my shoulders and is concerned only with my utmost welfare. A wealth of warmth and understanding springs from this straightforward, level and gentle command. And it is immediately obvious to me. This is the only thing I can do.

Feeling as though a great weight has been lifted from me, I'm eased and comforted for a moment and, although I don't yet know what following this voice truly entails, I'm sure I'll be able to work it out…

… My eyes open wide at the memory, catching frantically at the fleeting strand, for I now know with absolute certainty, although I don't want to be there, that I have to relive this bit of my life; it is really, really important.

'Her eyes are open, can she see us?'

'I don't think so, she looks very far away. Gran, can you see us?'

Don't disturb me… please, don't disturb me… leave me alone.' They mean well but I can't expect them to understand this.

'You must follow your heart.' I've often thought about that voice and how it changed my life and the lives of those around me forever. I've never been particularly religious. Not that I didn't accept the existence of something far greater than myself, especially after my brushes with death. But, as a child, simple logic told me that this thing could not belong exclusively to any one group of people. It just didn't make sense that Christians should be more right about

God than anyone else, if He was what they said He was.

As an adult, I took an even more sceptical view as I began to appreciate how, time and again, the clarity and pure ideas of one good person are taken over by followers or users until, through interpretation and reinterpretation, fundamentalism, ceremony, tradition, power and law, the medium of delivery eventually over-shadows the message. The medium becomes the message, whatever religion you're talking about. Me, I believed the messages, they were so simple. They were pure and to the point. You didn't have to join a particular religious group to get them; they were universal.

The message of Christianity was a wonderful gift when I ran a church school. There was many a time I'd be able to sort out the most complex of the moral dilemmas that we're capable of creating for ourselves by asking one simple question…

'I wonder what Jesus would have said about that?'

'We can't possibly have a woman priest!'

'You must teach the doctrine of the Trinity.'

'I don't think we should admit Jehovah's Witness children to the school.'

'She can't be an unmarried mother and a teacher at a church school.'

All these protests were stunned to silence by that simple ques-tion. I just stuck to the messages. I loved them in their simplicity. Jesus, Buddha, Mohammed, the God of Abraham, the search for the centre of things and even lack of a God figure in Taoism — all of them. They all brought me to the point where I stood in that cathedral and I believed in that voice.

But what did I believe? Focus. You changed too many lives to let this one go. It wasn't an old bloke on a cloud in the sky speaking to me then, or even any of his prophets. It wasn't an epiphany, a road to Damascus moment, either. The voice was far too kind and level and quiet for that. It wasn't that at all.

I try to pull from that remembered voice what I felt, why I was so sure, screwing up my face with the effort. My granddaughter, leaning over my bed, attempts to give me a comforting hug but it's another arm that curls around me now. It is that of my husband and as he pulls me to him, the great bells of the cathedral begin to toll the hour, finishing with that glorious, swaggering peal that only English bells can produce. I know today that they are truly tolling for me and tears begin to fill my eyes as the realisation of what I must choose begins to dawn.

My husband kisses me fondly on the nose but by the time the last note has died, I have pulled away from him and, trembling inside, at the bidding of that voice, I have begun to think the unthinkable. What we can think becomes possible. What is possible we can –eventually — do.

My heart lurches. It's not the pneumonia, it's the memory. Harriet's remembered cry is carrying me straight there…

… It's some weeks later and I haven't dared listen properly to that voice yet. I've driven home from an illicit meeting with the man I love; a meeting where we agree to do the honourable, the sensible thing and end the relationship. It was a numb, wooden rendezvous where neither of us dared touch or look at the other, and we voiced the words that society and duty expected of us, like mummers in some ritual play. I don't think I saw the road on the way home, only the night. I moaned softly into the blackness, unable to take in the finality of the lines we'd spoken.

Just, only just, held in control, I creep through the slumbering quiet of our house to peep in on my two children, each sleeping in their accustomed positions; my beautiful six-year-old daughter on her stomach and my beloved four-year-old son spread-eagled on his back, Growler clutched firmly in one hand, mouth open and snoring gently because of yet another ear infection. They are the best thing I have ever done; the only really good thing I have ever done in my miserable, crabbed life. Something inside me hollows and tears a space with a knife that is serrated by pure anguish. It is a hole as black and deep as a well and I feel that it will never be filled again as I realise the hopelessness of my situation.

I back out of their room as if I have been punched and I fall to my knees on the rough carpet of the landing, winded by grief and bewilderment. Control now abandoned, some detached part of me finds the carpet with hands that scrabble and claw and, finding no purchase there, I grab my hair and I pull out handfuls, again and again. I stare at the strands, uncomprehending, from the pool-dark bottom of despair. Desolation brims over and begins to rise inside me on the crest of a silent scream and, with my head thrown abruptly back, I mouth sounds that are not so much words as stifled animal howls of full blooded loss, for I know I am going lose something that is dearer than my life, whatever happens.

Fist thrust in my mouth to stem the gasping, I am on the stairs now and I head for the dark and private stillness of the outhouse, where I crumple to the floor once more and suck on air that holds no life. Almost delirious with grief, I imagine many desolate future scenarios with never a glimpse of a way out. In one of them there is a woman in ragged and blood-stained clothing holding a dead baby in her arms. Like me, she has her head thrown back in a long and soundless howl of loss and, unquestioningly, I join with her in pouring my misery into the night. Silently we suck on air, again and again as though we will never breathe out, until finally we can hold in no more grief and a thin animal wail winds its way upwards, pulling on and on and on. I don't know why she should be sharing my grief, but it helps a little up to the point where the pain is so great that I instinctively know that the only way to gain relief is through greater pain. As I beat my head against the cold bricks, the visions of desolation retreat and a kind of relief finally comes.

'Are you coming to bed yet?'

A distant, irritable and sleepy voice breaks through the night. The woman, whoever she was, has gone and I am utterly alone. I cannot answer. My mouth will not make any sense at first and it is some time before I eventually croak out, 'Soon, go to sleep.'

Slumped on the outhouse floor, I realise that I am filthy, bleeding and warmly wet. I have soiled myself in my moments of frenzied self-abuse. My fists are full of hair I dimly recognise as my own and I stroke it absently, gathering it into one thick lock, folding and pleating it again and again, demented now beyond tears. I rock backwards and forwards, waiting, remembering from childhood the place beyond tears. I know that welcome numbness will eventually follow and fill tomorrow.

Tomorrow.

How can there be any tomorrow that means anything?

I cannot leave and support my children on my own even if my husband would let me take them, which he will not; he has already forbidden me to take my tiny daughter to see her German grand-parents in the dark days after my mother died. No, there is no question of my taking the children. Marriage is sacrosanct and I have violated its sanctity. I am an adulteress and society would sooner metaphorically stone me than help me.

I cannot ask for support from the man I love, or even go to him, because he will not be a part of this rending.

I cannot have the two things I love more than my life, together in one place.

I cannot bear the slow death by suffocation that is life with my husband.

I cannot expect help from either my family or his.

I cannot bear to put my children through what I went through as a child, by staying with their father and trying to make the impossible work.

I cannot face the social censure that will follow when all this becomes known, as it inevitably will.

Worst of all is the knowledge that I must somehow choose between my children and the man I love and whatever I choose I am damned. I cannot choose. How can I choose?

With each 'cannot' I keen and rock but my wails are quiet now as if each one is a nail closing down my coffin lid, muffling life and hope.

Quiet at last and finally numb, I struggle to my feet. Life goes on even if I don't expect it to. A bath will be a return to existence, an excuse to stay out of that bedroom and a chance to try and gather up the remnants of my rapidly scattering wits. I mop the floor with an old towel and, returning to the bathroom, stuff it in the linen basket and flush the handful of hair down the toilet. As the taps run, I feel at my forehead where sticky grazes stand out in an accusatory cluster. I begin to frame the story of a fall on our long, dimly lit drive. I soak myself in lack of any feeling, and welcome the deadness that washes over me; the drips of the tap are my whole existence. I stay a long time in the warm, womb comfort of the dark bathroom, filling the bath over and over, relaxing into half sleep until the early hours of the morning.

In the half-light of a summer dawn, I hear the voice again.

'Follow your heart.'

I know now. An understanding filters in with the soft light. It is a voice I ignored all my life because I was taught to ignore it and subdue the way things made me feel. It really is the voice, not just of my heart, but of the whole human heart, heard clearly above all my despair and confusion. It is a voice of love — simple unconditional love; the voice of the person I would be if I was complete, whole and at one with the universe and myself, not this stunted, waspish, half-grown thing that I am. It is the wonderful voice I have heard before, beckoning me from my ball of light. I understand this for only a few moments in the diffuse light of morning but it is enough…

… A cough, and I mist faint breath into the oxygen mask once more. There. I had forgotten that moment and its feeling of utter completeness. That's what made me so sure.

In the end, it was my heart that chose the unthinkable because my mind could not. It's not a choice any mother thinks she will ever have to make; giving up her children. It goes against what being a mother is all about. It's an abomination, incongruous, a contradiction, a paradox. But sometimes, just sometimes, being a mother means that it's kinder and better for the children that way, whatever her own natural instincts may be.

A gentler, more forgiving self grasped, if only for an instant, that there was a greater love at stake here than parenthood, passion, romance, marriage or anything else I had met so far in life. In fact it was the framework within which all these must operate.

I chose to leave my children and my husband and live on my own.

# 12

## LOSING

The piper always, always has to be paid, my Gran said.
And I paid.

Granny Rose was right. In leaving that marriage I left a great part
of myself behind; my wonderful, beautiful children. They were the
best thing I'd ever done in my miserable life and up until that terrible day, their welfare had always come before mine. So, I became
that small bird; tumbling, tumbling, unable to land, unable to find
a hold on anything.

Even now, the memory slides cold steel into the warmth of this
July day and I shiver with the remembered frosts of a winter long
ago, diving deep down to a chill Christmas Day, white rimed and
foggy, which has lain its heavy mantle around my thin old shoulders.

Bony trees, dressed in a delicate skin of frost slowly fade into the
gloom outside as the remnants of daylight disappear. Not bothering
to switch on the lights, I am settling into the gloom, my face
flicker-lit by a muted TV's glow and the dirty yellow of a small gas

fire. An illustration in grey and ochre, I am flat, insubstantial and incomplete, contemplating the ashes of my former life. Everything has tumbled into chaos and uncertainty by what I've done, and insidious tendrils of grief and remorse creep across the ruins, tightening their grip on my weak resolve.

It's a couple of months since I came to lodge here in a single damp room at the back of this dark and narrow Victorian terrace. Soon after that night, I walked out on my husband in just about what I stood up in, leaving behind nine years of marriage, a house and two small children. I've taken only some photographs and baby keepsakes, together with a small brass and pewter snuffbox given to me by my mother-in-law. It has no value except that my little boy loves it and continually flips the lid chanting, '*Best powder*,' over and over to himself.

'Strange,' I think, flipping the lid open and closed now as I remember my leaving, 'strange the things you grab when you run for shelter.'

The house I'm in now belongs to a single lady lawyer who advertised for a lodger and companion; a bolt-hole just when I needed one. I help pay her mortgage and she gives me a roof and an impartial ear in my loneliness, for I just can't face my family and necessity has forced them, in turn, to abandon me for the moment. What else could they do? Grandparents have no rights of access and my husband's utterly crushed pride needs for *everyone* to point their fingers my way as the villain of the piece.

Anyway, I can't expect my old Gran to avoid the scolding tongues and ride the bus all the way from Scugton to Barton on the Aumber to see *me*. It's a painful, trundling hour's journey, the cold, draughty bus calling at every village and hamlet along the winding route. Then there's the long, uphill walk from the bus stop… no I couldn't have asked her to do it, she's too frail. I phoned her at Mrs Travers' from a call box once but was so ashamed by the woman's stiff, disapproving voice when I asked her to fetch my Gran that I never called again, although I did write to her, jabbering on about choices and children, falling in love and failure, all the while never giving her my address so she couldn't write back.

My dad doesn't drive. Not that he'd come here. His views on children and marriage are draconian. I have sinned and I must be punished. My friends don't want to know either, and my work colleagues whisper behind their hands in the staff room.

'She left her children, you know. How could any woman, let alone a teacher, do that?' Barton is a bleak enough place at this time of year to match my grief. It has the one advantage of being the place where I work so I don't need money for travel but it is also a small, parochial town where most of my friends and colleagues travel life's voyage — they 'tackle and trim their gear', their certainties and sails billowing with righteous indignation. At me.

A walk down the main street brings a stiff embarrassed hello, or if they see me coming, a swift sidestep across the road, their eyes fixed elsewhere in order to avoid me as I approach. I even saw one friend call to a non-existent companion as she turned the other way and ran. A visit to one of the cafés or public houses brings down a sudden silence akin to the 'baddie' standing in the saloon door. If it didn't add so much to my isolation, it would be funny. I want to shout to them, 'Hey, have I got two heads or something?' but in their eyes I probably have.

Instead I go down to the banks of the wide Aumber where the wind swirls the shallow waves into long sad whispers, and rain clouds snag the shores of the estuary. There I sigh out my loss to the autumn winds, the grey waters and the marsh grasses, returning through the network of fishing ponds so as not to be seen. Each time I tread those shores in utter misery, I do find some grain of comfort, as if I'm wrapped briefly in a warm blanket and, in that desolate place where curlews bubble their mournful call, there's always a quiet voice saying, 'I know.'

It was her! My eyelids flicker but stay closed. I never knew until now. Just as I never knew it was her weeping with me on that most awful of nights sixty-seven years ago. Is this where it's all going? Harriet's grief and my own loss are framed side by side in my mind, two identical silhouettes; two shadows of losing, two voices carried away by the estuary winds. Was she always there with me? Was I always connected to her in ways that I never recognised at the time? Is she the wind that is blowing this wrecked vessel home? I try to focus on Harriet once more but she is as elusive as ever and I'm drawn unhappily back among threads of memory that are barbed, sharp and cruelly bright.

From time to time I managed to be with my little family, I tried to have fun with them, tried to keep up some semblance of normality, all the while shrieking to myself, 'Why I am doing this?' Holding my children close, so close I could melt them into me, I murmur that I love them, how none of it is their fault and that this has to be better than all the falling out and shouting that has gone before but they get caught up in the novelty of a day out and are too young to take it in. They just want me back and cry when I don't go home with them. My husband is angry and cautious but tries to be affectionate, tries to woo me back.

It breaks my heart. He hasn't a chance.

The man I love is also caught up in the storm. We're both teachers and supposedly beyond reproach. Some outraged colleague — some 'Mrs Angry' who has wind of what has been going on — has made a complaint to the local Education Department and now he's left for a job in London where people don't know or just wouldn't care about our transgression. I'm fast coming to this point, too, but I have to get through Christmas. It has loomed darkly and heavily on my horizon for weeks and now it is here and I'm brooding on Christmases past while festive joy mocks away on the silent screen.

Staring into the glow of the gas fire I realise that, for the first time in my life, I am truly alone. My landlady has travelled home to her family and the house is empty, undecorated, cheerless, childless and still. The excited, chattering owners of new bicycles and roller skates and scooters passed my window this morning in a joyful procession that jabbed painful accusation my way, even though there was never going to be any question of seeing the children today. I've accepted it as my punishment, designed to let me know exactly what I'm missing.

In any event, the house has no telephone, I don't have money for presents or even for travelling back home to see my Gran. Most of my salary goes to my husband for the children, the rest goes on food and rent. Just surviving, dug into my bunker, I'm trying to weather this war of attrition, feeling its slow destruction grind at my soul. I am the unspeakable, the harridan, the whore, that thing most abhorrent and contradictory to nature — a mother who has abandoned her children.

Getting up to close the curtains and veil my misery from the outside world, I look around the tiny front room and take it all in, the whole sorry lot. An empty can of baked beans sits on the floor by a gas fire that is about to go out as I've no money to feed the meter. I couldn't even be bothered to put the beans on a plate and spooned them cold from the tin, following them with half a packet of Rich Tea biscuits, the paper from which I've twisted into a cracker shape, with the remaining biscuits in the middle. My one festive luxury is a bottle of sherry; I've always had my father's taste for alcohol and, though I rarely drink, oblivion is what I need now and I'm halfway down it, feeling the worse for wear and utterly, utterly humiliated.

Still, I deserve it all; every bit of it. I should really go to bed and wake up tomorrow when Christmas Day has passed but I feel sick and the room is making crazy half turns around my head. With a sputter and a pop, the gas fire gives up on me too, so I blow my nose and sit back down in the dark, silently accepting my lot…

… 'Don't cry, Gran, it'll be all right.'

'Can't you give her a sedative or something?'

Those frightful days have flashed through my consciousness in, perhaps, seconds but the memory has left my sheets soaked and my face wet with tears. Just like Harriet, I was carved out by loss, but it was a loss of my own choosing and I never realised just how deep that hole would be and how much love it would take to fill it. That came later.

A nurse is called but I shake my head vigorously on the pillow. I know it will be much easier for them if I don't appear to be suffering but there is little enough time left to sort my thoughts; I don't want to waste it in drugged sleep and slip away, conveniently peaceful. I want to see it all, feel it all, tidy it up, finish it all. There is a fussing and scraping of chairs as someone suggests my family takes a breath of fresh air while they make me more comfortable. More scraping of chairs and murmurs of subdued assent and they leave me in peace.

My sheets are deftly and gently changed, I'm wiped clean and a fresh pad eased under my old body. The trauma of memory seems to have echoed itself in my bodily functions, or perhaps it's just the progress of letting go; the dying body releasing hold of its processes one by one.

'I think you still want to stay with it, don't you?'

A tired but kindly face swims into view and cool fingers push back my sweat soaked hair. It disturbs that scent of old woman that I hate so much but I'm past caring now. I nod my head and do my best, with thin, fumbling fingers, to squeeze the professional hand smoothing my sheets.

'Ok, but you can change your mind at any time, you know. Anyway, to give you a bit of peace I'll tell them they can go off for a couple of hours while you have a sleep. Buzz if you need us or if you want anyone to sit with you.'

The call button is placed in my hand. Peace.

Nurses who have seen death so many times know its processes, so I am grateful for this breathing space. There is so much to be settled, especially around Harriet, whose memories fit so feather-sleek among my own. Our thoughts and feelings are the roots of two trees that are now entwined and are no longer separable.

I would rather be with her now but I cannot summon her presence and so I close my eyes and let events unfold, uneasily following this particular tangled strand to its completion…

… 'It's the worst day of my life,' I complain to my bottle of sherry, adding in a moan of self-pity, 'and nobody cares'.

Part of me sits outside of myself, dimly aware that I am, even now, at thirty years old, that hard shelled, insecure little girl who has never unfolded enough to truly empathise with anybody, but the greater part of me can still only think of my pain right now, and the flicker of the TV screen is giving me a really bad headache. I petulantly slam the 'off' switch with my foot and sit in total darkness, with loss, loneliness and misery as my leering companions.

And yet, against all the odds that Christmas afternoon, there's a knock at the door that changes everything. I open its chipped facade on to winter darkness but it is as if sunshine has just streamed into the hall. I step back, blinking and scuffing my face where I know my mascara has run grotesquely, overcome with shame at my predicament but glad that someone, at least someone, has forgiven me enough to come here today. It is Granny Rose, hopping up and down on the frost sparkling doorstep, arms wide and face beaming.

'Well, Mia Pia, here you are at last! Peg here has driven me over from Scugton and we have knocked on nearly every bloody door in this street trying to find you! No one at home knew your exact address. What a time, the roads are really bad and the folks round here even worse!'

Trailing Christmas cheer in her shopping trolley, she delivers one of her tickly kisses, and puffs and breezes in as though nothing is amiss. Merriment and joyfulness flow from her as she deposits her burdens one by one on the kitchen table, rubbing her hands. Her presence seems to light up the whole house.

'Where's the party, then?' she quips, adjusting her wig to a rakish angle that says quite clearly that neither she nor aunt Peg are here to condemn. Speechless, I hug them both before they begin bustling about, melting my bleak Christmas with care and concern.

'You didn't think we'd forgotten you?' chides aunt Peg, planting another kiss on my tear-streaked cheek and proffering her hanky. It smells of the wonderful holidays I spent with her as a child, safely away from the battlefield of home.

'There's no gas, Peg,' Gran pronounces, fiddling with the knobs on the oven. Purses are tipped out, the necessary change is found and the meter fed.

'It's all right. Really it is. I've eaten.'

'Humph!' snorts my Gran, picking up the empty can of beans as she hobbles around, switching lights on and plonking a ridiculously tiny artificial Christmas tree on the kitchen table.

'Oh, I see you brought Arty Fischl.' I can't help a grin at the name we bestowed on the pathetic plastic green sprout that comes out annually. We love it dearly and laugh at its inadequacy every year but it is Christmas incarnate and spreads festive cheer even now in this cold, gloomy house.

'I've brought you some food — and some common sense my girl, as well.'

Small talk flows as a dinner, sandwiched between two plates, is pushed into the oven, three glasses are found for the remains of the sherry and some leftover Christmas pudding is set to steam on the cooker top. My aunt is wreathed in encouraging smiles and Gran keeps patting my arm but I get the feeling they're just filling the silence with chat and waiting for me to start talking; really talking.

'Gran… I can't…'

The words are lost in tears and then I'm folded up between these two wise women who have stood by the mores of society all their grown lives but who have now decided, from the depth of their hearts, to stand by me instead. They hug me and pat me, and my nostrils fill with the remembered scent of comfort found squeezed tightly in those arms when no other could be found. Their love hangs tangibly, expectantly, in the air as the words fail to come once more.

'You're not going back, then?'

I shake my head. They visibly relax and exchange meaningful glances, turning to dish up my Christmas meal. The oven door is left open to take the chill from the air as I eat the carefully plated leftovers; and I make a good show of it, the roast potatoes, the turkey and the sprouts mopping up the excess alcohol so that my head gradually clears as I chew.

'I love you both so much!' The words spill out between mouthfuls of turkey, and they just nod. They know. Two indulgent smiles and a contemplative silence follow while I scrape the last of the Christmas pudding from my dish, savouring, with undue relish, my Gran's brandy sauce, a taste of childhood.

'There's no mending it?' My aunt queries, peering over her sherry glass in a final check before she reconciles things in her head.

'No. It's like I said in my letter. We're far too different. I just can't do it any more. Even if I hadn't met someone else it would all have come to grief pretty soon.'

I think how it had been coming to grief for several years and that even having children still didn't forge the bond between us that I'd hoped it would. In fact it drove us further apart as I immersed myself totally in bringing them up. How naïve I was! How selfish.

'No question of having the children?' Granny Rose grasps both my hands in hers, peering into my face for final confirmation as I put my spoon down. My face goes into in my hands and my shoulders shake once more. 'Look at this dump! This is good for what I earn. I've done the sums. I earn too much to qualify for Family Income Supplement. All I would get is Family Allowance, so that doesn't give me the money for any place where they could come with me and have what they have now, and anyway, their dad won't entertain it because of…'

'Him.' Aunt Peg finishes the sentence for me, quietly. Another silence. Mention of the third party, in their eyes the catalyst of all this trouble, hangs like a tangible shadow in the room.

'Are you going to live with this man?'

'No.' The simple word hides whole boxes of used tissues, countless sleepless nights, bitten nails, half-written notes screwed up and thrown away, figures added again and again, and hours and hours of agonising among the marshes and reeds of the riverbank, over what to do next.

'What will you do, then?' I push my tangled hair back from my face, take a deep breath and tell them the decision I've come to.

'I'm leaving here for a better job, that's a start. I've managed to get a promotion down in London, near him, and I can go to university part time there as well. There's no chance of getting on in this area.' I tell them about the busybody, to underline matters.

'Do you know,' my Gran pipes up indignantly, 'there was this one door we knocked on tonight and the bloke shouts back to his missus, "ere! Gladys! There's two folks 'ere looking for that school-teacher woman who left her kids.' Cheek of it! The woman comes out, ugly as a box of frogs, looks us up and down and just shuts the door in our faces.'

'Oh Gran, I'm so sorry, but it's no more than I deserve.'

'Don't you go putting yourself down; there's plenty as will do it for you for free. You need to get a better sense of who you are and what you're worth,' Gran wags her finger at me, almost knocking over her glass of sherry.

'Gran, right now I'm not worth anything. I've done the unforgivable and, what's worse, I'd do it again, I love him so much. It's like I said when I wrote to you, I've never felt anything like this before. I just have to go and be near him.'

A sharp intake of breath and two strangely triumphant smiles.

'That is just what I've been waiting to hear, Mia Pia!' Gran smiles tersely but triumphantly, licking the spilled sherry from her fingers and dabbing at the table with her hanky. 'Now I know you're on the right path. All these bloody years it's taken! At last!'

'What?'

Aunt Peg raises her eyebrows knowingly at me as I protest, and inclines her head towards Gran. Mother and daughter, they're of one mind and I'm about to get a piece of it.

'Don't think we didn't know right from the beginning this marriage wasn't going to work but you have to go ahead sometimes and make your own mistakes. It's how it is. Sometimes folks just make the best of it but you haven't had a proper life yet, so you were never going to do that. It's a crying shame you waited until you had children, though, to decide you couldn't do it.'

Gran's finger is still wagging and, staring at the table, I've nothing to say until I manage a hesitant, 'What do you mean 'a proper life'?'

'Well, apart from those bairns, you've never really loved anything much until now. People wrapped up in themselves and their problems make very small parcels and you are one tiny person. Now don't start on!' She raises a hand to silence me. 'You'll see what it's all about; it'll change you beyond recognition, loving will. You need a bloody good dose of it, I'd say!'

Aunt Peg nods in agreement and then, as my mouth opens again, she utters an uncharacteristically sharp, 'Listen to what she's saying!'

I shuffle uncomfortably on my chair like a child, wipe my finger around my pudding plate and draw doodles in the trails of salt on the table. I hadn't expected this. Gran sits back and folds her arms in silence until she's quite sure she has my attention. I can't help smiling inwardly for a moment, despite my embarrassment and confusion, as I copy this trick often when I'm teaching.

'You have to survive and make the best job of it you can,' she continues finally, her chin sticking out for emphasis.

'Make your mistakes work for you. It's no good staying here, like you say. I'm so glad about your new job; bloody waste of brains it is in this place and married to him, good man though he may be.' She sets her wig straight to show how serious she is.

'So go to London and get a place where you can start again and have the children when you're able. Be with your new man whenever you can. Just love him; hold on to him if he's the one, and I'm sure he is from what you've said. Loving won't half sort you out and prune your excesses, my girl. My, how you'll grow! You always wanted that career to take off, so now is as good a time as any to embark on it. Who knows, you could even be a headmistress one day — now wouldn't that be something?' She slaps the table for emphasis, nearly spilling her sherry again and beaming encouragingly after her lecture.

There's an emotionally charged pause as we sit around the table, we three women. Three generations and one heart again. Women like them have paved the road for women like me, and I'm grateful beyond words. They're launching me this night into a world they can only guess at, knowing only that before anything is going to work for me at all, I need to move on, start again and live a life that fits me better. But mention of the children almost tips me off the tightrope of control where I now wobble.

'H... how are they?' I venture. 'Have you seen them?'

'Angry is how they are,' my Gran spits, taking the hanky from up her sleeve again and blowing her nose for emphasis. Her mood has darkened abruptly. 'Somebody's telling them that you don't love them and they're all mixed up. I've tried to put them right on that one, but you know how it is. I never thought to see my own great grandchildren taken up and used in such a way! It's wicked.'

'Now mam, you said you wouldn't,' aunt Peg mutters, clearing the table.

Gran does the washing up and is up to her elbows in suds in the sink. I can see her thin old arms twitching in and out like they do when she's really indignant. Aunt Peg is slowly and deliberately drying a plate over and over again, rubbing at the pattern as if it needs removing. The moment is thick with anger and accusation. What can I say? I've decided that I will never, ever, speak out against my husband or his family to anyone, and especially not to the children. None of this is his fault, anyway. What he does and says is the indirect result of my own actions, so I simply murmur, 'Thanks for telling me'…

… I surface from the agony of this memory to hear that my daughter has arrived; she's talking to a nurse. I feel an unhappy lurch. I left her before and I will have to leave her again. She's seventy-seven now, almost an old woman herself, not a child, but I've always felt so protective towards her. She felt it harder than my son, I think, being that little bit older and wiser in the ways of the world.

'She may well wait until she's alone you know,' comes the soothing reply. 'They often do. It's a journey you have to make on your own. I should go and get some air. We've got your mobile number if anything changes.'

Don't they know? I'm changing all the time now. A chrysalis turning in my white cocoon, I'm being transformed, made complete, brought to an understanding as these memories flow together in a painful stream. I grimace and bubble once more. If I thought that Christmas Day was my nadir, I was wrong. There was more to come. And more and more.

Harriet, where are you?

# 13

## PARTINGS

Abruptly, I see the face of my little boy at the railway station, sleepy from the London train, as I hand him back to his father. The baby smell of his hair is in my nose and his four-year-old food-encrusted cheek brushes mine. I feel the splash of his tears as he realises what's happening and his fists grab at the air. I squeeze the crabbed fist of my daughter, who doesn't even say goodbye because she can't. She pulls her fingers roughly from mine as she gets in the car, staring resolutely ahead, while my little boy cries into his father's shoulder.

And then they're gone for another few weeks and I'm standing here alone on the platform of the station wondering at a high insistent noise that fills my head, blotting out all thought. I turn to find somewhere, anywhere private, because I realise that the noise is coming from me.

I am silently screaming, screaming. I am howling once more with that animal anguish which engulfs and overwhelms me. I beat my forehead against the cold tiles of the tiny, rank station toilet, my hands tearing my hair as I collapse, my mouth stuffed with a muffling tissue, on to the filthy bowl. Sitting there, I think that I am feeling all the anguish of all the mothers who have ever lost children.

I was kidding myself. Others have suffered more, even if it felt bad to me then. It was by far my most painful memory, though. The one thing in all my life that still breaks my heart here on my deathbed. How long did I sit there like that, covering my mouth to still the howls? That's gone, thankfully, scattered somewhere along a long, long road and forgotten. I know somebody was fetched eventually to ask if I was ok and a glass of water was pushed under the door. The rest has vanished, but my little boy's tears, the sound of his cry and the grasping hands that could not find me, has not…

… I motion for someone to moisten my lips and a little pink sponge on a stick is brought close to my face. The oxygen mask is lifted and cool moisture is dabbed onto my eager tongue. Memories tumble about wildly and I can't control them as I careen headlong down a shadowy, interminable corridor of such partings, ricocheting from one to the next. I find them strewn haphazardly along the next seven years of my life; small doorways of reprieve that open briefly, only to slam again in my face. Like the sailors whose old scars and sword wounds were opened up by scurvy, death is unseaming sorrows that I healed many years ago.

I shake my head at the next proffered sponge…

… That first year in London! I don't know what I expected — a little peace perhaps? I sort through a bundled rag heap of thoughts to try and find some order to it all.

'Harriet, where are you?' I whisper her name but she doesn't come. Just this miserable heap of memories that I can't stop now they've started.

By day, thankfully, I had no time to remember I was a mother. I was on the steep learning curve of teaching in my first multi-ethnic community at a time when this country was waking up to the fact that it was no longer white, Anglo Saxon and Protestant. Every day was a different, though satisfying, educational challenge and it took my mind off my loss. I learned a lot of Yiddish, found out exactly what you had to do to get a six foot, stubborn Nigerian girl to knuckle down to work and why Bangladeshi girls needed to wear a full body leotard for swimming. I learned that those angel faced children wearing their long hair up in a bun were boys, Sikh boys who on no account could be asked to remove their bracelets for PE and that Wesak was a time for giving. I drank down the dish of sour milk brought to my desk without batting an eyelid and put the flower garland around my neck, wearing it all day.

What a narrow life I'd led up to this point! How naïve I was in the ways of the world, within my slag-stained northern upbringing. I felt humbled by these remarkable children who spoke one language at home, another in the classroom and yet another out in the playground.

But most nights I took the grimy Central Line from Leyton, returning alone to a single, rented room. I had an alcoholic footballer for a neighbour and a landlord who groped my backside every time I paid my rent, requiring weekly athletic avoidance tactics; and empty bottles smashed against walls punctuated my sleep each night.

And, just to underline the fact that, no matter how far away

I might flee, I was still a pariah, 'Mrs Angry' from up north, the outraged woman whose complaint had precipitated this move, still dogged my life. With mystifying and vituperous persistence she'd carefully traced my whereabouts and laced her self-righteousness with regular silent phone calls. *Schadenfreude* — does she gain pleasure from this? Rough justice? Reporting back? Who knows what her objective was? The calls continued until I traced her number and returned the compliment. That was very satisfying, as was the time I deliberately stood with my back to my landlord, and then, tottering as his hands made contact, 'accidentally' ground my stiletto heel into his foot.

Access to my children from this shaky base was impossible. If I wanted that, I had to persuade the love of my life to move out of his shabby, cramped fifth floor council flat temporarily, while I moved in for a few days with the children. He wasn't to be allowed near them if I wanted access. He was filth. So the three of us lived out of suitcases and took the stairs to avoid the large Rasta who found it absolutely necessary to pee in the lift every morning. Visits were necessarily infrequent and restricted to school holidays. Sometimes, though, desperation compelled me to take the day off work and drive the 180 miles north, arriving just at lunchtime outside their school playground. I sat in a borrowed car for an hour, hiding myself and slaking my thirst on little glimpses before I turned back for London to arrive home at the end of the day as though nothing had happened.

My love and I both made it through that year in tatters, exhausted by the initial effort of learning to teach all over again in the educational war zone that was the East End and emotionally wrecked by the sheer bile directed at our fleeing backs.

'I heard you were living in London with your lover,' quipped an acquaintance I decided to look up, just for the chance to talk to somebody — anybody — about my situation. She made it sound so glamorous.

Yes, it was at the end of 1978, a year whose serrated edge I can still feel against my old flesh, that we bought a house and first lived together as a couple, sharing the place with the stream of lodgers that we needed to take in to make ends meet. But it wasn't good enough. He still had to disappear for the duration of each access visit until, three years later, I finally filed for divorce and married the man for whom I had willingly remade my entire life. And I loved him still through all of it; deeply, truly and to distraction, just like my Gran said I would.

Yet they were still hard times. The splashback of my leaving still tainted us both. We might have been respectable in go-ahead London but, back up north where the map still said, *Here, There Be Dragons*, we would always be the enemy, the disgraced objects of suspicion, confounding belief systems and established views. I had no excuses to offer anyone and anyway, what was the point? Everyone from my past life had gradually sidled away. Finally, the few friends I had were new ones and they hadn't a clue about my past. It was easier that way. It's not something you bring up in casual conversation, that you left your children.

There was never any question of custody and it never got any easier. All I could do was continue to acknowledge it all as a continued and well-deserved sentence. While my solicitor shook his head in despair, I let my ex keep the house, everything. I paid off hire purchase bills he didn't even know we had, as he tried to keep his head above water financially. I certainly wasn't about to make matters worse for my children in a courtroom battle over maintenance and access. Instead, I told them as often as I could that I loved them but I'm not sure they understood back then. But of course they didn't. How could they? I break out into a cold sweat at the thought of the disruption I brought to their little lives…

… A welcome breeze stirs the thick atmosphere of the early afternoon ward, wafting warm air along the beds and stirring the curtains. There's some sort of orderly speaking to my daughter, who's hovering about still, but I can only make out the deep burgundy of his uniform. Things are progressing; I can't seem to see much else but shapes and colours now…

… That burgundy, yes, the exact colour of the velvet suit I was married in, posing for wedding photographs in the grounds of Barkingside Register Office. I remember I made my daughter a fashionable leisure suit out of all the trimmings that were left over when I'd finished sewing. She looked lovely and, stupidly, I fancied that I'd created a mother and daughter bit of togetherness when we wore our matching outfits.

I'm standing, sun warmed and happy for a moment, in the garden of our house in London. I remember my conceit now. My long red curls are swept in a sideways ponytail and my daughter has plaited her fine blonde hair so that it is pulled away from her delicate pale face. Mother and daughter dolled up to the nines. It's going to be perfect. It's a beautiful, honey-warm August evening and we're posing for a photo in our matching velvet outfits, beautifully dressed and ready to go to the ballet, every little girl's dream.

I feel like a real mum, holding her hand, grinning and waving at the camera, but she can't be persuaded to smile, despite my new husband's silly jokes.

'Knock, Knock!'

'Who's there?'

'Eva.'

'Eva brick at the window.'

Nothing, not even a smile. So we give up and settle for a picture of her scowling, hand on hip, into the camera lens.

Disappointed, he finally ambles off down the garden to inspect his vegetables. He's growing Jerusalem artichokes, the only thing that can be persuaded to thrive on ground that was once landfill. Laughing again, I call rudely after him, because this unfortunate vegetable gives us both terrible wind. It's a perfect moment and I'm utterly blind and deaf to the unintended consequences of my happiness.

Bending down to tell my little girl about the artichokes, I take a sudden step backwards. She has begun to scream angrily into my face, quite unprovoked and so ferociously that her eyes bolt and roll. The scream goes on and on and turns into an angry roar that produces white dots of spittle at the corners of her mouth. Finally she just stands there, shaking, and all I can do is to try and hold her but she won't be held, her slight form all angles and corners, backing rigidly away from my arms…

… That scream is still ringing in my ears as I try to adjust my oxygen mask. The tape is cutting in behind my ears, adding one more discomfort to my dying. I remember how she refused to enjoy the ballet, refused to talk to me, and refused each one of my attempts to be her mum that holiday. What a wake-up call that was.

But I did what I could to make their lives easier, buying clothes and little treats whenever there was money enough. Eventually it got to the point where they would never take them home because it caused too much ill-feeling. I understood. It looked as though I was the good fairy, swanning in to create all the nice times, while my ex got the rest. So I packed Christmas and birthday presents, cards and holiday souvenirs discreetly in their bags for them to take back for dad, grandma and grandpa. I spent just the right amount and wrapped them badly enough to make it look as though they'd been bought by a child and hoped the two of them didn't let on where they'd come from.

Bolting wildly now, my thoughts panic and flee back to the other times the children had been allowed to come and stay with us as a couple, in this place where we'd eventually won our anonymity, the vast sprawl of London. It was a warm, comforting anthill where no one cared about the rules we'd broken as they rushed about their tasks. But there was always that long miserable drive back north after each visit, when tempers had crabbed and frayed by the mile and they couldn't kiss me goodbye when we got there in case anyone saw. And it was always the same — weekends and school holidays strewn with tearful partings.

I didn't let you down, though, Granny Rose. I filled the long, aching gaps in between with a part-time degree, a Masters degree and more promotion. For both my new husband and myself, two rocketing careers propelled us into school after school and absorbed our time, mopping up the pain of those partings. He was learning to be a father and he hurt, too...

… My heels ache so.

I don't seem able to move my legs on the mattress enough to keep my circulation going and the rippling hasn't helped much. They were as black and shiny as damsons when I caught a glimpse of them the other day, another sign of this old body shutting down. Still, I won't be walking anywhere anymore…

… I walked a thousand miles pacing the floor, though, trying to understand the reasoning behind the severity of my sentence. Why was there never a Christmas together, never so much as a card, never a lost tooth to keep, never a painting to pin up in the kitchen, never a birthday party, never a school concert or school report, never any indication of childhood milestones passed? The answer was always the same. You don't deserve any of these things.

All I could do in the end was to come not to expect them any more. They were the things I gave up in exchange for having my soul mate and a career. In the days when women certainly couldn't 'have it all', I reconciled myself to the fact that I had more than most and that what I did have was so selfishly come by, I had no right to expect anything else.

The years slid by and my first husband remarried, too. I was so glad for him at the time, knowing he needed mending; he needed the balm of someone who would love him as unconditionally as I came to love. I cherished the hope that it would help him change and soften but he was too badly hurt. When he lost me, he lost his pride and he had to learn to cope as a single father at a time when northern men, especially those from Scugton, had only just become brave enough to push prams, let alone bring up a family. He once asked me, when I was pleading to see the children, why he should comply. 'What have you given me but misery?'

'I've given you half my life,' I replied. I met him at fifteen and left him fifteen years later when I'd given him half and more of everything that I was. I'd given him our time together, the life we shared, the places we'd gone, the things we'd done, the children I'd borne.

But it wasn't enough. I was a thorn, a bad memory, an uncomfortable presence. I wasn't required.

'Well, when can I see them? When can they come and stay?'

Shuddering even now at the awfulness of it, I remember his reply, and the words that stung like biblical stones. 'It would be best for the children if you don't see them for a good while and that's what they both want, too. You're causing too much chaos in their lives.' Then I screamed and paced the floor a few thousand miles more.

'They don't deserve the fallout of your hate; if you could stop hating, there wouldn't *be* all this chaos!' I bellowed at walls that bore the marks of my fingernails.

But he couldn't and didn't stop hating and, in the end, I could see only one way to provide a fallout shelter for my babies.

Yes, what we can eventually bear to contemplate becomes possible, what is possible we can do; and so, to give them all a chance at some sort of stability, I remember how I choked back my selfish need and finally consented to vanish from the picture.

Hearts can do no more.

# 14

## FINDING HARRIET

I feel so chill and weary now, still here, clinging on by only the will to know what Harriet is saying to me. But those five words have chilled me even more. There is some faint echo about them I catch that has a real significance to today and my dying, yet my old and muttering brain can't quite spell it out.

I never wanted to be this old. I wanted to go long before this; long before I became so fragile and helpless. I didn't want to relive those awful times, either, but I can see a bit of the purpose of it now. It's not simply Harriet reminding me just how closely my life followed hers, I know there's more she's going to tell me and it must have to do with all the things I felt when I left my children. Perhaps there's a final resolution to face. I feel so slight, so insubstantial; I hope she tells me soon.

'Being *really* old is a bit of a bitch,' Granny Rose used to say, 'but being not too old is ok; quite good in fact!' On her eighty-third birthday, when she'd decided that she'd had quite enough of being bedridden, in constant pain and totally dependant upon others, she died. She said she would go on her birthday and she did. Eighty-three is no age these days but at that time, like most of her peers, she had seen through two World Wars, untold poverty and hard work and she was worn out.

Well, old age *was* quite good! I loved being released from the passions, torments and urgencies that drive you when you're younger. A much older friend had once told me that if could get through the inevitable and frustrating decline in capabilities, I'd find the best was yet to come, and it was certainly true in many ways. I was freed up to do what it was I most wanted to do. Unfettered, unembarrassed, articulate and with the wisdom of years, the world was laid open and fresh in a way that it never was when I danced almost entirely to the tune of lust, the need to breed, motherhood, a career, fame, fortune, fashion and all the rest. It's such a strident orchestra that fills your head when you're younger. That's not to say I gave up on *any* of these, not at all. It's just that they seemed to assume their proper proportions. What's more, I experienced an acuteness of simple satisfactions and joys that I'd never felt since I was a child.

And in the autumn years with John, our needs were small and we had each other, which was all we needed. In the clear light of spring and autumn, things look so much simpler than in the heat and shimmer of your summer years. But the winter, ah the winter years; you don't stray far from your chair by the fire and memories are your constant companion. I think if I hadn't found Harriet long before then, that guilt and the dreadful memories that she laid out before me would have finished me well before my time.

Finding Harriet. Yes, that changed so much.

'But first I found myself and then I found my children,' I think as I drift willingly along the vivid, pulsating highway of the many things I have found, glad to be feeling a memory that is more substantial than I am…

… The rain hammers insistently and gravel-hard on the roof, and against the windows which my breath mists, obscuring the iron-grey day outside. I'm staring, unseeing, from the warmth of a solitary car parked behind wild sea dunes; a piece of scoured driftwood, washed up, totally spent and worn clean. I have walked the shore for the last half hour or so, unburdening my soul to the earth, sea and sky, because it's four months since I've seen my children and each day the finality of loss stamps itself hoof hard and heavy, upon my shoulders. It's the heaviest, most bruising thing that I have carried so far.

I remember how I used to tell the pupils I taught the tale of a princess whose children were enchanted away. If ever she spoke of her grief she would never see them again and so, each night, she would creep out of the palace and dig a hole in the gardens. Into this hole she poured all her sorrows, screaming and howling into its depths. Then she carefully covered it once more, taking care to dig in a different place every night.

On the seaward side of the dunes, the waves foam over the traces of the many deep holes that sand dapple the length of these dreary-skied, desolate North Sea beaches. Some are the remnants of bait diggers' excavations, where fishermen with furiously flashing spades hope to lay bare a ragworm or two. Others are made by me. If you dig down just a little into the depressions in the wet shifting sands, a faint cry will rise up and fragment on the spray, its echoes coiling and drifting their way across dune and field to find my children. Like the princess of my stories, I bury the loss deeply so that no one will hear or know.

Stuffing a final tissue into the ashtray and wiping the window with my sleeve, I peer at the dunes and tell myself that it has to be buried now, down on the forgiving shore, hidden far down, where no one can see or hear. I can't burden anyone else with it. My father doesn't want to know, Granny Rose is dead and my new husband just doesn't do weepy women and this was my choice, after all. As for friends, well, how do you begin to say I ran after my lover leaving my four-year-old son and six-year-old daughter with their father? Those are the facts, regardless of the pain, the story or the justification behind them.

So, returning wet-kneed and temporarily anaesthetised by these solitary excursions I tell myself that I was, after all, the cause of all these problems and no one else but me should feel responsible for this new sorrow. I should bear it alone. And I do…

… Surfacing for a while but not really fully in the ward or the warmth of the day, I shiver and remember how that hurt; the sheer aloneness of it, as well as the loss. But the tides wash everything away, scouring the soul and the heart as clean as the North Sea sand. Just like Harriet whitening her misdemeanors with her washing, my slate was wiped a little cleaner each time I made that trip.

For nearly a year, when the loss got too acute, I made those journeys down to the shore, laying my head upon the shoulders of the sea and the sky, burying my cries in the bosom of the sand and returning each time to immerse my heart in my job and my marriage.

Turning these leaden thoughts round and round, I try to find some point on my pillows that doesn't make my thin, old shoulders burn and ache with the simple effort of lying here. My chest is so sore now and my breaths come fast and rapid as my heart tries to do its job against impossible odds.

Yes, it was a bad time, a time of bereavement, made worse by the fact that, to all outward appearances I was living it up, having a man, a career and a good time in London. My first husband had often said so; my father pointed it out rather regularly and, the few folks from up north who still had no choice but to associate with me occasionally, let the thought drop in peevish asides.

'Well you're ok at least. You should think about the children.'

'Thanks. That's all I ever do.'

Whichever way you look at it, though, my job and my marriage were my salvation, bringing me to my senses. No matter how badly your heart is broken, the world doesn't stop for your grief, so I had to get on with living and as I did, I changed. You can't love someone with all your heart and soul and still keep putting your own needs first. It doesn't work that way. And you can't be responsible for so many ethnically diverse young lives and not begin to empathise with their problems too. So the cold hollow inside began to thaw and fill with warmth, and it wasn't just the passage of time. No, this was something different. This healing was to be found in my inner self, uncrumpling from the hard carapace where I'd hidden it all those years. I was learning how to love, just like my Gran said I would.

'Empty hearts have room for nothing. In a full heart there's always room for more,' she used to say to me.

Giving with no thought of return, seeking compromise instead of victory, accepting hurts and turning them to good, biting my tongue and saying something quiet when a barbed criticism reared up — these gentled and smoothed my spiky corners and filled my heart. Learning that it was better to be kind than right, always forgiving and forgiving and forgiving again, and especially never saying a word of harm about my ex, were very good lessons in restraint that expanded the cramped space within with every effort I made.

But the world is how you see it, and the cracked glass of hurt and humiliation makes people say the most appalling things. It wasn't my first husband's fault and he probably never knew, lashing out in pain, that his words were almost as great a trial as the loss, opening up profound wounds that would take half a lifetime to heal. But then again, I know that *his* wounds never did. They festered and soured and scabbed over the years but they never healed. Listening to it all, I forgave and never said a word. I never said a word when my ex told everyone that I'd suggested he send the children to an orphanage. I never said a word when I found out they'd been told I had abandoned them for good. I never said a word when the love of my life was reviled and made out to be someone evil. I just kept quiet, kept away, kept sending money and kept praying my babies wouldn't forget me.

And the strange thing was, that in doing all this I actually began to like who I was becoming. The strident, insecure me that had clumped, heavy-footed, through my earlier life was slowly brought into check. Lord, what a stroppy little madam I was before! Afraid of everybody, trusting few and disguising it all with a hard brassy shell, I bit the heads off anyone who came too close. It seems such a stunningly simple thing but I suppose that, first of all, you have to learn to like yourself. It's absolutely necessary before you can like, accept and tolerate others.

When I began to feel at home in my own skin I grew to love and understand everyone else a bit more, travelling a long and painful road from humiliation to humility until, bit by bit, losing became finding. I grew into my soul a little better, just as Gran said I would.

Yes, it was a time of finding. At peace again now and a little warmer, my memory settles on a bright point, a day that brought a small measure of tranquillity at last. It gleams like a lighthouse, drawing me exhausted from the storm of those days towards calmer waters.

And here I am at last on a warm May day that is drowsy with the promise of things to come. I'm thirty-six years old and I feel as though I've survived a devastating, dark journey through a twisting tunnel of sorrow and emerged miraculously transformed at the other side. In fact, it's been a perfectly circular voyage. In the very place where I once thought nothing could grow, least of all me, here I sit in charge of helping others to bloom and flourish. I hardly recognise the person I used to be and I wonder if anyone else will, for I have indeed come full circle and I'm back in my home town of Scugton once more.

I'm in my very own office; a headteacher in the first school that I can call my own. If you could see me now, Granny Rose!

There's a jubilant shout, a leap and a punch into the air as Benjamin Morley is the first one to make it out into the playground. Strange how I can still remember his name over sixty years later. I wonder if he's still as exuberant? More children follow, their babbling voices borne in on the gentle breeze filtering through my open window. A swallow twitters under overhanging eaves and the air is heavy with laurel and hawthorn. I am totally tranquil, all dilemmas pushed far, far away.

I've at last found that room with quiet whitewashed walls. It is real. Slant sunshine does indeed fall onto warm boards this bright spring day, emptying my mind ready for the challenge of my new job. I have so much love that I want to share with these steelworkers' kids; it's a second chance, a second shot at my life in the place where it began. I want to make a real and positive difference to these young lives, where I failed so badly with my own little ones. Life has been very kind in giving me another go at having children, albeit there are nearly two hundred of them to care for. This moment is a hiatus of pure peace and contentment, a pause for breath before another part of my life begins, setting me off on a fresh voyage where, once more, all things are possible.

Looking around my first office, I'm ridiculously amazed and humbled to be here. On the wall, next to a picture of my Gran, wig slightly askew, are my new certificates and hard won qualifications, framed and hung with such pride. And on my desk, gleaming softly against the dark mahogany, are a shiny new fountain pen from my father, a china handled letter opener from aunt Peg and a photograph of my new husband, leaning long-legged and smiling against a sunny Mediterranean wall. They were all so proud of me when I got this job and, at long last, I am proud of myself.

Running my hand over the polished wood on which these objects sit, I pause. There is just that momentary sad little niggle that there are no pictures of my children arranged there; too painful to see, too difficult to explain to anyone right now that they are sealed away in my heart, someone else's babies, no longer mine. I know how I remember them but I don't even know how much they've grown. There has been no communication, no contact, no photos, no phone calls, no updates, no acknowledgement of my continued financial support, nothing. No matter. I've learned to live with it and now I can go some small way to making amends in this world. I breathe out the pain in a great long sigh, turning it to hope at the start of this great new adventure.

A whistle blows and the babble gradually subsides as the school settles down for the rest of the afternoon. In the muffling, drowsy warmth a telephone rings, seemingly a long way away but only in the adjacent office. Low voices take on a perplexed note. A door opens and closes. Further discussion and then my own door opens and the deputy head stands in the threshold, filling the door frame with his lanky, cadaverous form, running a nervous hand through wavy black hair while he holds an apologetic cup of tea in the other.

'I'm very sorry. There's someone on the telephone who claims to be the headmistress's daughter,' he finally blurts out, stepping forward to put the cup of tea on the corner of my desk. My heart doesn't lurch or leap or stop or falter; it opens like a flower, a speed frame blossoming of a water lily, spread star-like in instant joy.

'Thank you for the tea. Would you put the call through, please?' The words are barely more than a whisper. There is no room in my chest for air. He backs out and closes the door. He's seen my face.

She's fourteen and lost, adrift on an ocean of hormones, hostility, hate and confusion. It's been such a while since I heard her voice, she sounds older but at the same time just like the tiny little girl

I knew before I left.

'Can I come and live with you, mum?'

There's no preamble, just the bare request but the voice carries so much. It tells, without speaking, that she's been informed this will be a waste of time; that I won't want her, that I'm far too busy with my career to bother with her, that we're strangers now; that I never loved her, that if she goes ahead she'll have to change schools and lose all her friends, but most of all it tells me that she's angry, yet still hoping I care.

The world hangs on that moment, suspended in its turning for all time, it seems. In reality there's not a second of hesitation, not a single doubt in my reply, which flows honey warm and open-armed back to her.

'Of course you can.'

The sorrow of years is gone in that instant. I am whole once more. I am a mother again and I can speak of my children. I can hold a hand in the darkness and do the things I've longed to do. I can show photographs, I can tell stories proudly, and I can love and dare now to hope that I am loved back, just a little…

… The moment coalesces into the bright blur of the sunlit ward. Smiling as I surface once more to this other drowsy afternoon, I find I'm still alone with no visitors at the moment, and I'm grateful for it as I turn the memory lovingly and shift to try and find a cool place on my pillow once again. Such a wonderful day that was; I'm still filled with the warm glow of it.

I found so much again that day. Not vindication, then, or even in the years to follow, for vindication is not possible; I will never have the moral high ground, nor do I want it for it is not mine to own. What I found that day was simply a gentle acceptance that things were as they were; and I found both my children once more, for my son came to join us not quite a year after…

… I can't resist following his galloping, twelve-year-old footsteps as he catapults through the ramshackle four storey Georgian house, on the edge of the Wolds, that I've just bought for us all to live in together as a family.

'Can I have any room?'

'Well, all except those that have been claimed already.'

My daughter has staked out the entire basement, and we have a bedroom and ensuite bathroom on the third floor, but there are still plenty to go at.

'Any room?'

'Yes!'

He charges from the top to the bottom of the empty, clattery house again and again, thundering on bare boards and cornering recklessly around twisting mahogany banisters before I hear a scrape, a crash and a far away voice that sounds as though it's coming from outside.

'I'm having this one!'

Staggering up to the fourth floor, I find him hanging out of a broken sash window, his voice carried off by the wind as he admires the view from four floors up, flushed and excited.

He found his retreat, his home, the eagle's eyrie that would see him through teenage years, a first job, many, many girlfriends and the beginnings of a life made around using his large capable hands and remarkable mind, before he finally left, eighteen years on, to make a home of his own.

No, there was no vindication, just the full and precious joys of family, sometimes Christmases, small achievements and, above all, the amazement of finding just what unfathomable love that hollow inside would hold. In losing, I found so, so much…

… I laugh in my heart at the joy of it, my eyes wide open and full of tears that run down the side of my mask and under my chin. I sigh and fumble to adjust the elastic of my mask and wipe away the tears before anyone sees. Quiet joys, wonderful moments, an amazingly happy marriage and great memories expanded and grew to fill every corner of that old house. I made sure the children kept in regular touch with their father but it still became a safe harbour for us all.

Quietly happy, the certainty of that gentle voice in Wells Cathedral sustained me over the years. I had followed my heart and accepted all that so doing entailed. Deeply scoured out, hollowed and emptied by sorrow, I was now capable of more love than I believed possible. My decision had been the right one and I never once doubted it.

And then I had grandchildren. As I held each one in turn, cherishing each small new personality, marvelling at their perfection, the steps they made, the fun, the laughter and even the sleepless nights of it all; through it all a question kept coming back to haunt me.

'How could I have done it? How could I have walked away from two tiny children?'

It was guilt, returning like a thief in the night. I'd just neatly sidestepped it over the years. I packed it away and never brought it out. And as I cradled the soft warmth of my grandchildren's heads to my face, the guilt took over big time. Underneath everything, I still felt I deserved to be punished for as long as I lived. That day at the gym, the day I behaved so badly towards Coral, countless soul searching, sleepless nights; all of it brought me slowly to the point where I realised that I was *still* paying for what I did and that I would always be paying unless I could find a way to stop the guilt.

Now I think I know why I've had to remember all this. Painful though it's been, it has taken me straight to what Harriet really meant to me, what she did for me all those years ago.

My fingers stroke the sheets as an enigmatic face in an old photograph swims into view…

… A photo of a family wedding sits on our dining room table between me and my wonderful, old aunt Peg. I think, as I stare across at her, how she always used to be a bit of a guardian angel to me but nowadays it seems to be the other way around. Since my uncle died she visits every week or so, standing on my doorstep to enquire, 'Well, Mia, have I got it together?' as she smoothes down an outfit carefully selected to make the best of her slender figure. At eighty-three, she's a real doll, interested in everything and still the great fun that she's always been.

We're laughing and drinking coffee as she points out the photo's faded faces, while a casserole for lunch bubbles away on the old wood burner that warms our backs. The cat is folded as carefully as he can be around the stove, only an occasional lift of the head and twitch of the nose indicating that he's waiting for the casserole to come to fruition. Scribbling furiously on a scrap of paper; I'm finding my aunt's reminiscences are hard to extract but they're often the only clues I have had to go on in my search for Harriet. Bless her heart. She loves the chase as much as I do and together we've searched and dug about and ferreted out so much information about her family that we've been amazed.

She takes off her rimless spectacles to polish them and bestows me with a broad and demonstrative grin. Never having had children until very late, when she finally adopted, aunt Peg has always shown special affection towards me and I've loved her dearly for as long as I can remember.

'Ooooh, there's aunty Mary!' she says, returning her glasses to the end of her long nose. I peer at the sepia print over the top of her fuzzy white hairdo, so reminiscent of Granny Rose's cotton wool mop. She calls her wispy hair style, held fast with perm after relentless perm, a 'fur trapper's helmet'. And, I have to admit, as I look down on its spot welded woolly precision, that I can see the similarity but I keep quiet and listen to the story that, like all family stories, is fascinating.

Great aunt Edith's sister-in-law has done something quite remarkable for Scugton in the first years of the twentieth century. She has married a 'coloured' gentlemen; a much esteemed local character and learned chap who ran a grocery store, by all accounts. Aunt Peg carefully unfolds the article, an ancient brown newspaper cutting that tells the story of the wedding and of the slave who became a gentleman, pointing out the family members in the photo as she reads. There's my granddad aged fifteen, his hair slicked back, and standing very upright inside his tight Edwardian shirt collar. There are my great aunts Gertie, Mary, Edith and Alice, with Clara on the back row obviously married and holding a child. Amazing! I never cease to be enthralled by any snapshot of these serious faced young women. It doesn't fit at all with the mad old birds I remembered from my childhood. I couldn't possibly imagine that they were ever young at that time but then again, what young person does look at a stooped, elderly frame and see the fire of youth hidden deep inside?

The bride sits primly on the front row with her wide brimmed Edwardian hat, while the groom, the only dark face in a sea of white ones, stands proudly behind her. What really grabs my attention, however, is the woman standing stiffly next to my granddad. A calculated guess puts her in her fifties and, although the sepia doesn't show red hair, she has the selfsame square jaw I see in the mirror every day, raised in defiance towards the photographer.

'And there's my granny!'

'Is that Harriet?' I breathe in excitement. It is my first glimpse of her.

'Yes, there she is. A terribly thin and miserable old lady as I remember. I once pulled my knickers down for a dare and she didn't half paste my backside with a wooden spoon, which was a bit harsh now I think of it, considering all that we've found out about her goings on!'

'So what *was* she like then?'

'Well, as I've always told you, a bit of a misery. Upright, uptight and spiteful. Don't forget that your granddad was the only one in the family who'd have anything to do with her, so I only saw her on the odd occasion that she came visiting, and there weren't many of those. I was only twelve when she died, you know.'

I don't know what I expected, but looking at Harriet now as she stares out at us from that old photo in her dark, high-necked

Edwardian gown, I can't help but be struck by her supreme fragility despite the look of fierce defiance on her face. She's not at all the bruised, careworn creature I'd imagined from my research, but then again neither does she look at all like the woman aunt Peg is describing. Then something odd strikes me.

'But if she was *persona non grata* in the family, how come she's on this family photo?' I query of aunt Peg. Her memory's not always reliable and her stories change from time to time in the telling and retelling, but of this one thing she seems quite sure.

'Well, from what I was told, she was there because he insisted on it,' aunt Peg replies, running a knobbly finger around Harriet's face. She puts her coffee cup down and picks up the photo with both hands, squinting at it over hooked nose and spectacles. She's so like my Gran, it's spooky.

'Who insisted? My granddad?'

'No, the groom,' she chuckles, putting the photo down on the table and tapping it thoughtfully.

'Your granddad always told me that the groom thought that elders should be honoured and respected and, if the son and daughters of the family were coming to the wedding, then so was their mother. He said it caused a bit of ill feeling but people were very well behaved on the day and Harriet just stuck it out. Even got on the wedding photo — look at her!'

She slaps her thigh for emphasis, before primly straightening her skirt and pulling it well down over her knees. It tickles my aunt to call her grandmother Harriet, because even if you knew a grown up's Christian name in those days, you certainly didn't address them by it. And aunt Peg never knew much at all about Harriet until I started digging. I'm just amazed, staring hungrily and for a long, long time, at that face.

Harriet. At last! I've really found you.

Later that day, after an agreeable lunch and an afternoon spent scouring the local shops for just the right colour scarf, aunt Peg climbs in her old Skoda and drives it at a rock steady 45 mph all the way back home, incurring a speeding ticket in a 30 mph limit. I spend ages on the phone to her trying to smooth down her flustered feathers, it being the first time she's ever been stopped by the police, something she points out over and over again. She's outraged but at the same time aghast, and a steady clucking is coming from the other end of the phone.

'Young upstart! There he was barking at me like a robber's dog and asking how old I was. I had my licence with me so I stuck it under his nose but that didn't stop him, oh no! I've got to go down to the station with all my insurance details. Me! A little old lady!'

Now she's about as far from being a little old lady as I am from being the Queen, but it's a mantle she chooses to adopt from time to time. It clearly hasn't worked on this occasion, though, and maybe it's just as well.

'Aunt Peg, you're eighty-three; you should wear this as a badge of honour. Just pay the fine and forget it.'

'Me with a criminal record!'

'Oh, I'm proud to have an eighty-three-year-old aunt who's got done for speeding. I can dine out forever on that one,' I joke, although secretly I wonder if her driving capabilities are finally failing. That old car has been her lifeline since uncle died; it would be awful if she had to give it up.

As I make endless soothing noises down the phone, wandering up and down the hall while I try to pacify her, I pick up the photograph and newspaper clipping that she left for me on the hall table. Inspired, I try a change of subject.

'Just going back to that photograph for a minute, are you sure it was the groom's idea to invite Harriet to the wedding?'

'What?' She's been stopped in full flow. I repeat my question just to see if this recollection will stay the same but about this she's adamant.

'It was just before your granddad lied about his age, joined the army and found himself in the middle of the First World War. He remembered it so well because he went and joined up the day after the wedding.'

More soothing and much ear bending later, I've left John to take over at the telephone. The clucking has risen to a crescendo once or twice but in his expert way with all women of whatever age, he manages to find the words to make everything better. He always does.

I'm still fired up with today's first glimpse of her face and to have fitted more pieces into the puzzle that is Harriet. My current search is for Kate Ogley Blanchard, the missing daughter she had the year after Edward died and the third child Harriet bore in her liaison with William Ogley. Any descendents of Kate's would be full blood cousins of aunt Peg and that would be so wonderful for her. She has an amazing retinue of friends but little in the way of family apart from me. I would just love to find her a cousin or two.

My aunt has finally been dispatched to bed, promising that she'll dose herself with a medicinal cup of whisky and hot milk but I know she'll sit propped on her pillows for a good couple of hours, retelling her indignation to one friend after another until she's all talked out. The cat is curled up uncomfortably on my knee and the house is quiet apart from the creaks and clicks of its old bones. I sit in the peace of this spring evening, quietly marvelling at the generosity of a long dead black man, born a slave; a man who had so much forgiveness in his heart that he could push aside family feuding to honour Harriet and invite her to his wedding. After the events of the day, this simple act of generosity from someone who might have had little cause to be generous has finally sunk in and I wish I could thank him for giving me my long awaited first glimpse of Harriet's face. The sepia print sits propped up against my computer, my great grandmother seemingly staring quizzically out at me.

'Harriet, what are you telling me now?'

'Think I'll just do a little bit more hunting,' I say, depositing a length of moaning and disgruntled Siamese onto my husband's knee. There is a vaguely huffy sigh from behind the book in the opposite chair. He knows just how long a little hunting can stretch to but he's patient with my obsession, knowing that it's something I must do.

So far, after weeks of trying to find Kate, my granddad's only full blood sister, I've drawn a blank, but I think tonight I'll have one more go, sifting through family trees on the website instead of combing official records. The search engine, unhelpfully, keeps on turning up the name Katie Bowers which I've discarded a number of times, especially since I've already followed this particular trail to a dead end in an emigration across the Atlantic to America. Irritation more than curiosity takes over for a moment; I will close this dead end once and for all and silence the computer. You could take a Glock to these machines sometimes and they'd still ask, with a slight sneer, 'are you sure'?

Over the third cup of tea that's been placed with a wordless smile at my side, I decide to stem this electronic pestering and have a look at the details on the public family tree page that will tell me all about this girl Katie. She can't possibly be Harriet's Kate, who vanished at only one year old from public record. What would Harriet's Kate be doing in America? The name is wrong, anyway. The impartial ancestry search engine is annoying like that, throwing in all sorts of unrelated rubbish in your path. Well, here goes.

It takes a while for what I see to sink in. There are the emigration details of her parents, the name of the ship, the parents' previous address and other notes added by the tree owner. I look again to make sure. There's no mistake. They'd lived in Scugton, in Sereton Terrace and their daughter was adopted. Her previous name — Kate Ogley Blanchard. I am utterly stunned.

'Harriet! What happened?'

I stare at her face for a long time, trying to imagine what could have led to Harriet and Will's third child being carried off to America. But she's not giving me any answers and there's no way of finding out much more at the moment until I contact the ancestry tree owner. Still, I sit for ages going over the possibilities in my mind. What could have happened?

Later, watching shadows cast by passing traffic loom along our bedroom walls, I ponder this new mystery long into the night. At the time that the wedding photo was taken, Harriet had an illegitimate son, my granddad, a thirteen-year-old daughter in America given up long ago for adoption, and possibly also a grown up illegitimate son she'd never seen since he was a baby. Three children, four if you count Edward, born out of wedlock and now two children whom she's given away. No wonder the family had such a hard time with her antics. Turning it all over in my mind, I can't condemn her or even be shocked. I wasn't there and I don't know what she went through. Wiping hot tears from my face I simply forgive Harriet and, as I do, I forgive myself, remembering that black smiling countenance on the photo and its owner's simple generosity of spirit.

In that calm space between being asleep and awake the other, kinder, complete me that I remember from so long ago in Wells Cathedral, surfaces for a moment. It reminds me that guilt doesn't take you forwards; it is the act of forgiving yourself and accepting your mistakes as part of who you are which does. I forgive myself and embrace the idea that I'm not perfect and it's not something I should beat myself up about. I'm here to learn and grow and continue to be fashioned, along with all my mistakes, into the pattern that is me. Once I am fixed in my form, there will be no more learning, no more growth.

I turn to embrace the sleeping form at my side; my husband, the potter, who would be well satisfied with how I've grown. I think, that night, that I may even tell him all this one day.

I remember the great curve of his broad back and shoulders, the curls in the nape of his neck and the soft breathing of his sleeping form…

… My hand reaches out across the white hospital sheets for him but I drift instead towards the snows of a Christmas long ago.

It happened not too long after I first saw Harriet's face and shortly after I forgave myself and finally moved on. It was a magical moment, as brilliant and enchanting as only Christmas can be. I catch at its tinkling and murmuring and pull the glittering threads towards me…

… I am sitting in a school hall amid a glorious chaos of mums, grannies, beaming dads, fractious toddlers, tinsel streamers and pictures of angels, painted stars and Santas. I'm waiting for a concert to begin; the first one ever that I've watched as a member of the audience. The very first one.

No one ever thought to invite me to one when my children were small. I often wondered if my children looked for me and what they were told about why I wasn't there. Oh, I attended plenty of concerts when I was working; I was always chief usher and shusher, hovering at the fringes, waiting to thank everyone at the end, sweeping up strays, walking the corridors with restless toddlers, rocking crying babies and wiping away tears. It wasn't the same, though. There's nothing like watching your own children and having them know how proud you are of them; I know because I saw it each Christmas on the rapt faces of the audience.

There's a hush and the nursery children file onto the stage with their not-quite-grown-into plimsolls and puppy dog waggling gait. They immediately stand transfixed by the audience, like rabbits in a headlight, but gradually begin to thaw as they wait for the rest of the cast, swinging their arms and fiddling with their costumes. One little one spots his mum and waves, another shouts, 'HELLO MUM!' and a ripple of laughter runs round the audience.

Angels hitch up their tights and knickers with no regard for modesty; the class clown has been typecast and is pinging the mask of his harlequin suit on to his nose, while someone at his side drops a tambourine and causes a scuffle. There's a loud wail as the third shepherd is overcome by the sheer enormity of what's being expected of him and is sobbing for his mum as a helper comes to lead him away. Baby Jesus is tucked, with more firmness than is really warranted, into the manger and the stars' tinsel headdresses are adjusted before everyone is finally assembled.

I've spotted my grandson on the back row dressed as a bowler-hatted snowman, wound around with an enormous stripy scarf. I desperately hope he remembers his actions while everyone bawls out, 'The snowman's got his hat on, hip, hip, hip hooray,' but, despite all my anticipation, I don't really see any of what follows, my eyes are too full of tears. It's not the sentimentality that used to catch me out every time I heard *Away in a Manger*, it's something more. I think it's because I feel so humbled and grateful to be here. I was actually invited to come and a coveted seat was saved for me. It's as if my debt has finally been paid and, although my hands are clapping the snowman furiously, my heart is overwhelmed by humility and gratitude. Finally, I am at peace. I am accepted by my family as a real person, a proper granny and a mum, no longer a harridan, a whore and abandoner of children. I can really move on. I wish I'd understood what mistakes are all about much earlier in my life, but then if I had, maybe I wouldn't have made another very important one.

# 15

## MISTAKES, SIGNS
## AND PATTERNS

My eyes are full of tears even now as I remember how I put all this behind me long ago; there was simply no point in flogging myself with it any more. In the end you put the burden down or your life stalls. I really didn't want to relive it all, today of all days; leaving my children was so hard and not something I'm proud of, even though it seemed like the right thing to do at the time.

Well, perhaps this is what death does for us; stands us way above our lives so that we can see the whole picture. More like the whole album, I suppose, not just odd snapshots of the bits we remember, and Harriet has been turning its pages for me, reminding me of my debt to her. Revisiting these memories in this order, in this delicate chain of detail, reveals a significance that I missed when I was so close to it all. My great grandmother has evidently been teaching me from beyond the grave for most of my life. And me, a teacher! I would like to smile at the elegance of it but my face seems not to be able to move anymore.

But, whatever else, she's *still* not revealing to me the significance of my memories from earlier today, when I realised that we always shared something else, too; the memory of a chilling and gruesome face, mask-like and charred, leering at us through billowing clouds of slag smoke. The thing that catapulted me straight into Harriet's life, the sight of that skeletal hand excavated on the steelworks, is also part of our joint design. Maybe it's even the key to what she wants me to know.

'Hurry up Harriet,' my lips mouth weakly.

*'Soon. There's one more thing you need to understand first.'*

It's Harriet's voice and I don't question how. I'm beyond struggling and fretting, so I pay attention instead. Death is a real education.

Somewhere in the hospital ward a child is chattering and my faltering heart swells with joy at the sound. How I have loved children! Straining to hear properly, I think it is a little boy. Among the scrape of chairs, the murmured, pleasant drones and low buzz of Sunday afternoon visiting, a higher voice pipes. Yes, it's a boy of about nine years old, my long practised ear says. He's brought in an encyclopedia to relieve the boredom of visiting elderly ladies and now reads aloud, in the halting style of unsure readers, about mimicry in nature. The words are many syllabled and complex and it's hard for him to pronounce them, let alone grasp their meaning but eventually, with everyone encouraging him, he has the sense of it.

'Con... convergent evolution is an excellent example of the effect that smile... ('similar,' a voice prompts)... similar en... vir... onments, environments can have on widely diving... ('divergent')

divergent species,' he reads. 'For example,' he continues, gaining confidence, 'many widely div… erse creatures will develop on their bodies the markings of the large eyes of a predator. Pot… ential threats are thus dis… couraged. Several un… related mammals have dev… developed prickles on their skin and possums have a thumb, like that of to... totally un… related primates.'

I can hear the little catch of satisfaction in his voice as he continues to read and the adults with him remark how clever he is. I drink this in greedily; how I've loved teaching and the pleasure it brings when some little scrap of humanity takes a step in learning. It's like holding the hands of a baby taking those first steps. You hold, you support, you point the way, you steady the totter and comfort the fall and then — they're off on their own, getting better and better. A warm pool of satisfaction floods through my being as I fondle the memories of children long grown. Yet it was a big mistake, how I came to be a teacher, but I expect you know that, Harriet…

… I'm staring a handmade rug Granny Rose and I put together when I was eighteen. It started off terribly but it ended beautifully and I'm staring at it over her shoulder, biting my lip, because I've something awful to tell my Gran and I don't know how to start.

I look down on the soft cotton wool of her hair, the wig tossed onto the floor at the side of her chair. My Gran values education above all things and she'll think I've gone and thrown a chance away.

She may look like a frail old lady but she's an amazingly clever, wise and self-taught woman. Nobody in our family has ever done much at school so far, she always says. My granddad had no choice but to work from being nine years old, and he lied his way into the army and the First World War at fifteen. My dad, born between the wars, missed so much Elementary School due to tuberculosis that there was no point to secondary education and he began work in Scugton iron foundry at thirteen, despite showing signs of a greedy, agile mind.

My Gran is determined that I'm worth more. These are the 1960s and anything is possible; we don't quite know what, but it is. After all, my granddad's sister, aunt Alice, has two sons who went to Oxford, so there must be brains somewhere in the family, she says. I don't want to go to Oxford, or even university. I have an escape plan. A perfect plan, but I don't know how to tell her.

She was so pleased when I passed the exam for the Grammar School, turning pink with pleasure and exclaiming, 'Mia Pia!' Then she did a little dance around her living room, clasped my face in her hands to deliver a scratchy kiss and went and raided the Christmas club money to help buy my uniform. I was pleased too; I'd achieved something. There were only thirteen out of the forty-eight of us in my class at Junior School who passed, and my best friend Gloria Whitely cried all the way home from school the day they told us, because she didn't. But I didn't care. I thought I'd been unhappy up to this point, and that Grammar School would change everything.

Finally, here was a chance to make my parents proud of me! In the angry turmoil of their lives together, they'd neglected to show me that they were proud of me already. How was I to know? My dad had even said he would buy me a bike if I made it to Grammar School but when I did, he just said, 'Now you'll have to work really hard. That's because you're working class and they're all middle class and have advantages you don't. You'll have to try harder than them to get to the same place.' And I did.

I didn't get the bike but I did try harder. Yet when I fell in love with music and wanted to take up piano lessons and when I wanted to go on the school ski trip to France, he still said it was too middle class and not for me. That was when I knew that I would never amount to anything unless I could get away from home. My father was his own self-fulfilling prophecy and I was a hostage to all his fears and prejudices. The drink, my mother's temper and his social conscience, worn like a badge, put the brakes on all the opportunities that presented themselves, both to him and to me.

I studied hard, and I didn't leave school at fifteen to work in Woolworth's store like he prophesied that I would when I first started going out with my boyfriend. I didn't leave because I had a plan.

'Well, I'm waiting, how did you do?' says my Gran, putting the rug down with great ceremony and peering anxiously over her glasses up into my face.

How do I explain? How do I explain that I really want to work in the sciences, maybe marine biology, and not literature like my dad wants me to? He just can't understand a girl wanting to do science, so I've messed up my French A level just enough to prevent me from taking up my place to read English and French at a university two hundred miles away. How can I explain to Granny Rose that I need a ticket out of here? How can I tell her I want to get married as soon as possible because marriage is that ticket?

'Did you get the grades you needed in French?'

'Well, I only got an 'O', not an 'A' at French, so it wasn't good enough.'

I shuffle my feet and stare at the horrid size eight Start-rite shoes that I still have to wear at eighteen. There's more I should tell her.

'Well, it's ok Gran,' I continue quickly. 'I can go to college only forty miles from here and come home most weekends. My grades in Biology are fine, they said. I've got a place there. I could even get married! He has a good job now not too far from the college. And, if I go there, I can do science like I really want to.'

So that's my escape plan but today it's all gone wrong. I strode to the telephone box on the common, too proud to let the teachers see my so-called demise, secured my college place there and then and came home with a *fait accompli*, expecting some disappointment and maybe even a few beer sodden recriminations from my father, but not this!

'Gran, he's gone and telephoned the university and got them to put me on a waiting list and there'll probably be a place for me!' I blurt out, twisting the brand new engagement ring on my finger.

As soon as I'd left school in June I'd got engaged. It was just perfect. Both families smiled benevolently on us and encouraged the romance. We had, after all, been going out together since I was fifteen. It was my ultimate moment of triumph over the girls at Grammar School who, for seven long years had made my life a misery, first for being poor and working class, then for being clever and pretty. It was my plan. It was my way out. It was brilliant. Marriage! A ticket out, status and independence. Stick that in your pipes and smoke it, you bitches! But it's all going wrong and I can't bear the thought of not being out of this place for good, not being able to have the freedom I want. I need to study science. I love its calm and order and sheer persistent logic. I need to get married and be my own mistress.

Something seems to hit the back of my head, dizzying me as I stand and then the unbidden thought brings me straight back to my senses, whispering insistently, 'You've been here before!' That's stupid; I haven't; but the thought persists and I shake my head to bring the world into my own sharp focus, pushing away the image of myself sitting in the branches of an old ash tree, kicking my feet in cracked black boots and fingering a velvet ribbon.

'Soft as a mouldywarp,' I murmur and then continue, 'my own mistress.' It sounds so comfortable and familiar…

… The shock of that buried memory is enough to spit me back into the ward, flapping, lurching and gasping for air. That's it! *That's* where Harriet and I were one person for the very first time and I'd dismissed it as a silly illogical thought, just as I always did. I didn't even bother to run it past all those other odd memories I'd had. How could I have been so naïve and arrogant? If only I'd not been so determined to see my world through eyes that ignored all but the concrete and scientifically provable.

The beeping of an alarm, footsteps across the ward and then a professional hand smoothes covers that have been flung back in frustration, stills my plucking hands and dabs tears from my face. The beeping stops…

… 'So why are you crying, then?' Gran breaks my thoughts and with it some odd idea I had of time shifting around me. It's no good thinking like that, it doesn't get you anywhere. It doesn't help. Calmness and a life structure get you through a crisis, not half-baked ideas.

Granny Rose is making a rug for me. She usually makes rugs

from rags but as soon as I became engaged she raided the Christmas money yet again, scraping the bottom of the Bulwark Cut Plug tobacco tin until it was bare. She bought proper wools to make me a modern fireside rug. She knows I like modern things. Now she picks up her hooking again with her head cocked on one side at me like a bird.

She never says a word while I fling myself down on her old settee and pour it all out, twisting and twisting that ring, my symbol in this 'marriage or nothing' world, that I have become somebody. Even if I'd failed every subject, I still had that ring. Granny Rose senses that this is even more of a crisis than a simple matter of higher education. She carries on with her rug-hooking, silent and deep in thought. Finally she looks up over her glasses and says the thing I least expect.

'Come and help me with this rug, Mia Pia.'

I sit down on my little childhood stool at her side, relieved to have got it out in the open but wondering where all this is leading. I want to go to college. I want to do biology. I don't want to go to a university two hundred miles away from my fiancé. I begin to push strands of wool through the gridded canvas. The rug is a lovely pattern of black circles with red segments on a beige background and I begin a new segment, pushing the red strands through the netting, all the while waiting for the barbed truth to fall from my Gran's lips. I'm concentrating so hard on what I'll say in reply that I make a silly mistake with the pattern and I tell her that I'll have to pull it out. Her bony hand grasps mine to stop me.

'You know, we can turn this into something that will be a real focus point on these bloody, plain, boring modern shapes,' she declares, and within ten minutes or so of deft pulls, while I watch in silence, she has manufactured a set of fat, red, open lips from my error.

'Mick Jagger!' she quips.

A load lifts from me and we laugh hysterically and begin to sing Rolling Stones hits, my Gran squeaking, 'I can't get no-oo satisfaction,' in her cracked voice. 'Wah, waaah, wa-wa, waaah, wa-wa, wa-wa-wa,' I intone in an approximation of the guitar riff.

Standing up, I begin to wiggle my hips and stick my bum out, while doing the exaggerated and hallmark handclap. I pick up her tortoise, Bullet, and sing into the rear end of his shell as if it's a microphone while Granny Rose uses the rug hooks as drumsticks on the hood of the gas fire.

'You know, there's the thing about making rugs,' she says, her eyes bright and intense behind her glasses as I pause for breath. I put a surprised and withdrawn Bullet down by his pile of lettuce again and perch back on my stool, still laughing. Gran hands back the rug hook.

'What thing?'

'Your mistakes can always be turned into part of your pattern.'

'What?'

'It's the best way. No sense in going back and trying to undo things. Not big things. What's done is done. Better to make your mistake work for you; make it part of your pattern and who you are. You know, Mia, that's what God does for us and it's a good way of going on. Just recognise it as a mistake, that's all, and don't make the same mistake again. Now about this college business; is that what you really, truly want?' I look at her in amazement. I don't really see this as a mistake but I'll go along with one of her signs if she's on my side.

'I've been planning it for three years!'

'All right, that's it. I'll talk to your dad, then. An education is an education, no matter what.'

And that was it; plan accomplished!

Except it wasn't, was it? I was *so* naïve back then, I think, snatching at my sheets again. I was so blinkered, so hot for marriage and intent on shaking the dust of Scugton from my feet. Oh, you madam! You thought you were so clever, but you weren't, were you?

I drift back again to that first day at college. Books had been bought, clothes were packed and my ancient, second-hand steamer trunk from great aunt Gertie's honeymoon cruise was sent off by special delivery as we didn't have a car. Kisses were kissed, dreams dreamed and goodbyes said, and before I know it, it is my first morning at college.

I'm turning the events of the last twenty-four hours over and over in my mind as I sit waiting for the welcome address to two hundred or so of us new students. The forty or so miles it took to get here yesterday was an adventure in itself, travelled by three buses, a journey which took all day. And I've met Coral Gray, my roommate. My first proper friend in years! We've clicked instantly, clattering downstairs to the refectory to eat our evening meal together last night. There I showed off my engagement ring to an admiring crowd and later, we hosted more new friends in our room, talking long into the small hours, brimful with the newness of it all and the feeling of belonging somewhere at last.

We're all seated in the main hall as the late September sun

streams through stained glass windows, puddling colours upon the newly polished parquet floor. Row upon row of green canvas and metal chairs creak as their owners lean forward in anticipation. Shields that are supposed to represent something I know nothing about as yet, line the walls, impressing on us all that this is an important day in an important place. The Principal is about to address us, and I'm so excited that everything is going to plan. Just waking up today in a different room, unafraid for the first time in my life, seemed like a minor miracle in itself.

There's a welcome, which I miss because I'm too busy staring at the array of lecturers, wondering who I'll get. Then I come into sudden, sharp, horrified focus.

'Now that you are all here at Seaton to train as teachers...'

'Teachers!' I choke to myself and sit bolt upright. I must have misheard it. I thought this place was just a lesser form of university; a place where you got a certificate that wasn't quite as good as a degree but which still opened doors. The dearth of careers education at school hadn't informed me otherwise. Women can go to university, college or secretarial school, they'd said in their single, ten-minute careers advice lesson. I've never even heard of Colleges of Education.

I listen, dazed, to a glowing description of how I'm going to help form young minds. There's no mistake, I'm at a teacher training college. I'm dumbfounded. How stupid could I be? Why did no one tell me? Why didn't they say at school? Didn't my dad know? Why would I want to go back into schools, for goodness sake? What an awful mistake! I was in such a rush to get away that I overlooked the fine — and most important — detail of where exactly I was running to.

The cold, clammy, sweatiness of the moment is all-consuming. My mind races, rattling around the shields on the wall, beating against the ranks of hopeful trainee teachers, looking for any way out but there is none. Too late to do anything about it now, I would just look stupid, and anyway, it would ruin the plan.

'I don't want to be a teacher!' The words creep out, small and ashamed, darting furtively round the hall and coming to rest at my anxiously scuffing feet. I'm a solitary blemish amidst all these faces of hope and enthusiasm.

'Well, what are you doing here, then? It's a bit late now to chicken out,' whispers Coral at my side, squeezing my hand in support. 'It's just nerves, silly'…

… 'If only you knew, Coral!' I think, panting into my mask in breaths that are ever shallower. Still, Granny Rose was right, as usual. That mistake really worked for me and became a fundamental part of my pattern, for teaching runs up my backbone like Blackpool through rock, an act that was, for me, as natural as breathing. It's what my analytical mind and sense of order was made for. I was born to teach. There wasn't a child I couldn't reach and teach in some way or other, and no more fulfilling job I could have done. Yet it was all a mistake. But it was a long, long time before I learned that mistakes are not an unforgivable blot on your copybook; they're life's best lessons if you use them well…

… '*You're nearly there,*' whispers Harriet.

I am with her now, remembering. There she is at last, come to tell me what it's all about. Having finished her washing, she's on her knees scrubbing the flags of her tiny kitchen floor with some of the washday leavings of warm water, strands of red hair plastered to her sweating forehead. Pleased with her day's work, she stands up for a moment to ease her joints, apron hanging damply from a thin waist, below which there is a suspicion of the child swelling inside her. The back of her hand pushes away her hair and then itches at a drip which has fallen on to her nose, escaping from the brush she holds. What is she looking at?

On her worn boots a water-soaked lace has come undone, making the knot into a conundrum for tired fingers. Pulling a pin from her hair, Harriet bends and picks at the wet knot with it, persisting until it comes loose. The lace has broken so many times, the knots upon bows and bows upon knots finally giving way under the stretching and straining of dragging heavy buckets to the gutter.

'Bend to the situation. Carefully unpick it bit by bit, then mek the best of it you can, my girl,' she mutters at her broken laces.

'We've done it before, we can do it again. Just think it through. An answer 'as to be there.'

I catch an image in her mind of her children; Will's own four, her five girls, Fred and the unborn child that is on the way so soon after she buried Edward.

'I'm going to 'ave to bend me back even 'arder now. So is Will, an' Lord knows 'e all but breks 'is 'un seven days a week at the furnaces,' she sighs.

With red and cracked washday fingers that smart with every pressure, she knots her boot once more and then freezes, still bent double, wearing the familiar vacant gaze I saw on her child's face in the orchard.

A blink and she watches, fascinated, as the water she has just thrown across the floor spreads over the dusty flagstones. Wherever it moves, the stones become clear and bright, their colours glowing. Ahead of its flow, the stones remain dusty and undefined. A tidal rim of dust, pieces of fluff, a red hair, fabric threads and bread-crumbs crusts the edge of the flow.

'There's no fresh starts in life.'

She's haunted by something. I clutch at the thought and we think it together.

'Ay, you carry with you all that you've bin. All the kelter an' stuff from what you've done, it's allus there no matter what. Aaaaah, no!'

We rub at our forehead to erase a swelling horror but it won't go. 'Stop it! Will yer leave me alone, for God's sake?' we moan as the familiar horrific face looms into memory. I notice for the first time as I mentally back away from this apparition that the eye sockets are turned down at the corners, as if there is enormous sadness behind them. The mouth is almost pleading, too. It's a face not of menace but of utter devastation.

And Harriet, Harriet. She is being punished for it far more severely than I ever was for what I did.

'What is it Harriet, what is it? What did you do?' I push the thought at her, sensing a great tangled ball of heaviness inside her but I can't unravel it, and then her mood changes abruptly and the face and her sense of guilt are gone, replaced by a moment of abso-lute wonder.

She stands stock still for an age, bent over the spreading water swilled from her bucket.

'That's how I live,' she finally whispers, staring at the advancing edge of water which now pools towards her feet. 'That's how me time is. I live on th' edge where it's all 'azy and unsure. I can only vaguely reckon at owt in front. Behind, everything's clear, an' mebbe I can get the measure of it.'

She pauses for what seems another age as her thoughts come together.

'Who we are, well it's right 'ere now, runnin' wi' that edge. We're now, not yesterday or termorrer. But then both are still a little bit of us, they're still there. Oh, it's so, so beautiful!' She gives a little skip and clasps the brush in both hands.

This gaunt, tired woman feels such satisfaction at this understanding that I, too, am aglow with it, despite the crawling horror of a few moments ago. A portion of her life has slid into place, sorrows and fears have been pushed away and another item will be added to her list. Finally she stands chuckling as she straightens and arches her back.

'One. On me father's grave; it has to be — ONE! And now don't you go frettin' on the past and dreadin' tomorrow, 'Arriet my girl, because it's all 'ere now. Where you are is it. There's on'y today, nowt else. What you need will come to you; it always 'as and, if it dun't, you'll mek the best on it you can'…

… I'm stunned. A wheezing lurch of the chest brings me back to the present and I'm trembling, more in excitement than anything else. She has shown me the simple, elegant insight about time that she put at the very top of her lists, above Charles, Fred, everything. Is this what she's reminding me of as I'm being remade and reformed inside my white cocoon; that I shouldn't regret or fret over my past, no matter how awful it was? Or is she saying that it's all here now? This is the sum total of all that life comes to, rounded and finished here on a deathbed. That's some of it, Harriet, but there's more, isn't there?

Across the ward, chairs scrape and rearrange. Visitors arrive, visitors depart and life goes on.

'There are only so many ways for life to find a solution to similar problems of exist… existence and they, too, all tend to be similar,' a voice reads. The little boy has started reading out loud again about convergent evolution.

How could I have missed it? Granny Rose's signs weren't silly superstitions at all. They, too, were nothing more than this wonderful gift we have for seeing beautiful patterns everywhere, especially comparisons between the patterns of the world out there and the situations of our lives. Nature does only have a certain number of answers. Surviving in similar situations does require similar solutions. The universe has its own impeccable logic and laws that operate at all levels if *only* we will look.

It was Harriet's religion, maybe the deep understanding behind all religions. Is this what we do on our deathbeds, appreciate the logic of the universe? I always thought that it was fear that so often drives us into the arms of religion at the very end.

# 16

# TAPPING DAY

The whisper of my oxygen takes on a gentle hypnotic quality. Feeling remote, tranquil and complete now, and still humbled by the remarkable insights a simple Victorian washerwoman has laid before me, I guess I'm finally ready. I turn thankfully upon the peaceful folds of death and settle back. It won't be long now.

But there's an uncomfortable lump in my tranquillity. Like the princess with the pea under her mattress, I can't quite settle. It's like that wonderful, brief moment when you wake from a deep sleep and all your troubles have vanished, before reality comes flooding back and you realise, in a cold sweat, the awful things that are waiting for you that day.

This is just another stepping stone. She hasn't told me about the mask.

But does it matter now?

I'm too weary.

I just want to go.

Trickling between shallow breaths, the thought gathers into an insistent drip. If Granny Rose could do it when she'd had enough, I can.

This is it.

My hand gropes for the call button. It won't take more than a little morphine to help me on my way and my family will be so comforted that I've asked for pain relief. I find the raised button but my fingers are like wet string as I try to make it work. Fumbling and fumbling, I try to press down. There, I've done it.

But nothing happens. Nothing except a thought, heavy and insistent, more substantial even than this vestige of a person upon my hospital bed. Why was Harriet being punished when it was her very life that taught me about self-forgiveness? The question repeats itself over and over and gathers strength, re-infusing me with a little willingness to follow her one more time.

Learning from mistakes is part of forgiving yourself, I suppose; and what a precious gift that is. Forgiving others is nearly as hard as forgiving yourself and what we don't realise, is that this is also a gift to ourselves. I should have forgiven my father before he died but I just couldn't. It took me years to do that. The wounds were too deep and he was still carving at them, even in his final years. Every time the hollows filled with just enough love to extend a hand to him, he scored out more, deeper and deeper, until in the end it was just easier to back away and leave him be. I haven't thought of him in so long until today.

*'Yes, carry on.'* It's Harriet. I try to conjure up my father's face but it's red and bloated from alcohol and he's saying something vicious, as was his habit in drink.

*'Don't stop.'*

Why was he always like that? I can see him now on tapping day, a Thursday, which was always payday, too, so he's come home flushed from two open hearths; the furnace at Scugton Foundry and the *Open Hearth* pub. His flat cap is studded with solidified gobs of metal which he won't let my mother remove because he says it reminds him how dangerous the job is, and to keep sharp. He smells of smoke, metal, dirt, sweat and beer and I hate that stench above all others. Its mingled beer-soaked reek always means trouble.

*'You're there!'*

I can almost smell that stench now and, as I inhale that bitter tang, my mind is swept, unwillingly, along a blood red filament of light…

…The filament brightens and becomes a sunbeam shafting through a hole in a rusty corrugated roof, fixing him in dusty yellow where he kneels, illuminated, in the sand of the moulding floor. He is readying his tools for the gush of molten metal that will soon fill his prepared copes and drags to make three glowing, white-hot machine cogs.

Copes and drags; the tops and bottoms of his boxed sand moulds. How the words of his trade run around his mind, ticked off one by one as he waits for the casting, tensed and taut. He has, with infinite care, strickled the sand in the boxes around his patterns so that every single grain is in place. Then he's added central 'chills', so that the inner diameter of the cog will harden properly. The heavy steel plates are ready by his side to top the moulds and stop them floating up as they cool. A dowel lies upon the sand at his other side, cast down from where he's used it to make a sprue, a channel into which the molten steel will flow. The air shimmers slightly, full of heat and sweat and oaths.

'Stamp! Git yer bloody 'at on!'

'Fuck off! I'll put it on when I'm ready!'

'We're ready now, gret wazuk!'

'Blanchard! If yer get much more metal on that 'at of yours you won't need a crash helmet on your bloody motor bike.'

My father laughs and momentarily doffs his flat cap to Jack Stamp. He has casually pulled it on sideways in an attempt at comedy. His insides, however, are sucked in tightly and his breathing is rapid. To relieve the tension he wipes the dowel on his leather apron and taps it against his strickling tool in a steady rhythm, whistling tunelessly through his teeth as he does so. I never once saw my father at his workplace, so this isn't a memory but I can't stop the flow of images that sizzle, molten red, behind my eyes.

There's real tension on the moulding floor, as five kneeling craftsmen moulders like himself wait for the tiny open hearthed furnace to be ready. Eventually a shout goes up and a hooter sounds. The large open- topped ladle shudders and squeals as it's drawn, on its chains, towards the small furnace. Sparks and heat rise up from the tapping hole, bringing down a flurry of pigeons that have been roosting above. My father always said that folks think of iron and steel as something akin to lava, but it's slicker and brighter and quicker and far more dangerous than that. It's bright yellow and impossible to look at directly; moving faster than water, it demands your respect and if you don't give it due deference, it will be the end of you.

'Git yer bloody goggles on!' a shout goes up to the man standing with his rod by the furnace.

My father carefully resites his battered cap and blows through his teeth. This is it. The cooler waste products from the bottom of the furnace are run off through the tapping hole before the furnace is plugged and the temperature ratcheted up. When it is judged to be ready, a rod will clear the tapping hole once more and the tilting ladle hoisted on its chain will receive the first of the steel as it spews from the furnace. The men's edginess is suddenly released. They can soon begin to fill their own smaller ladles and go about their work.

''Ere she comes!'

But my father stiffens and it takes him all the bravado he can muster to stay poised by his moulds. I mentally recoil, too, at the awful and horrid familiarity, for there in the first crusted run off is that familiar face, its mouth sloping down to one side, running loose and finally disappearing into the sand of the foundry floor. As he wipes his gauntlet covered arm across his sweating face, I know that he's seen it too, not once but many times. It haunts his every casting day, leering out at him from the furnace, no matter whether it's iron, steel, bronze or brass that they're casting. But there's no time to dwell on it for long as the crucible empties its searing contents into each of the moulders' sprues and the frenetic activity begins to make sure the moulds are properly filled…

… Appalled, I am anchored to my bed with it; awake and with my skin crawling and cold, all thoughts of morphine, dying and forgiveness are forgotten in the shock of the moment. I have witnessed this shape so many times today and now it seems as though my father saw it, too. Ever rational, my younger self had dismissed it each time it slid its menace into my life, and I had willfully ignored any significance I could have gleaned from it. It seems that my father could not ignore it. I can still feel the wall-climbing, gibbering horror he felt as it poured itself into the sand.

'Harriet! Harriet! What's this about?' Skeletal hands claw their way around my skull and prise open my mouth to let out my panic.

'What about Harriet, mum? Can you see her?'

My daughter is again by my side; she strokes my hand and remarks how cold I am, pulling the blanket up around me. Despite the pneumonia and the remembered heat of the moulding floor, I feel as though I have an inner core of ice and I begin to shake once more. There's a call for the blower to be switched back on and a warm current of air circulates under the covers, soothing, gentling and eventually stilling my old body in its tremors.

I turn my head to mouth a 'thank you' and, as if in answer to the name I called out, I see Harriet's head pillowed beside me.

At last.

I willingly let my mind mingle with hers this time but she's drifting into sleep and I'm drawn along the pleasant hum and tumble of her drowsy thoughts. In that calm space between being awake and falling asleep, she sees things. Sometimes it's just a flash, a glimpse of a brilliant and intricate pattern which she tries to hold on to, weaving it mentally into a piece of silk or damask, maybe even a fine woollen shawl. Sometimes it's a garden but not like any she's seen — its colour pale and faded like a much-washed dress — with stone pillars, columns and fountains forming a long avenue. Everywhere there is the sound of water and she knows without a doubt that it is a place of great love.

Then there is the house. Ever since she was a tiny child it has been her escape. When her list of beautiful things could not soothe, she scampers along the lane from the cottage up on to the Wold top and to her imaginary little house in the woods, far away from the crush of Shiloh's dank dwelling and the incessant shriek of her mother.

Over the years her house has grown, in her mind, from a small hut with a straw mattress on the floor and a fireplace for warmth, into a secluded mansion set in the grounds of a beautiful garden. In the beginning, her imaginings are all about gathering firewood and setting rabbit snares so that she can eat. She gathers berries and filberts from the hedgerows in the autumn and sneaks out to pick field mushrooms and penny buns on dewy mornings. In the spring, she wraps her arms in cloth and gathers nettles and wild garlic for soup. She steals washing laid upon the hedges for blankets and clothes and sneaks into the kitchen of the Hall to take scraps of bread.

Gradually her mind's eye fills the little hut with things she's found or stolen. A cup, an old saucepan, a jug, her three-legged stool, are all placed with care in their proper place in her tiny refuge. Later on, however, when it has grown to a mansion, she simply fills it with all the treasures she's ever seen: crystal vases, stained glass windows like the ones in St John's Church, fine Persian rugs from the houses she's visited, glittering silver, and her very own journal on a lady's desk. Outside is a fine kitchen garden where she grows white, black and redcurrants, herbs and vegetables.

There's a room in her house for each person who has left her life, each appropriately furnished. Old Shiloh sits forever in his rocking chair by the window, dreaming of the days when he could milk cows and tend to their needs, rather than dig red clay for brick making as he was forced to do in his latter days, walking the long miles to Barton on the Aumber each morning and coming home again, clay-caked each night. A beloved aunt sits by a fire, stirring an ever-bubbling stew and throwing her arms wide whenever Harriet opens the door to her room.

There is her sister Hellen's firstborn swaddled safely in a wash basket in a bright and airy room that flows with pure white billowing muslin, as white as the bindings that wrapped him in death. He's sleeping peacefully now and alongside him, in his own basket, is Harriet's precious firstborn, Charles. Her waspish mother Anne occupies a basement kitchen that she seldom visits but there is, of course, also a room for John Henry. She visits each room in turn to talk and spend a while and she's with John Henry now in the calm space where I, too, am lingering.

'I 'ad ter do it, John.'

John Henry has his back to her and makes no reply. In her imagination Harriet has dressed him in his working clothes; he has laid his flat cap on the bed and is taking off his boots, pulling painfully at the laces but making no progress.

'I just couldn't see yer like that.'

I feel tears and an enormous sense of guilt and horror welling up in Harriet. Something awful lurks, a dark smouldering shadow occupying the space between Harriet standing in the doorway and her dead husband. I recognise what it is.

'Forgive me.'

John turns. He has no face, only burnt red meat where an iron worker's ruddy, sweat streaked countenance should be. There is no hair, just a red skullcap of flesh, with sightless eye sockets and a red jag of a mouth. His fingers have been charred to the bone and he cannot grasp the laces of his boots.

With a reeling mind that careens wildly from one gut-wrenching episode of her life to another, Harriet tosses on the pillow and remembers the cause of all her guilt. I am pulled along with her to the smoky rooftops of Sereton Terrace where she's pegging out her washing in the back yard, half an ear cocked to young Mary playing out the front with the Ogley's youngest, Betsey. Clashing and grinding from the nearby Appleton Works is the main thing she hears but against its background, the high voices of the two girls reassure her. She has made them both peg dollies from scraps of fabric and wool and they're being put to bed under a floor cloth in an old rectangular enamel pie dish.

The noise from the Appleton Works, together with its gassy smells and ugly cloud-smearing red glow from either furnace tapping or slag tipping, are her constant back yard companions. The ore is so close at hand that the men dig it from long pits to the east of the Terrace and then stagger with enormous barrows along walkways right to the top of the furnaces to fill them. The furnaces are hand loaded by large, two- wheeled barrows that carry limestone, coke and ore. Time after time the barrows are pushed up to the men on the walkway around the furnace's rim. Again and again workmen heave the barrows upwards, blowing and exclaiming, for the furnace is always hungry. The proportions of the mix have to be carefully worked out or it becomes very volatile when it is smelted, for the ore here is very poor. Under the shade of her hand, Harriet can pick out their progress most days, a steady stream of ants climbing up from the mine gulleys, pushing their loads before them.

The squeal of the iron barrows and the workers' grunts and banter carry on the wind when it blows from the west, but today one of the furnaces is close to tapping time and the barrows are temporarily still. A hooter sounds, a charge blows out the tap hole to number one and the furnace discharges its first load of molten iron into the pig bed, along the sand gully sows and into the preformed sand moulds of the pigs.

Harriet clicks her tongue over smuts that have landed on sheets, nightdresses and pinafores, floating down in the smoke that pumps acridly from the furnace tops. Nobody else here washes on tapping day or when the furnaces are blasting except Harriet, who takes in a little laundry to pay her household bills and shoe her four girls. She cannot rely on steady money from John Henry unless she meets him outside the works with her girls in tow on pay night. Like most of the ironworkers, he maintains that it's a job that generates a terrible thirst but for him it's one that can only be slaked by beer, and John Henry's thirst is more deep and powerful than most.

Away to the south, at the edge of the Frodsby Works, a lone labourer is sprigging the wheels of the empty slag trucks, checking them prior to tipping. At any works, once the iron has been run off, the slag that has floated above it must also be drained and disposed of. They don't run it into pigs like they do here but into bucket shaped railway trucks. Each truck swings sideways on its bed with a metallic shriek, an operation that must work efficiently or the molten slag will tip with a jagged lurch and splash the mechanism of the slag trucks. When the slag is finally tipped over the end of the slag heap, the glow of its malevolent red mass slurping down the side of the slag heap can be seen for miles, day or night. It lights all the bedrooms of Sereton Terrace and terrifies the children at night. Clank, shriek, clank, shriek, the noise goes on down the line of waiting trucks.

Works noise is such a normal background to lives in Sereton Terrace that it is some minutes before anyone notices that the quality of the shouts and clatter has changed. Like a persistent wasp, the odd noise finally penetrates Harriet's washday musings. Something has gone wrong with number two blast furnace and from her back door, Harriet can see that several men have been sent up to the walkway that surrounds the open-topped structure to investigate.

'They shouldn't be there so close to tappin',' Harriet mouths in horror. 'What in God's name… who sent the buggers up there?'

With a pounding heart, she can see that the men must have received warning of something awful about to take place and, knowing full well the terrible consequences of an explosion in mid smelting, they are running around on the walkway that surrounds the top of the furnace, shouting and gesticulating to those below. Harriet freezes. John Henry is a pig iron carrier and will be waiting below for the furnace to be tapped and pour its contents into the pigs.

There is a sudden noise that is almost akin to being hit around the head, so intense is its feel, and as Harriet stares in horror, part of the skyward edge of the furnace seems to crumble in slow motion and tumble down its side. Another deafening explosion follows and the furnace flames shoot skywards. Clouds of glistening red cinders, lumps of slag and molten metal rise up and begin to rain down around the furnace and on to the rooftops of Sereton Terrace.

Harriet cannot move. Even her tongue has stuck fast to the roof of her mouth and her throat will not carry sound. As she watches, the workmen up aloft make vain efforts to conceal their bodies under the walkway and shriek after shriek comes from the top of the furnace, followed by equally heart-rending sounds from below. A wave of howling humanity flows up over the rise of the ground nearby and away from the erupting furnace, making its way towards the sanctuary of Sereton Terrace and home.

Harriet turns and runs, too, to gather up the two little girls. Once safely inside, she rushes distractedly from her back door to her front door, time and again, with little Mary gathered up on one hip and Betsey Ogley on the other. She is utterly terrified by the rattling on the roof and the hissing of her washing which is being caught by hot falling slag. Peering from the back windows she can see men running towards the shelter of home as the furnace continues to roar into the grey skies. Up and down Sereton Terrace women are screaming and babies, infected by the commotion, start crying too.

Gradually, over what seems like an age, the uproar subsides and Harriet plucks up the courage to peer out of the back door. A piece of slag has embedded itself in the woodwork and is still glowing hot, charring the wood. Setting the girls down and wielding the coal shovel in both hands, she prises it free and kicks it down the path. She scoops a bucket of water from her rinsing barrel to cool the blackened wood before she turns to soothe the girls, who have picked up on the panic in the air and are crying in high pitched voices. I can feel Harriet's rising panic too, a stifling, prickling burr in her chest, as she fumbles to cut a half slice of bread with a smear of jam for them both. Betsey throws hers down and continues her cries but hungry Mary is appeased at once.

'There, there, duck… it's all right,' Harriet croons, with a confidence she does not feel, picking the child up once more, to dandle her on one hip, rocking and swaying and swirling around in that motion that only a mother can perfect.

The rumbling furnace has settled itself now and most of the men who made it back as far as the Terrace are standing in the middle of the street, dashing lumps of hot metal from their hats and jackets. Some are knocking smouldering lumps of slag from outhouse and privy roofs with clothes props and sweeping brushes, thanking heaven that their wives and babies are safe. Others are just silently embracing their weeping wives. Shouts go down the row of houses as more arrive.

'Tell 'er I'm all right, duck.'

'My God, 'ave yer seen my Jack at all?'

'Go git our Annie from school. Her dad's been 'urt!'

'What's 'appened t' men on top?'

'Where's Albert?'

'Yer 'at's on fire lad, git it off quick!'

Cries of pain, bewilderment and horror mingle with the subsiding roar of the furnace which glows a dull red at its upper margins. A choking metallic smell picks at nostrils and stings at eyes so that it is hard to see who is crying and who is not.

Pointing and turning again towards the works, the surviving workmen begin slapping each other on the back, amazed by their good fortune. As Harriet watches, torn between the need to get down to the Ogleys and reassure her friend that little Betsey is all right, and wondering if she dare ask after John Henry, a few other workers, clearly injured and supported by their workmates now begin to arrive, limping towards home. One soul is being carried, writhing and jerking on a broken door, towards Harriet.

Moaning softly to herself, Harriet sets Betsey down on the kitchen floor, retrieves her piece of bread to keep her quiet and, with trembling hands, clears the kitchen table. As she turns, I find myself inexorably pulled into her in spite of my horror. I don't want to look but I know I have to see this. It is what has eaten at her for so long; the horror that has lurked, hiding, at the back of her mind and which is perhaps the cause of the apparition my father used to see in the pouring slag on tapping day.

We can smell the cooked flesh as the men loom in the doorway with what remains of John Henry. He has his neck scarf tied around his face and flaps at it with hands that are little better than charred claws.

"E got a big bit full i' the face and down 'is wikins, missus. There's nowt to be done, so we've brung 'im 'ome.'

'Set 'im on the table then,' we whisper, held in tightly; so tightly we're again loose inside our stays.

'Is there owt we can do?' the men query, backing off, removing their flat caps and slurring their feet awkwardly on the kitchen flags. The sickly smell is clogging their nostrils. After a moment of terse silence in which I feel Harriet's whirling mind is rapidly reviewing her options, we look up from the twitching figure on the table.

'Is Will Ogley alright?'

'Yes missus, 'e was in the coke shed when it blew.'

'Tek the bairns to Mrs Ogley down eight doors, then, an' tell 'er what's 'appened. She'll be worried sick after little Betsey and Will.'

One of the workmen picks up the broken door that served as a stretcher and the other gently gathers up little Mary, and young Betsey with her chunk of bread, handing his cap to his mate. Harriet notices vaguely that the peak is burned right off and there's an angry red hole the size of a sixpence in his brow where molten metal has been prised out.

'An' go git that seen to.'

When the little girls are safely away, we turn to what remains of John Henry. Nearing the table, it becomes apparent that most of the front of his torso and legs are badly burned. Blackened toes peer from charred boots, and in places along his shins, metal has joined with flesh to produce a glistening, carbuncular red mass. But it is the face we both fear, unwinding the hanky with one shaking hand and holding away John Henry's weakly flapping hands with the other.

It's too much. I have to get out of her!

Dry, voiceless clicks from his burned throat, and a red oozing mass where forehead and eyes used to be tell her all she needs to know. Can she feel my recoiling horror as I pull away? I want to wake up but I know I have to be here and know what she knows. There is nothing to be done with what remains of John Henry. He is beyond help.

Pacing the room wildly, she grabs at her hair and tugs her scalp back and forth as if to clear her thoughts.

'Can you 'ear me, John?' she asks over and over but there is no response, just the continued twitching and writhing. A moan of despair finally tears its way upwards and breaks free from her gaping mouth in a long and sustained 'Noooo! NO! No, no, no, no.' She chants over and over as she paces the tiny kitchen, casting herself down from time to time on one of the chairs before leaping up again to continue her pacing. At one point she makes as if to tear some clean sheets from a freshly laundered pile, for bandages, but looking at the expanse of fused flesh, metal and slag on the table, she flings them back on the ironing pile again and covers her face with her hands. I can feel disgust and a terrible loathing pressing up inside her as she stares at this wrecked piece of humanity who is still clinging impossibly to life on the kitchen table.

'John, mek a sign if you know I'm here.'

There is only the continued writhing and shuddering from the table, with no sign that he is anything other than a heap of incinerated meat. She shakes him by what remains of his shoulders and repeats her plea.

'John, just lift a hand, owt to let me know you're there, if I can mek you more comfy.'

Nothing.

Finally she stands stock still for an age before making for the stairs, then clatters abruptly back down, clutching a pillow. And then I catch the full force of the memory, sobbing with her as she places the pillow, not under John Henry's head but hard over her husband's face.

When she is done, it bears the imprint of a burnt mask and I understand fully and at last.

It is the same mask that I saw so many times as a child, leering from slag stained clouds; the same mask my father saw and the mask Harriet will see in those boiling clouds for the rest of her life. She must have tried to reach both of us with that vision and, who knows, maybe my granddad as well. Having no success with my drunken father, she tried me and had even less success. Until now.

'Harriet, it's all right! I know why you did it,' I call out, trying to let her know I understand.

I know she can't look after both her family and the lingering, charred body that is now the corpse of her husband, but I've learned as I've watched her real life unfold today that she is, above all else, a practical woman and a survivor. I sense this as she wipes her eyes defiantly on a fine lace handkerchief that she intends to launder again and return to its rightful owner after the funeral.

When she finally moves from John Henry's side where she has remained for an aching expanse of time, inert and defeated like a heap of her washing crumpled upon the floor, her first thought is, as ever, of survival and then, once more, the means to survive.

'Let's 'ave a look at what money there is to bury yer.'

Trembling, she makes her way to the jam jar she keeps hidden in one of the hearth ovens, moving aside the kindling to bend and peer at where she has so carefully concealed it. The jam jar is there but its contents are not. John Henry has found her secret hoard, the produce of all her bone cracking hours of washing, mangling and ironing and she knows he has drunk the proceeds. As the jar smashes on the flagged floor, I catch such a wave of despair now welling up in her that I wonder how she will overcome all this. She turns and beats feebly at the inert form of John Henry which squelches and heaves like a hot water bottle. She can still feel the heat from some of the cooling, flesh-congealed metal.

'Bastard! Bastard! Bastard! Yer bugger! Yer drank it all!'

I sense no grief, no sense of loss, only anger and hatred towards

John Henry for leaving her in this mess. There is no money for a funeral; he will have to go in a pauper's grave. She has endured so much shame in her life already, that having to beg leave for a doctor to arrive, unpaid, to pronounce him dead, beg again for someone to lay out the body, stand before old Bainton and register the fact of the death, then beg again for the body to be removed and buried with little ceremony, no coffin and no mark, seems too much too bear. And what is there to lay out, anyway? The bairns shouldn't see that. There's no money even for a cart to take her and the girls and their belongings to some new abode, nothing except what she can earn at her washing and that won't put a roof over their heads.

'I'm not facing me mam wi' this!'

She will not go back to her parents, and staying with Mary Ann is out of the question. The ache of losing little Charles is still so fresh in her, even after all this time, and she will not ask for the charity that amounted to slavery which was all that was on offer from her sister. Handing the girls into the care of relatives is not, I can sense, an option she wants to consider.

'Nobody's 'avin' 'em but me. I'll not ask for charity again,' she hisses fiercely to herself.

I catch echoes of a tumult of thoughts as they writhe, one by one, to the surface of her mind. Harriet knows full well that if the works management decides that it's the barrow men's fault that the furnace blew, there'll be no wages owed either. If they and their foremen had miscalculated the proportions in the mix, despite being told of the new proposals for smelting, all would pay the penalty until the number two furnace was blown back in. Dead or injured workers' families would have to get out of the tied houses at the end of the week, for there would always be new men and new families waiting step into their shoes. The relentless maws of the furnaces must be filled and iron smelted once more. Sereton Terrace, she knew, would probably soon echo daily to the sound of carts hauling away injured men and belongings, and women weeping and cursing.

But Harriet has a plan, I know she has. I can feel a little stirring of hope. Stitched carefully into the hem of her only other dress are two florins she has been keeping for a winter bonnet and shoes. They won't buy a funeral but they might buy her some time to work out what to do.

'Now how much beer and spirits will that get me? Think! How much? Enough to do it, I reckon. Enough. It's got to be enough,' she mutters as she paces her tiny kitchen, flapping her apron up and down distractedly as she turns…

… Exhausted by the direness of the last hour, I feel myself expanding towards consciousness and I fight to stay where I am. I have to stay now! But I hear another voice; it's quite close and I can feel its warm breath upon my face as my eyelids are lifted one by one. Someone shines a light into my pupils but I'm only vaguely aware of its brightness, as if it is far away at the end of a very long tunnel.

'It's only a matter of hours, I think.'

That's me they're talking about and I'm not ready! I'm so close to ending this puzzle.

'There's a little pupil response but not much. I should prepare yourselves.'

That's just what I'm trying to do; prepare myself. Let me alone to go back to Harriet…

… The ragged, charred, fag end of the day's shift finds her down at the *Blue Bell*, waiting outside by the door with the coins clutched in her hand inside her pinafore pocket. She knows that this is the first place that the workers from this ill-fated shift will go before ever they head homewards again; and she's waiting for two men in particular.

'Buy yer a pint, Stan? Where's 'Erbert? Oh, 'ere 'e comes.'

'My God Mrs B! What's tha doin' 'ere? 'Ow's poor John? Shun't tha be at 'ome wi' 'im?' The first worker pulls off his cap and pumps it anxiously in his hands, while his mate stares at the ground and scuffs at it in embarrassment with his boot.

Harriet composes her features into a picture of worry and concern and stares into the two red and filthy faces of the workmen. I can feel her biting back the words, 'Ay, and shouldn't you be at home?' and instead she says, baldly, 'It wain't John Henry. Yer brought me some other mawk.'

'But missus, we were sure…'

So that's your plan, Harriet.

'Come in an' 'ave a pint, lads, and ah'll tell yer what's to do.' She speaks more roughly and broadly than she would normally do, in an attempt to gain their confidence.

Inside the *Blue Bell* the usual stink of beer, urine and tobacco is overlaid by the metal and charred cloth reek of the day's tragic shift at Appleton. Once all three are seated at a table and the ale is flowing in generous quantities, she loosens her shawl, leans forward and repeats her story. Her hands pick nervously at its fringe under the table but her face is defiant.

'I've left all me bairns wi' Betty Ogley to come down 'ere and tell yer that yer brought me some other mawk. It weren't 'im.'

The *Blue Bell* is now ringing to the angry sound of workers drowning their sorrows and discussing the day's awful happenings. Hands thump wood and caps are cast to the floor in anger. Every time the name of a foreman or manager is mentioned, there is a united spit into the sawdust. Surfacing momentarily from his pint, a bemused and stunned Stan gapes for a moment, then turns and calls across to the other side of the bar,

''As any bugger seen John Blanchard?'

Harriet knows that John Henry was not a popular or gregarious man, preferring a solitary drink to the company of mates, and she's counting on this fact. A chorus of negatives and one lone affirmative greet the question.

'Ay, the bastard 'ad bin 'idin' by the tap charges just a while afore it blew. Cyril Fussy 'ad 'em all ready for the tappin' when it went and there's nowt at all left of him barrin' 'is 'at. I took it to 'is missus. Awful bad she took it, with another bairn in the oven. Di'n't see what 'appened to Blanchard, though.'

Stan turns back to Harriet and takes the handkerchief from around his neck to wipe his perspiring face and dab at the hole in his forehead, now grown angry and swollen at its margins like a small volcano. He looks meaningfully at his empty glass, grasped in the grimy calloused hands of a barrow man, and cocks his head towards Herbert's glass as well.

Herbert seems to be in some sort of state and is ashen beneath his ruddy cheeks, trembling violently. Once the beers are ordered, Harriet sits at his side and takes off his handkerchief too, muttering soothing words while she gently wipes at a burned eyebrow. Then she stands up abruptly and, hands on hips, hisses, 'So where's my John Henry and who is the mawk yer brought me? I don't want a strange mawk in me kitchen!'.

Stan takes a while and a few draws at his pint to digest this statement before querying, 'Ow do yer know? 'Ow can you be sure it wa'n't 'im? It were 'is jacket reet enough.'

'Oh it were 'is jacket all right, the drunken bastard gev it and 'is second best apron *and* 'is work boots to a new bloke that stayed with us last night before startin' fresh today. Don't even know the bugger's name, 'e came so late last night. Reelin' in from drinkin' wi' their arms around each other, they were. And I've got no lodging money to show for it. Any road, does hayther of you two know oo 'e was?'

Her mind is working quickly now, skipping from idea to idea, extrapolating and testing each one before discarding it or holding it up for further reference. It's common knowledge that many single young men turn up at the works site each week hoping for a job and find lodgings with the families of Sereton Terrace. They come from all over the county and beyond, and are a good source of extra income for whoever takes them in. Stan and Herbert shake their heads in unison, while Harriet looks covertly at the remaining coins in her apron pocket. Just enough left to get the two well and truly fuddled.

'So where is John Henry? And what are we going to do wi' that mawk yer brought me?' she persists, all the while keeping the ale and talk of the days events flowing so that she can judge whether her plan will work.

Finally, with a boldness even she did not know she had, she stands on a chair and addresses the entire clientele of the *Blue Bell*.

'HAS ANYONE SEEN JOHN HENRY BLANCHARD?'

There is a momentary silence as the question is digested once more. Pipes are sucked on and heads scratched.

'No missus, more than likely 'e ran off frit!'

'He was a bit of a nobbut when it came to tappin' and castin' anyway!'

'He mebbe got the shits like he usually does when owd man slag starts a pourin'. Try the shithouse!'

There is a titter of agreement, the odd guffaw and much nodding of heads as the men resume their conversations. Harriet didn't know he was disliked so much.

Climbing down, with an exaggerated air of defeat, Harriet turns once more to a bleary Stan and Herbert. She may look defeated but I sense a glow of hope inside her. Just a couple of weeks is all she needs. A couple of weeks to get some sort of plan and a bit of money together. Her apron pocket is empty, so it's now or never.

'Well you two can just come back wi' me, then, an' git rid o' this bloody mawk.'

Stan and Herbert stagger to their feet and Harriet pushes them to the door with mock fury. More guffaws sound but as they move outside she notices that some of the men are quietly weeping and some are simply shaking and staring into an untouched pint.

Reality does not bite until the three are actually in Harriet's kitchen, staring at the sheeted corpse.

'Weear are we goin' to tek him, Missus?' slurs Stan, only dimly aware of his surroundings, while Herbert just stares at the red stain at the head end of the sheet.

'Back ovver to the works offices. They'll know what to do with 'im. They'll bury 'im. Whativver 'appens, 'e's not stayin' the night 'ere and that's final.'

Harriet is exhausted but she keeps up the act of indignation until the door is firmly closed and locked, John Henry having been carried outside and she off up the street to her friend Betsey Ogley's. When she finally stands in front of the door she is shaking with tears of disbelief at what she has done. Now there are *more* lies to be told.

Drawing a deep and shuddering breath she hesitates, then knocks softly.

'Oh at last; come in, duck. What's to do?'

The big protective hand of William Ogley steers her into the kitchen where his wife Betsey sits rocking Mary by the embers of a fire. The child's eyes are red raw and tears are still upon her lashes but her face is the transparent white that babies and young children assume when they are in deep sleep. Harriet takes her from Betsey and buries her face in Mary's dark hair, pacing the floor and composing herself among the ebony strands, so different from her own red locks. Just like John Henry's hair, she thinks, but then sees with a shudder, the charred skullcap.

'The rest are upstairs with ours love, but Mary wouldn't settle. She's on'y just nicely gone off,' says Will, stirring the embers with a poker. 'Will you have a cup of tea, duckie? I can soon get the kettle on.'

Shaking her head, Harriet begins to spin her tale, finishing with a plaintive, 'You haven't seen him, have you?'

To a chorus of nos, and where can he be? She finally explains that the two workmates are just taking the unfortunate and unknown corpse over to the works.

'Well, they can't turn you out just yet, duckie: missing men's families get two weeks' notice, not the weekend shove out that the rest of these poor buggers will get.'

This is definitely Harriet's plan; two weeks' grace to think of a way to keep her little family together.

'Listen Betsey. I get paid for me washin' tomorrow so I can just about mek the rent. ''Ow would it be if I came and 'elped you with the bairns, did some cookin' and your washin', too? You know you're not well and can 'ardly get out of bed some days. In return, if you could just spare me and the kids a bite or two of bread and jam...'

'We'll do more than that, duckie. If tha' cooks it tha'll yet it as well. Bread and jam indeed! Ovver my dead body!' exclaims Betsey.

I feel Harriet overcome at last with a mixture of relief, grief, gratitude, fear and weariness. With Mary still in her arms, she bends down to give Betsey Ogley a kiss on the cheek, tears dripping on to the tired woman's hands. She notices the dark circles under her eyes and the bloodstained hanky tucked into her sleeve that are the marks of the consumptive. There's nothing much to be done for Betsey, except care for her and hope the children don't get taken with it. Harriet and Betsey have grown up together in Ellenby and, as the wives of iron workers, have reunited in adversity on Sereton Terrace. I can feel a strong and sympathetic bond between them, forged fast by the hard circumstances, the smoke and heat of the Appleton Works.

'Ah'll do me best for yer,' she sobs.

'An' we will for thee, lass,' returns Will, patting her heaving shoulders. 'Now don't go disturbin' the bairns. Come ovver in t'mornin' and get 'em, an' tha can mek us all a breakfas'.'

Back in her own cottage, Harriet puts Mary to sleep on John Henry's side of the bed and stirs up a little fire in the bedroom grate to ward off the chill of the cold February night. It's a luxury but she feels in need of some comfort tonight.

'Just a bit o' comfort,' she says to herself and then, thinking out loud, begins to tick off her immediate problems as she rocks to and fro on the edge of the bed. 'Well, at least there's a couple o' weeks afore they twig on and turn me out.'

She has warded off disaster for now, then she knows she'll have to leave Sereton Terrace and find somewhere to live with her girls.

'Then there's the question o' the mawk, though I'm sure 'e couldn't be telled apart from a pig on a butcher's 'ook. An' what about Betsey? Poor lass, she looks nigh gone.'

Her brain just cannot encompass any more tonight but, in spite of the warmth of the fire, sleep will not come. And so she does what she does best, going downstairs once more to find numbing comfort in activity.

First the kitchen table is scrubbed clean of blood, metal and grime until its deal boards glow white in the dim candlelight. Then she sets to, to swill the kitchen floor where John Henry voided his bladder in his final agonies. Next, the broken jam jar pieces are picked up carefully from the floor and thrown into the night, far down the garden.

'Bastard!' she mutters again, as she latches the back door, shutting out little eddies of snow that have begun to obscure the remains of the distant and dully glowing blast furnace hearth. Dark figures scurry backwards and forwards, silhouetted against its glow, working far into the night to secure the wreckage.

In the cold and quiet of the early hours, pillow seams are unpicked with numb fingers and the feathers tied carefully in sackcloth, so that she can put the bloodstained ticking to soak in lye. The ash is carefully mixed in a bucket in just the right quantities, with water, soap shavings and salt until she has a mixture that she thinks will do the job. Holding up the pillow ticking, and before plunging it up and down in the bucket, she crumples momentarily, seeing that it still bears the imprint of John Henry's scorched, faceless mask, the mouth open in a twisted, beseeching jag of a shape. The eye socket rims burn accusation into Harriet's jittering mind as she goes over and over the events of the day, repeating her explanations again and again to herself until she is satisfied that she has left no loopholes. The mask's accusation stays with her as she finally heaves her way up the stairs and climbs wearily and fully dressed into bed next to a sleeping Mary. She stares for a long time at the embers of the bedroom fire where she fancies she can still see that face, the empty eye sockets black against red glowing flesh.

She turns in her half sleep now and I turn with her.

'I 'ad ter do it, John. 'Ah just couldn't see yer like that.'

Her consciousness finally finds some closure for the events of the day, in setting up a room for John Henry in her imaginary house, a place where she can go and speak to him as she will. She furnishes it with a bed and a comfy chair, a coat stand on which to hang his cap and leather apron, and she places a bottle of beer and a candle on the stand by his bed. Not wanting him to be cold, she adds a small grate as an afterthought before finally shutting the door of her imagination on the awful sight of his face. Curling around Mary, she falls into a superficial, fitful sleep.

Down by the spoil tips of the open cast mines, two shadowy figures heave a sheet draped corpse into a shallow grave. Leaving Harriet, I trickle down among their thoughts. A little more sober now, Stan and Herbert have forgone the inevitable inquiry that would have taken place had they taken a faceless corpse to the management's offices. If they can smell a rat in their state, they reason, somebody else certainly will. Best for the corpse to vanish, keep quiet and let Mrs B sort it out as best she will. No harm done. But the flailing hand of John Henry Blanchard will not submit to the grave, and even when, with a sickening crack they are forced to dislocate his shoulder, the clawed fingers still lay mere inches from the surface.

'Aw bugger it! They'll be tippin' 'ere in t'mornin, Stan. Leave the mawk and forget it. Lets us git 'ome, lad. She'll niver know 'e 'ad no proper burial and we b'aint be about to tell 'er.'

'It were 'im.'

'There's nowt to be gained by sayin' that, Stan.'

'But it were!'

As the argument fades into the night, I catch sight of a pale face staring from an upper window on Sereton Terrace. It is Harriet, awake once more and staring after Stan and Herbert as they stumble home. She must have known what they had done.

The shock propels me into reluctant consciousness once more, all too painfully aware now of the significance of the mask that has haunted my final hours, and which probably haunted my father for most of his life.

Harriet, my great grandmother, killed her husband and allowed his body to be buried on the steelworks where it remained, in all likelihood, until it was discovered just yesterday, nearly one hundred and forty years later.

# 17

## ANOTHER CHOICE

Death, you continue to surprise me just when I thought you held no more secrets. Turning John Henry's dreadful demise in my mind, I really expect to be shocked by Harriet's part in it but I'm not. She was simply a survivor, not a victim. On this day of days, when I've come to know her thoughts so well, I've never once caught the remotest thread of a victim mentality running through her thoughts. She knew that whatever happened in her life, she was the one who had to deal with it, so rather than condemning her, I acknowledge instead the backbone of steel and will of iron that propelled her on, marvelling at her determination to survive which drove her to hasten her husband's imminent death, and then to claim he was someone else.

The accident explains so many things. I'll never know whether the family had any idea of what she did but in her small world there must have been rumours. And John Henry's clawing hand! That was the start of all this; the skeletal hand on the television last night was where this turbulent day of recollections and realisations began.

I know that the hand in the news report just has to be his. That's probably why there was no record to be found of his death, no matter how hard I looked.

The thought is insistent. Why is *his* death so significant now? Why did Harriet repeatedly, and throughout our lives, try to tell both my father and myself about what she'd done? As always with Harriet, I've solved one mystery, only to uncover several more.

'Well you'd better hurry up, girl, I haven't got much time left. The time for conundrums and mysteries is over. Whatever it is that you want me to learn before I go, you need to make it plain,' I sigh to myself, the thought escaping in a sound somewhere between a cough and a snort of exasperation.

'I'm saying this to a woman who has been dead for over a hundred years!' one small remnant of my logic protests, waving this fact like a flag of weary defeat to my semi-conscious self. But in my mind's eye that skeletal hand is beckoning, drawing me to a time when my great grandmother's life finally unravels. I can see the threads, loose and livid, hanging, tangling and throbbing about her head. There are bells ringing. Is it still Sunday? It's not my Sunday…

… It's a sunny Sunday morning in a place far from here and long ago. The bells of St John's Church drift over a lunar landscape of ironworks, excavations and slag tips; up and over grimy patched rooftops and playing children, to Sereton Terrace. There I find Harriet standing once more in her cottage yard, stirring her steeping barrels. Her calendar tells me it is April, 1901. I should know why that date is important; it should tell me something but its significance is lost for the moment as I watch her stirring. It seems obvious to me for the moment. I've picked up her story again at the point where she has survived the death of John Henry Blanchard by moving in with Will Ogley after Betsey died of TB. This is the yard where I first saw her, earlier today.

Was it only today? I seem to have lived two whole lifetimes in a few short hours. I never thought death would take so long to ease me out of this wrecked frame. But I'm pleased that long after the other grieving widows have left, Harriet is clinging on in Sereton Terrace Perhaps she's going to show me what happened in the months after John Henry's death. I'm wary now, though, about becoming too closely entwined with her thoughts, so I stand in a corner of the yard, beaming love and comfort towards her stooping back.

She pauses for a moment in her toils to watch the arrival of the sand martins as they pipe and shriek along the discarded open cast mine faces, searching for the holes they vacated last year. Her worn face even affords itself a little smile as she watches their swooping flight.

'Four hundred and ninety,' she breathes into the sky.

The moment is abruptly shattered by a clatter at the gate as the latch lifts. Too late, I'm Harriet. I'm Harriet, feeling our stomach lurch as the hair on the back of our neck rises like a cat's.

A pale, cleanly shaven almost polished face peers into the tiny yard. It wears a smile that barely twitches the mouth corners, by-passing the owner's eyes entirely. Meeting their gaze we give an involuntary shudder. We know we see the world differently to most people but these eyes see a whole other place, a covert world where beauty hides in shame, and pleasure lies in guilt. Humourless and ashen, the face is surmounted by an immaculate, black stovepipe hat that lends Jacob Churchill's thin features more bile than the gravitas he hopes to exude. Out of hiding, a leer scuttles across his face, underlined by a lift of the hat that lets fall a lock of colourless, lank hair. This is swiftly swept back by a bony, fluttering hand that flies to his pocket when he sees our furious expression and the incline of the head towards our daughters.

Jacob immediately replaces his hat and hides his face in a crisp, white handkerchief, blowing his nose with great ceremony, flushing at the thought that he had almost been caught out. I sense that, for this character, propriety and public appearances have to be observed no matter what, even in front of children.

'I shall be collecting the rent, as usual, this Sunday night, Mrs Blanchard,' he says, stuffing his handkerchief up his sleeve in a manner he believes demonstrates both breeding and delicacy. His statement is followed by the slight involuntary escape of air, almost a groan, which we know he gives whenever he is forced to say something he feels to be somewhat embarrassing or uncomfortable.

Jacob has now fully entered the yard and stands with his jacket open and thumbs hooked into his Sunday best paisley waistcoat. The effect of this stance upon his narrow shoulders and pigeon chest is, again, not exactly what he intends, giving him a strut like a magpie. His attempt at a pleasant smile further smears the picture. Alice and Edith stare, fascinated, at the disappearing handkerchief and smother their giggles.

'I shall have it ready.'

'That you will, Mrs. Blanchard, a widow cannot have tenure in a works house without she pays her dues. Never forget you are here by my favour and my favour alone. There are many who have a greater right to these premises than you and your ill-assorted family.'

'Yes Mr Churchill,' we murmur, bobbing in only the bare semblance of a curtsey, head still erect and a glare tightly in place. The rent on the iron workers' houses of Sereton Terrace is usually collected on Fridays but as a widow, we have had to make another arrangement.

Jacob Churchill is now striding around the yard with jerky, long-legged steps, peering suspiciously into Harriet's barrels. Edith and Alice, meanwhile, have retrieved dirty lace handkerchiefs from a washing pile indoors and are busy stuffing them up their sleeves with fluttering hands and taking prancing steps in line behind him. The rent collector stops, vaguely aware that he's being mocked behind his back, and attempts to puff himself up with importance.

'And will my shirts also be ready?' he enquires, swinging round and fingering his necktie, newly stitched for him by another widow of his acquaintance. 'There is much virtue in a clean shirt; a good, fine, well-got-up shirt showing plenty of collar, front and wristbands. Many a man has been indebted to his washerwoman, not only in the little amount of her bill but also for subsequent fame and fortune.'

Clara has, by now, appeared in the kitchen doorway to scoop up Alice and Edith's hands and pull them back into the house. Licking his thin, dry lips, Jacob gazes after the retreating children and remarks, 'My! I see your Clara is fully grown of late. A fine young woman! Let us hope the rest show such promise.' Another involuntary groan follows his last remark and Harriet takes his meaning exactly.

'Whitecurrant stems,' we mutter into our pinafore as we dry our hands and, when our head comes up, our face wears a smile of such power and warmth that Jacob takes a step backwards towards the gate, abashed.

'They'll be ready sir, hand fittin' for a man such as yourself,' we pronounce, in the most refined voice we can muster. Sensing her sarcasm, Jacob Churchill flushes once more, this time in anger.

'T... tonight then, madam!' he snaps.

We don't reply, our smile a continuing barb to his pride, prodding him all the while with its sheer presence to the gate and out of our sight. We don't stop smiling until we hear his receding footsteps on the cobbled ten-foot behind the house, then we turn with a click of the tongue back to our steeping barrels.

Though she is outwardly calm, I grasp the despair and revulsion in what she's thinking and I surface momentarily in cold, sickly shock. This is not what I expected to see. What *is* happening? Harriet is alone once more and desperate. Where is Will Ogley? Have I got the time frame wrong?

From the cottage a thin wailing cry can be heard and Clara emerges carrying an undersized baby girl of about a year old.

'She's 'ungry, mam,' Clara frowns. 'She needs milk.'

'There's nowt until tomorrow,' Harriet snaps. 'Give 'er the last bit o' sugar and some water in the titty bottle.'

Clara comes back out again a few moments later carrying the child and a banana shaped glass bottle surmounted by a red rubber teat at each end. The child is screaming so loudly by now, however, that she will not feed. She throws herself back in Clara's arms and the girl can hardly hold her.

'Give 'er 'ere duck, an' you do this.' Harriet motions for Clara to take over at the steeping barrels.

Seated on the doorstep, Harriet shushes and rocks the child until she will take the bottle. 'Now then our Kate. That's it. There's a good bairn. You drink it up. That's the last o' the sugar until tomorrow, though. It'll be the owd Godfrey's Cordial at bedtime. 'Appen we'll all need it tonight as there's nowt in at all to yet for supper. There's a good girl. Yes, that's it. Yer daddy would turn in 'is grave if 'e 'eard you bealing like that,' she intones. This entire, dismal story is murmured in a low singsong voice as if it is a lullaby of the tenderest words. Rocking and rocking the child, Harriet sings until little Kate finishes the bottle and is quite peaceful again.

'He didn't mean to leave us. It weren't 'is fault, duck. Don't tek on so, Kate. Be good for your mam, there's work enough wi'out all this.'

The full significance of the calendar date suddenly sinks home. I should have realised. This time frame is after Fred, after little Edward, after her liaison with the man who was my great grandfather. Harriet is alone once more because Will Ogley is also now dead. Her fortunes have taken a turn for the worse yet again. I remember how finally, after many months of searching, I managed to trace my great grandfather's death certificate. How I sighed then over the few short years of their partnership. This isn't the relatively happy time I expected to find. This is the time during which my great grandmother will eventually have to give up yet another child. Yet Kate is still with Harriet for now; maybe the Ogley children are too.

'I miss the others, mam, even though it were more mouths to feed,' says Clara over her shoulder to her mother, answering my unspoken thought.

'They were good girls and young Arthur played wi' Fred a treat,' agrees Harriet. 'But they're better off wi' a full belly and clothes on their backs. Their granny can give 'em that at least.'

'Will we ivver see 'em any more?' asks Edith in a plaintive voice. 'Betsey helped me a lot at school, mam.'

'I doubt we'll cast eyes on 'em ivver again.'

The abrupt reply hides so many things that I am drowned in them. Regret at having to send the Ogley children to live with their grandparents, sorrow at Will's death, which was the cause of the parting, and despair at still having just too many mouths to feed. I sense that little Kate's incessant hungry wail is particularly heart-rending. Harriet's milk dried up early with the shock of Will's death and there is never enough food in the house to feed the child.

'Harriet, was there ever a time in your life when you didn't have to struggle?' I wonder, watching the sad little tableau in the yard. Here they are yet again, clinging to goodness knows what life raft. Are they about to be thrown out of their cottage?...

... There's a tight squeeze on my arm that brings me, wobbling and faint, back to the ward as my blood pressure cuff is inflated. I feel utterly wretched and disappointed by what I've just seen but equally unhappy to be back here on my bed and subject to the gentle indifferences of the hospital and the world I will shortly be leaving. I don't want the ache of the sad company that I sense is circled around me. I can do nothing with or for their sorrow. How strange that the continuation of my own life means so little to me now, other than as a tool for solving a mystery. I shouldn't think like that; they can't help it.

The staff need to know how far gone I am, I suppose. That's all it is. There's nothing they can do for me other than this palliative care. My family should leave me be but they all have to show me that they love me and that they're doing the right thing. They have this great horror of me dying alone but that's how it works. They can't come with me.

No, I really shouldn't think like that. With my eyes still closed, I try and shut out the world of which I am now barely a part and ponder on this latest scene from my great grandmother's hard existence. When I was doing that ancestry stuff all those years ago, I remember how I gradually forgot about Harriet once she'd done her work of introducing a little self forgiveness into my life. I was content. I could move on at last and look to the future once more, and so the one person who really began to hold my attention was Kate. Baby Kate, my granddad's true sister.

After I discovered that she'd been adopted and taken to America with the Bowers family, there was always the tantalizing possibility that she'd married and had had children of her own and that they, or their descendants, might still be alive. The search took on a new urgency after my lovely aunt Peg died and I became, to all intents and purposes, the Ogley-Blanchard family elder. It was such a small family and with so much that was still unknown, I wasn't ready to take on the mantle. It made me feel so alone. There was no one left who knew me as a child, no one who knew the people I knew then, no one with whom I could have a meaningful conversation about folks from the past. Oh, your children are always vaguely interested, but like anyone of a different generation, it's only the people whom they can remember that they really want to hear about. They don't need to find their real roots until much later on when uncertainty and doubt begin their delicate work of unstitching what you thought was the meaning of your life.

It was in looking for my own roots that I eventually found Kate's only surviving child and another whole branch of my family. She lived in Iowa and had no children of her own, so family history really did revolve around just us two then. Imagine finding that your grandparents and all of their family are really nothing to do with you at all. She took it well and, at eighty years of age, bought a computer so that we could correspond more easily. Dear, sweet, gentle aunt Ruth, I loved you from the first moment I saw you. You were the gift in the middle of Harriet's tragic tale, but then ancestry research is full of such wonderful surprises.

'Did you ever wonder, Harriet, if anyone would find Kate for you? Is that why I'm seeing her now? Is that why you showed me Charles too?'

I think about the photos I received from aunt Ruth: Kate as a child, a young woman, a bride, a mother and, in later years, a formidable female activist, meeting the American President and leaving her own mark on history. Harriet would have been so proud of her fine, intelligent daughter; perhaps now she is about to show me what she remembers of her. I drowse a little more happily and pick up the threads of that day in Harriet's tiny yard.

It is long past midnight when a furtive knock at the back door marks the return of the rent collector, who lets himself into the tiny kitchen to face an ashen, tight-lipped Harriet. We have been waiting for him on a stool by the fire embers.

'A light, madam, if you please. I cannot collect my dues in darkness, as well you know.'

Shocked and appalled, I leave Harriet immediately, backing away in disgust from what I now realise is about to take place. By the light of two candles, Jacob holds Harriet down by her hair over the kitchen table and lifts her skirts. Harriet parts her breeches and waits, thankful at least that he takes her this way and there will be no offspring as the result of this vile pairing. She knows he will take some time and effort to be ready and there is absolutely nothing she is prepared to do to help.

'Are you clean?'

Harriet does not reply but buries her head in her apron which she has spread on the table before her, waiting for the brief pounding, the twist of her hair and the gasp that will signify her rent is paid for another week.

When he is done, I feel humiliated. How could I presume to know what Harriet needs to show me? Hopelessly entangled in her shame and engulfed by a feeling of dirtiness and absolute despair, I look out into the night and follow the dim silhouette of Jacob Churchill's retreating form. Harriet stares with me and we wonder together how long she can go on paying her rent like this. The act itself is bad enough, but then there's all the rest. I read in her thoughts that it does not, of course, escape the notice of the rest of Sereton Terrace that she, a widow, is still residing in an iron worker's cottage long after other widows have been turned out. But, as she is not dependent upon idle tongues for the income that feeds and clothes her girls, she learns to ignore the daily cat calls hurled her way by neighbours, the abuse at the grocery store and the leers from other iron workers as they leave their shifts.

'Got owt left ovver for us, duck?'

It's not the first or even the second time she's been called a whore. Maybe everyone is right about her, after all.

'No Harriet, No.'

'An' mebbe I should 'ave moved away when Will died but where was there to go?' she sighs despairingly to herself.

I can see her square jaw clamp and tighten as she gathers her resolve to carry on. Her mind flickers briefly over the alternatives, as it does every Sunday night when she feels so low and defiled. Her sister in Derby said housing was cheaper there but with so many mouths to feed, what good would a cheaper rent be?

'No, best endure it 'ere until summats else turns up,' she concludes. But her heart aches for her girls who also have to endure whispers and sniggers in the playground, as the children copy their parents' derision, though thankfully in ignorance of the cause of it all.

With the rent dues paid and the collector gone, Harriet stands astride a bucket of water in the kitchen to clean herself. When she's done, the water is thrown down the garden She cannot even bear to empty it in her stone sink. Her face is blank and expressionless now, betraying little emotion. All I can read is a feeling that she has a roof over her head and she can just about feed her children. She is luckier than some and she knows it, but how long will her luck last?

'As long as the bugger still comes to dip 'is wick,' she says out loud, answering her own question.

The last job for the night is to prepare the only food she has in the house so they can all eat in the morning. She intends to cut up stale bread from a loaf she has hidden in the oven. She cuts up thin slices of bread each night and soaks them in a little water to make them edible. Sometimes she can manage to find a bit of jam or even weak tea for them to drink as well; but not tomorrow. The last of the teapot dregs were baked in a flour and water crust two days ago. With a bit of sugar sprinkled on it they'd all pretended it was a plum pie. Tomorrow she has to buy more soap, and with so much on tick already at the grocers' she'll have to be careful she's not refused.

Harriet bends to open the oven door and notices it is unlatched. Casting the iron door wide open her worst fears are realised. The bread has gone.

'Well it was a nobbut 'idin' place. They've done this afore. They're 'ungry, the wretched bairns. Waited until me back was tonned and then smuggled it up under someone's pinny to bed. There'll not be a skerrick left by now. Lord, I on'y hope Kate got some.'

She sits down heavily at the table and puts her head in her hands, a weariness almost visible around her like a shawl. No matter how many times she pastes them all with the washing tongs, leaving red welt marks on their backsides, hunger gets the better of them. They always find whatever food she has hidden away, no matter where she hides it. She just can't keep pace with it.

'One more thing to worry about tomorrow,' she voices to the ceiling and the sleeping children above, her tones sharp and accusatory. This isn't like the Harriet I have come to know on this day.

Her hands are spread on the white deal table top, suddenly

slapped down there in frustration. Red raw and cracked, with skin peeling from the caustic lye, those hands, together with her will to go on, are all that is holding her little family together. They look like butcher's meat in the candlelight.

'Better see to you, then,' she mutters and rises abruptly to cross the tiny kitchen and rub her fingers through a knot of sheep's wool that hangs by a string on the back door. 'But Lord I 'ate the smell on it. Me owd 'ands stink o' tow every night.'

She crinkles her face and sits at the table once more, massaging the lanolin into and around her fingers, wincing as she catches the deep, open fissures at the corners of her thumb and forefinger. Then she tilts one of the candles before blowing them both out and rubs the liquid tallow into her hands too. Job done, she sits by the light of the last glowing coal and begins to recite her lists.

'Sand martins arrived for the summer... '

But it won't work tonight; nothing brings her peace or provides her with a useful metaphor for her problems.

'Will's gret 'ands... ' she whispers, but the image touches a spot even more raw in memory than her own hands and she can only weep.

It is an age before she moves again. The meagre fire has gone out and the house is chill this April night. I expect to find fierce resolution driving her on as usual but, as she finally mounts the stairs to her bed, I catch only despair, despair and more despair. I felt this only once before; when she took that pillow to John Henry and I know that Harriet is about to use desperate measures to get through this. As she lays her head upon the pillow, I sense the veiled bones of another plan forming in her mind and a feeling I know only too well.

Drifting with her into sleep, I am suddenly and unwillingly plucked into the here and now by five murmured and familiar heart broken words.

'Hearts can do no more.' Now I know what she means to do.

'Harriet… '

'Harriet, we were *so* close, you and I.'

Hearts can do no more. To tear a child from your bosom and leave it to a probable better future than you can provide is a pain no one can know until they've had to do it. I think I know now why she wanted me to relive that same misery from my own life, here today. There was no point to remembering it all again except that it was to be reminded of what Harriet endured. I only hope she found the forgiveness that I did. I know that despite all her efforts to keep her family together she has resigned herself to losing at least some of them. But how do you choose which ones? At least I didn't have to face that, Harriet.

Before any of the girls or Fred are up the next day, she has combed and tidied her hair, washed her face and put on a fresh apron. Creeping upstairs, she scoops up Kate and takes the sleepy child downstairs to wash her and change her soiled wrappings. Rummaging through one of her baskets of dirty laundry she finds a reasonably clean bonnet, a coat and smocked nightdress. None of the items are hers and she will have to find time to launder and return them by Thursday but she needs to make Kate look present-able today.

Kate, laid softly in a basket of laundry on the kitchen table, is now beginning to stir and start her high-pitched, hungry wail as Harriet smartens her up. A last lick on the corner of her apron and

Harriet scrubs a sticky, grimy ring and a few breadcrumbs from around the protesting little girl's mouth. She'll do. Covering her with kisses, and hugging her tightly, she starts the song that always gets a laugh, while grabbing a ragged and worn pile of muslins and making for the front door.

'Atishoo! Atishoo! We all fall dooown!' Harriet sings as she makes her way round to the house next door.

Kate shrieks and gurgles, her thin little features lighting up to produce a pretty smile just as the Bowers' front door opens. She looks quite fetching under her lace bonnet and her neighbours do love her so. Harriet is counting on this fact.

The Bowers are already up and about, as Jim is on early shifts this week. A childless couple, Syringa and James are always more than happy to look after baby Kate for Harriet. Harriet, meanwhile, knows that it is the only way Kate will be fed this morning. She can't bear to listen to those hungry screams while she's doing the washing. The older ones will just have to suffer but Kate, her darling girl, and young Fred don't understand why she has nothing to give them.

'Come in,' calls James from the kitchen, as Harriet makes her way in with a beaming Kate.

'I'd swear that tha' was a dadda if I didn't know different,' smiles Harriet, depositing Kate in his arms and setting the muslin wrappings upon the table. James blushes, dandling Kate and enquiring how he and his wife can be of service to Harriet. She sits down heavily at the kitchen table, smoothing the folds of her worn dress and neatening her apron. She looks distracted as she begins to ask if Mrs Bowers will mind Kate for the day.

'It's like this, duck. The bairn just wain't settle and I 'ave Mrs Duffelen's linen to do. You know how particular she is; sent a load back unpaid for the other week.'

She is about to pluck up the courage to press on further when I feel something inside her crumple and wilt. Although I'm sure she had no intention of playing it this way, she puts her face in her hands, unable to finish her request. Her shoulders begin to shake and, finally, with a huge and shuddering sigh she lifts her head, grasping her hair in both hands in a gesture I remember so well.

'Who am I to ask such a thing of you good folks? 'Aven't you 'eard what the entire Terrace is sayin' about me?' she wails. 'No one can 'elp me! I do what I 'ave to do but it i'n't enough! The bairns are hungry, there's no milk for Kate and no matter what I do, I can't keep up. What's to become of us all?'

The Bowers look at each other in stunned shock, waiting for the outburst to subside. Harriet has always been so resolute. She seemed to manage to carry on when her husband disappeared in the accident, she buried Betsey Ogley and then took on her brood of four, she took up with Will Ogley and seemed stalwart and invincible even when Will died. She gave him a decent funeral, she made sure his children were cared for until their grandparents sent a cart for them, she kept on with her washing, she even worked out an arrangement with that wretched rent collector avoiding, for a second time, the inevitable eviction that follows the death of a man and provider on Sereton Terrace. They had come to regard her indomitable spirit with real admiration, and not the derision shown by many in the street. Now here she is, a broken woman, sitting helpless at their kitchen table. This is not the Harriet they've come to know.

'Have you really no family who could help?' says James gently, handing Kate to his wife and laying a gentle hand on Harriet's heaving shoulder. Harriet wipes her face on her clean apron, smoothes her hair back into place and faces James Bowers squarely as he sits down across the table from her. She gratefully accepts the cup of tea that is brought and then looks at little Kate, only to start crying all over again.

'Shall I give her milk, then?' Mrs Bowers enquires, setting the teapot down in embarrassment and nodding towards Kate who has got over all the attention by now and is beginning to grizzle and wrestle about in her arms.

'Oh please duck, if you could; if you don't mind,' whispers Harriet. I feel her resolve stiffen as she remembers her plan, and turns to James who is pulling up a chair next to her. It takes a few sips of her tea, however, before she feels calm enough to speak.

'Well, I've another sister, Alice, in Derby, who dotes on Edith and would give her an 'ome,' she says, staring into space. 'Then Gertie's money helps a bit, an' she gets board and lodge wherivver she's in service, so that's another mouth less. I could mebbe manage Mary, Fred and Alice if they could get from under me feet and get some schooling. Clara is such an 'elp wi' the washing I couldn't lose her, but it's Kate who is the tie when I'm working. She has to go without food or upbringing when I'm at the dolly tub, poor mite.'

Both of them nod gravely and encourage Harriet to go on, while Kate slurps greedily at a cup of warm, fresh milk bought not a half an hour ago from the milkman doing his rounds with his horse and cart.

'I've a mind to send to her and ask if she can find us lodgings in Derby on'y, on'y… '

There is a heavy silence broken only by Kate's gasping and slurping as she drains the cup.

James and Syringa exchange glances before Mrs Bowers breaks the silence and speaks.

'Would you like us to look after Kate for you for a bit?' I sense that they have both been almost hoping for this. They have no child of their own and looking after little Kate fills a huge gap in Syringa's life. 'She loves coming here and we could take her if you decide to go to Derby, you know.'

'It would make me so happy to see her well looked after. It breks me 'eart to see 'er go 'ungry day after day. But… '

'Look Harriet, give notice on the rent for next week, and get yourself off to Derby tomorrow with Clara to see what that sister can do. We'll take the children while you sort it all out. Anything has to be better that this and the pickle with Jacob Churchill.'

Harriet's face colours deeply and she hides it in her apron.

'Everyone knows, love.'

'Well it can't get much worse then, can it?' sobs Harriet quietly. ''Appen it's time to move on at last. Come 'ere duck!'

Reaching her arms out for Kate, she smothers the child's milky face with kisses and the baby, now satisfied at last, goos and coos in her arms.

'I'll 'ave to get all me washing done first.'

'And I'll help you with that too,' soothes Syringa.

'So a child's future is remade,' I think as I watch my great grandmother already mentally saying goodbye to her baby. What we can think becomes possible. What is possible we can, eventually, do.

'Mam! Mam!'

There is a thunderous kick at the back door and Harriet jumps to her feet, Kate still clutched in her arms.

It's Fred, my granddad, still in his nightshirt and bawling at the top of his lungs.

'Mam I'm huuuuungry!'

# 18

## FALLING SLOWLY

How I wished, as I did my ancestry research, that my granddad had spoken about his childhood; how he had had to leave school at nine years old to provide for the family, how and when they all left Derby and came back home to Scugton again, how he ran away to join the army and exactly what he ran from. I found him in lodgings in the 1911 census, when he was fourteen. The record says he was an iron worker and that Harriet and Alice were visiting that day. The next public mention of him is in First World War records, and then he came home and married Granny Rose. No one ever heard him talk of those early years, except that they were very hard.

'How could I ever have thought that this life of mine was difficult? Is that the sum of it, Harriet?' My faint breath mists the oxygen mask but my words are soundless. I'm still reeling from the shock of those other five familiar words and their significance. My heart recovered in the end. Did Harriet's, I wonder?

My dear old granddad. He died as he had lived, poor. Poor and physically ruined by the demands of iron and steel, a price many thousands like him paid then. He was no one all, just an echo in history, a number in the army and a small detail in records of the Scugton Steelworks. After he came home from the trenches, they recorded forty years of sweat, burns, bronchitis and unbroken service with a stainless steel plaque as shiny and as sterile as he was grimed and broken. He was no one. No one until, that is, I placed his photos on my family tree on the ancestry site. A couple of weeks passed and I found my photos of him on another family tree, then another and another. As the months and years went by, the pictures appeared everywhere. It seemed that he was a part, indirectly, of so many stories and so many lives.

It was the same with Harriet. As I uploaded her photos and I told her story, it bounced around the world and back again, ensuring that she would never be forgotten. I kept my vow to her in the end and showed the world a little of her beloved Fred, too.

'We're all connected, Harriet, did you know that?'…

… 'What did she say? She just turned over. Is she all right?'

By some Herculean effort I've turned on my rippling mattress so that I'm laying on my right side. This seems to make my breathing a bit easier for the moment and I find the strength to open my eyes a little. I fancy I can see the shapes of my daughter and granddaughter side by side, peering into my face. I can't really see them any more but I feel their presence and, for once on this day of days, I find comfort in having people around me.

'Can you see us, gran?'

My granddaughter is French and bilingual from being a tiny little girl but I still detect that faint other language twang in her voice when she's upset. I waggle a finger as a sign of recognition.

'Gran, we're here for as long as you want us.'

At last! Some realisation that dying is my business and is my journey alone to make. This is such a relief to me that I close my eyes again and manage to lift a hand in gratitude. I'm so close to it now, so close to an understanding but my mind wanders not to Harriet, where I want to be, but momentarily to France and then on to another death.

France, yes. In the small Lyonnaise village of Seyssuel, the inhabitants can stand high above the Rhone and, in the distance, take in the French Alps. Wearing its white cloak, Mont Blanc towers above the surrounding peaks and is only visible on a very clear day, a fact that causes the villagers to shake their heads, suck in their breath and bemoan the vile weather that will inevitably follow. Beauty and calm before the beast, they say. I suppose I should have seen it coming.

'No, not this one, Harriet!'

We've just returned from the holiday of a lifetime and are bathed in that wonderful glow that lingers after a great experience. The family is, for once, settled and peaceful, John having had very few heart problems even at quite strenuous points during our travels. Three weeks ago we had been climbing the sea cliffs of Madeira and now, suddenly, sitting in his old blue leather armchair, he's breathless, his lips surrounded by a band of white that I haven't seen before.

As usual, we arrange a trip down to Papworth, a strange elongated village strung along part of Ermine Street but home to a wonderful heart research and teaching hospital. We've been here many times before and each time we leave reassured and helped along our way by the amazing skills of the staff who work there. An early start in the dark of a raw December morning, a drive down the A1, skilfully avoiding one of the terrible blockages that used to stop the A14 in its tracks, and we arrive in good spirits; a little early but confident that, as usual, all will be fixed or, failing that, mended as well as possible.

Papworth was once a TB isolation hospital, so the site is spread out and disjointed. The day ward is through a rabbit warren of other wards bearing the names of past great and good. We're on Varrier Jones ward but all the names bear testimony to the marvellous work that has been done here. The nurses will organise and oversee up to twenty angiograms every day. They're practiced and calm as one by one the patents return, some needing a prolonged pressure point over the breeched femoral artery in their groin where a fine catheter has been introduced into the arteries of their heart; others relatively sprightly and up and about quite quickly after a femoral plug.

In the male section of the ward, wives wait by empty beds, walk about the corridors or take an uninteresting tour of the village. I've walked this part of Ermine Street so many times now — through the white knuckle, lip biting, waiting hours of one by-pass operation to mend John's ailing heart, and then another some years later — that I'm content just to sit by his bed and trust to this wonderful place.

I can't read here, though, my mind won't focus, returning again and again to the theatre where my love lies. I sift the 'what ifs' over and over. It's not his first angiogram and we're always informed in advance that it's a procedure with some risk but your mind, ever optimistic and hopeful at the start of this new journey, blanks out all but the smallest doubt. What will the test reveal? Will there be another operation? What will this mean for our lives together?

We've been partners for so long now; John and I, that you'd think that some of the passion of our lives together might have worn off. Not a bit of it. As he was wheeled away, his parting words, accompanied by a twinkle of those intense blue eyes that unwrap me down to my soul were, 'Keep it hot!' My big, bad handsome man!

I'm giggling inwardly now at the memory, when something suddenly stops me short. I'm instantly aware that part of me is suddenly missing. It's that feeling I had when I gave up the children. It's an aching hollowness and incompleteness, a vacuum that is as heavy as a stone.

And then a pause. An exhalation and I feel whole once more. I know instantly what's happened and I make for the ward sister's desk.

'He's been a long time; he's having problems, isn't he? Would you go and ask for me, please?'

I don't hear the soothing noises she makes because I'm swamped by that feeling once more. This time it doesn't go away and my face betrays my panic because she doesn't pick up the phone, she gets up from her seat and makes her way swiftly down the corridor as I stand helpless at the nurses' station, not even trying to hold back the tears. When we're apart, we're like two halves of an apple, raw, split and incomplete. This is far worse. There's just nothing there at all.

I'm used to waiting by now but this wait is the purest sweat forming agony because my heart knows what's coming at the end of it. Yet still we always hope against hope, as I do now, twisting my handbag handles in my hand and walking back and forth from the desk to the window, and the window to the desk. But I can feel this hope slipping away with the last of the fading light on this dark December afternoon. Someone comes up and brings a chair and puts an arm around my shoulders but I can't sit down; I'm desperately catching on to the very tail end of hope and I need to hold it fast. I put my bag on the chair for a moment, hold my forehead and with my other hand over my mouth, I weep unashamedly in the hospital corridor, gasping in great lungfuls of air and the remnants of the forty-five years of life I have known with him.

Finally, the waiting comes to an end. The sister reappears from a side door some way away, together with the surgeon who performed the procedure. He has taken off his scrubs and is in his shirtsleeves, rolling them down as he walks the interminable length of the corridor towards me. It is such an ordinary, insignificant, but terribly final act.

As they approach, the sister points me out and he turns his head from her to find my face. He quickly looks away again and that's all the confirmation I need. If he'd smiled, or given some gesture of recognition I might have thought that this terrible, terrible hole in my chest that is stopping me from breathing was down to simple, irrational fear.

Their steps slow and slow, as though they don't really want to reach me and break the news: I don't want them to reach me. As long as I don't have this final confirmation there's still hope. We can go home and still have a future, still be the world's last two great lovers and curl up tonight in bed as we do every night, in each others' arms. But finally they're in front of me. 'Don't, don't, don't, please don't. Not yet. I'm not ready!' Can we ever be ready for this moment, losing someone we love? Someone who has been my whole life for the best part of my life?...

… My chest heaves as I open my eyes and I let my swimming gaze finally wobble around the shape that is my daughter. Will she be ready when I go? She's seventy-seven and has seen death before but I know this is different for her. There's so much baggage surrounding our relationship. Many years ago, when she'd had children of her own and finally reconciled herself to the fact that I was not some sort of monster, she bought me a locket and had it engraved: Lost and Found. It both touched and shocked me, for I had never once lost her, clinging on all those years through thick and thin. I never understood why she thought she'd lost me. She's always been the best part of what I am; a gentler, less strident me.

Now she will lose me.

Forever.

My chest tries to lift but it won't and I think it's just memories and sorrow that are heaving at it, even though my body is thrashing on the pillows.

'They sometimes do this near the end, don't worry.'

I'm sheet lifted up the bed, propped higher up on my pillows and turned on to my back again. I don't want to return to where I've just been in my mind but I do, finding myself standing in front of the man who has just been beside my husband…

… This is the man who threaded a delicate cannula through an incision in his groin, guiding it to his heart. This is the man who injected dye and then watched the heart unexpectedly lurch, flounder and stop. This is the man who took charged paddles and tried again and again to bring his heart to life before eventually, and with great sorrow at losing a patient, calling a time of death. Out of protocol, he asks my name, even though he knows, it and then says, 'I have some very bad news for you.'

He's done it a hundred times before, given the relatives the bad news, but it's the first and most awful of times for me.

'Nooooo!'

I want to stop each word as it falls from his lips and stuff it back in his mouth again, so that this thing has not happened.

Taken into a side room and seated between them, I am gently told the details of my husband's death. The words fall through me and gradually erase me, bit by bit, until I am insubstantial and barely there at all.

'At his age... '

'So many procedures before... '

'A clot... '

'He didn't know anything about it... '

I suppose those are the words I'm waiting to hear, if any words can be welcome at this time. I can't bear to think of him slipping away alone and frightened and without me at his side, where I have always been. I seize hold of this crumb of comfort and carry it numbly through that blank, empty night at the hospital, and all the awfulness that follows a death until you can at last close your door and cry.

And I did...

… Someone lifts my mask and wipes away what must be tears, for my eyes and face are yet again wet with memory.

'It's all right. Everything's all right, mum. We're here.'

The voice of my son soothes a passage through my sorrow and brings me back safe but exhausted to his side. We're so alike, he and I. I've always understood the way he thinks and he, instinctively always reads me.

'Is he reading me now in death?' I wonder.

I can't see his face but, searching for the direction of his voice, I attempt a brief movement of my hand. It's the greatest weight I have ever lifted, that thin old hand of mine; it makes me sweat and pant with the pure effort of it. It falls to my side and slides, unbidden over the side of the bed, from where he lifts it gently to my side again in his great calloused and cracked fingers, fingers which soothe the last remains of my being with rough, warm, living skin. A momentary reprieve, I cling to it for its sheer immediacy; a life raft that bears up my ebbing spirit while my body falls slowly down through another layer of dying. He feels so real that I am just a shadow by comparison, a ghostly smudge of half-life, less than that, even; a trace of a trace of a thing that was once whole. But I can't go yet. The clawed, skeletal hand from last night is heaving the rest of its charred remains from a shallow grave, pointing me towards a final glimpsed answer.

Gathering what little determination I am still capable of, I slake my spirits once more on my son's great hand to find that, somehow, I am folding it up in both my own, kissing the rough finger tips and letting my tears fall freely upon its coarse warmth…

… But it isn't my son's hand I am holding, it is Will Ogley's and

I am Harriet, gathering the folds of my apron to wipe my eyes, kneeling, weeping, at his side. We kneel by the kitchen table in Will's house on Sereton Terrace where Harriet has spent the years since Betsey Ogley died, bringing up John Henry's girls, Will's four children and her own beloved Fred and Kate. Her thoughts are serrated and saw so painfully at her heart that I gasp out loud. How can this woman carry on?

'It's only four years since I laid out Betsey on this very table, placing the pennies on her eyes, tying her jaw and washing her wasted mawk,' her mind whispers to itself.

She remembers how she had looked after Betsey for just a few short months after the Ogleys had taken her in. The consumption got the better of her so quickly, despite Harriet's tender care of her childhood friend.

'Coughing up her lights she was, bless her dear sweet soul.'

She and Will had clung to each other that night, first in shared grief and then in passion, as they both sought comfort from their loss. That was the beginning of their immeasurable love for each other.

'With Betsey hardly cold in her coffin in the kitchen below.'

Harriet's mind scuttles painfully from the thought. In her heart of hearts that night she felt that no good could come of this union and yet she had had the four happiest years of her life with Will.

We take his enormous hand in ours once more; the hand Will gave to my granddad, my father, me, my son and even one of my grandsons. Its hard and capable roughness rubs against our cheek, triggering a thousand, thousand memories and overwhelming us with the joy, the completeness, the tenderness of it all. This broad shouldered Yorkshire iron worker and plain country lass were a match made in heaven.

The back door latch clicks and a woman slides quietly and respectfully into the kitchen, smoothing her apron and her hair. It's Mrs Bowers from next door. She stands beside us, silently twisting a handkerchief in her hand before speaking.

'How did it happen, love?'

'He fell from a chain, duck, on number two furnace top,' we choke out, turning to look up at Syringa Bowers.

I pull away, startled by what Harriet has just said. I know that! I have his death certificate. I read the words and tried to imagine what they would mean for Harriet. But we never know what it's really like until we've been there ourselves.

'God love us! What was he doing up there in the first place?' Mrs Bowers replies, holding her apron up to her face in horror and surprise.

''Elpin' out. He was allus 'elpin' out. You know Will,' she replies tenderly, with no bitterness. The body on the table has belonged to a good and gentle man, someone to be proud of. Mrs Bowers simply puts a hand on her shoulder and waits quietly for a time before speaking again.

'The children are all tucked up safely next door. James is doing a grand job as a father. You'd think he'd been doing it all along. And I took the liberty of sending word to Betsey's mother and father.'

'Why would that be?' Harriet asks sharply, scuffing tears away with a sleeve. But she already knows; she's been here before.

There is a shudder that runs through her as she drags herself from Will's side to think about more pressing matters. Standing up, she turns to face Mrs Bowers, all the while holding on to the table for support. I feel we are falling into an abyss, as she grips the table edge tightly, her red hands white at the knuckles and thoughts of John Henry's death boring through her brain.

'Now it's time to pay. The piper always, always has to be paid.'

I am Harriet. I am thinking the thought that was in her mind, feeling her hands upon the hard deal table, crying her tears; tears I cried when I had to pay. I can't escape it. My guilt and hers tumble together in one thought.

'I should be punished, for all the things I've done. It's my fault and mine alone to bear.'

The thought is so familiar, so lead heavy, it shocks me with its customary iron weight and habitual burden. I said those very same words to myself so many times in the past until I learned to put the burden down. I try and detach myself to protest.

'No Harriet; don't do that, don't say that. It will never go away if you do.'

'What did you just say?'

'I didn't say anything, love,' replies Mrs Bowers.

I am Harriet again, shaking my head. I could have sworn I heard someone talking to me.

'I've got kids to feed, washin' to do an' a funeral to sort out. The last thing I need is voices in me 'ead. Steady now girl.'

She heard me! Harriet actually heard me!

But in my complete astonishment I lose her and fall back through layers of memory and currents of time to become myself once more. My hand upon the white deal table blurs to become the smudged shape of my hand clutching the white hospital sheet.

Tossed on this sea of memories, I'm flotsam now. No more. Enough! I want to go, yet I hold fast to the one thought that bears me up and cushions me along its length. Harriet heard me. All those years ago she heard me from the future just as I, in my own lifetime, felt her presence from the past. We were always connected and I never knew it, never guessed how our lives mirrored, *Spiegel im Spiegel.* Odd how I came to love that piece of music by the same name. It seemed to echo the stories of all our ancestors, told over and over back down the years, each of us with familiar and ever repeating flaws that made up our own unique story. How perfectly neat. How circular. How satisfying.

My son's hand holds mine once more and I think of hands again, my husband's hands. My husband, the potter. His beautiful hands produced proud and practical pieces, where form, glaze and function married to produce a perfect pot. Clay is such primal stuff and the potter is a god in his own little world throwing, fettling, firing and glazing until he has a piece that is permanent and can last forever. Well, it's taken me a long time to become that finished piece but I'm finally fettled and ready now, too. He would be satisfied with me; what I've become now makes me ready at last for the kiln. I laugh deep down inside; he would have appreciated the joke, too.

I want to be with him so badly now. The harbour of his arms was always where all my journeys ended; I want to go there now and hear his voice, to feel those beautiful hands on my body.

I try and visualise his broad back, his bear-like hug and gentle chuckle but other, more mundane sounds intrude.

# 19

## MOVING ON

A rattle of teacups and clatter of wheels announces the arrival of the afternoon tea trolley. It's usually the most welcome of sounds on any hospital ward but it doesn't interest me now. I'm too far gone for tea. I just want to go. I hear a scrape of chairs as family members stand up and make for that welcome break. When you're sitting with the dying you're glad of any distraction…

… 'Would you like a biscuit with that?'

The woman pushing the train's refreshment trolley puts two plastic mugs of industrial strength tea on the table top that separates us from two other passengers on the London bound train. Coral and I survey the unappetising selection of savouries and confection on the most inaptly named of objects, the refreshment trolley, then decline…

… I don't want this now, this intrusion on my thoughts. It was all coming together. I was ready. I don't want to see Coral. There's so little time left. Do I have a choice in this? My knees draw up as I try to cough but there's just a helpless fluttering of my diaphragm.

Nothing more…

… 'That'll be £3.50 then, please,' the woman pipes, her voice rising in that characteristic squeak that's meant to be bright and breezy and oh so customer friendly.

'£3.50!' Coral's voice rises to an even higher note. She may be the world's keenest shopper but resents bitterly paying more for anything that she can get cheaper anywhere else. I kind of agree with her but I hate tea from a flask and the effort of bringing one along just isn't worth it. So I cut short her outrage by placing the right coinage in the woman's hand and the trolley trundles on before further damage is caused. We settle down to watch the scenery gliding by and sip our teas thoughtfully as our two fellow passengers decide to get up and seek refreshment further up the train in the dining car.

'Thank goodness for that. I hate people listening to my conversations.'

I decline to comment. We've had this discussion so many times. No matter where we are Coral will always assume that there are spies on hand ready to tap into her life and who will rush off and divulge its secrets to the world. So unlike my aunt Peg, who would announce chirpily to every checkout girl, 'I've just lost my husband, you know.'

But anyone trying to get to know Coral by asking a few sympathetic questions is given the brush off immediately. This has not helped matters at all since she has been a widow. When she most needed sympathy and support and could have done with a few more shoulders other than mine to cry on, she has fallen out with all-comers one by one. I don't remember her being like this when we were younger, or perhaps I just didn't notice then. Anyway, people change and we did spend the middle years of our lives out of touch with each other. Many blows have knocked both of us into different shapes in those years in between.

I twist my mug around, grimacing at the brown scum ring inside but manage to finish the last dregs of the bitter brew as the train begins to slow.

'Peaborough,' I remark, looking at the recently renovated Victorian station. A metal roof, coat of dark blue paint and new ticket offices seem to have done little to bring this mainline station into the 21st century. A few spatters of late spring rain on the carriage windows add to the gloomy picture. It's a relief to pull away again and try to cheer up the conversation, but a thought insinuates itself, cat-like around my heart. It's been four years since our friendship first began to cool, I muse, as the rain soaked countryside whizzes by and we pick up speed for the last leg of the journey.

Horizontal rain hisses against the windows as a bearded young man and his tiny pink clad daughter, who've just boarded the train, make their way to the seats over the aisle. He seems to be very keen and nervous, making a great fuss of taking her coat off, of settling her down with paper and crayons and plying her with sweets and toys from his back pack. He stows her Hello Kitty suitcase in the luggage rack, keeping up a stream of talk that is more characteristic of the enthusiasm of a grandparent than a young dad. My ears always prick up when there are children about — I do so love listening to their babble. But the drift of the conversation indicates that the little girl is on a two day access visit to stay with him and her eyes are large and her face anxious under dark curls, as she keeps asking if mummy will come to London to take her home. It's a familiar tale these days but I never did tell Coral about my own earlier problems. There were always too many of hers to listen to. Maybe I can repair this friendship. There are too many broken things in this world.

'Oooh! You weren't listening in, were you?' grins Coral as I turn back to her. I don't quite know whether she's being short these days or not. We still make an effort to rub along for old time's sake as much as anything, bringing humour into our situation. I call her my ever so slightly psychotic friend and she calls me a didactic old fart, but each of us is now wary as to how we conduct our conversations, which is why I can't really understand what I say next.

'Did I ever tell you that when I left James, he kept the children and not me?' Just like that; banal, nonchalant and chit chattery, a secret that I've kept from her for years lies naked on the tea stained table between us. It may have been the little girl who struck a chord or even, I suppose, the fact that having finally been compassionate enough with myself to set that burden of guilt down, it doesn't seem too awful to speak the words now. But, whatever else, I sense that what I'm really doing is trying to heal this friendship by offering closeness, a confidence, something only strong friends would share.

Coral has turned towards me and is staring hard into my face, halfway through trying, while fighting the rhythm of the swaying train, to apply lipstick with the aid of her small handbag mirror.

'Reeeeally?' Half lipsticked, her mouth has dropped into its aghast letterbox shape and her chin is drawn back. At that familiar sight I feel a sudden sinking inside. I shouldn't have gone there.

'It was difficult… I didn't want to repeat my parents' mistakes… I left to live on my own…'

I expect she might be a bit sympathetic or ask for more details but instead she slowly and deliberately finishes applying her lipstick, puts everything with uncharacteristic care back in her handbag and then takes out a brush to smooth her lustrous dark hair. Finally, and with great precision, the brush is put away too, and she turns to me.

'You *never* said.' The tone is accusatory.

'I couldn't bring myself to tell anyone until recently. It's not the sort of thing you go around talking about to everyone. How do you say, I walked out on my first husband and left my kids with him? It's a bit of a conversation stopper; it even brought you up short just then.'

There is a hard-edged smile by way of acknowledgement. I can't quite read her yet.

'So when did they come to you, then?'

I try and condense seven turbulent years and what they meant to me, into the miles that flash by on our day trip to London. She mostly stares unseeing at the countryside but, as we pass through a tunnel I catch sight of her face in the darkened glass and see it is set in an expression of mild disgust. Finally I pause and finish with, 'You never really know what you'll do until the time comes when you have to do something — anything — just to survive.'

It's an excuse. Why am I excusing myself? I resolved all this four years ago and I certainly don't need to excuse my actions any more. I feel myself becoming hot and angry and her eventual rejoinder after a long pause only makes it worse.

'I could never have left the girls, you know.'

I flush darkly with anger and frustration; I can feel their hand slap upon my cheeks, pushing me to retaliate.

'We're not talking about you, though, Coral are we? This isn't about you,' I say as gently as I can muster. I should shut up right now and so should she, but now *she's* on a mission.

'Well, just know I could never have done it!' she snaps.

'Never say never.'

'Oh… the thought of those little girls crying for me breaks my heart!'

'Do you think mine wasn't broken?' I manage, in barely a whisper. 'I could tell you all about that if you like.'

The couple from the two opposite seats return, full of laughter, and chewing on a bacon bap each. They ease themselves into their seats and there is an embarrassed pause; a chance for Coral and I to regroup maybe. I smile at them but inwardly I'm seething.

'They look good.'

'We were just so hungry!' giggles the woman, looking at her travelling companion with doe eyes.

Why do I get the feeling that they've been doing something else, apart from just fetching bacon baps? Even this delightful thought, however, doesn't stem my annoyance. For anyone else, that confessional moment would have been an invitation to extend some friendly support and concern and just sit and listen. But not Coral. I finally begin to see that she is wholly lacking in empathy and perfectly incapable of seeing beyond her own life and her own concerns for more than a moment. A pair of friends adds up to more than two; it's a symbiosis that expands all the time. This relationship is imploding, focusing around the needs and the opinions of one.

'Surely you could have taken them with you?' she persists in hissed undertones that still carry shock and disgust. The couple opposite looks at her in mild surprise, and then they busy themselves with their bacon.

'Just take it on faith, Coral, that I couldn't. I did what anyone does, the best they know how at the time. Anyhow, I shouldn't have said anything; let's decide which museum we're going to.' My tone is bright but my heart is heavy because she's flying beyond my reach as quickly as the fading scenery outside.

But it's not until we're standing, later that day, in among the twisting columns and marble balustrades of one of the beautiful upper galleries of the V&A, that I finally, and with great sorrow, realise that it's over.

'Wow Coral! Just look at that view!' I enthuse, peering over the balustrade at the galleries below.

'He was just like his mother, you know, 'she says, trotting up behind me and glancing perfunctorily over the cool marble edge. 'I worked my fingers to the bone for that man and where did it get me?'

Five years after Geoff's death, and it's still the same old, same old; she still hasn't moved on a single step, I reflect sadly, all too painfully aware of what's coming next. I try to let it all wash over me and become part of the background noise of London as we retrace our steps to the Tube.

'He never once lifted a finger to help...'

Through the gift shop.

'Whenever we went out he just couldn't wait to start drinking...'

Along the Brompton Road.

'And I've lost count of the times on holiday when he tried to drive me and the girls around half pissed.'

Back to South Kensington Underground.

'And when he retired, he sat at that laptop day after day, watching me dig the garden and move great rocks about…'

Wave after wave of her well-worn story overcomes any sense of enjoyment I might have had in this outing. I love London, despite those rough early days, and I remember my time here with affection, as well as the occasional hot gush of pain. Coming back as often as I can is usually a real treat. But not today.

Scoring my fork miserably on the red checked tablecloth in Joe Allen's restaurant off the Strand, a place I usually love to eat at before the theatre, I try to chat while Coral chooses her meal.

'John and I used to come here in the late seventies when it was a proper American burger bar. You know, before McDonald's and everything,' I remark lightly, looking at the signed photographs from Theatreland dotted around the homely, bare brick walls.

'That's a long while ago. Did you have the children with you then?'

I ignore her question. If she'd been listening on the train, she would have known that I didn't. But she doesn't listen.

'It hasn't changed a bit from the days when we used to look out for famous faces and enjoy a glass of wine. A pianist used to play lazy weekend music; it was lovely.'

'It's a bit expensive for what it is. I don't suppose we're getting a pianist for our money tonight.'

'Mmm,' I mutter noncommittally, trying to disguise another

surge of growing irritation.

'I brought up the girls entirely on my own, you know.'

Here we go again! And this time it's laced with a little barbed self righteousness.

'Geoff still supported you, though, Coral; and he was there even if he didn't do much. You know you never wanted for anything,' I parry. The subject of my past decisions is closed and not up for discussion.

'He moaned at every penny I spent; said I was always shopping.'

I should be enjoying this evening but even the meal, when it comes, is spoiled by the continuing monologue. I don't know whether to be hurt by or despair over the way she is. Friendship should be more than this.

We've booked to see the evening performance of *The War Horse* at the National Theatre which both of us have looked forward to for ages. The performance is spellbinding as the tale of Joey, a farm horse put to service on the battlefields of the First World War, unfolds. The lifelike horses are worked by puppeteers but after a while the tale holds your attention so completely that the puppeteers become invisible. Watching the horses move around the stage, twitching their flanks, and rearing and tossing their heads, I wonder about the invisible forces that move us all and shape our lives. Are we puppets like Joey? Can we help who we become or are we all a simple brew of genes and environment from the very beginning? Would I have turned out differently if my parents had cared more? Would Coral have been a different person if her spirit had been expanded by love? And Harriet? What about her?

Choose a chocolate bar,' Coral whispers, nudging me and

displaying several she has in her bag, blissfully as unaware, as ever, of my discomfort. I know not a single bite of chocolate will pass her lips, however. She keeps them there in her bag to make people think she eats what she likes.

'It's all a matter of choice,' I continue to myself, thinking of my childhood. 'You get what you get. It's how you choose to live it that counts.'

The moment the thought enters my head I'm almost knocked sideways once more by an overpowering sense of *presque vu*.

'I know this. It's what my life has all been about!' I breathe to myself. This time I will hold on to it; I will discover the enormous truth that is about to be revealed. Pulled into a giddying maelstrom of 'almost' ideas, I close my eyes in the darkened theatre and repeat the words, pressing my back into the seat and the thought into my mind.

'You get what you get... '

I daren't think about anything else because I know the feeling will vanish like it has done so many times before when I seemed to be on the point of an epiphany. I feel that I'm standing up but I know I'm not; part of me still feels the press of the red plush seat in my back and my coat across my lap. A flash of gunfire on stage fills my head with thunder and a light behind my closed eyelids. I don't so much hear it as feel it, trying to shut out the world inside the theatre.

The pulsing whiteness finally settles into a frozen grey and it takes a few moments before I realise that the overbearing greyness is an iron sky, a sky swept by bitter winter winds. And I am stand-ing for a fleeting moment in a tiny back yard, stirring half barrels of washing with one red, cracked hand and clutching my belly with the other. I think I have wind and then it dawns, with a smile, with the croon of a sitting dove and a honey warm glow, that it is a child moving inside me. I stroke the small mound beneath my clothes. Deep, sharp, stinging cracks at the corners of my thumbnails catch on my dress and make me wince. Why do my hands feel so sore? The pain is so real that I look down at my own hands to find that I'm cradling my stomach, here in the theatre.

'Which one do you want?' hisses Coral, nudging me insistently. It's gone.

'Damn!' I make as if to drop the chocolate bars and, bending down, silently shriek, 'Damn you Coral!' into the seat well of the next row. Moments pass and I'm outwardly composed, sitting with a bar of plain dark chocolate unopened on my lap. But my heart is fluttering wildly in my chest as though it would leap out as I wonder what on earth it was that I just experienced. Maybe I was just falling asleep but the performance has been too riveting for that.

Gradually, despite trying to concentrate on what it was I saw and felt, I'm drawn into the play again as Joey and Albert are finally reunited, so that by the time I have a real chance to think about that extraordinary flash of experience, it's just the vague remains of a feeling. It was so important. It told me so much that I needed to understand, I know it did…

… There's another flash as my eyelids are prised open once more and my pupils examined. My chest is pumping up and down now so rapidly that I think my heart will leap out of it. Surely it can't be very long now? I feel so close both to death and to an understanding.

Yes! I do remember that moment now I'm here at the end. Slip sliding unawares into Harriet's world for just an instant, I was totally unaware of what it meant then. How could I have forgotten on this most momentous of days, that the experience in the theatre was the second time Harriet and I were as one?

But I haven't forgotten, have I? It comes slowly, with that inescapable urge to follow, to take in the meaning and to fully understand and then, with a rush of brilliance that lights up every last fibre of this dying body, I am on fire with it. Understanding streams over me, through me and from my very finger ends. How unreceptive I was, compared to Harriet, when it came to making connections.

I have remembered, today on my dying day, exactly all the times when Harriet's world and mine collided. Fractions of moments that passed, were forgotten and whirled on into history, are dancing like a circle of bright lights around my head. Lincoln railway station, falling out of the window, the eve of my first wedding, the robin outside the gym, that afternoon in the pottery studio, on the way to the crematorium, the marshes down by the Aumber, the white-currant bush. All those moments have lined themselves up in my head today to focus my attention on one monumental thing.

This dying process has, after all, been about Harriet, not about me. From the moment I saw that skeletal hand it was always about her.

'Harriet? What did you need to say? What am I supposed to have learned about you?' I can feel my lips moving but nothing is coming out.

'Is she trying to say something?'

'What is it, mum?'

'Can you hear us?'

'The train,' I mouth silently…

… On the late train home, as the miles towards home sped by, I closed my eyes and feigned sleep, just as I do now on my hospital pillow. It came to me then from something I'd once read, that my life, being less than a thousand months long, should not be spent in the enormous effort of trying to maintain a toxic and mutually unsupportive relationship, simply for want of making a break. If Coral couldn't or wouldn't do it, I would. The next day I sent her a final email and we never spoke again. The relief was tremendous, palpable and like one more burden set down. I think that Coral, a once dear friend, ended up for me as a valuable lesson in economy of effort. It was over.

Many years later I decided to tell Coral, just before she died, what she'd once been to me; I thought it might reconcile things, I thought she might still care about what we once were to each other. But I was too late and probably not high on her list of priorities, so I laid her to rest among the gentle remains of all things that I wish had been different.

Yet here she is still, in my dying moments. There has to be a reason. She never moved on.

'I know that. I know that.' Once again I feel myself mouthing the words to an uncomprehending audience. I've lived a lot longer than a thousand months now and I know quite well who has mattered enough in my life to make it here to my final moments; their faces flow around me in memory, smiling. But there, still looking pained in the background, is Coral. She never moved on and got on with her life. Why is this significant now?

I manage a jagged sigh and feel my rapid breaths slow now and become further and further apart. I'm not struggling to breathe now. I don't even want to breathe, sinking into somewhere that is not quite here. It's a serene pause, a peaceful blank, a space before I gather myself to go. I can feel all the strands of my life being pulled slowly into a glowing sphere.

It's here.

'No man is an island unto himself.

Every man is a piece of the continent, a part of the main.'

My father's voice speaking his favourite poem blows like a wind across the embers of my life, rekindling them momentarily. I know I should try and think why this has all been about Harriet and not me, but I can feel hands upon me now, stroking and soothing. Quiet voices speak of their love, their ties to me, their sadness. They urge me to go when I'm ready, smoothing my hair, holding my feet, stroking my cheek. I feel cradled in love; rocked like Harriet was in my great grandfather's arms. My beloved family is at last reconciled to my imminent end and trying to help me go peacefully. I am content for them now, and happy that they are all here to wish me well on my journey.

Except that I still cannot go. My father's breath stirs the embers again.

'All mankind is of one author, and is of one volume;

When one man dies, one chapter is not torn out of the book,

But translated into a better language.'

There are still connections to understand, I know there are. Spent as I am, I will not be quite finished until I know *why* this has been about her. The dregs of me remain, here on this quietly whispering mattress because Harriet has one last thing to say. My mind wanders to her death. It wasn't like this.

'And therefore never send to ask for whom the bell tolls,' my father intones, as he always did, with great ceremony…

… I am at her bedside where she lays on an iron bed in a long narrow ward of about thirty or so others. Only a few beds are occupied, overlooked at the end of the room by an enormous plain black and white clock, its ticking sounding out in the silence. It ticks out the last minutes until five o'clock, when there should be comfort; there should be tea and pillows plumped and shaken, but there is nothing. The walls are white tiled and cold, reflecting a baleful light from a high window opposite. A cough, a moan from somewhere seemingly far away, is all that breaks the chilling, ticking silence. This is a place devoid of comfort, where the poor come to die when no one will care for them.

It is near the end for her too. You can tell when you've met death before. Harriet lies on her side, her knees drawn up under chin in a foetal position and white knuckled, bony hands curled tightly in under her chin. She is so thin. Her shoulder blades stick out through the worn, pink flannelette nightdress, the sleeves of which I can see are stained with dark green bile as she has vomited where she lies. There are also marks on her rough blankets, brown stains where fluids have ebbed, dried and remained, and her head lying upon the pillow is a delicate eggshell in shape, plastered over by thin wispy strands of grey hair that are knotted untidily at the nape of her neck. A pale scalp, whiter than the hair, shines luminously through the strands and is already the colour of a corpse.

Her features no longer bear any resemblance to that determined square jawed woman that I've seen in my photos and memories; but then death changes and reduces us so before we expand in our welcome going, struggling from the cramped, crusted chrysalis of flesh into flights of joy.

She's so close to death. Her breaths are ragged and uneven and a long way apart, hardly moving the frail body that is my great grandmother. She looks so ancient, withered and dried out, yet I know she is only seventy-three, younger than my daughter. My heart goes out to her once more; it always was hers from the first moment I found her.

'I've found you now, Harriet. I'm here, even if no one else is.' I peer at her sunken eyes, closed fast beneath purple lids, and at her jutting bony brow. Am I supposed to comfort her, to ease her passing? What is it I am supposed to see and do? Will I see that bright sphere come for her?

I gaze in wonder and anticipation at the small figure upon the bed but, as I do so, with great sorrow in my heart at her hard life; although not at her imminent death.

'Harriet, this will be the most wonderful thing that has ever happened to you. Better than your lists, better even than Will, Harriet.'

An age passes while I transmit all the peace, love and life and laughter that I know will shortly be hers, down to that hunched form. If I could hold her I would. Another age, even though the clock hands have hardly moved. Something seems not quite right. I reach out and feel her presence once more, very faintly; a flickering light that is about to be extinguished. Expecting to feel some sort of peace and reconciliation, all I sense is great disappointment.

Disappointment in her family, in Fred, her beloved son, who should be here, disappointment in herself and in her life.

'Oh Harriet, what about your lists? Have you forgotten how beautiful life is, despite everything? What about the tiny puff of a robin's breath on a frosty morning and the feathers on a starling's throat? What about whitecurrant stems and a baby's head on your cheek? What about number one, knowing that everything you are is always here, now?' I recite as much as I can remember of her lists, hoping their residual beauty will reach her but it doesn't.

There's not a trace of the joy I found in the younger Harriet, just a sense of barren emptiness. And there's something else there too.

Self-loathing.

In the moment where my heart opens out to her, as it did when my daughter returned to me, I grasp what is happening as Harriet drifts, unmourned, towards her departure from this world. She has never forgiven herself and neither has anyone else forgiven her.

'Hearts can do no more.'

That moment when she finally had nothing left to give to herself, was the moment she began to wither inside. She has never been able to forgive herself for John Henry. The loss of Edward and giving away Charles and Kate are nothing to the guilt she feels about this death. The woman whose life taught me to forgive and accept my own mistakes, has no forgiveness in her heart for herself. The sadness of it is unspeakable; a weight so heavy it almost pulls me down with it.

'I should have known, Harriet. That hand was John Henry; it couldn't have been anyone else. You knew, I'm sure, that he never had a proper burial and that he was buried in the open cast mines.'

Looking down on the fast ebbing life of my great grandmother, I finally now know what my own dying process is all about and, with a numbingly beautiful moment of clarity, I understand, at last, Coral's place in my memories, too. Everything has led me here to Harriet; everything, including Coral. My friend never made the choice to change her life. She stuck fast, repeating her mistakes over and over, living her life as though she would never die, and dying as though she had never lived. Her daughter told me, in a chance meeting years later, that those words were on her lips at the end.

'I've never really lived.'

And Harriet, poor Harriet, snubbed and reviled by everyone, you have never been able to move on either. You, too, are stuck fast, mired by the self-revulsion that is guilt, always feeling that you should be punished for what you have done. I remember that feeling only too well. Knowing that my great grandmother had also faced difficult choices about her children when it came to just surviving, helped me see that these are the choices women have always had to make; I wasn't a monster and neither was she.

Now it is my turn to help you, Harriet. This is it. I gather myself, thinking that I am going to be able to perform some miraculous act of forgiveness for Harriet and set her free to enter the love as it comes for her but as I watch, someone in uniform comes instead, and pulls the blankets up over her head.

'Wait!'

This can't be right. There was no joyfulness, no surge of raptured passing, no brilliance; nothing.

'She hasn't gone, she can't have. I'm here to save her.'

But I know she has. A time of death is noted and a stretcher sent for.

I've lost her. Why did I come so far, why did I come here if I couldn't help?...

... In the remoteness of the here and now, my own wasted form momentarily convulses with grief and frustration on my hospital bed.

'Sshhhh. It's ok, mum, you can go,' soothes my daughter and I am cradled once more in love as a great rough hand is laid upon my cheek.

And then it comes to me in a molten white hot surge.

I know where to find her. I know where she is.

Somewhere outside a bell tolls the hour. Five o'clock on a Sunday in July.

'It tolls for thee.'

# EPILOGUE

'It will all be all right,'

It's my daughter. I wish she could see me now; *really* see me as my own dissolution becomes a crowning spiritual act. Death is so beautiful.

'It's all right mum, we're all here with you.'

Somewhere, my father is reciting poetry once more.

Donne's *No Man is an Island unto Himself* rings out again, slowly and deliberately in his sonorous tones and I am overwhelmed and shot through with love for him. He showed me all of all this when I barely reached his knee. Did he understand, I wonder, in among his drunken efforts to blot out the horrors of the war, and then that mask, exactly how we are all connected, as Donne said? Was it the extreme disconnection and apartness of humanity at war that finally destroyed him? I can only guess. But as he finishes with his favourite lines,

'Send not to ask not for whom the bell tolls, It tolls for thee,' I realise that my take on death has been a ridiculous conceit.

I am part of humankind, not an island, not the capsule that I have thought of as me. I was never a human *being*, but a human *becoming*. Perhaps we can only discover this unity in death, for I am now finally approaching humankind's hidden completeness and it is staggering, awe inspiring and uplifting in its perfection. If I could kneel, I would kneel before it. If I could bow my head, I would offer it my humility. I am ready to give up all that is or was me.

'It's all right…'

It *is* all right. It is pure happiness. It is being one. It is love. It is reaching out. It is life.

'I think it's time to play *Spiegel im Spiegel*; she wanted that, at the end.'

A pause, a breath, a quietness; and then the single hesitant piano notes and trembling vibrato of the violin fill me up, as I see Harriet and all the mirror-echoed people of my story and her story, and all of our stories back to the beginning of stories, unfold like mirrors in a mirror until they reach around in infinity and begin once more.

I have reached my glowing ball at last and the longing is over. The greatest thirst is slaked, the keenest hunger is filled, the deepest lust quiesced, the purest love realised. Hesitantly at first and then with a rip tide of joy, I propel all that I am and have become towards its spinning light, entering with a heart burst of brilliance.

When it clears, I am standing in the centre of a glowing stream of time, inextricably part of the past, present and the future, and close to me stands Harriet. I had expected to see the man I have loved for nearly seventy years, but I remember again that this isn't about me, it's always been about her.

Time streams from me, through me, beyond me and I realise, at once, the universal fiction that is our worldly view of time. There is only one life, one time and we all share it, just like Harriet said. And as I look, I can see that the living stream is, in fact, my sphere. It is part of a larger sphere, through and over which time flows in multitudes of incandescent strands.

Aware suddenly, with an overwhelming rush of love, that I am connected to every other person who ever had a moment of life or who would ever be alive, this feeling of being loved, supported and watched wraps me up and swaddles me in its brilliance. I concentrate on those around me. There is Harriet but there are also entities — I cannot call them faces — that I love and know and some who are less clear but, without exception, they are 'family', they are 'for me', although that hardly describes our connection. Some of them flow to the surface of the sphere and turn again inwards. Some flow as sparks along branched strands which meet up with the whole again but all the while there remains about me those who are familiar, numbered in the thousands of thousands.

I know now that what we call birth and death are irrelevant as I swoop and twist up and over and above and back to join where I have been. Those whom I know rearrange themselves once more close by; Harriet, momentarily, the closest of all.

I am my ball, my beautiful ball at last, and I cannot conceive of anything I would rather be.

I want to move through to the larger sphere but I become aware of the small spaces within the tangle of threads and that they are not, after all, spaces. They are filled with a softer glow that resolves itself into an uncountable myriad of smaller spheres. An age or maybe just a moment rolls by before I understand and make the connection, a sharp clarity of understanding that comes with a dream and fades as I try to grasp it once more. But I have it now. Now and for all time.

It's the living host of all other life played out at all times and forever. Each bacterium, each bird, each coral polyp, each plant, each person… the vastness and greatness of it makes me weep for pure joy and amazement. I turn to Harriet who is at my side again, smiling. She has red hair like my own and her hands are clean and new and whole again.

'Yes,' she says; and I understand it all.

Everything.

At last.

Harriet stretches out her hand to me and points to where peace is waiting. Gratefully, I take it but she will not come and holds back. I appreciate instantly that she never was translated into a better language. She is stuck; she cannot move on.

There is one more thing to do and it has been waiting for me my whole life long. I just never grasped it until now. Perhaps I really was not meant to grasp it until now.

In the grand scheme of things, whatever choices and mistakes we make, we are still loved by whatever it is that we choose to call our God. We just have to live with the consequences, that is all. We mostly do what seems the best at the time, but the real crime is not to learn and especially not to learn to love and honour ourselves. Finding Harriet showed me that all those years ago, but finding her again has shown me so much more. Now I must help her to find her own way home.

What are the words that can take away a lifetime of guilt? How tender is the embrace that can assuage it? What medicine can heal a shattered heart? I have no answers. I can only offer Harriet what I discovered in finding her all those years ago; self-forgiveness, that gentle voice that I now know arises from this beautiful place.

I offer it to her and gaze in wonderment as all that she is dissolves into a bright ball of light that hesitates for a moment before me, then whirls away to join the rest.

And, as the final notes of *Spiegel im Spiegel* curl around what is left of me, I follow her into the great sphere of life.

# GLOSSARY OF DIALECT TERMS

A
afe — half
ain't — haven't
any road — anyway
allus — always
an' all — as well

B
bairns — children
bealing — calling out, like a calf to its mother
besling — calf
besling's puddin' — a pudding made with cow's colostrum after
    calving
boak — heave or retch
bod — bird
bumfits — fifteen

C
clagged, claggy — dirty
cowd — cold

chamber-lees — urine, as in a chamber pot

## D
dancin' 'awk — buzzard
doggerybaw — nonsense
dooer — door
dowter — daughter
dozzen 'eaded — dozy, stupid
dun't — doesn't

## E
ead — head

## F
fat bacon — slabs of pig fat hung up to smoke
fethera — four
fost — first
frit — frightened
fumad — ferret
far weltered — on your back unable to rise (as in a sheep)

## G
gawpin' — staring in a stupid manner
git — get
gither — gather
gress — grass
goas — goes
gret — great

## H
hask — ask
hayther — either
hoppen — open

I

ivver — ever

issen — himself

J

jiggered — surprised, or worn out as in tired

K

kelchin'– falling violently

kelter — rubbish

kit — baby ferret

L

liggin' — lying down

M

mawk — corpse

mebbe — maybe

mek — make

mouldywarp — mole

N

niver — never

night soil bucket — bucket used for evacuating the bowels at night

nobbut — nothing but, or not amounting to much

nowt — nothing

O

on — of, as in on 'em, of them

ovver much — too much

owd — old

owt — anything

**P**

petty 'ole — toilet, wooden seated and ground dug

pethera — five

**Q**

queer — funny, amusing or different

**R**

ran — one

reet — right, really

roarin' — crying

**S**

scutch (n) — smack or hit, as in a person

sen — self

sharp set — hungry

skerrick — tiny scrap or crumb

spang — bang, as in door

squad and blather — muddy

summats — something

swath — bacon fat or rind

**T**

tan — two

tek — take

ten-foot — alleyway

tethera — three

thowt — thought

throttle — throat

ton — turn

tow — strands of sheep's wool found caught in hedges

trollops — prostitute or low woman

U
ugly — angry
un'eppen — clumsy

W
wain't — will not
whoaar — whore
wikins — front or insides of the body

Y
yet — eat